Leave No Trace

Leave No Trace

Take only photographs, leave only footprints...

(if you don't want to be found)

A Novel

by

Tim Mulholland

Leave No Trace

First published, November, 2021, Print Edition
by Illuminata Photo

ISBN = 979-8-9852889-1-9

TimMulholland.com

_____Acknowledgements

Fall, 2021

Thank you for purchasing and reading this book!

I started writing _Leave No Trace_ in the Fall of 2020. For a long time, I've wanted to write something more meaningful than a formal letter or a technical report. To my credit, I have prepared a couple of relatively large "documents" that helped me to hone this craft, as well as recognize how much effort is involved in something like this, but they were much shorter and factual, not fiction.

At heart, I'm a creative person who enjoys being outdoors. My primary vocation over the past fifteen plus years has been as a landscape photographer. After an aborted backpacking trip during the COVID pandemic, I realized that I had a fair amount of backpacking knowledge and experience, as well as a pent-up desire to be out in the wilderness. Like many people during the pandemic, I spent my time somewhat bored as well as entertaining myself reading books and learning and relearning skills. Trying to figure out what I might do next to entertain myself, the thought of writing a book started to worm itself into my soul. For the genre I most enjoy - outdoor crime novels - and various writers whom I most enjoy reading - Nevada Barr, CJ Box, Margaret Cole, Tom Corcoran, Car Hiaasen, Tony Hillerman, Craig Johnson, William Kent Krueger, Aimée & David Thurlow, and Randy Wayne White, to name several - I realized that no one really wrote about a crime that involved backpacking. Yes, these various authors place their novels in lots of great outdoor settings (I'm thankful to several of them for exposing me to new places to explore and backpack) and frequently involve interesting outdoor talents other than backpacking, but there's a certain solitude and relative lack of technology involved in escaping a criminal that's unique if the situation involves backpacking. Over a few days, the basic outline of the Leave No Trace pretty much appeared to me. It took two months to write the first draft and another month to edit it a few times.

My next steps involved sharing the draft of *Leave No Trace* with several friends and family, to whom I am deeply grateful. Tom Thoreson, a retired game warden, provided insight regarding the law enforcement and investigative aspects of this book. Melissa and Colin Anglin are great friends and experienced backpackers who highlighted many of the weaknesses in my early draft. My wife, Asta, is also a backpacker - thank goodness! - who provided insights and edits. My friend Ed Nelson basically told me that he didn't like *Leave No Trace*, that it didn't grab him, and that comment was as valuable as any; I hope that Ed will enjoy it now. Robb Seal helped me to better understand body injuries and issues that I could incorporate. Lastly, another sort of failed backpacking trip to Colorado in the summer of 2021 made me realize that I romanticize backpacking too much, and the final version benefited from this experience and realization.

Again, I want to express my appreciation to my reviewers as well as a whole host of other friends and family - backpacking and normal - who helped provide me experiences on which to draw in writing this book.

Remember, *Leave No Trace* - take on photographs, leave only footprints.

Tim Mulholland

Table of Contents

Chapter 1

Fred sat back, the nearly still lake in front of him, sun going down, his left cheek cool and his right cheek warm. The setting sun created stunningly beautiful pink and orange pastels on the mountains and snow reflected in the lake – another picturesque forever memory. He was tired and sore. The granite against which he sat was rough and not precisely shaped to his back, but it radiated warmth, and the stone's surface was hitting his sore muscles in mostly the right places. It was the best he could likely get if he wanted a back rub.

It had been another long, fulfilling day of backpacking in the Sierras. He always loved this time of evening. It was a chance to sit back, relax, reflect and relive the adventures of the day - vistas seen, steps taken, pitfalls avoided, injuries sustained, and strangers made friends. His mind wandered, and he was looking forward to sleep, eyelids drooping just a bit already. Over the lake, he could make out insects flying – likely those damn, annoying mosquitoes – and trout rising to take in one last morsel before darkness fell.

No two days of backpacking were ever the same. The spectacular views never grew old and created memories to carry Fred into the many years left in his life. Some days there was rain, grey clouds, wind, and cold. Most days were clear, sunny, and warm – just like today. There had been the typical climbing and descending; unstable rocks; sweating and grunting; clear, cool streams; and squeaking marmots. Yep, it had been a pretty typical day – except for one little thing. Well, not so little after all.

Fred turned nonchalantly to his right and raised an eyebrow.

"So, what's a pretty girl like you doing in a place like this?" Fred asked.

Kim looked at him, shook her head, and rolled her eyes. "Do your kids enjoy your stupid dad jokes, or is my response similar to theirs? I mean, you remind me so much of my father."

Fred grinned, happy for the company, happy to entertain the company, and missing his wife and kids.

The view to the southwest was spectacular and beautiful. Nothing was moving, other than the insects, trout, and the slight swaying of the few pine trees in the gentle breeze, which was just the way they liked it at this point. Kim and Fred were comfortable but very cautious.

"The good news," said Fred, "is that I don't see anyone following us."

Kim gave a quick smile and said, "Let's keep it that way. I would much prefer being the hunter than the hunted."

Chapter 2

Aw, it feels good to be out of the city. Driving alone, soaking in the sun, the wind rushing through the windows, cleansing you with fresh, sweet, warm air. Much better than sitting in an office.

Though this was his second backpacking trip of the summer, Fred always felt the same excitement and anxiety at the beginning of his adventures. Excited to leave, to get away, to be alone. Anxious about going, getting away, and being lonely. The weeks, the months of planning, dehydrating food, pouring over maps, thinking about this and that possibility. Thinking about the mistakes he'd made and the lessons learned from past trips. Checking equipment. Making last-minute decisions about what to stow in the backpack, what to bring if he changed his mind before he set out, and what to leave at home. Planning his possible meals, filling boxes with food, and mailing them to be picked up along the way on a three-week-long trip in the Sierras like this one. Making sufficient arrangements for work and family issues while he was away rebuilding his sanity and spirit.

Fred was lucky to have such a wonderful and caring family. As much as they loved him and he loved them, they all knew that he was a better – and more tolerable – person if he was able to get away for some quiet time in the mountains. He spent much of his free time over fall, winter, and spring planning and anticipating his wilderness time. There were hours and hours of walking in the neighborhood, on trails with and without his backpack. Fred also was in the gym, strengthening the muscles and joints that he would make sore each day on his trip. Some years, he didn't get out too much, like last year. Sometimes, family plans or work got in the way. Last year was different, though. Coronavirus had shut down his dreams. If he lived closer to the Sierras, then it might have been tolerable for everyone not involved in the backpacking part but involved in the staying-at-home-and-worrying part. There had been too many variables a year ago, too many opportunities for things to go from bad to worse in the wrong place.

His first trip this season had taken him to the high country of the Wind River Range. It had been late spring there, with some snow still hanging around in high places and shadowed nooks and crannies, but the mosquitoes had been gloriously tame. The four days in the Winds had been a warm-up and shakedown to get his feet back under him after not being deep in the wilderness for nearly two years. Central Wyoming was closer to home than the Sierras, so it was easier to get there. The Winds are almost as beautiful as the Sierras, too. One of the drawbacks of the Winds was the grizzlies, but he'd been lucky never to see one while he was out in their territory. The few days at altitude had reminded him that being a flatlander was not beneficial in the mountains. His hips and shoulders were sore the first couple of days, but his feet felt good. He'd taken his time getting into the mountains and up to elevation, and he hadn't suffered. Yes, he felt the effects of altitude at times, but he knew how to pace himself and enjoy the moment. He missed his family for those few days, and he never fully let go of civilization. The cutthroat trout he'd landed while in the Titcomb Basin were one of the best backpacking meals he'd ever enjoyed. Fishing was a new skill for his trips this summer. Enjoying the sunrise in one of his favorite places on earth, The Cirque of the Towers, had been his favorite part of the trip. The memories that he gathered would carry him into old age when he couldn't make it up the mountains anymore.

Now, though, this would be his fourth trip to the Sierras. He had had a couple of less than successful backpacking trips in this area, and he'd also had one of the best trips of his life when his teenage son, Will, joined him on the John Muir Trail a couple of years ago. The Sierras are much busier than the Winds since they're so much closer to California's big cities. The internet made the Range of Light more popular every year. There is something magical about the Sierras that he had not found anywhere else in his many backcountry trips. While there were more people in the Sierras, there were also more like-minded people that he came across. Getting away from it all was one reason he so enjoyed backpacking but running into some of the most agreeable people in the world – in the middle of nowhere – was also enjoyable.

Friends and family asked Fred *why* he enjoyed backpacking, and the question always made him smile and confused him at the same time. He'd always been drawn to the outdoors. The peace he found there just felt right. As a teenager, he'd gone for long walks to get away and spend time with himself. In college, he'd been able to travel, camp, and hike in a great many places. His early career had taken him to the big city, and he spent weekends camping and hiking when he could. The 'call of the wild' had echoed within him, and he had cautiously begun to explore the wild world. Over time, as he chose work and family responsibilities, he felt the need to get further away and deeper into the wilderness to keep his balance, and backpacking provided that avenue. He also became more comfortable with his skills, that he could take care of himself "out there." He'd pushed himself in midlife, slowly at first, taking short solo trips and then more prolonged and profound trips. Now, his kids were teenagers and growing more independent, and his wife knew that he had this particular yearning.

Backpacking wasn't that dangerous, but it seemed to be when separated from home's comforts and society's safety. But being too safe was also risky for someone like Fred. As John Muir once wrote to his sister, *the mountains are calling, and I must go.* The high that he felt after a backpacking trip carried him through the autumn months, and by the depths of winter, he felt the hunger to start planning his next wilderness journey, the next high. Even his wife Asta didn't fully understand – but she did. She knew how important being in the wilderness was for Fred and made him a better person, husband, and partner. Over time, he felt like he'd found a balance between his needs for adventure and wilderness renewal and his family's needs for him to be in their lives, providing the succor that they required. He appreciated that his family also enjoyed their time deep in the out of doors.

Every one of his backpacking trips brought back different memories. Early backpacking trips seem to have been as much suffer fests as fantastic scenery. He had learned a lot over the years, traveled smarter and more manageably, and had lightened his pack weight by nearly half. The memories of clouds of mosquitoes, drenching rains and booming thunder, slipping on suncups, and being cold and soaked to his core were not endearing. But those memories were more than well balanced by the occasional deer, elk and mountain goat, sunrises and glorious sunsets, stars so bright and seemingly near that he thought that he could pick them like grapes. Going to bed dead tired, recounting the travails of the day, and falling fast asleep. Waking to the morning songs of the birds and new opportunities. Simply sitting on a rock with a view for miles that he'd never see again. The more he backpacked, the more comfortable he became in the wilderness and the easier and more pleasant it was for him.

Fred was looking forward to this trip, to making more memories, to rejuvenating.

**Chapter 3**

Walking through, in and around the city thrilled Kim. There was so much activity, so much for the eyes and ears to absorb. Her neighborhood was tight but not crowded. The corner grocery store provided for most of her needs along with the weekly farmer's market. It seemed like there was a coffee house on every corner. The aroma of freshly roasted coffee and baked goods on her morning walks was one of the things that she most loved about getting up and out. Even on those many cold, dreary mornings, the aromas may not be as intense, but the hot java invigorated her.

On this venture out, she had not purchased a whole lot of fresh produce, just enough to get her through the next few days. Vacation was coming up. The work week was almost over and she was relaxing and packing her bags, sorting out her clothes. A long-awaited trip to Europe was just around the corner. Coronavirus had nixed her plans the previous year, but not this year. Europe was open again, and she was going to enjoy her time in Vilnius and London, along with a stop in Amsterdam. Kim hadn't traveled as much as usual over the previous eighteen months, so it was time to make up for it. San Francisco and Vilnius were so similar and so different. Both were hilly, rustic, and vibrant. While San Francisco was a Pacific melting pot of cultures, Vilnius was more typically European and cosmopolitan. Amsterdam was, well, Amsterdam - a mixture of cultures, canals, and food. It was a feast for the eyes, palate and soul!

Work kept her busy through the pandemic. She could quickly bury herself in projects that enthralled her, but it was always good to step away and see the more significant and natural world. Kim enjoyed sitting in her home office, looking out onto the world from her windows. She had always been interested in computers and the things behind them that you couldn't see. Her first computer was a hand-me-down from her father, who had been a programmer. He had taught her about logic and the beauty and simplicity of making electrons do what you want, about the endless puzzles that coding a program can bring, as well as the satisfaction of solving the puzzles. While there was frustration in debugging programs, there was excitement in solving the problem – and then moving onto the next puzzle. These puzzles were her challenges, the challenges that sometimes kept her up long into the night, kept her searching for answers when she should be sleeping.

In college, Kim excelled in her computer, math, and logic classes but hadn't been as strong of a student in her social science classes or social life. She was an attractive, competitive, feisty, athletic woman but didn't find the same attraction in others. Being an introvert had its strengths and weaknesses. She had plenty of male friends, primarily through work, but no one close. After her Ph.D. program, she made her way towards Silicon Valley and quickly found her skills needed and appreciated. Different businesses had wooed her with enticing offers, some with great prestige and salaries. Still, she enjoyed her work and her employer, even if she couldn't tell family or friends for whom she worked or what she did. She spent most of her workdays in the formal offices with her teammates. Occasionally, *'they'* permitted her to work from home, but only on non-sensitive issues. Here, she was able to work at her own pace with fewer interruptions from co-workers. Working from home was a perk that she hadn't thought would be permitted. Still, she convinced her supervisors that she could safely perform her tasks here without compromising security, especially since most of her work from home involved management issues like approving time sheets, hiring, performance reviews, and the like. Today, she would be clearing accumulated office chores from her task list, like submitting a request for reimbursement for her last work trip. Kim had created a seemingly safe and comfortable rut for herself, living and working in San Francisco and exploring the area, its cultures, and cuisine. Her occasional forays into Napa Valley fed her sense of adventure.

However, work consumed her as much as she let it, and it usually managed to dominate her life, which was fine by her – to a point. Lately, work had been dragging her down more than a little bit. Her "projects" had increasingly dark undertones. As much as she liked solving her computer puzzles, the puzzles involved more and more security issues, chasing hackers and their efforts to infiltrate computer systems. Early in her career, Kim's security work for industrial and commercial clients created great value for them by protecting their intellectual property and processes. Her work for private clients caught the attention of her current employer who had made her an even better offer and a chance to be more useful to more people. As the world became more complex, connected and digitized, bad actors became a more significant issue. Kim now spent less time creating value, it felt, and more time preventing problems. She knew that she was good at what she did, but it was still sapping some of her spirits away, trying to stay steps ahead of the next big problem. In her time, Kim had thwarted more issues than several people combined, and there was satisfaction in that. She, though, was someone who tended to see the good in people and society, so it bothered her that she spent so much of her time putting out human-made fires caused by greed, hunger for power, and maliciousness. Drawn to computers and the internet with the hope of creating a better world, she now spent much of her energy and time trying to outsmart intelligent people on the dark side of the internet. On the other end of her computer screen, Kim knew there were people similar to her – some female, primarily male, and presumably well paid by whomever to create havoc in the world. She couldn't understand the *why*, though. There was so much creativity in what these people did; why couldn't they use their efforts to make the world a better place?

More and more, she had been sitting back from her work and pondering these more philosophical, existential questions. Her morning walks for coffee, groceries, and flowers had been longer and more meandering. The long walks in her neighborhood were the physical manifestations of the long walks in her mind. Today's walk was longer than many in part because the morning sun felt so good on her cheeks, and yesterday's rains had cleansed the air and made everything fresh again. The lightness that she felt today and the pleasure from the sun and smells took her away from her work broodings. She stood on her front stoop, turned around and looked back over her neighborhood, took a sip of coffee and one last breath of fresh air before she put her head down to head into her home and get a good start on the day. *Where did I put those hotel receipts?* she thought to herself. Her thumb rested on the electronic sensor on the door, while she twisted the key in what appeared to be an analog lock. Opening her front door, Kim was so lost in her pleasant morning thoughts that she didn't notice that the umbrella wasn't where she had picked it up and then set it down when she left home an hour earlier.

Chapter 4

Approaching Fresno, Fred felt himself grow tense. The cross-country drive had been pleasant and uneventful. Not being comfortable in big cities, he tried to avoid them as much as possible. He always found it curious that they all seemed pretty similar when he drove or walked in cities. They all looked the same, smelled the same, and gave him the same jitters when so many indifferent people and cars surrounded him. Being in a city was in contrast to how he felt being in the wilderness where everything felt so vibrant, unforgettable, and new, even if he was visiting someplace for the umpteenth time. Fred knew that the risks he took to be in the wilderness were similar or maybe higher than being in a city but tweaking an ankle or even possibly running into a bear seemed to be 'natural' risks compared to being mugged on the street. Nature seemed to look different to him in every moment. The light changed the landscape; clouds flew across the sky; the wind breathed life into him. He knew that light, shadows, and wind existed in the city, but they didn't animate him there.

Fred found the little house on the cul-de-sac with the help of his GPS. His college roommate and wife had lived in this house for twenty years, carving a different niche in life from his own life. Gary wasn't home today but had left Fred instructions on parking his car and stashing his keys. After his car was safely in the driveway, Fred unloaded his pack from the back seat and rifled through the last bit of equipment in the car trunk. Before leaving home, he had scheduled an Uber to take him into the Sierras, and it should be here in a few minutes. Final decisions needed to be made about what to pack and what to leave in the car. It was one of his weird rituals where he needed to decide whether to bring a warmer coat or another shirt, thinking about what the weather might be over the next few weeks and how things had worked out on previous trips. And it didn't seem to make much difference. He always brought a couple of things that were dead weight, and there were always a few items for which he'd be longing over next weeks, but they'll be here in the trunk.

Soon, a small car with a large U decal in the windshield crawled down the street, and Fred could see the searching driver from where he stood. He waved and got the driver's attention. The Uber pulled to the curb, and Fred raised a finger to signal that he needed just a minute more. He could spend another hour trying to decide what to bring and what to leave, and it wouldn't make a whole lot of difference. He wouldn't know if he'd made the right decisions for another few weeks. Fred shrugged, hoped that he'd chosen the right equipment, closed the car trunk, and then hid his car keys where Gary would find them, and strode towards the idling Uber.

Fred tucked his pack into the backseat, and then he followed with his lanky frame. Before leaving the neighborhood and getting onto the main road, the driver introduced herself as Heather.

"So," Heather said, "from the order, it looks like we're taking a long drive east to the mountains, but you're not coming back with me. What's up with that? I take it from seeing your pack that you're going for a long walk."

Fred smiled a little smile because he always enjoyed the curiosity of the incredulous. "Yep, I'm heading into the Sierras for long-needed vacation."

"Vacation!? With a backpack? Sweating your butt off? Heaving your lungs out? Knees feeling like aching rocks? Eating burnt food over a fire? Worrying about critters getting into the tent? That's not my idea of a vacation. Take me over to the coast, some wine or brewskis, relaxing in the sand and surf. Now, that's a vacation."

Fred smiled even more, having had similar conversations many times before.

"I understand. Everyone has their definition of relaxing and vacation. I've been to the coast, too, with my family and when I was in college. I've enjoyed my time there, but there's something unique and magical about the mountains that you can't get anywhere else. For me, it's like a drug, a high that I only get to enjoy once or twice a year."

"Well, this is California. I can hook you up with similar experiences on a more frequent basis if you need. But I understand. Like you sorta said – different strokes for different folks."

They rode for a few miles in silence, Fred still thinking about the things that he might have forgotten. Every time he went through his mental list, he came up with the same answer – *I'm good*. He'd been backpacking so many times that he had his trip preparations pretty well down and also knew that if he had forgotten something that it probably wasn't that important.

The miles through the farmland east of Fresno seemed monotonous to Fred and reminded him that he was a part of something larger than himself. His natural side knew that he could not separate from the artificial side that depended on monoculture farming and the other aspects of modern life upon which he relied. He would hardly know how to survive if the world suddenly changed from how we know it now. He wished that the world had taken a different path; he knew that this is the path we all traveled, and he was thankful that the way was slowly changing for the better. In his own life, he recycled, had an electric car as his second car, used water reasonably efficiently, and shunned pesticides for his lawn. But he also owned a gas SUV, frequently flew to see his clients, and watched his children spend endless time entertaining themselves with social media on the internet. The problem of modern life weighed on him, but he would be away from these issues for much of the next three weeks so that he would better appreciate everyday life when he returned.

Heather had the radio on, softly humming to herself, being a modestly attentive host but also trying to do her job and drive Fred to his destination. Fortunately for Fred, she was enjoying California public radio, which suited him just fine. The hourly news came on, touting more progress on the economy, conflict in the Middle East, and a feel-good story about how windmills grew in Iowa like corn. When the programming switched to the local scene, some clamor was about the weather and a new restaurant trend in LA. Fred was zoning out, watching the rows of fruits and nuts fly by, and enjoying a quiet moment of not being in control, not driving, not refereeing sibling disagreements, but not yet hiking in the mountains.

The further east he rode, the bigger the Sierras appeared, and the more he felt excitement growing inside of him. He drove over the Sierras a day ago while on I-80 but had not been in them. Now he was getting ready to enter them, breathe them deeply, and experience them as few people did – the lucky people. No matter how many times Fred went backpacking, there was always this excitement and anxiousness before taking those first few steps. The enthusiasm that it was finally becoming real after months of planning, prepping, and hoping. He was slightly anxious, knowing that he had canceled other trips because of life events like sick kids and a pandemic, which he hoped were behind him for this trip. Anxious about what might go wrong or the difficulties that he might face over the coming weeks. And there was always that element of his mortality that he felt. He knew that he was taking risks to enter the wilderness alone, which scared him and his wife, Asta. But he also knew that these risks invigorated him and made life worth living.

Shaking his head to bring himself back from his daydreaming, Fred realized that they were entering the foothills, making their way towards Sequoia National Park and that the mountains appeared larger. He'd been this way once before and knew the road was slow and winding. The change in velocity was welcome, slowing him to meet the speed of the world that he was entering. There were fewer big trucks here, more cars, and families on vacations enjoying their summer plans. He smiled and felt it sincerely as he entered the world about which he had been dreaming for months.

The crowds around Grant Grove Village were what he had expected. Heather quietly cursed as tourists jumped into the road from between cars, doing their best to ruin her day and their vacations. Fred needed a break and asked Heather if they could make a quick stop. She was ready for a break, too. Finding a parking spot was a chore with the hordes of holidaymakers. Fred took his time, enjoying maybe his last moments among crowds, feeling almost lonely while surrounded by people. Again, he smiled and knew that in three weeks or so, he'd be cursing when he next encountered crowds like these because he'd be used to being alone. He enjoyed a soda and ice cream and picked up a lighter that he realized that he'd forgotten to pack – just in case.

Back on the road, Heather was equally glad to be away from the crowds of people, but she didn't have the same attitude as Fred. In a few hours, she'd be back here, dodging possible victims and then flowing downhill, back to Fresno and her life.

"So, tell me more about why you escape to these mountains. What's the draw?" Heather asked.

"Well, it's hard to describe, even if I knew you better. I live and work in a world that's similar to yours, I guess – I have a family who loves me and whom I dearly love. I have a great career that I usually enjoy. But there's a part of me that feels like I was born a hundred years too late, that I would have been happier with fewer modern luxuries, more simplicity, and wilderness. I know that I'm fortunate to be living in this day and age, but I'm also wistful for simpler times that I don't know. I escape to the mountains for my spiritual sustenance and to recognize how poorly I'd likely survive without all of our modern conveniences. Recognizing my weaknesses in the wilderness helps me to appreciate civilization better, I guess. I don't feel like I'm avoiding anything as much as I feel like I'm filling a void from an unknown source. Does that make sense?"

"Well," Heather slowly responded, "yes and no. I can sort of relate to who you are and how you live your life in the modern world. But I don't have any desire for my life to be more difficult. It's difficult enough already! For whatever reason, I hear what you're saying that you need to test yourself to appreciate who you are and where you are. I can sort of feel what you're saying, but I can't fully understand it. I'm younger than you and have different experiences that have molded me. I'm fighting to survive in Fresno, it feels like, without having to fight in a mountain world that's so foreign to me. Maybe when I get older and am tired of living in the city, I'll look for a challenge in the mountains – or on the beach!" she said with a laugh.

Fred smiled, knowing that he, too, had slowly come to these realizations about himself and knowing that he wouldn't appreciate where he was if he hadn't also gone through trials in his life, just as Heather was experiencing. Shoot, he likely hadn't yet experienced the worst that life could throw at you since he was still relatively healthy for a middle-aged man and living a decent but modest life. He knew that he was lucky for his health and happiness, for having Asta in his life, three beautiful kids, and the relative luxury of being able to take a few weeks off from work and family.

After a few more quiet miles, they dropped into the Kings River Valley. Fred was feeling more comfortable, excited and anxious. Heather's reaction was a bit more outward.

"WOW! I've never been here before! This view is spectacular! The river looks so powerful the closer that we get to it!"

"Yes, this is a beautiful place. And the further up the canyon we drive, the better it gets. When we stop, I'd suggest that you take a few photos. Maybe we'll get you off the coast and to the mountains yet," Fred said teasingly. "If you'd like, I could drive so that you can gawk. This road winds a lot, and it would be easy to end up in the river. I almost drove into the Colorado River once because I was watching the scenery too much."

"No, no, that won't be necessary. I'll keep my driver's eyes open and make some mental notes about places to stop on the way back," she said.

"A few miles up the road, we'll find the Kings Canyon Visitor Center at Cedar Grove. There's a small lodge with a convenience store and grill – I'll buy you a late lunch. I want to pick up a few snacks to tide me over this afternoon and evening. This store will be my last opportunity for good junk food for several days," Fred said with a grin.

They continued in silence, but now there was a peacefulness in the car that they hadn't felt down by Fresno. The old mountain magic was growing stronger. Fifteen minutes later, they parked by the Cedar Grove Lodge and checked out the store's offerings. They ordered burgers, fries and sodas, and extras for Fred and then sat on the deck overlooking the Kings River.

"So, I better understand what draws you here," started Heather, "what with all of the beauty and fresh air, but I still don't get why you want to get so far away from everybody and everything. Why can't you just be happy staying closer to the road, closer to civilization?"

Fred paused a moment before responding. "There was a time in my life when being this far from civilization, like at a national park visitor center or on nearby trails, was good enough. As I got older and better understood myself, I realized that I needed challenges and wanted to go deeper, farther into the wilderness. I've always enjoyed hiking and wanted to try backpacking. My first few trips were relatively easy and simple compared to what I do now. It's hard to explain *why* I want to get deep in the wilderness. There are sights that I see there that I know that few other people will ever see. It's generally pretty peaceful when

I'm backpacking. There's a certain odd pleasure that comes from hiking, working, climbing, sweating all day, and then relaxing by a mountain lake for supper and sunset. Now that I'm middle-aged, I wish that I had started sooner. One of my favorite things to do is to share these experiences with my family. Three years ago, my son and I backpacked the John Muir Trail here in the Sierras for more than two weeks. It was one of the best trips of my life! I just don't know what else to compare it to in a way that might make sense to you. I hope that helps."

Heather sat at the picnic table, looking over the trees and river, sipping on her soda. Finally, she responded. "Again, it does, and it doesn't help. I respect that you have this desire, but that particular bug hasn't bitten me."

They gathered their wrapping papers and cups and tossed them in the trash bins, and Fred pointed out to Heather that the road kept going a few more miles to the east – that's where he wanted to be let out.

Over the last stretch of road, Heather continued to take in the scenery with amazement. When they reached the traffic circle at the end of the pavement, Fred pointed to an open parking spot. He extracted himself and his pack from the car while Heather got out to take in more of the overwhelming view.

Fred pointed to the trailhead, and then his outstretched arm slowly moved upward. Heather frowned, not entirely understanding what he meant.

"Now is when I start the hard part – walking. I'll head up the trail and spend the night somewhere up there and enjoy my extra sandwich and chips. It's a long uphill hike for the next day or so." Fred grinned and grimaced simultaneously, knowing that there was a lot of work to be had before he enjoyed the reward.

"I wish you well, and I'm glad that you shared this bit of your trip with me. Driving people around Fresno has its ups and downs, but I've never had a client who brought me so far away from the city and who made me feel a bit of envy for their particular journey. From your ride request on the Uber app, I have your details, so I hope that you don't mind if I check in with you in a month to see how it went."

"That would be fine, and I hope for you that you'll be able to get back here sometime and explore this area a bit further from your car."

Heather got into her car and slowly drove away, head hanging out the window. A few hundred feet down the road, she stopped, got out, pulled out her phone, and took a few photos. The last thing she did was give Fred one more big wave and a smile, and she was gone. Fred began to feel his anxiousness again. He felt like an abandoned puppy left by the side of the road – which was sort of accurate.

Fred picked up his pack, sauntered away from the parking area with a smile on his face, and found the Copper Creek Trail. His adventure had begun!

Chapter 5

Kim's head was down when she stepped into her home, focused on the purchases and keys in her hands, the pleasure of her morning walk on her mind. As she kicked the door close with her heel and fumbled with her coffee cup, a firm hand closed over her mouth, and a dark hood draped over her head. The dropped cup bounced off her left shoe and warm coffee splashed against her pants, wall and floor, and keys clattered on the foyer tile. With cloth bags of fruit dangling from her wrists, her hands reached up and back, searching to find an ear, an eye, a neck, but without success. She struggled, tried to wrest herself from arms much heftier and more potent than hers. Her heel searched for feet, too, but to no avail. Her attacker didn't hurt Kim but only subdued her. After a bit more useless wrestling, she relaxed, took a breath, remained silent, and waited for instructions. She had trained for a situation like this but never really expected it to happen.

Someone slowly guided her through her home and up the flight of stairs to her office. There was some mumbling, indistinct quiet male voices and more verbal commands by her captors – *there were at least two of them, right?* – than clear directions, telling her to watch her step, where to walk. Her captors settled and took a breath now that they had her under control. Presumably, Kim would be let in on the little secret, especially since she had a central role.

Her office had a nice window that looked out to the city from her desk's left side. The room was well equipped and neat. There was very little paper around her office, a telling sign that she worked in a primarily digital world rather than analog. Her computer desk was modest, with several ancillary data storage units and two monitors aligned side by side. The panic button under her desk wasn't doing her any good from where it sat across the room. She was guided to her comfy chair in front of the window and slowly allowed to settle into it. The scent of her flowering jasmine on the table next to her chair gave her a bit of comfort.

After a few minutes and a bit more shuffling, a shadow moved over her, and then somebody gently removed the hood from her head. After she blinked a few times and smoothed her hair, Kim found two large men in her home office, wearing dark clothing and hoods. Their presence was not threatening but certainly not calming. *Someone wants something pretty badly to enter my home and wear costumes,* she thought to herself. Being a straightforward and keen woman, Kim decided to take charge, even though it wouldn't likely get her anywhere.

"Well, welcome to my home, and can you please tell me what the hell I might do for you?" she started.

The dark hoods looked at her for a moment and then turned to each other. In their way, they were also trying to assert themselves, quietly, confidently, even though they were obviously in control.

After a moment of hesitation, one of the darkened hoods finally spoke.

"Dr. Johnson, we have been asked to inquire about your recent work. Our colleagues would like to know more about your projects and hope you'd be willing to share your work with them. You have come to their attention recently as your digital poking around is raising concerns."

"Well, that doesn't give me a whole lot to go on," Kim responded. "And, just how did you get into my home, as my security system is a bit more sophisticated than most and is supposed to keep creeps like you out?" She could see that they had found the panic button and covered it to keep it from being intentionally or accidentally triggered.

"We don't know much about your work and how it has come to the attention of our colleagues, but they will be communicating with us shortly so that we can better direct your responses. Likely, you'll speak directly with our technical colleagues rather than with us. As for how we let ourselves in, we've been carefully and quietly watching you for the past several days. Your daily behavioral patterns are reasonably predictable. We scanned your security system and realized that its primary security identifier is a chip that it senses, either on or in you. We placed a small receiver by your front door the other day, and it was relatively easy to wait for your chip to emit its signal and then copy the frequency and code."

"Well done," Kim responded. "So, how long do we have to wait for directions? And what do I call you two? Do you have names so that we don't get confused? Tweedledee and Tweedledum?"

"I apologize, Dr. Johnson, for not properly introducing ourselves. You may call me Alpha, and this is my colleague, Beta. We are to assist you with logging into your computer, and then we'll contact our other colleagues for their directions."

"So, what's my motivation for logging into my computer? I don't quite get how that part's going to work," she said with a very slight bit of snark in her voice.

"You're correct," said Alpha. "Our leverage is rather limited, but not entirely. Our colleagues have various alternatives to consider depending upon how well you cooperate. The alternatives escalate in their degrees of freedom and how we all continue our 'relationship' from here on out."

While Beta was the larger of the two men, Alpha so far was in control. Allowing only one person to talk and be in authority seemed to be a reasonable strategy, Kim thought. Both men were relatively large, well-built, and their posture spoke that they expected compliance. They didn't move much, seemed respectful towards her, so far, and they appeared to be comfortable in their command of the situation. Kim had no illusion that she would be able to out muscle these two or outrun them. She knew that her strength existed in her mind and maintaining her composure. Kim also knew that this was not going to be a quick meet-and-greet and that she was going to be with these two gentleman goons for some time, so she'd better behave and hope that at some point, they let their guard down.

"Well, you can see that I haven't started my computer for the day, so do you want the honors, or do they fall to me?" Kim asked.

"Please," said Alpha, "be our guest. However, so that we're all on the same page, please do not do anything that signals to someone that you are entertaining company. That would not be a helpful move."

"No, I won't, though the thought had crossed my mind. I don't see how it's going to help me in the short or long term. May I move to my chair and desk?"

"Yes, carefully and slowly, no sudden moves. While you were away, we searched your home for alarms and weapons. Your steak knives were the most dangerous things we found, and they're now secured. You also noticed that we secured your panic button."

"Oh, you just never know what a computer scientist could do for a weapon. I just might have a ninja robot with lasers waiting in the closet," Kim said.

Alpha chuckled. "We checked for ninja robots, cameras, motion sensors, guns, and several other possible weapons. Let's just say that we neutralized the cameras and microphones before you arrived, so we're not too worried until you start your computer."

"You two and your colleagues seem to be well versed in your methods. You're better at this stuff than me, it seems. Again, I just don't understand why I even turn on my computer. I'm not going to give you access to whatever it is that you think you want. The files with which I work aren't stored here, and the layers of security that I go through to get to files and programs are just too many for me to just open things for you without alerting somebody and locking down the systems. When I remotely log into the systems you want me to enter, alerts are sent to management. It will look very odd to them because I've never logged into those systems from anywhere but my office. The system will protect itself and sacrifice me, and then we all hope for the best."

"That's sort of how we expected this scenario to unfold," said Alpha, with a bit of a sigh. "We know that you have a high-level security clearance, scrambled communication systems and that the system isn't going to allow us to enter without your cooperation. Our colleagues are also aware of your strong personality, so everything is unfolding as anticipated. That means that we move onto the next step of the plan."

"Well, please don't keep me in suspense!" Kim said. "And, my two cups of coffee have already filtered through me, so that will also need some attention soon."

For the time being, they all waited, Kim less patiently than Alpha and Beta. Beta sat in her desk chair and kept a watch on her while Alpha busied himself seemingly communicating with someone on his cellphone, typing messages, and keeping busy with whatever it is that kidnappers need to do. Kim wasn't immediately let in on the plan and passed her time trying to catch up on the reading that she'd put off for the past several months, but her mind wasn't really into it. She frequently sighed or groaned her displeasure with her situation, but her keepers didn't respond to her. This went on for several hours, all three sitting around her office. Alpha told her that they were all just being quiet and patient until evening. Kim took this to mean that they were going to take her somewhere, and Alpha agreed. She was allowed to pack a small bag of toiletries and a couple of changes of clothes, and that was it. They kept Kim as a prisoner in her office and only permitted her to move around her own home with an escort. Alpha and Beta took turns watching her, the other going to the kitchen and making snacks and sandwiches for all of them and enjoying the fruit that she had purchased this morning. Watching them eat her food really rankled Kim.

For as much as Kim enjoyed being alone, being alone with Alpha and Beta was not her idea of a good time. The magazines that she had slowly been making her way through sat on her lap. Occasionally, Kim read and flipped pages, but just as often, she sat there and tried to figure out how to get away and on who's toes she might have stepped. There were too many questions flying through her mind and very few answers.

By mid-afternoon, Kim couldn't stand the quiet, the unknowns, any longer, her bit of patience worn thin. "Could one of you please tell me what the hell is going on? Who do you work for? What did I supposedly do to piss them off? What are we waiting for?"

She rose from her chair, not knowing where she might go but also wanting to test her captors' reactions. They stood up with her and blocked any exit from her office but did so in a way that wouldn't hurt her. They were firm and in control but didn't feel the need to be heavy-handed about it.

Kim sighed, looked around dejectedly, shook her head, and plopped back into her chair. "You know, I'd like to beat the shit out of both of you right now and get on with my life, but I know that's very unlikely."

Alpha and Beta looked at each other, a slight grin rising under their hoods.

"Dr. Johnson," Alpha began, "our colleague, Omega, is in charge. We've kept him abreast of the situation, that you're not cooperative, and that's what he expected. We're a portion of Omega's extended security team, and we don't know the particulars of why we're here to gather you. Our job is to secure you and move you tonight to a safer location. Our orders are not to harm you and to treat you respectfully. We don't want any trouble from you, but we also very experienced in how to manage various difficult situations. About all that I can tell you is that you're not to be released until Omega approves, and he's not likely to approve until you cooperate. We prepared for a long-term assignment as your escorts because Omega anticipated that you would not initially cooperate."

Kim was mad, frustrated, and discouraged. "Well, who is *Omega,* and what does he want with me? Again, what have I supposedly done to piss him off?"

"Ma'am," said Alpha, "we're not at liberty to reveal who Omega is and who he represents. In fact, we've never met him, nor do we know his real identity and don't know where he's located. He prefers his anonymity. And, as I just told you, we do not know why we're securing you."

Kim just shook her head and slumped in her chair. "Well, shit," she muttered.

There were many, many possible people and groups whose wrath she might have incurred with her work. Kim kept an eye on all of the up-and-coming computer security risks and what hacker groups were employing which tools. Through her skills and her employers' tools, Kim had access to the more extensive, nefarious internet that few knew existed. Exploring the dark side of the internet is why she was tired of putting out fires. Kim knew that many people were just as intelligent and more motivated by greed and power than her. Somewhere along the way, she must have made a mistake, taken some bait, left a trail. One of the groups that her systems followed now had taken her hostage. Her systems operated on secure computers, not here in her home, but a lot of the *hows* and the *whys* of the strategies she'd help create were running around in her head. She figured that she must be more value alive than dead but shouldn't be too cavalier about that view. And she knew that her composure and health were her more significant assets at the moment.

Darkness doesn't arrive until late this time of year. It was a long, slow, dull afternoon for all three, and especially glum for Kim. She sat in her chair, but also took spells standing, stretching and laying on the floor, and looking out the window, wistfully longing for the freedom that the birds enjoyed as they occasionally flew by. Growing clouds also darkened her mood.

Outside, it grew drearier as a grey drizzle fell over the darkening city. Alpha and Beta busied themselves, gathered a few things and placed them near the front door. Kim took this to mean that the next part of their journey together was about to begin.

After the streetlights flickered on, Beta gathered Kim and her few belongings, placed a dark cloth over her head, and then helped her pull on her lightweight raincoat. He drew the raincoat's hood over her head to better hide her face. Kim heard the front door open and smelled the moist summer air and, after a few moments, someone took her by the arm, and they started walking down the street. They warned her to behave, and she had told them that she would, but she didn't feel like being compliant. Kim had her wits about her, but there wasn't much she could easily do about her situation with minimal vision through the dark cloth. Even if she managed to pull away and remove the hood, she'd be quickly re-captured. At this point, it was more rational to go along to get along.

Yes, it was more rational to go along, but Kim wasn't feeling so logical since her life was threatened. Not surprisingly, her survival instinct was overriding her logical side.

After they walked up the street and around the corner, Kim could make out through the cloth over her head that they were approaching a van or truck. The taillights glared through the hood, but there wasn't much other detail. Many of the homes along this street had wrought-iron fences, walls, hedges, and short driveways leading to closed garage doors, so she was hemmed in by these as well as cars. Beta reached for the handle to open the door on the side of the van, but it didn't easily budge, so he let go of Kim's arm to use both hands and gave it a firm tug.

Kim snatched the dark cloth off her head and ran behind the van and into the street. She didn't know which way to run in the damp gloom, but gravity helped to pull her down the street that she'd just walked up. She'd gotten a couple of car lengths downhill before Alpha stepped into the street and blocked her escape.

"GODDAMN IT!" she screamed and then exhaled a small, sad breath of defeat.

"Dr. Johnson, you're not behaving as you said you would," Alpha declared flatly. While he was moving toward her, he had been carrying a backpack in his left hand. With his right hand, he deftly removed something small from his jacket pocket, put it in front of Kim's face, and squeezed it. Kim inhaled a puff of vapor and felt lightheaded. A moment later, she collapsed on the pavement.

A light twinkled on from above a stoop, and an older, gray-haired man's head popped out a door. "Is everything OK out there? I heard a scream."

Alpha was standing over Kim, starting to lift her. "It's my girl-friend. Sorry to have bothered you, sir. She got a job promotion today and celebrated way too much. We'll be OK once I get her home."

Alpha easily picked up Kim's limp form and sort of carried her in his right arm, her head laying over his shoulder. The backpack was still in his left hand, and he lumbered towards the van. Behind him, Alpha could hear the alerted gentleman's front door close and saw his shadow disappear when the light turned off.

Beta had the van door open, waiting for Alpha and his freight, the overhead light off. They gently placed Kim in the middle seat of the van. Beta placed his hand on her head to guide it downward so that she wouldn't hit the door frame. Before Alpha closed the door, Beta climbed into the back seat, fastened Kim's seatbelt, and laid her on her side.

"I told you we shoulda tied her wrists," Beta said to Alpha.

"Yea, I trusted her too much. Let's not let that happen again," was Alpha's response as he climbed into the front passenger seat.

The truck quickly started and took off into the night. As they moved, Beta cinched Kim's wrists and ankles with zip ties. She wasn't going anywhere now without some assistance.

———————

Kim slowly returned to a groggy consciousness but continued to quietly lay still on the bench seat, the van gently rocking with *swoosh clack swoosh clack* sounds over the pavement. The sounds the tires made reminded her of crossing one of the Bay area's bridges, but she couldn't tell for sure from her horizontal position. The dark cloth was over on her head again, blocking much of her vision. She could make out the twin rows of streetlights which strengthened her belief about being on a bridge. There was a wet spot on her left cheek from where she had drooled. *Great*, she thought to herself, *there goes a bit of my dignity.* She continued to lay there, hoping that someone would say something and reveal their location, but no one spoke.

Try as she might, Kim couldn't keep track of the turns, how long they were driving in any particular direction, stops at streetlights and stop signs, and myriad other details that she knew that a well-trained hostage learned to do. She'd been knocked out and had no idea how long they'd been driving. Eventually, she gave out a slight groan, belatedly announcing her return to reality.

"Sounds like Sleeping Beauty might be waking up," said Beta with a bit of a sarcastic inflection in his voice.

Alpha turned around in the front seat in time to see Kim slowly raise herself on her left elbow, wrists tied together, stopping there for a moment to collect herself. Kim gave out a cough to clear her throat and better sell her seemingly recent wakefulness. Beta reached forward from his seat behind her, grabbed the right shoulder of her raincoat, and helped to sit up. Through the face covering, Kim rubbed her face with her hands, swiped the drool off of her left cheek, blinked her eyes, and sat there, acting as if she was just coming back to reality.

Alpha watched her. All that Kim could make out was his fuzzy silhouette. "Dr. Johnson, I hope that we don't have to go through something like that again or something even more traumatic. Do you understand?"

Kim sat there, wobbling a bit with the van's movement, head drooped, and nodded her understanding.

Alpha continued. "Thank you for your compliance – we appreciate it. Now, the drug that I used on you is short-acting and doesn't have any side effects. However, one possible consequence of using it is loss of bladder control. We haven't noticed that that might have been an issue for you, but I want to check."

Briefly, Kim felt thankful that she'd used the toilet before leaving the house. "No," she weakly uttered, "I'm OK in that department, although my elbow hurts, and my head, too."

"Ah, you must have hit them on the street when you collapsed. Yes, there are those side effects, too," Alpha said. "Are you bleeding?"

"No, I don't think so. I'm just dizzy and sore."

"OK, then, if you'll just sit back, we're going to be on the road for a while longer. Our driver also used a similar but longer acting version of the drug on someone who we think was watching your house." Alpha turned to face forward, and Kim could hear Beta relaxing behind her. Kim realized that there must be a third person driving the van.

After what seemed like a couple of hours of twisting, turning, braking, and starting, they finally stopped. Alpha cut the zip ties on her ankles, the van door opened, and Kim was slowly led on a hard path, climbed a short set of steps, and stood on a porch or deck for a moment in the cool evening air. A door opened, and she was led into a musty-smelling building, tripping a bit on the slight step up. She was walking on thick carpet or a rug, so she guessed she was more likely in a house. The snick of a light switch caught her attention, and a bit of soft light filtered under and through her hood. The door closed behind her, followed by the latching of a lock. They left Kim to stand alone while she heard footsteps moving around her, but she felt they were watching, so making a move now was a flawed idea, especially with her wrists still bound.

A few minutes later, she heard a door open and another light switch snick. Heavy footsteps faded down a set of stairs, and she listened to a door opening and something – *furniture?* – sliding and scraping across a floor. Another set of footsteps moved elsewhere about the house without any words spoken. She also heard footsteps in a nearby room – a kitchen? – but wasn't confident whether these footsteps were from the second or third person. Soon, footsteps thudded back up the steps and headed towards her.

"Come with me," she heard Alpha say, and he took her by her arm, guiding her somewhere.

"You're standing at the top of a set of stairs. If you screw up, it's easy for me to push you down. I'm going to take your hood off, and then we're going down the stairs."

Alpha gently removed her hood, and Kim raised her bound hands to smooth messy hair. The harsh light on the stairs took her aback, but after adjusting she began to slowly walk down into a typical empty basement with a laundry room and furnace. Nothing remarkable. The few cobwebs reminded her of her own basement, although this one smelled slightly better. To her right was a door that opened to a basement bedroom, and Alpha herded her in. In the room was a twin bed with a shabby pillow, sheets and a blanket and a single naked light bulb – nothing else. The musty smell was less pungent here, but it wasn't a dirty room. There was a small window near the ceiling but too small through which to crawl.

Alpha had his hood on, so she still couldn't get a look at him. He told her that this is where she'd be staying until she decided to be more cooperative with her information or Omega made other plans for her. Alpha said that there were a utility sink and toilet near the laundry area, so she'd have opportunities to take care of herself. They would bring her meals regularly, but nothing special.

Before he could leave, Kim said, "Alpha, right? You haven't told me what information it is that your colleagues want me to provide, so how can I possibly be helpful?"

"Yes, ma'am, I know. I haven't told you because no one has told me. I've only heard from Omega that we were to move you to this place. Tomorrow, maybe the next day, I'll receive my next orders, and if they involve you, I'll let you know. The only other part of my orders that are important to you is that I'm to take care of you and not let you escape. I didn't know that this place existed until the driver brought us here. We're all on a need-to-know basis."

With that, Alpha asked Kim if she needed the toilet or a drink before he shut the room and left. She decided it best to use the facilities because who knew how long it might be before she had the next opportunity.

After cutting off the zip ties around her wrists and Kim rubbing her sore joints, Alpha was a gentleman and gave Kim her privacy as much as possible. When she finished, she returned to her room-*cum*-cell. About that time, she heard footsteps coming down the steps.

"You can leave the light on if you wish if you're scared of the dark or whatever. We'll be around, so don't get too excited about trying to go out for an unsupervised walk."

28

Alpha backed out of the room and locked the door. She could hear his footsteps climbing the stairs, which meant that there was probably Beta or the driver sitting outside her room.

Kim turned off the light and laid down on the bed. It creaked a bit, which meant that they had an idea if she was on it or not. She had no idea what time it was, just that she was tired, and her elbow and head hurt. Laying there, Kim took stock of her situation. She'd been kidnapped by two men and now a third person. She'd been taken away from San Francisco, probably someplace east of the Bay Area, across bridges, but she had no idea of where in the area. She was in a small basement room of a house, she presumed, and not threatened. Well, not threatened other than being held captive. She'd pissed off someone, somewhere, but she had no idea of exactly who or why, but she had a good guess as to the how.

So, yeah, she was rummaging around in a typical situation, flying blind. This time, though, the problem was more personal and physical than digital. In a way, this indeed was a familiar position. She explored the internet's dark corners in her computer world but was never really physically threatened or at risk. Tonight, well, the threats were much more significant, and she had no idea of their intentions. As long as she kept her composure, then her chances were decent. She was behind in the game for the foreseeable future, but the game was far from over.

As long as she kept calm.

Chapter 6

When Fred got his late start on the Copper Creek Trail, he was already a bit tired. It had been a long day of traveling and there were still miles to go before he slept. The middle of the afternoon was the hottest part of the day out here and he didn't like starting out in these conditions, but that's the way it was.

One step at a time, one foot in front of the other. For Fred, during the first few miles and hours of a backpacking trip, there was always this recognition of how long the journey would take. This trip might last three weeks, and this was just the first few minutes. If he let them, these types of thoughts could overwhelm him. But it was just like eating an elephant – one bite at a time.

One step at a time, one foot in front of the other. Within fifteen minutes, he was plenty warm and hitting his stride. After sitting in his car and then the Uber for so long, his muscles argued with him, hoping for a bit more kindness than he offered.

One step at a time, one foot in front of the other. After another fifteen minutes, the sweat beaded on his forehead, and he could feel damp spots in several spots on his body, mainly where his pack rested on his back. He was barely damp yet, but he was looking forward to washing with a bit of soap and cold water this evening. He was still holding onto his citified version of hygiene; he'd be over that in a few days.

One step at a time, one foot in front of the other. There wasn't a lot to see this afternoon. He had his head down, focused on the trail, avoiding loose rocks and tree roots. The afternoon winds were blowing up canyon, at his back. A squirrel chittered a warning. There were trees all around him and not a lot of anything else to see. Trees, rocks, dirt, and the trail zigzagged upward. He looked forward to maybe having a better view tonight and a spectacular star show – if he stayed awake long enough. There was a gentle rhythm he heard listening to his footsteps in the trail grit.

After an hour, he figured that he might have climbed a thousand feet or so. His clothes dripped with sweat from his exertions. Fred took a break, ate a granola bar and some nuts, and slaked his thirst with a long draw of water from his hydration pack. He had filled his water bottle and bladder at the visitor center, but he knew that there was a stream nearby from which he could gather more water and cool himself when he needed.

One step at a time, one foot in front of the other. Fred pulled out his phone and earbuds. It was time for some music to take his mind off of his plodding and labors. He was lost in his thoughts of work, Asta, the kids, the chores needed his attention when he returned home. The good news is that the duties and work would be out of his mind as he took in more spectacular scenery over the coming days. The old tunes in his music library brought back memories. He thought of good times in college. A college friend who had passed away a few years ago was on his mind now, someone who had died too young, not getting to enjoy life. Despite his uphill struggles this day, Fred was glad to be on the trail, busting his ass, rather than working or dead. Thankful is what he felt, grateful to be here in this moment, no matter how difficult.

The next time he checked his phone, it was nearly five o'clock and time for another snack. Fred had been on the trail for a couple of hours and climbed about two thousand feet. His previous best day of climbing while backpacking had been thirty-five hundred feet, and he still had more altitude to gain today. When Fred was in college thirty years ago, he took a field geology trip to explore the Colorado Plateau. On that trip, Fred and some of his fellow students took an overnight trip to Phantom Ranch at the bottom of the Grand Canyon. It had been a fun and easy day going down, and they had lots of time to loll around. The next day, they arose early and climbed back to Bright Angel Lodge. He remembered how difficult that five-thousand-foot climb had been and how he had fallen asleep in their van that afternoon. Today and tomorrow were going to be similar, except his pack was heavier, his body heavier, and he was thirty years older, and there'd be no seat cushion at the end.

One step at a time, one foot in front of the other. He normally stopped for the day by five or six when he backpacked, so his body was telling him to stop, even though he had just started. His steps were coming a bit slower. Breathing was becoming more difficult as he gained altitude. Fred maintained a decent pace despite the thinning air.

Even though he mostly had his head down, he appreciated all that was around him. The round leaves and thin, red bark of manzanita had made him smile earlier in the afternoon, reminding him that he was back in the Sierras. Mostly though, he was surrounded and shaded by Ponderosa pine trees – tall and straight. Nearer Copper Creek, to his right, he could make out willows through the gaps in the foliage. He wasn't great at identifying plants and animals away from home, but it kept his mind busy. Red fir now supplanted the Ponderosa pines. And he always, always enjoyed seeing flowers blooming in the high country.

The sun wasn't setting, at least in the astronomical sense, but it was dipping behind the mountains when he made his way into Lower Tent Meadow. Fred was more than tired and felt a sense of accomplishment. He had made the tiniest of dents in his long trip. There were a few decent places left to stake his tent; this would likely be the last time he'd be amongst other backpackers for several nights. After his tent was up, he wandered down to Copper Creek to wash up – at least as well as he could amongst blood-thirsty mosquitoes. The good news is that his supper was pre-made tonight, the sandwich and chips that he hauled from the visitor center. He didn't need his stove and didn't need to wash dishes tonight. It was a lazy way to start a backpacking trip and he didn't complain.

Fred took a few minutes to check in with his neighbors, about their plans, weather reports, trail conditions and the like. Everyone else was in pretty much the same boat as him – starting their trips – but they had started earlier in the day than him. Everything was pretty much as expected – no surprises, but since most of them were just starting they didn't have a lot of information to offer on the trail above. And most of them would be staying on their various trails and that wasn't his plan. He might see some of these neighbors over the next day or two, but after that he'd be on his own. This was nice for him, enjoying a gentle easing from civilization.

Fred bedded down a bit earlier than he expected since he didn't need to put so much effort into making dinner. He scrolled through the photos in his phone, missing his family. These moments of loneliness were the times of his trips that he didn't enjoy, particularly early on. He knew that this was typical for his excursions and the longer he was out on the trail, the more occupied he would be with his surroundings and in the moment. It wasn't long before his eyelids sagged and he was out.

The next morning dawned early. Fred wasn't the first person out of their tent, but nearly so. When he heard the first stove hissing from his neighbors, he was ready to get on with the day; he'd already been awake for a bit, snuggled in his cocoon, enjoying the warmth and dreading the morning cold. His muscles were a bit stiff and sore, but not as bad as if he'd tried to tackle the whole five thousand feet of this climb in one day. He may be getting older but he was also smarter. He wasn't lugging around as much machismo anymore. Hot tea and oatmeal warmed him on the inside while he packed his gear.

The morning calm broke when he realized that he hadn't sent a text message to Asta the night before. Fred turned on his satellite transceiver and a message loaded from her:

> *Haven't heard from you but guess ur trashed. We hope that ur doing well; love you and miss you!*

Fred quickly sent a message to Asta:

> *36.82356; -118.58022; I'm fine. Sorry for not writing last night. Yes, long day yesterday – driving and hiking. Today should be better. Luv U!*

He smiled when he heard the *tweet-tweet* signal when the transmitter sent the message.

Since Fred didn't have a traveling partner on this trip, he moved a bit more quickly than his neighbors. He wasn't talking like his neighbors, wasn't complaining about how a tent mate snored. He enjoyed hearing the patter about him and not participating in it. He appreciated the quiet of the morning on the trail, like he savored his morning quiet at home. He was the first one on the trail this morning and bid his camp mates adieu.

With about half of the big climb done, he was glad to start the

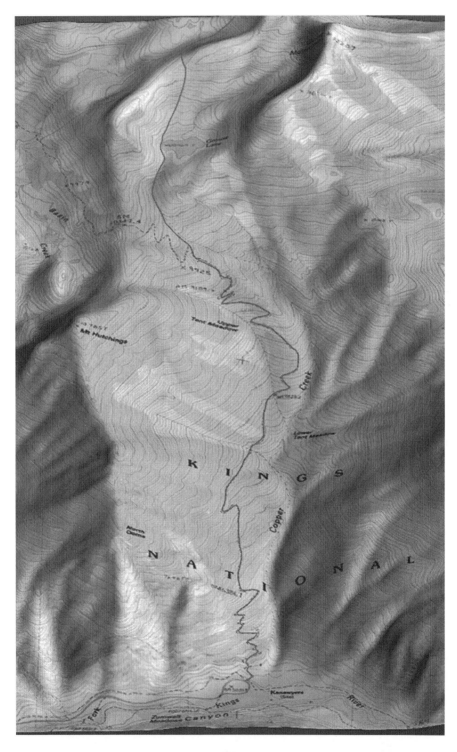

second half in the cool of the morning. He could feel the altitude getting to him a bit, which was another good reason to take a couple of days to get to the high country. He trudged upward like he had yesterday afternoon, head down. He smiled as his body warmed but knew that he wouldn't be feeling quite so happy again until he made it up to the Monarch Divide. There were occasional stops for snacks and water and to turn around and look across the Kings River Valley behind him – it was a glorious morning!

By late morning, he made it to Grouse Lake. The bulk of the climb was done, but there was still a bit more. There was water here and a great view – an ideal spot to eat even though it was early. He had put in a hard morning and deserved lunch. He chilled as the breeze dried his wet shirt, while the sun roasted his exposed skin – quite the contrast.

By noon, the sun beat down on him and beat him down. It was very warm, but not hot. An hour after lunch he finished the worst of the climb for today and for the whole of the trip. There would be long climbs in the days ahead, but not long like he had just accomplished. Fred turned and gazed over the grand vista overlooking Grouse Lake and the Kings River Valley and took a photo, another way to etch this moment into his memory.

From here, his path veered north and east. Actually, there wasn't much of path at all. He was moving off-trail, cross country towards today's goal. The walking was pleasant, meandering between a few trees and around many rocks, occasionally checking his GPS so that he knew he was headed in the right direction. Up here, it seemed like he could see forever. All he really needed to do was make certain that he chose the correct landmarks and keep himself pointed towards them.

A couple hours after lunch, Fred skirted the Glacier Lakes and dropped lower in elevation. Trees blocked his views again and he had to be more careful about maintaining his heading. Before leaving the Glacier Lakes basin he made certain to carefully check the topography and landmarks to help keep himself on the right track through Glacier Valley. He knew that if he headed down this valley he should run into his next landmark – the trail to State Lakes. A gentle hour later, Fred was at Lower State Lake. It was only mid-afternoon, and he had plenty of energy in him to cover the short distance to Upper State Lake which would be his home for the night.

When he got to the lake, he dropped his pack and found a nice rock to sit on. Fred splayed out with the sun hitting him hard while the wind cooled him. After resting and regaining some of his energy he returned to his backpack and pulled out his tent, sleeping pad and quilt. After the tent was set up, he laid the quilt over it so that it could air out. With an early stop today, he had the opportunity to test his luck with the trout!

Fred pulled out his small, light tenkara rod and tied on one of his favorite flies. While he had done his research about what the trout might bite on up here, he didn't want to think about it too much. This moment was as much about catching a meal as it was about resting and relaxing, taking his mind off backpacking. If he didn't catch anything, that was fine by him. He could rest and then not have to worry about cleaning and cooking the trout.

Today, he earned a little of both – rest and food. It took some time and many casts, but he had a couple of nice, fat trout for supper. After cleaning the fish, he got his stove and pot ready, poured some water in his pot and then poached the fish. A few minutes later, they were well cooked and nearly ready to eat. A little packet of lemon juice from his bear cannister made all the difference with the trout!

On his second night, he took a more relaxed approach to bedding down. He'd had a longer day than yesterday but had made it to camp much earlier, more in line with how he liked the rhythm of his days to unfold. His chores were finished, bear cannister stored, and he was ready for sleep just as the sun went down. He had enough energy left to find a big flat rock by Upper State Lake and simply lay back on it and take in the heavenly show that was slowly appearing. The stars here were so bright and the moon was waxing; this is a show that he didn't get to enjoy nearly as much at home and he was going to take it in as many times as he could on this trip – if he could stay awake.

The last thing he did before turning in for the night was to send a message home to Asta. She wanted to be reassured that he was alive and well, and it also helped him to track his progress when he got home.

Good to know that you're busy, having fun. We still love you and miss you!

;)

Fred sent a message to Asta:

36.92914; -118.56897; Second day was better. Got to camp early; trout for supper. Enjoyed the stars. Off to bed Luv U

Chapter 7

The following day, well after sunrise, Kim awoke on a squeaky bed, trying to figure out why she wasn't under her warm, down comforter. After a moment, she remembered, sighed, and then curled up more deeply under the blanket, trying to block out reality. She laid there for a few minutes, trying to think about what might be expected of her today and how she might respond. Upstairs, the floorboards creaked with heavy footsteps that didn't seem to be in a hurry to go anywhere. She caught a whiff of coffee and realized she was hungry.

Rolling out of bed, she went to the door and tried to turn the handle. No luck, but that's what she expected. She gently rapped on the door, hoping to catch the attention of whomever she figured must be on the other side. A moment later, "Yes?"

"I need to use the toilet, and I'd like to freshen up, if I may," she asked.

A low voice responded. "Give me a minute to get Alpha and have him come down."

Footsteps dully thudded up the stairs, the whooshing of an opening door, and then more footsteps and muffled voices above her.

After a few more shuffling steps, Kim heard someone coming down the basement stairs. She stood back from the door to not appear in a hurry or threatening, but not cowering either. She gathered herself, her courage, hoping to appear stronger, more together than she felt. The key clicked in the lock, and the door slowly opened, a hooded head surveyed the scene, ready for trouble if necessary. After finding no threat, the whole, dark body filled the doorway.

"Good morning, Dr. Johnson," said Alpha. "I understand that you'd like to take care of yourself. I'll escort you, return you to your room, and then get you some breakfast. Also, how are your elbow and head feeling this morning?"

"Yes, Alpha. I'd appreciate that. My elbow is sore and I have a bit of a lump on my head, but I'm otherwise fine. Maybe after breakfast, I can go for a long walk."

After Kim finished and returned to her room, Alpha quietly closed the bedroom door and locked it. Kim heard him take the stairs and then the sound of shuffling feet above her. More muffled, unintelligible voices filtered down to her. A few minutes later, the stairs creaked, then there was a light knock on her door, and Alpha unlocked the door. When the door opened, Alpha held a small tray with a cup of coffee, a store-bought danish, and a banana.

"Wow!" Kim said sarcastically, "room service. I seldom get this kind of treatment. When can I schedule my mani/pedi?"

Kim could tell by the slight change in Alpha's body language, how his shoulders relaxed ever so slightly, that she had gotten to him, just a bit. She'd made him smile, she thought, if only under his hood.

"I apologize for inconveniencing you like this. As I said earlier, you have come to the attention of the people I work with, and they want to learn more about what you know. I wish you no harm, and I hope that you feel that we are treating you decently."

"Well, this has to be the worst first date ever," she said and just shook her head.

Again, she could see Alpha's body language change, loosen, that he was holding something inside of himself, maybe trying to keep from laughing at her. She knew that she was getting to him ever so little, letting him know that she was human and friendly, even if he couldn't acknowledge it. She didn't know how, but she hoped that this slight advantage might help her in the future. She knew that she was better off trying to build a relationship with Alpha and the others, no matter how she had gotten into this situation. In her training for these possibilities, teachers told students to build relationships but watch out that they didn't develop Stockholm Syndrome. Even though she had tried to escape last evening, Kim still hoped that she could convince him that she was now going to be more docile, even if it wasn't true. Trying to balance playing nice and planning her next escape was challenging. Lying had never been her strong suit, but she excelled at not fully revealing the truth – just ask her parents.

Clearing his throat, Alpha said, "My colleagues will be calling you later today. They didn't tell me exactly when to expect the call. Until then, you'll have to wait here. I have a newspaper that I can bring to you if you wish, but that's about all that I can offer for entertainment."

"Yes, I'd appreciate that. And, if it has a crossword puzzle, could you please bring me a pencil, too? I promise not to stab myself with it."

Again, there was the slightest twitch in Alpha's shoulders, trying not to laugh or to let Kim get to him. But she was, and she knew it. She was pleased with herself – at least, as pleased as a captive can feel.

A few minutes later, someone walked down the stairs and slid a copy of today's edition of the *San Francisco Chronicle* under her door along with a pencil. She presumed that she was still somewhere in the Bay Area but likely to the east. She wasn't the first to read this paper; she could tell. Not that it made any difference to her. But it did tell her that her captors were likely potentially interesting people and that the people who held her cared about things more significant than themselves. Just as she had gotten to Alpha a bit, she tried to learn as much as possible about these men from the few pieces of information provided.

Kim lazily read the *Chronicle* at a slow pace. It had been years since she had read the paper cover to cover. She put the paper down for a few minutes, then picked it up and turned to the crossword puzzle. She surely must be bored or trying to ignore reality, likely the latter.

While she had her mind buried in the puzzle, she heard steps moving down the basement stairs. A light tap on the door let her know she had company, and then the door opened. Surprisingly, it wasn't Alpha because this hooded person was slightly larger and broader. Kim asked, "Is that you, Beta?"

"Yes, ma'am."

It was the first time that Kim had heard him speak, at least without the door between them. There was nothing distinctive about his voice, though. Beta had brought her lunch: another cup of coffee, carrot sticks, another banana, and a peanut butter and jelly sandwich.

"I do have to say that for being the bad guys, you do seem to be eating fairly healthy."

There was no evident emotion, no change in body language from Beta. She'd have to keep working on him.

Beta left the tray on her bed, straightened and backed out of her room, and locked the door behind him.

"Beta! Wait! May I please use the toilet? That first cup of coffee has already gone through me, and this one will make it worse."

The door reopened, and Beta stood aside while Kim walked out. He just stood there while she walked toward the toilet.

"Uh, no peeksies, OK? Alpha nicely stands at the top of the stairs while I do my duty."

Almost sheepishly, Beta clomped up the stairs. *So,* she thought to herself, *I'm getting to him, too.*

After she washed her hands and returned to her room, Beta locked the door behind her. While eating her little lunch, Kim was thinking to herself about her captors. They had been, so far, pleasant and respectful, read a good newspaper, and had not been mean or threatening. They had treated her decently and didn't inflict any unnecessary pain or consequences when she had tried to escape last night. She didn't quite know what all of this meant. It wasn't safe to take these past twenty-four hours of mostly decent behavior and extrapolate it to whatever the future might hold, nor safe to extend Alpha's and Beta's behavior to their "colleagues." She felt a little safer, though, and didn't feel like they would rape or kill her. If they were going to kill her, maybe they'd do so humanely. But she wouldn't rule out any particular torture methods yet.

However, appearing to play friendly with them while also trying to figure out how to escape did take a lot of energy and stealth not to reveal how she really felt. *These guys may be bastards, but at least their nice bastards,* she thought to herself. *While I try to lull them into a mistake, I need to keep up my façade of niceness, as well as be ready for whenever they might slip up.*

After lunch, she continued working on the crossword puzzle as there wasn't anything else to do. Letting her mind settle on her current state didn't do her any good. She completed most of the puzzle. She was thankful that it wasn't the *New York Times* crossword puzzle, or she'd complete a lot less.

The stairs creaked again. Through the door, Kim heard a voice say, "I've received a message that your phone conversation will be within the hour." It was Alpha's voice.

"Thank you, Alpha. In the meantime, I'll be diligently prepping for the call. Hey, Alpha, could you let me out for a few minutes so that I can brush my teeth? I forgot to do that since this isn't my normal morning routine."

After a brief pause, Alpha said, "Yes, Dr. Johnson. Let me go upstairs for a moment, and I'll be right back."

A few minutes later, after Kim had retrieved her toothbrush from her pack, Alpha opened the door, stood back to let her pass, and then took his position at the top of the stairs. As she brushed her teeth, Kim thought to herself how odd it was that they were all learning their roles in this scenario after a little more than a day. People can be so predictable, pleasant, and understanding, even in the worst of times. Or else Alpha, Beta, and the driver were being very well paid by someone. It could be both, she thought. She also realized that she, too, needed to appear to be nice and predictable until opportunity knocked.

After returning to her room, Kim sat on the floor in the corner of the room, knees pulled to her chin, thinking about the situation and the players. *Why were these guys halfway decent?* She guessed that was their nature, but did it also reflect on the 'colleagues' with whom she'd be talking? In her perusing of various groups' digital skeletons and footprints, had there been any group that seemed more human, more refined than others? It struck her as an odd way to view the inanimate, digital world she explored. But, every group, every scheme, every hacker that she had ever encountered in her work were sterile and evasive. They focused on money, information, power, or all of the above.

As she mulled over the organization's personality that she seemed to have offended, she remembered that the group had kidnapped her and wanted something from her. She didn't need or want to play nice, although that's what she most wanted to project. It might be just their game plan to play as pleasant as possible so that she might, eventually, give up whatever secrets that they wanted from her. It was likely as smart for them to play her as it was for her to play them while she thought about her escape.

Kim had one major project on her plate and several smaller ones, and she couldn't figure out which of these projects had irritated someone. In reality, they were all designed to thwart the interests of the objects of her attention. If groups were behaving nicely and putting good before evil and greed on the internet, then they didn't have anything to fear from her. The good actors didn't even know she existed, and that's how she wanted it to be. She had been following so many digital villains that she couldn't come up with any one group that might want to pursue her. And she didn't really follow individuals and groups as much as she followed tools, patterns, and trends, which lead her to the groups behind them. Every nefarious group she had identified would like to figure out who she was – and someone had found her. Some groups that Kim chased likely didn't have the resources to engage in an elaborate kidnapping and more. Other groups did have the resources, but she figured that they viewed her as just a chess piece on the other side of the board. *What had she done and to whom to cause her current situation?* As she pondered that question, Kim just smiled to herself because whatever it was, it must be good! Her computer programs must be working as intended and maybe even better than she had hoped. In a way, she was proud of herself, and that made her feel slightly better. A smile crossed her face. Her captors had the edge on her because they'd been planning her capture for some time. Was there a way for her to get up to speed and even ahead of these people?

After enjoying her moment of basking in her glory, she heard footsteps on the treads, and Kim snapped back to reality, realizing that, ah, yes, she was being held somewhere in a basement against her will. There was a light knock on the door. The door unlocked, and there was Alpha's hooded head. She could tell it was Alpha because he wore his hood slightly further back on his head than Beta, a little more loosely, in an almost jaunty fashion.

The hood looked toward Kim, still sitting in the corner. Alpha set a cellphone on the bed.

"In about five minutes, this phone will ring, and my colleagues would like to speak with you."

"And, what if I don't want to talk with them?" she retorted. *That was a little snarky of me*, she thought to herself. *Oh well.*

"Um, I don't know, ma'am. How you respond is up to you, and how my colleagues respond is up to them. I know my role, and I'm just filling it. But I do know that if you don't cooperate, then the ordeal continues."

"Thank you, Alpha. I'm sorry – but not sorry – to snipe at you, but I hope that you realize that you're the 'face' of your employers, even if you're wearing a mask."

Again, there was a slight loosening in Alpha's shoulders. "Yes,

Dr. Johnson, I understand. I would be frustrated, too, if I were in your shoes." He continued to stand in the doorway, watching her to make certain that she didn't make any unnecessary phone calls.

Alpha did have some empathy – she knew it! This thought buoyed her ever so slightly. It was a small victory, and she was going to enjoy it.

A few minutes later, the phone on the bed beeped. Kim picked up the phone, saw *unknown number* on the display, took a deep breath to gather herself, and then pressed the button to take the call.

"Yes, this is Dr. Kim Johnson. To whom am I speaking?" She had taken the initiative, and she felt her power.

There was a brief pause on the line that seemed to be caused as much by distance and circuits as by the caller taking their time.

"Dr. Johnson, you may call me Omega. I am one of the colleagues of whom Alpha has been telling you. We hope that Alpha and Beta are treating you well, given the circumstances."

"Yes, they've been perfect gentlemen, other than keeping me confined against my will."

There was a slightly delayed chuckle on the other end of the line.

Again, taking the initiative, Kim said, "Can you please tell me why you're holding me? I've wracked my brain and can't figure out who would want me or why."

Another pause.

"Well, Dr. Johnson, we have been following you for some time. We have reviewed your academic history, your papers, and your awards. We know who you work for."

Pause. Did Kim hear a faint accent in the voice?

"I work for myself. I have secured independent research grants from various governments, nonprofits, and corporations over the years. I don't understand why my research into computer security systems has brought on your attention."

Omega continued. "Dr. Johnson, I have a limited amount of time to speak with you tonight, so I'll get to the point. We also have been able to track some of your wanderings around the internet. Your work in computer security systems is much more than that, especially to us. While you may have grants and contracts, we also know that a particular U.S. security agency directly employs you.

"In your work, you appear to have created a very effective tool.

But a tool is simply a tool. It has no intrinsic negative or positive value. A hammer can build a home or break a window. A chemical can be nutritious or toxic, depending on the quantity. So, too, is your work on computer security systems. For some, your work is helpful, while for others, it is quite an interference. Most computer security systems are defensive, but the tool you created is new, unique, special. It seems to be an offensive computer security system that we've never before encountered. And to be perfectly frank, we don't know how to work around it or defeat it, and it's impeding our efforts."

Ah, Kim thought to herself, *I guess that it's working – better than I'd thought!* She was glad that Omega couldn't see her smiling.

"Yes, I understand your point. Different tools have different values depending upon your perspective. And, from my perspective, the tools that I create with my team and use are very valuable to the greater good of society because we prevent intrusions and thefts of information and wealth. However, you seem to be confusing my work with someone else's work and giving me credit they deserve. I'm not clear why you think our security systems are causing you any more problems than any other security system. Again, I'm just trying to keep unauthorized people out of computers. We're just responding to attacks. There's nothing aggressive about our work."

The pause again, the tiniest bit of a crackle in the connection.

"Dr. Johnson, you do seem to see the dichotomies that exist in the world, the *yin* and *yang.* When we choose one side, we feel that we are choosing the right side, we hope. However, both sides are necessary. There cannot be life without death. Nothing lives forever. There cannot be good without bad."

"Yes, I understand the dualities of life, of existence. But you aren't helping me to understand my role and how my role is affecting your efforts. You're blaming me for the efforts of others, as I said. And, you're blaming me for your ineffectiveness. We've designed our tools to prevent unauthorized people and groups like you from getting into computer systems, just like every other person who works on computer security. You and I are in an ongoing struggle: I create better locks, you pick those locks, and then we go around again. That's the game we're in and now you've elevated the stakes by kidnapping me. It's like you've now decided to kidnap the locksmith rather than learn how to pick the lock. If it's not me and my lock that impedes you, then it will be somebody else. You're quite obtuse, making this more difficult than it needs to be."

The pause was longer this time as if gathering thoughts. And, maybe Kim heard a sigh on the other end.

"Dr. Johnson, when you took on your current role, was that a conscious decision?" asked Omega.

"I'd like to think so. I'd like to think that it was a conscious decision made over the course of many smaller decisions. I feel that I took stock of my world, the world, and my role in it and chose a course that was fitting for me."

"Good, good," said Omega. "We, too, have been through similar times of reflection as you, made similar choices, and believe that we are making our choices for the greater good. Towards this end, we search the world for opportunities. Our search tools involve computer systems and the data, information, and knowledge they store, gleaning from these systems and combining this information in novel ways.

"Throughout our searches, we have come across your work many times. We feel that we may have similar aims as yours and that there could be fruitfulness in combining our efforts."

"I must say that I am confused," responded Kim. "I've never had someone approach me about working with them by kidnapping me. The requests for introductions that I typically get are at conferences or via email and phone calls. Knowing what I work on and how you introduced yourself to me strikes me as an opportunity that I would not find inviting. Is there something that I'm missing here? Am I unaware of ways that I could be a bigger, better contributor to society?"

"We believe that we could put someone with your talents to more effective and more lucrative uses for everyone involved. You see, your worldview is rather one-sided. In the duality, one side is not necessarily only exemplary and the other only wrong. Roles can change over time, like the tides in an estuary. Positions are mixed and fuzzy. Have you not done something wrong one moment, like treating someone poorly, and then turn around and help the same person? This duality exists equally in ourselves and our societies, although we most often see it in how we view others, but not as frequently in how we view ourselves.

"In our view, we seek to restore balance to these roles that have gotten out of balance. Resources have been hoarded by the proverbial good side, leaving one side poorer and weaker. We only seek to create better balance so that all societies benefit, so that all people have an equal and fair chance in life."

"OK, I'm listening and thinking," she said. "I understand your philosophy as being similar to mine, I hope. But it feels like *how* you implement your philosophy is likely different from how I fulfill my values. For example, I can't find in my philosophy how kidnapping someone is beneficial to the greater good." Kim was trying to keep herself calm, but there certainly was an edge to her voice, an indignant edge.

"Yes, yes, we have pursued methods that we previously thought were beyond us. We'd like to think of this moment not as forced detention but rather as a transition period to a new beginning."

Now, Kim was getting a little hot. She was holding her tongue, wanting to spout off, but knew that it wasn't in her best interest since she didn't seem to be holding a strong hand at the moment. "Go on," she said, "you obviously have my undivided attention." *Drat,* she thought to herself, *that was a slip.*

"We aren't at all clear on your methods, but we are clear on your impacts on our gleaning. We feel that you could be more productive, more beneficial to all involved if we could use your methods to improve our gleaning. We would like you to work for us. You could live and work anywhere you wish, as long as you maintain an extremely high level of secrecy, more so than you do now. And, of course, you would be abundantly rewarded for your efforts. Best of all, you would be addressing your desires for achieving the highest good, and more people would be better off and have better lives.

"Well, Alpha, you're going to have to be more specific with me about how I can be of more help to more people," said Kim.

"At the moment, I don't have the time to go into more detail, as I have other pressing matters with which to deal. I'll call tomorrow, likely earlier in the day so that it's convenient for the both of us, to further discuss our proposition. In the meantime, what might you like for supper? Please tell Alpha, and I'll have him see to it that you have it."

"Well, OK, Omega, we'll talk tomorrow, I guess. But I still feel nearly as clueless as when we started, as well as perplexed by not knowing what you're blaming on me."

The phone went silent, leaving Kim confused and frustrated, dwelling on her thoughts. On the surface, the opportunity held some intrigue, but not much. She was a person who usually liked to hear people out, even if she hadn't previously agreed with them, because she knew that she didn't have perfect knowledge and that there was much she could learn from other people, their experiences, and perspectives. Work had been burning her out a bit, especially when she hadn't been able to see or feel the effectiveness of her efforts. Sometimes, completing a household repair was more fulfilling than her work because there was a clear start and finish, as well as pride in fixing squeaky wheels. Life might be better, more comfortable with Alpha; maybe the grass might be greener on the other side of the fence.

On the other hand, and much more dominating, this situation and this approach didn't feel at all right. Omega had talked calmly and smoothly, even philosophically, appealing to the best parts of Kim. He obviously knew Kim better than she knew him; he'd done his research on her, and he hadn't revealed much of anything about his organization. There was too little detail in what Omega wanted her to do and too little detail in how she interfered with his current efforts, although she had a pretty good idea. That's what she most strongly felt. If Omega had a marketing brochure or website, she would look at it, but that's not the world in which he operated. Her inner voice said that she had barely scratched the surface with Omega and that all was not as he presented it. His worldview was at odds with hers and likely couldn't be reconciled. Her inner voice felt quite strongly that Omega's offers weren't nearly as good for her as they might seem. She was getting a little irritated with herself for even trying to find the opportunities in whatever Alpha was attempting to peddle.

No big deal, she told herself. Kim rethought that attitude – it was a big deal because they'd kidnapped her. I'll keep listening, asking a few questions to keep the game going, but she didn't feel like she would fold. The longer that she could extend this then the more likely she was to find opportunities to escape. That was about the only redeeming feature that she could find in continuing to play this game. Also, the longer they played this game, the more likely Alpha's crew might make a mistake or someone would rescue her.

She was lost in her thoughts, considering the various possibilities, sitting on the bed. Alpha had been quietly waiting for her to finish the call, watching from the dark basement outside the small bedroom. Finally, he appeared in the doorway, startling Kim out of her assessment of Omega's offer. He extended his hand towards the cellphone and she gave it to him. She'd been so busy thinking about Omega that she'd forgotten that she held in her hands an opportunity to call for help. She could have easily and quietly dialed *911. God, I'm so stupid sometimes,* she dejectedly thought to herself.

Alpha's words pulled her from her despair, but barely. "Before he called, Omega told me that he wanted me to check in with you about what you might like for supper. What can I get for you? I can order about anything, and I'm a decent cook."

Kim sighed. "You know, Alpha, a nice bottle of wine and a supreme pizza would make me happy right now," she answered. "Comfort food and sedatives. Something to help me forget."

"Yes, ma'am. I'll be back in a couple of hours and bring you supper."

Kim felt that she was building a minimal relationship with Alpha and, hopefully, could do the same with Beta. She doubted that she was anything more to Omega than a tool to help him achieve his disreputable goals, another functionary.

Left with her thoughts and feelings again, Kim just couldn't shake the idea, the intense feeling, that Omega's values were inconsistent with hers. Her work might be similar, but how Omega used it would be out of her control. Since it seemed that her work frustrated Omega and his group, the tools that she and her team had created must be more advanced, more effective than they knew. How she could twist her security system to help Omega wasn't clear and that was fine by her. In fact, to work with Omega, Kim would have to come up with ways to thwart her security tools, and her team was already working on that, trying to stay ahead of the competition. She had felt this sort of a conundrum earlier in her career as she weighed her opportunities. No matter who creates an invention, it's usually the business people who got rich off it and directed its use in the world. Many scientists had made discoveries or inventions, feeling that they were doing something good for the world, only to find later that their creations were not employed as the scientists and inventors intended. Alfred Nobel came to Kim's mind at that moment.

A while later, Alpha delivered the pizza and a couple of plastic cups of a decent chianti. Kim slowly ate and drank, lost in her thoughts, and bored by her surroundings. She tapped on the door to signal that she wanted to use the bathroom. After brushing her teeth and washing, Kim returned to the cell and laid in the dark with her thoughts, knowing her likely direction. She strongly felt she was on her path, a good path for her, and Omega wanted to divert her to something that wouldn't be right for her.

It was going to be a long and restless night.

**Chapter 8**

Fred slept like a rock his second night on the trail. The first day had been invigorating, but draining, and he had a modest, fulfilling second day. There were a couple of times during the night when he woke up, gasping for air. Moving so quickly to a much higher altitude had its consequences. Fortunately, he had no headaches, so acute mountain sickness was not much of a worry but something to keep a watch on. He wasn't in a hurry to get up this morning but was awake around sunrise – being hungry has that effect on a person. His body was still in the earlier time zone of home. At first, he just laid in his snug, warm quilt, enjoying the sounds of the morning birds. He slowly started to move, figuring out which parts of him were stiff, painful, or both. His back and shoulders hurt a bit, and his legs felt tight. His hips were plenty sore; carrying a backpack for a long distance always caused him pain in his hip muscles until they got used to be used so much. His throat was a bit sensitive, but he figured that he must have been snoring after being so tired last night, as well as the dry air. Finally, there was a tingling warmth on his calves and arms, which he figured meant that he'd been in the sun too much the past couple of days. He found his clothes in his stuff sack pillow and pulled them into his quilt to warm a bit. After a few minutes, he started his morning contortions of dressing himself in his warm cocoon. After he felt that he had most of the clothing sorted, he laid there for a moment more to relish the warmth before bursting into the cold, morning air, as well as to enjoy the satisfaction of this adventure. Two days down, nineteen or so more to go.

Fred found his shoes, crawled out of the tent, and smiled with the beautiful morning colors. He stood to face the rising sun and take on a little solar heat. His arms stretched as high as he could make them, and he heard a couple of vertebrae pop – *oh, that feels good!* The bear canister was where he had left it. Bringing it back near his tent, he found his breakfast and boiled water for tea and oatmeal. Fred ate while packing his quilt, pad, and tent. About forty-five minutes after waking, he was loaded and ready to go. He let out a very audible groan when he pulled the pack up and onto his right leg and then slung it onto his shoulders and back. Moving around camp and stretching had loosened his muscles and reduced some of his pains, but not all of them.

The third day would also be relatively short and easy. Fred had planned the trip around various obstacles, like mountain passes, and opportunities to camp by beautiful lakes. He had a couple of big obstacles coming up tomorrow and today was a day for him to keep on acclimating. No use burning himself out too early, pushing his body harder than it needed to be pushed. The going today wasn't too difficult but it wasn't easy, either. He was off-trail again and that caused him to move slowly and carefully. The topography was the typical up and down stuff. At high points, he'd pick out his landmarks and guide himself by those, hoping that he'd still be able to keep sight of these natural signposts when he was at lower altitudes in the forest.

All in all, the third day was pretty unremarkable. Fred's body felt a bit better; breathing was coming easier for him. There might be a couple of blisters developing on his heals, but he was paying attention to those hot spots. His shoulders and hips ached less than yesterday, which was a sign of his improving shape and the loss of weight in his bear canister.

This was another day of about ten miles – maybe less. Fred had the energy to go farther but if he did, he'd have to get over a mountain pass and then a few miles farther to find a decent camping spot – not worth it. By mid-afternoon, he passed Marion Lake and it looked like a beautiful place to camp, but there was still plenty of daylight left. In the Lake Basin, there were several quaint lakes that each had their own charm and great views – and mosquitoes. Fred eventually chose a location where he had great views all around. There was plenty of time for him to wash his clothes a little better than normal and enjoy a relaxing supper. He wasn't in the mood to try to fish in these small lakes and he still had plenty of food to get him to his first resupply. Fred would be able to enjoy the sunset to the west and the play of pastel twilight on Vennacher Needle to his northeast. Tomorrow could be grueling, so best to relax, rest and let his body recover.

To Asta: *36.98603; -118.50359; @Lake Basin; good day; relaxing; enjoying sunset. Luv U!*

To Fred: *Glad to live vicariously through you! Kids miss you too! Looks like you might get wet tonight. Luv U!!*

Asta was right. Near midnight, the winds picked up and the storm hit hard a half-hour later. Fred laid in his warm quilt, enjoying how his tent flapped and swayed in the wind, comfortable that he was out of the worst of the weather but annoyed that some of the stray water droplets blew beneath the edges of his tent and around the door flaps. He'd brought a small, lightweight, one-person tent held up by his hiking pole, and it was best suited for calm summer nights in the mountains. Packing such a light-weight tent meant that it provided a bit less protection in conditions like these than a heavier tent; there were always trade offs. The tent was designed to keep him a little warmer and protect him from wind, rain, and insects. There was just enough room in the tent for Fred's backpack, pad, quilt, and him. The ability of the tent to keep him dry was proportional to how securely he placed the stakes in rocky soils and sand. He'd been lucky tonight that he'd set the stakes well, but the wind still drove some cold droplets onto him. The quilt was getting a bit wet; if it didn't get any worse and didn't last too long, his body heat would dry it in due time. Unfortunately, the storm continued strong for another couple of hours, and Fred coped by pulling the tent edges down with his fingers and using his pack to block the upwind edge. While not miserable, Fred knew that you had to take the good with the bad while backpacking as in life. As it turned out, it wasn't the worst night that he had ever spent outdoors and the pitter-patter of rain on his tent put him into a sound sleep.

Fred awoke later than he had expected the following day, but it had been a long night. The rain lasted until early morning before the winds calmed. Some of his gear was damp this morning, but nothing drenched. When he peeked out the tent flap, sunlight mixed with clouds, and the clouds were thinning in the west, but it was still cold and damp. It looked to be a decent day.

While the weather appeared to be improving, it would still be one of his more challenging days. Fred had made this choice while planning this route, and he was sticking to it. After a hot breakfast that he savored in the chilly, fresh morning air, he packed, struck out, and headed upward and eastward. Forty-five minutes later, he was well above the trees and walking in difficult, unstable scree and talus. The loose footing slowed him. It took him another hour of carefully picking his way through sketchy footing to reach the top of Frozen Lake Pass. Before he took a step in the scree and talus, he made sure that the rocks weren't going to shift beneath him; he didn't need a sprained or broken ankle out here in the middle of nowhere. When he made it to the pass, the view was spectacular! The sun was still relatively low in the east, casting cool, dark shadows across the landscape. Looking westward, he could see where he had hiked the past couple of days and the several small lakes near where he had spent last night. Looking east and north, laid out before him were his next challenges. He first had to scramble down similarly treacherous footing on the east side of the pass. In another hour, he'd be on the John Muir Trail that he had shared with his son a couple of years before. He distinctly remembered the long, smooth stretch of trail in the upcoming basin. Further east still, he could easily make out the apparent profile of Split Mountain, another memorable landmark. The vertical spire of harsh Vennacher Needle was just to his southeast. Sitting here and snacking wasn't getting him any closer to his next camp, so off he went. It was always a balance between moving and making progress juxtaposed against soaking in the views, taking photos, and making memories.

He was soon hoofing it northward on the JMT. When he descended into the basin and its better soil, he was delighted to see all the alpine flowers in bloom! Sedges, monkeyflower, sorrel, lilies, a few daisies, and violets, all decorated by lingering rain beads. Their colors contrasted so wonderfully against the tawny soil, sand, and rocks. He thought about stopping for an early lunch but decided to keep going. It was nice to be back on a decent trail and moving a little faster and more comfortably, even if it would only be for a few miles. In the last two days of this trip, Fred hadn't seen another soul. Now, the trail seemed

like a highway. Southbound backpackers were mainly on a JMT trip, while northbound hikers were on their much longer Pacific Crest Trail adventures. It was nice to see smiling faces worn by people who knew how fortunate they were to be out here in this starkly beautiful, remote wilderness.

Fred didn't get to enjoy the new surroundings for very long before he was staring up the south side of Mather Pass. He figured he'd be up there in an hour or so, given his slow pace. With his head down, he put one foot in front of the other. Fred wasn't nearly as concerned on this ascent since it was only a mile or so and a climb of a thousand feet over several switchbacks. *Easy peasy compared to his first couple of days!*

He enjoyed a great but late lunch and the camaraderie of other backpackers on Mather Pass. Again, the vistas were breathtaking! Various shades of sterile taupe mountains were all around him, with some snow still caught in the shadowed northern recesses and other protected spots. The wind blew strong over the pass and he was glad to be wearing his coat and toasty stocking cap. The basin through which he had just walked was slightly greener than the surrounding country, but not a great deal. The next destination, the Palisade Lakes, was below and a few miles north. Fred sat there in awe of his surroundings, thankful to be able to take in this moment. The view from the pass was one that few people ever had the privilege to enjoy, and he smiled as he remembered being here with Will. Fred had another backpacker take a picture of him on Mather Pass, to later share with Will and the rest of his family.

Heading down the north side of Mather Pass was easy and pleasant; he was still on the trail and enjoying his pace. Fred felt for the backpackers he passed who were struggling their way up the pass, just as he had done an hour ago on the south side. The trail leveled out, and he was soon at the Palisade Lakes – a magnificent sight! His memories of being here from when he had been on the JMT with Will were not quite so pleasant. These memories were not distasteful because these lakes were less beautiful then, but because at that time, Fred and Will had been walking southward rather than northward and looking up at intimidating Mather Pass and the climb that it entailed. He enjoyed the contrast of his emotions by going in both directions on this section of the trail.

Following a break and afternoon snack by Upper Palisade Lake, Fred was back at it for his last segment of the day. Towards the north end of Lower Palisade Lake, he said goodbye to the ease of the trail and bushwhacked northeast and upward. It was getting later in the day, and Fred had already crossed two substantial passes. Since he felt good and had a couple of easy days before, he decided to press on rather than camp near Palisade Lakes. It took him another couple of hours of hiking and sweating before cresting Cirque Pass. He didn't stop for more than a quick blow and then headed to today's destination, a quiet little lake on the north side of Cirque Pass at the base of the Palisades, a spectacular and impressive vertical ridge of granite to the east.

The camping here was mainly on granite slabs, and he had some difficulty pitching his tent. His stakes were of little use, so he used rocks to tension his lines. Fortunately, there was still some time for fishing – after he rinsed out his sweaty clothes. Today, he had no luck as this lake was maybe a little too remote, cold, and sterile. The best part of the day was yet to come. After supper and cleanup, Fred sat outside his tent on the still-warm blocks of stone. He enjoyed the mesmerizing show of pastel pink and orange hues that illuminated the Palisades as the sun went down and reflected in the foreground lake – absolutely stunning! He'd remember this sundown forever, especially after capturing several photographs of it.

He checked for a text from Asta. She had written to him:

Hope that all is well — no news on this end. We miss and Luv U!

Fred responded with:

35.07320; -118.50360; Just enjoyed one of the most beautiful sunsets ever! Wish u were here to share. Luv 2 U all!

Fred sat there in the waning light, reflecting on his life as the colorful Palisades mirrored in the lake. He was very, very thankful. Appreciative. These thoughts and feelings had been coursing through him these past few quiet days while on the trail, along with some pangs of loneliness, but they were coalescing into a great and gratifying warmth. Now he missed Asta and the kids. They would love it here, he thought, especially with all of us together in this moment, laughing at and with each other. They always made terrific memories on their trips. But Fred also knew that he needed times like this to get away from the family so that they appreciated him and he them, and this was one of those times to savor being alone, but not lonely.

Lost in his thoughts and feelings, he realized that his toes were growing cold. Best to hop in the sack and enjoy warm thoughts while warming my body, he figured. He slid into the tent and quilt, quickly falling asleep with a fat grin on his face.

The next morning arrived early, clear and very cold. Fred took a bit longer to roll out of the sack and relished his cup of hot tea and oatmeal a bit more. While he had the privilege of enjoying the spectacular sunset on the walls of the Palisades last night, this morning he was in their cold, dark shadows for quite some time.

Today's hiking was going to be different. He'd arisen earlier than usual because he figured that this would be a long day. After a couple of hours of ups and downs, dodging boulders and skirting small lakes at the base of the Palisades on his right and Dusy Basin on his left, Fred was near Bishop Pass. It was just mid-morning. He scrambled over the pass and made his way down to Saddlerock Lake. Fred ate a modest lunch, put up his tent, and shoved in his quilt, pad, and clothes. He set the bear canister a few hundred feet away and put his accumulated rubbish into his pack. He was headed down to Parcher's Resort for his first resupply and hopefully some well-deserved junk food!

Fred made it to Parcher's in a couple of hours since it was downhill and he was carrying hardly anything with him. When he got there, Fred's first thing was to check in with the staff to claim his resupply package. Surprisingly, two boxes were waiting for him; one was a small package covered with hearts he hadn't sent. Fred had a big smile on his face and missed Asta dearly!

The next thing was to order a big cheeseburger and fries and wash them down with a cold soda. Fred enjoyed returning to civilization from the wilderness, how something so simple as savoring a burger, sit-

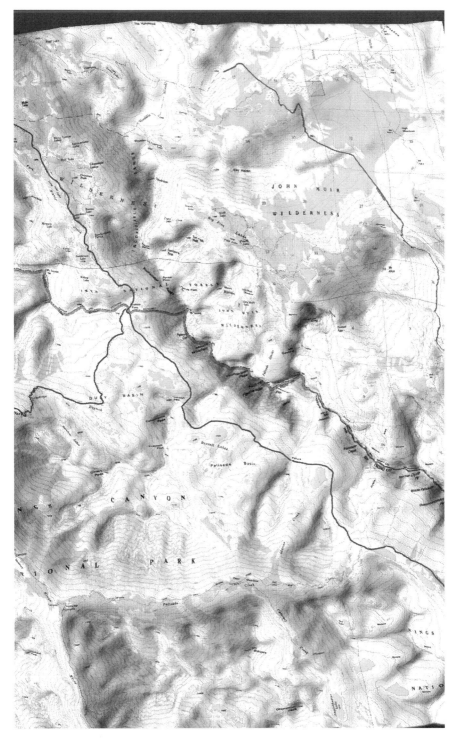

ting in a chair, and leaning on a table seemed like luxuries compared to how he had been living the past few days. And he contrasted that with how he'd be ensconced in civilization in another couple of weeks, only able to return to the remote wilderness after another long, cold winter. Yes, better to be here and relish this opportunity while he could. The last thing he had hoped to do was to call home and talk with anyone there, but he didn't have cell service here.

Now with a full stomach and a heavier pack, Fred slowly trudged back to the camp he had left at Saddlerock Lake. Leaving mid-afternoon meant that he'd likely be back to his camp before sundown. There would be time to wash and eat supper. With the bear canister reloaded for another several days in the wilderness, he realized that this had been his longest day of hiking. The morning jaunt from his last camp hadn't been strenuous but going down to Parcher's and then back up made for many miles and a long day.

Fred had a pleasant northward vista tonight, which made for a colorful, relaxing sunset. Sitting beside the lake, he checked his satellite transceiver and sent a message to Asta.

To Fred: *We hope you had a good day! Everything peachy here. We luv u and miss u!*

To Asta: *37.12536; -118.55126; Resupplied at Parchers. Thank u very much for the chocolates! Happy. Fulfilled. Taking in the sunset. Luv 2 u all!*

About fifty miles down and another hundred and fifty to go, he figured. His pace had been slightly slower than he wished, but Fred knew that he was still working his way into shape. Despite the many miles of hiking, he hadn't moved too far today, but he had made a great deal of progress.

Chapter 9

The morning 'dawned' in the dim, gray bedroom. Kim laid there, gathering herself and her thoughts. One of her realizations was that she'd been in the same clothes for three days and it was time for a change. After rapping on the door, feet shuffled on the floor, followed by the *snick* of the lock releasing. Beta carefully opened the door but not as cautiously as in the past. *Maybe they're becoming more comfortable with me*, Kim thought. She asked whether she could wash her clothes in the utility sink.

"Let me check in with Alpha. I'll be right back." He closed and locked the door and headed upstairs.

After several minutes of shuffling footsteps upstairs, Beta returned, opened the door, and presented Kim with a breakfast tray – coffee, a piece of fruit, and another convenience store pastry. And, without asking, this morning's *Chronicle* was under the fruit and pastry. She left the breakfast on her bed, made her way past Beta and headed towards the sink and toilet. Yes, Beta was learning his role, too, as he backed his way up the stairs, sitting in the doorway above. This morning, Kim could hear music playing but nothing that told her where they held her.

After using the toilet, she undressed to her underwear and warmed the water in the sink. It felt wonderful to wash more than her face! She dressed in her second set of clothes, her only other change, hand washed her dirty clothes, and wrung them out as best she could. Not quite knowing what to do with her damp clothes, she figured it was safe to hang them from the pipes and wiring in the floor joists above her; it wasn't likely anyone would steal them, and if they were taken, there were only three possible thieves from which to choose.

Back in her spartan cell, the coffee was still warm, and she took her time eating. As much as she wanted to act like this was a typical day, it wasn't. She wasn't home, she didn't feel safe and secure, and she didn't know what her future held. Kim checked the answers to yesterday's puzzle to figure out what she hadn't solved and tried to work on today's crossword puzzle. During this time, her mind wandered over the impending conversation with Omega and how he would react to the position she expected herself to take. *Was there anything that he could add that entice her to join his group?* No, nothing came to mind, she thought. And, since she wasn't willing to join them, then she didn't know what tomorrow would bring, other than more uncertainty.

Kim finished about half of the crossword puzzle and then retreated to the corner of the room where she had sat and contemplated life. It was a good place for that, with an additional day of familiarity. Yes, she could get out of this bind if she took Omega's offer; that was obvious. But could she live with herself? Kim doubted it; in fact, she knew that she couldn't fold and become one of "them." Whatever Omega was offering didn't feel right in her gut in any way. Maybe, just maybe, she could tolerate working for "them" for a year so that she could get out of her current detention, but then she'd want to get back to the life that she had been enjoying before all of this. How would she extricate herself from that mess and live to tell about it? Could she just vanish? If they had found her once, they'd probably be able to find her again. Even if Kim tried to disappear, how would she live and support herself? What about her extended family? She'd likely never see them again if she was living a forever hidden life.

Even though the decision was obvious, the consequences were unknown. OK, so I tell them *thank you very much for your kind offer, but I'm going to have to decline because of ethical concerns.* And, of course, they'll respond with *thank you very much for your consideration; we appreciate your time, here's the door, and we hope you have a nice life.*

How am I going to get out of this? What might they do with me? Even more fundamental, *I still don't know what I've done to piss 'em off. Gee,* she thought to herself, *if I were at home thinking about a significant problem, maybe I'd make some kind of decision matrix or something like that.* Good old logic. *Unfortunately, I don't understand this situation and the players on the other side. They're involved in something nefarious, and my computer tools have stumbled into it and deeply. My skills seem to be of interest to them, so that's a plus, but if I don't join them, then why would they allow me any freedom, let alone live?*

None of this made sense to Kim, and she didn't know what to do. The only thing that made sense to her was to continue playing along for the near future and see how it played out. They weren't overtly threatening her – *yet* – but that might change after her nearing talk with Omega. Maybe she could put off the call, claim that she was busy with another project or client. That made her nervously chuckle to herself. At least she still had her sense of humor.

Kim thought about how she might escape from this house. The casement window was about eight feet above the floor. The window looked to be solidly closed, maybe even screwed or welded shut. If she broke the glass, they'd surely hear the crashing, and she doubted that she could quickly squirm through before they recaptured her. When she'd been outside the room, she had noticed that the walls appeared sturdy and pleasantly finished. She figured there was a layer of wallboard on each side of the framing. She could probably kick a hole through one and then two layers, but the noise would alert her captors. She hadn't noticed a basement door that led outdoors. The only way out seemed to be up the stairs, which made sense if you were holding someone captive and only wanted to protect one escape route. There was no way she could subdue one of these guys, let alone all three people. The opportunity to escape didn't seem to be here. *Better to live to fight another day*, she thought to herself. That's about all that she could do, she figured. *I don't know what they're going to do with me, but I hope that there will be some moment where they let their guard down.*

And, if they don't let me go or I don't escape? Now, Kim was starting to get down. There didn't seem to be any escape at the moment, and she couldn't figure out why they'd keep her alive. Kim had had a mostly good life so far and had hoped for so much more. There were still too many places she wanted to visit. Hopefully, a future with someone special could yet unfold, and maybe children. Her mood was feeling as gloomy as this room was dark.

She tried to remember the last time that she'd been so down or when the odds were so stacked against her. She'd always been so successful at school and work that failure was rare in that realm. There had been that one music appreciation test in college that she had utterly bombed. And there was Keith in grad school. After dating for three years, she thought they were a good couple and would make a life together – until he decided that they weren't. Her friends had seen it coming, but she hadn't. The six months after that had been very bleak and difficult, and she had thrown herself into her research. Part of the reason she was such a great computer scientist was because she was such a poor social person. She had closed a part of herself off after Keith, and that part had not fully reopened.

Falling deeper into her pit of despair, Kim began to softly cry. *Why am I in this situation? I'm just one single person doing my job. These people aren't hurt; they're just greedy. But I'm paying the price for their greed.* She wiped her eyes on her sleeve and took a deep breath. *Gotta hold myself together because these people aren't going to save me,* she thought to herself. She only talked with her parents about every week, so they probably hadn't missed her yet. By now, the powers that be at work should have figured out that she wasn't on her computer or responding to calls or text messages, but they wouldn't know where to find her. Yep, this is quite the dismal situation.

Kim had never meditated in her life, but she thought this might be an excellent time to see if she could figure out how. She straightened her posture there in the corner, crossed her legs, took three deep breaths, and tried to open her mind to whatever. Kim heard footsteps upstairs, the floorboards creaking, water pipes banging. She tried harder to close off her mind to these distractions and open it to some source of inspiration. She didn't find any motivation, but she did find some comfort. Memories of her parents and how they had told her to be strong, how to deal with adversity, came back. Some funny little sayings popped into her head that she'd read on schmaltzy get-well cards, like *making lemonade out of lemons; if you're digging yourself into a hole, stop digging!* She remembered how her parents had cared for her when she'd had appendicitis as a teenager; how they had taken her to the emergency room when she broke her ankle while playing high school soccer. She had recovered from those hurts and been better than ever. Her parents weren't "here" right now, but they still were with her in spirit. She thought of her close friends from college, grad school, and San Francisco. They weren't here either, but they were. She was feeling better. She thought about the disastrous relationship with Keith and could feel herself being pulled back into the pit. Nope, not going there, at least not now. I'll deal with that after I get myself out of this mess. Her meditating lead her back to her strengths – her problem-solving skills – so she'd better dig deeper into herself that way.

She was feeling a bit better. She also realized that she was feeling hungry, didn't know what time it was, and that hunger contributed to her mood. She had been down in her life before but never really depressed. Kim could usually trace her poor spirits to things over which she had some control, like eating or lack of exercise. *Well, running laps around my cell probably wouldn't make me feel much better, so I guess that I'll ask for lunch.*

Rapping on the door, she thought she startled someone. Good, I'm getting my powers back, getting to them ever so slightly, she thought to herself, which almost made her giggle. She stifled it before the door opened.

Beta stood in the door frame, hood over his head as usual.

"Is it lunchtime yet? I'm starving. And I want to check my laundry. And, why hasn't Omega called? Could you please check in with him for me."

"Sure. You can check your clothes and then I'll take care of lunch for you," Beta said.

He worked his way up the stairs, sitting at the top, out of view, and left the door open for Kim. She walked over to the toilet and chose to be more observant this time. Nope, no obvious door leading to the outside, and her cell's interior walls appeared solid. The door was one of those cheap, hollow ones; with some effort, she'd likely be able to bust it down, but then what? After washing her hands, she found her clean clothes still damp, as she expected. She returned to the room and made sure that Beta saw her walk in.

Beta returned upstairs after locking her in. She could faintly hear music again, so he must have left the basement door open. If they could only be more careless, somehow, sometime, then she might have a chance. In a few minutes, he was back at her door with today's lunch – an apple, a chocolate chip cookie, a turkey sandwich, and a glass of lemonade. Kim took the tray with a smile and backed away from the door.

Lemonade. Kim smiled broadly, even gleefully. This had to be a good sign! And, even if it wasn't a sign from wherever, whomever, she was making it into one.

After eating lunch, she felt better, especially after feeling the drink's cool and tasty tang. She rested on the bed, eyes closed, feeling for her courage and grit. They were in her, but barely. She had a thought, a way to try to take a little control of the situation.

Kim knocked on the door and heard footsteps approaching. She stepped back and sat on the bed, trying to give the appearance of being in her place.

Beta opened the door carefully, a little more slowly than he had an hour ago. Kim approached him, holding the lunch tray out for him to take.

"Beta, any word from Omega?"

"Uh, yes, Dr. Johnson, I think that he's going to call in an hour or so, but I'll see what I can do. It's not up to me, though," he said.

"I understand, but could you please let him know that I'm ready to talk with him," she said, followed by a healthy smile.

Yeah, she was getting back some of her mojo and sass. How it would play out, she didn't know, but at least she was playing strong rather than cowering in the figurative corner.

Twenty minutes later, Alpha was at her door. He would have been easier to read if he wasn't wearing his hood, but how he handled himself gave her the sense that Alpha was a bit exasperated from being put in the middle between Kim and Omega.

"Omega said that he's not available to speak with you at the moment, like he had hoped, but that he will call within the next hour," Alpha said.

"Oh, thank you so much, Alpha, for contacting Omega and getting my message to him. I'll be here when he calls." Like, she'd be outside by the pool sunning herself.

When he did call, Kim figured that it had been a bit more than thirty minutes, but at least she wasn't going to be sitting around all afternoon wondering when he might call, like she was waiting for some high school boy to call for a date that her girlfriend said was going to happen.

"Good afternoon, Dr. Johnson. I trust you had a good supper last night, as well as have had a pleasant day thus far."

"Hello, Mr. Omega. Yes, supper last night was fine. Today has been dull and boring, as usual with your boys, sitting here anticipating your call. I've been seriously considering your offer and wonder if there are more details that you can provide. Like, what is it that you would expect of me? How many vacation days? Do you offer health benefits?" Oh yeah, she was feeling it again! She wasn't going to capitulate to Omega's expectations, but she was going to make the most of this moment to see if she could work it in her favor.

"Uh, well, let me think here for a moment. We would like you to continue what we believe to be your current line of work and redirect it to be beneficial to our needs. As we're not fully clear on your repertoire and you're not fully aware of ours, we feel that there would need to be some time to work together and come to a clearer agreement regarding your work with us."

"I'd like to be able to say *I see*, but actually, I don't see. You're still too nebulous about your group's efforts and how I might fit into that. Could you clarify those elements for me, please? Is this how you normally conduct a job interview?" Kim asked.

"As I said yesterday, we seek to identify areas of opportunity, invest our energies into those opportunities, and then share the harvest with people within our society."

"Still nebulous," Kim said. "You're not giving me much to go on. It seems that you're expecting me to trust you that everything will work out fine. Since you say that you'd want to work together to come to a clearer agreement regarding my work, I'm also not clear what would happen if we can't agree."

Today, there was still a digital pause on the line, but this pause was longer than a digital one.

"You have come prepared for this discussion today. Splendid!" exclaimed Omega. "I'm impressed. I'm not surprised, though, given your reputation. Please allow me a few moments to gather myself so that I can share with you what I can."

Kim was quiet, knowing the power of silence. She felt that Omega might be stepping back from the phone on his end of the line, conferring with others. She felt good that her chutzpah was back but somewhat directionless and seemed to be affecting their discussions. Actually, her energy wasn't directionless; it was just that she didn't expect that she could agree to whatever it is that Omega wanted. If this was her clout in action, then Kim at least was enjoying her fantasy.

Eventually, Omega was present on the line.

"Dr. Johnson, I needed a moment to confer with my colleagues. At this time, we're not at liberty to provide you with significantly more details of our operations. Knowingly or not, you have already interjected yourself into our work. If you know who we are, then you have a good idea of what we're asking and expecting of you. If you have not figured out who we are, we'd prefer to maintain our anonymity. Does that make sense?"

"Yes, it makes sense, but it's not at all satisfying. You want me to play ball for you, but you won't play ball with me is how I look at the situation."

"That's a fair evaluation of the situation, I believe," responded Omega.

More silence.

"Well," Kim said, "I have wracked my brain these past couple of days, and I have to honestly admit that I do not know on whose toes I have stepped. I don't know who your group is, who you are, where you're located, although I have a sense of your objectives. As I said yesterday, I have many different projects and interests. I can see how I might have intruded on others' efforts through my projects, but no one jumps out at me. Let's just say that I know that some of my methods, my tools, are reaching deeper than I was aware, and your organization and work must be one of those that are not fully evident to me."

There followed a substantial silence. Omega must also know the value of silence, Kim thought, or else he's as flummoxed as me.

"Give me another hour to talk further with my colleagues, Dr. Johnson. We seem to have hit a juncture that we did not fully anticipate on our end. We expected that you were aware of who we are, and that doesn't seem to be the case, presuming that you're being honest with us." The phone line was silent.

Kim thought about keeping the phone and seeing who she could call for help, but she figured it wouldn't do any good. Kim felt she had wrung about all that she could out of her situation and that this wasn't a moment when Omega, Alpha, or Beta had let their guard down so that she might run or at least call for the cavalry.

She went to the open door. Alpha sat at the bottom of the stairs, murkily checking his cellphone through his hood. She extended the cellphone that she'd been using to Alpha.

"I guess that Omega's going to call back in an hour or so. I figure that you should hang on to this so that I don't call 911."

Alpha's head jerked up, realizing that he hadn't been paying sufficient attention and that he'd left her alone with the possibility of calling for help. He reached out to take the phone from her, and Kim allowed her fingers to touch his palm. Again, there was the slightest hint of a reaction, of a pulling back by Alpha. Oh, yeah, she was feeling her energy again. She just hoped that it would lead to something useful to her.

Kim returned to the room and pulled the door closed behind her. She thought that she heard the lock click shut, but she wasn't sure. She wasn't going to check it out, didn't want to see if they were testing her, didn't want to tell them anymore than they were telling her.

She laid on the creaky bed, gathering her thoughts and how she might proceed with Omega. She really could not come up with any scenario that was in her favor, where she would knowingly come out ahead. The only card that she held in this game was whether she would work with Omega and his colleagues or not, and she hadn't gotten any better of a feeling from their recent conversation. She felt like she had him thinking that he might tell her more, but she doubted it. She figured that the hand that she was playing now was the best that she'd get. There wasn't any bluffing in her negotiating because she had little idea what the other side knew or was offering.

Based on what Omega said and didn't say, Kim guessed that her computer security work had found a significant hacking network about which she didn't know. That thought made her proud but still left her guessing. Her work aimed at better searching for hackers and security risks. The tools that she was using weren't unique. What was special is how she had configured those tools. She figured that she must be more successful than she knew. She had struck a nerve, a very sensitive nerve, one that was valuable enough that Omega felt that Kim needed to be kidnapped. The good news is that her computer tools were still working without her, and her team was monitoring the program's search results and seeing what it was finding and shutting down. He didn't know that, but she did. Maybe she had some leverage after all.

An hour and a half after handing the phone to Alpha, Beta was at the door to Kim's room. She didn't hear the lock, just the sound of the door handle. Maybe Alpha had left the door unlocked after all, she thought. Without saying a word, he handed the phone to her and left the door open.

"Yes, Dr. Johnson, this is Omega again. My colleagues and I have discussed your situation more, and we feel that there isn't anything more that we can tell you at this time. You'll just have to trust us in this negotiation."

Kim wasn't surprised. She had anticipated that response, but it wasn't that hard to figure out.

"Well, Omega, I feel that we're at an impasse. You've provided too little information for me to make an informed choice. And, even if you did tell me more about who you all are and what you're doing, I doubt that it's something that would appeal to me. Also, we both know that you have the stronger position since I'm not participating of my own free will."

"Yes, Dr. Johnson, I'm aware of the gulf between our positions, as well as the corner into which we've forced you. We had hoped that you'd see things our way with less encouragement, shall we say, and be willing to join efforts based on the information I've provided."

"I understand," she said. "My values are very different from yours, and without knowing more about your operations and methods, we're not going to come to a mutually satisfying agreement for my working for you. I recognize that you see the world through a philosophical lens that is very different from how I view the world. I just don't understand how your worldview is better for the world than my views of it. Most likely, I'd eventually want out of whatever it is that you're doing, and I don't see how you'd ever let me go. You've got me cornered. If I join you, I doubt that I could live with myself. I'd rather stick to my values and be able to live with myself, no matter the consequences with you."

"Well then, Dr. Johnson, I believe that our discussions are over."

"So, I'll be taken home, yes?" Kim inquired with just a bit of sarcasm in her voice.

"No, that won't be possible. Considering how we might spend our initial time with you, we felt that it was as likely as not that you'd be willing to work with us. Since joining us has not come to fruition, then we'll proceed with our alternate plan."

Kim didn't like the sound of 'alternate plan' but wasn't at all surprised.

"During our planning for your interview, we instructed Alpha on how to proceed if our negotiations were not mutually satisfactory. He knows what to do and will proceed," Omega stated.

Some of the wind left Kim's sails because she could only anticipate a morbid way that Alpha might proceed. She knew that she had one more move that she could make, and now was the time.

"Omega, over the last hour, I've thought more about my work and how it might be impacting your group. The good news is that I can only imagine that one of my projects is having an effect on any particular interest of yours," she said with a solid, strong voice. "The bad news is that I've programmed that tool to keep running, even when I'm away. If we're talking about the same thing, I'm guessing that you can run, but you can't hide. Even when I'm not around, the program runs, and my team is watching over the efforts and sharing results with our supervisors."

Kim took a big breath and hoped that Omega would not meet her thrust with a parry.

This time, the silence was even longer. Finally, after an audible sigh, Omega spoke.

"Dr. Johnson, we very much do seem to be at an impasse. I will need to confer with my colleagues regarding how to proceed and then possibly speak with you tomorrow. In the meantime…"

"Omega, one more thing," Kim interrupted.

"Yes, ma'am, what is it?"

"Could you please tell Alpha to bring me a Hawaiian pizza tonight?" Kim sarcastically asked.

The silence was deafening, and Kim loved it!

After Omega hung up on her, Kim took a moment to collect herself and consider her subsequent actions. A thought came to her and made her smile. She slung her knapsack over her shoulder and headed toward the door. With the phone still pressed against her ear, she fully opened the door and found Beta sitting on the stairs, which is what she hoped to see.

"Yes, Omega, I understand," Kim said to the silent phone. "I'll give Alpha and Beta the message and speak with you tomorrow. Thank you."

Beta sat there, giving Kim as curious of a look as he could muster under his hood while she handed him the phone.

Kim walked to her clothes that were drying nearby, plucked them from where they hung, and stuffed them into her bag. "Omega and I came to an agreement. You're to take me back to my home. Omega will call me tomorrow so that we can finalize the deal."

Kim walked past Beta and up the stairs to the kitchen. Alpha had heard them talking but didn't understand what was going on. Kim surprised him when she appeared in the kitchen — his hood was lying on a card table there. Beta scrambled to keep up with Kim and found Alpha with a confused look on his face.

"Like I just told Beta, Omega wants you two to take me home. We came to an agreement, and he's going to call me on my cellphone tomorrow to tie up the loose ends."

Kim turned toward the door that was off the kitchen, the one that she figured lead outdoors, and started to turn the knob to open the door.

"Not so fast, Dr. Johnson," said Alpha. He jumped up and placed a firm hand against the door to prevent it from opening.

"I need to check in with Omega to make certain that we're supposed to release you. This isn't my first rodeo, and I'm not about to let you go until I have confirmation from Omega."

Kim stood there, almost defiant, lips pursed and then her shoulders slowly slumped. She wanted to run but knew that Alpha was stopping her from leaving through the kitchen door and that Beta was blocking any exit through the front door. She slouched down onto the second chair at the card table, sighed, and hoped for better luck next time. At least she'd tried to escape.

"Well, shit," she muttered.

Chapter 10

Fred awoke a little later than usual; he slept in 'til 6:00 am! It was a clear, cold morning at Saddlerock Lake. He enjoyed how the world changed so much overnight, how it appeared one way at sunset, and how the shifting light and weather changed the landscape's appearance at sunrise. He took his time crawling out of the sack, making sure his joints and muscles worked as he expected. Except for a couple of smallish blisters around his heels and sore hips, he was in pretty good shape. He felt energized to be in the middle of nowhere.

This day was not going to be one of his favorites, he knew, but he had to do it, to get it over. This morning would be leisurely and the afternoon difficult. He much preferred having the problematic parts in the morning and coasting in the afternoon. Today's hiking took him down, down, down over three thousand feet, and then he'd slowly start to regain the altitude. He needed to remember to move at a decent but not too fast pace while walking the four miles downhill to protect his knees. He figured he'd be in the valley within a couple of hours. After a hearty breakfast, he pulled on his pack and groaned; he could feel that it was heavier than when he had hoisted it yesterday morning. Taking on a resupply had its benefits and costs.

By mid-morning, Fred found himself in LeConte Canyon. It was odd to have spent so many days above treeline and now surrounded by tall white pine trees, lush meadow grasses and various flowers. He knew that it was still relatively dry here in the mountains, but LeConte Canyon was warmer and more humid than anywhere he'd been for several days, and he broke a sweat. As he strode northward, the rise was gentle at first but grew steeper in ever so slight increments. He stopped for lunch in the shade of a small grove of pine trees, with the Kings River flowing nearby. One of the problems with more heat and water was more mosquitoes, which he detested like everyone else.

By mid-afternoon, his pace slowed as he walked upward on a similar grade that he enjoyed coming down in the morning. His heavier pack added to his burden. He knew that he could make it to Muir Pass if he chose, but then there'd a long walk to find a decent campsite beyond the pass. He remembered from his JMT trip a couple of years ago that there was a long, modest slope of desolate talus for the few miles north of Muir Pass and around Wanda Lake. There might be a campsite there, but he had plenty of sites here from which to choose, and water, too. He had covered a dozen miles today, which was good, but not great since he was on a trail all day. But he also had descended three thousand feet and gained much of it back. This was good enough. He figured that he should have a more relaxing day tomorrow. Besides, he could pull out his rod and hopefully land a trout or two for supper. Compared to some of his recent camps, Fred felt a bit walled in by the trees and mountains. The views weren't nearly as great here, but better to be in the wilderness than civilization.

Trout was on the menu this evening! His fishing prowess caught the eyes of his neighbors from a couple of tents a hundred meters away. Tonight was the first time he'd had neighbors since the first night of the trip, which felt odd. The presence of others altered the tranquility that he usually felt. He chided himself for being so selfish – there was plenty of wilderness, views, and solitude to go around. This deep in the backcountry, most backpackers were quiet and respectful; everyone was too tired from the effort it took to get so far into the wilderness to be awake much after sunset.

The last thing he did before hitting the sack was to check to see if there was a message from Asta, and there was:

Hope you had a good day. Nothing special on this end. We're living vicariously through you! XOXO!

Fred responded with:

37.12331; -118.64116; Hola! Pleasant morning, long afternoon. Feeling fine. Over Muir Pass in the morning. Luv U all!

The following day – *morning seven? Yes, seven!* – Fred was roused by the singing birds in the first bit of alpine light. He wished that he knew their songs well enough to identify them like birds back home. He had forgotten to notice, but the thin air hadn't wakened him since the second night. That was good; he was acclimating. Fred warmed water for tea and granola and quietly enjoyed the change from inky dawn to full-on sunrise. The other tents were still quiet. As the shadows opened more, Fred noticed a silent deer also enjoying its breakfast, not fifty feet from him. It amazed him that the deer seemed so relaxed with him nearby. This deep in the wilderness was not a place where wildlife feared for their lives from humans. It gave him a mild sense of kinship to blend into nature as a guest for a few weeks.

Just as Fred slung his pack onto his back, one of the other tents zipped open with a sleepy head poking out. Fred and the neighbor waved and smiled at each other. Fred gave the young woman with her mussed hair and stocking cap a thumbs up and pointed towards Muir Pass. The woman gave him a warm, knowing smile and silently mouthed *Good luck!*

As he expected, the first few miles were difficult. He dressed in shorts before he left camp this morning and stripped off his long-sleeve shirt within half an hour. It was a glorious morning to climb past Helen Lake and then up the south flank of Muir Pass. It took him ninety minutes to crest the pass. Fred clambered into Muir Hut and had it all to himself. The odor of smoke and charcoal reminded him that others had been here and warmed themselves. His warmth came from pulling his puffy coat over his damp shirt, a couple of granola bars, and a slug of water. Fred leaned against the doorway and looked to the north, making out several dark ants slowly lumbering his way. Before any of them arrived, Fred was back on the trail in the cool and soft, pleasant light. He was warmer if he kept moving this morning, at this altitude.

Fred saw a couple of rocky, exposed sites where he might have camped last night near Wanda Lake and was glad that he had chosen to camp where he had, a few miles south of here. It was pleasant here, in a stark, desolate way, but he preferred his last camp to these possibilities. A young couple packing a tent looked slightly worse for wear, he thought. That could easily be him and might yet be him on some of the nights to come, especially as the trail took a toll on his body and spirit.

Farther north and descending, Fred was on the trail that skirted above Sapphire Lake. He chuckled to himself as he looked down at the lake and remembered Will jumping off a tall rock into the frigid water. It made him shiver to think of that memory just as he had felt cold that afternoon a couple of years ago, feeling for his son's craziness. His son had come out of the lake with a big, blue chattering grin from ear to ear!

Fred was making good time this morning after getting over Muir Pass and moving downhill. The trail here was good, and it descended on a grade that was gentle on his knees. The stepping stones over Evolution Creek also reminded him of his son, and he was now becoming a bit lonely, thinking of all of the work and fond memories that they had shared on this trail. Looking at the crossing, he could easily see Will in his mind's eye as he carefully navigated this mild obstacle. It wasn't much longer before he was sitting on a slab overlooking Evolution Lake and taking time for a well-deserved rest and snack. The vista here was beautiful with the sun at his back, lighting the lake in front and dappled clouds and numerous peaks beyond. He stored another memory to carry him through the long winters of his future. This area would be a spectacular place to camp, he thought, maybe on a future trip.

All good things must come to an end, and just after Evolution Lake, Fred veered off-trail to the north and upwards towards Darwin Bench. It was going to be a long afternoon, he knew, but he was feeling pretty good. This part of the day was a slow, hot slog, warmer than most, it seemed. The sun was hot on his backside for much of this section. He figured that he might get sunburned again today since he had been lax about slathering up and covering today. An hour and a half after leaving Evolution Lake, Fred skirted a large, unnamed lake; Mt. Goethe leered above him on his left. After another ninety minutes, he was at the outlet for another lake in the shadows of Mt. Goethe and Muriel Peak. It was getting into late afternoon, and he didn't know if he had the energy or enthusiasm to go any farther. Fred stopped, checked his map, the time, and his body, and decided that this was good enough for the day. He had made about ten miles, which was his daily goal for his trip, so he was content. There might even be some trout in this lake, but he wasn't sure.

He made camp and threw his quilt over the tent to air out. Fred filtered water for a long drink and then washed in the frigid waters. When he bathed in the wilderness, he took water from a lake or stream away from the shore and soaped and rinsed. Since it had been a hot day, Fred first took a refreshing plunge into the lake. He was cold and tense in the lake, but slowly his body got used to the cold. Fred still needed to wash and didn't want to get too cold. He decided that instead of getting out and soaping up, he'd just rub the skin all over his body as best he could and hope he could remove the day's dirt and sweat. Besides, there wasn't anyone else around to enjoy his aroma! Fred dragged himself out of the lake, naked, and gathered the clothes he'd been wearing and took them back into the lake with him, rinsing them as best he could. He sort of enjoyed the patina of grime that his clothes developed after being on the trail for some time and not being adequately washed. The stains were signs of work and progress – a badge of honor. It was still plenty warm when Fred finished his laundry and laid his wet clothes out to dry. On the same slab, he laid himself out – the warmth of the rock and sun was terrific, and he was feeling very refreshed. It wasn't likely that he'd work up the energy to go fishing now, he thought to himself. It's nice to just laze around like this under the warm sun.

He briefly fell asleep. He hadn't taken a nap on the trip so far. A cool gust of wind startled him awake with a shiver, and his shirt nearly flew into the lake. He hadn't been paying attention, but it looked like the weather was changing on him. When he had made camp, the skies were brilliantly blue everywhere he looked. Now, though, to the north and west, he saw the beginning of some thickening clouds – that wasn't a good sign. He didn't know what was coming, but he decided that he had better boil some water for supper. He gathered his dry clothes and stuffed them into the tent, along with the quilt. While his dinner rehydrated, Fred checked his satellite transceiver for messages from home.

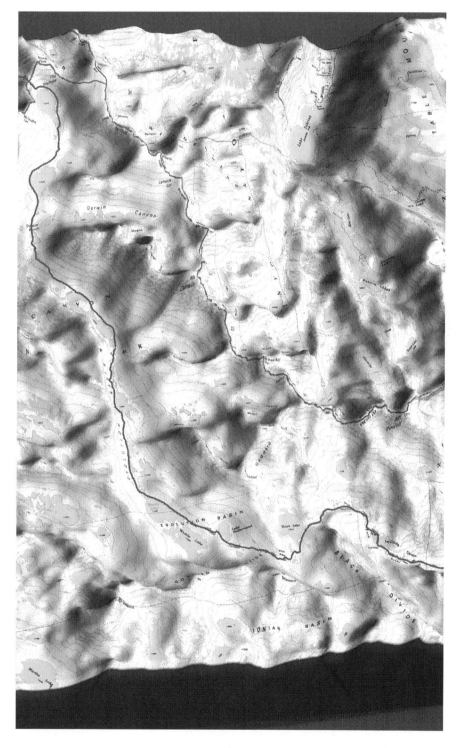

To Fred: *We hope you had a good day because it looks like you're in for a rough night and more. Storm likely headed your way, so be safe and smart. XOXO*

Fred wrote back:

37.20544; -118.69105; *Thanks for the heads up. I can feel the weather turning. I should be fine here. Good day of hiking. Luv 2 u all!*

He cleaned his spork after supper and checked his tent's lines. He decided to rotate his tent so that the opening was pointing southward, away from the north winds that were picking up. The soil was very thin here, and he hadn't been too thoughtful of his stakes when he pitched the tent. He found some good-sized rocks to hold down the stakes and lines and hoped for the best. Rather than set his bear canister far away from the tent, he kept it closer in case this was a bad storm, and he didn't feel like venturing out too far in the morning. He usually left his backpack in the tiny vestibule of his tent, but tonight he brought it in and placed it on the north side of the tent to block some of the wind lifting the edge. The more that he prepped, the more the wind picked up. When he had seen his last weather report before leaving Fresno, it had looked like good conditions for the next couple of weeks, but something had changed, which wasn't surprising. He had prepared well, he hoped.

He snuggled in his quilt with his rain gear and puffy jacket nearby. Gloves were in the pocket of his puffy, and his stocking cap pulled on tightly. Checking his phone's clock, he knew that sundown was still thirty minutes or more away, but it was already nearly dark. The tent flapped and strained at its lines. He hadn't been in a bad mountain storm in many years. He laid down, feeling the cold wind swirling on his face but warm most everywhere else except for a couple of drafts under his quilt edges. He could hear rumbling and figured the storm would be here in another hour or two. The wind was lulling him to sleep.

Half asleep, he half-heard a sizzling, crackling sound, and then *KABOOM!* that echoed off the walls of the cirque! He was awake now.

Chapter 11

Kim rolled over and the creaking of the bed pulled her out of her sleep. She laid there for a moment, recalling where she was and why. On her back now, she laid there hoping for a better day than the past several. *What day is this?* Is this her fourth day in captivity now? What's going to happen today? They weren't going to let her leave, she figured, so what's next? Had she overplayed her position with Omega, or did she play it well? When Kim finished speaking with Omega yesterday, she had felt pretty good about herself and how she had responded, and nothing had popped into her mind to change that feeling.

Kim knocked on the door to gain Alpha's or Beta's attention and to ask for breakfast. It was Beta who carefully opened the door and went upstairs. This morning, he wasn't keeping as tight of a watch over her as he had in the past. Maybe his attention was slipping, or perhaps he knew that there was no way for her to easily escape except to run upstairs and by him and Alpha to get out. She figured that it was the latter.

Alpha came downstairs with her breakfast tray and set it on the bed. He said to her, "I don't know what you and Omega discussed yesterday, but there's now quite a bit of discussion about next steps. I believe that Omega will be calling you today, but we'll see. I'll let you know when I hear more from him."

Kim just nodded her head that she understood and started on her breakfast. She wasn't any more hungry than usual. Kim had been disappointed last night when she didn't get her pizza, which made her chuckle to herself. Alpha had given her today's *Chronicle*, so she read some of it and took on the crossword puzzle challenge.

She didn't realize that she had become so engrossed in solving the puzzle until she heard her door unlocking. She hadn't heard anyone coming down the stairs, so maybe she was letting her guard down or becoming used to her situation. Neither thought was comforting for her. Alpha opened the door and made a gesture for Kim to give him the breakfast tray, which she did.

Finally, he spoke. "It sounds like Omega will call this afternoon, after lunch. There's also been a change in plans. We're going to be traveling rather than sitting tight. Omega told us that there's a chance that we've been discovered here. Beta has gone to pick up supplies for our trip."

"What trip?" Kim asked. "Do you know what's going on, what Omega is thinking to do with me?"

"I do have some sense of the next steps, but it's not my place to say. Since you haven't been providing the answers that Omega wants to hear and we need to keep you isolated, then we're moving onto other approaches to your accommodations."

"*Accommodations?*" Kim said, slightly incredulous. "I didn't ask for these 'accommodations' and would like to be released, taken home." Like that was going to happen, she thought to herself.

"Even if I knew more, I wouldn't be at liberty to divulge Omega's plans," Alpha said and then backed out the door.

Great, just fuckin' great, Kim thought to herself. *So, we're likely moving tomorrow to wherever. What does that mean? Are we off to another cell for me or to the slaughterhouse?* Her thoughts were becoming increasingly dreary about her prospects. It seemed that she did cause a change in the game with her responses to Omega yesterday, but likely not the kind of change she wanted. She would do her best to patiently wait for Omega's call, and she knew it wouldn't be easy.

For the first time, Kim paced in this small room. She figured the room was only about eight by ten feet, and she was crossing the length of the room every three to four steps and turning around. Kim did this for a long time. Pacing now was the most exercise that she'd had since her incarceration, and it felt pretty good. It felt better than sitting in the corner, contemplating her ambiguous future.

She forgot all about the crossword puzzle and focused on her bleak situation. If they were moving her, then there might be a chance to escape. Not likely, she realized, but she could always hope. What was wrong with this place? Why did they need to move her? Alpha had said something about possibly being discovered, so that gave her a little hope. Maybe someone was looking for her! But, she had so little awareness of her situation and realized again that she was just a pawn in someone else's game, in Omega's game. These thoughts didn't make it any easier on her.

Kim stopped her walking and took a deep breath. Sitting now on the bed, she tried her best to relax. It wasn't easy at first, but she could feel her shoulders relax. Kim took another deep breath and tried to let go of her confusion, fear, and desire to try to gain some control over her current state. All her thoughts came down to the fact that there wasn't much that she could do now; she needed to act on a moment's notice and maintain her sanity and composure to recognize the moment. Kim sarcastically thought this sounded like a great plan, but she knew it was the best she could do in her current circumstances.

She began to feel less anxious about her situation but not calm when she heard footsteps coming down the stairs. There was a light knock on the door, the click of the lock, and then it opened. Alpha stood in the doorway, and she could see Beta sitting on the stairs behind him, scrolling through his phone. Alpha handed her a cellphone and backed out of the room, leaving the door open.

The phone screen was glowing when she took it, and she could see OMEGA on the screen. Good to know that Alpha had Omega on speed dial on this phone, she thought. Putting the phone to her ear, Kim said, "Yes, Omega, I'm here."

"Good morning, Dr. Johnson. I'd like to discuss your future with us some more. Have you had further thoughts on the possibility of working with us?"

"Omega, I haven't changed my mind. I haven't heard anything from you about how it would be in my best interests to work with you other than I might somehow have more freedom than I'm currently enjoying. Nothing you have said makes your offer sound appealing."

"Ah, that's what I feared, Dr. Johnson." He was silent for a moment, maybe searching for words, but likely it was just a pause as he was about to change subjects.

"That being the case," he said, "we will be changing your accommodations."

Kim was beginning to severely dislike the word 'accommodation.' She just might have to banish it from her vocabulary.

She responded by saying, "Could you please be clearer about these changes?"

"I instructed Alpha and Beta to move you, and they are preparing now. Tomorrow they will take you elsewhere. That's all that I will tell you, except that they will take care of you, and we will not harm you."

Kim felt her shoulders relax a bit; at least there was the slightest bit of good news in what she had just heard.

"Omega, do you have long-term plans for me that you could share? How long do I have the pleasure of being your '*guest*?" she sarcastically asked.

"Our plans for you are flexible at this time, and we are not certain how long this will continue. We had hoped to convince you to work with us, and we hope you will yet change your mind. In the meantime, as we further evaluate the impacts of your work and tools on our efforts and how to neutralize these impacts, we will make additional modifications to your situation. You have cost us a great deal in terms of our harvesting as well as in how to respond to the tools you've created."

"That's just not as satisfying of an answer as I hoped," Kim responded. The reprieve from bodily harm had brought out her attitude again.

"Well, Dr. Johnson, let's just say that everything is quite dynamic right now. We initially expected that if we separated you from your computer systems, we would find that our efforts would be free from your interference. However, as you noted last time, your security tools are designed to continue without you being actively involved, so we are still feeling a great deal of pain. We were hoping that your systems were not autonomous, so this discovery has given us pause. Your systems are causing us more distress each day. For the time being, we feel that you should continue your vacation and stay away from computers. We're also looking into other, more forceful ways to convince you to work for us."

Kim hated dealing with bureaucrats and their obtuse way of speaking. Yes, Omega was some kind of grand manager for his scheme; that was obvious. He hid who 'they' were, what 'they' were doing, how her tools impacted 'their' efforts, and how all of this affected her future. Omega had given her very little information for all his talking, just like a good bureaucrat.

"OK, I guess I don't have much choice then, do I?" Kim said with a bit of exasperation. "I don't know any more today than I did yesterday or the day before. And I'm not really in a position to make or demand any changes. I hope that you all have an endpoint to this escapade," she said.

"Well, there are two or three possible endpoints," Omega said. "One endpoint is for you to work with us, but that does not appear to be happening anytime soon. Another possibility is that we keep you confined for who knows how long. We hope that you will change your mind. You can rest assured that we don't want this situation to continue any longer than necessary. We sincerely wish to return to the work we were doing before your systems started interfering with us a month or so ago. We are still trying to determine the best long-term approach to our various concerns."

"Oh, I do feel better that there's some unknown endpoint coming up," Kim replied. She regretted letting that slip out, but it was too late. On second thought, good to let them know that she still had her spunk.

"Dr. Johnson, I am as exasperated as you. One of the options that we originally considered was to offer you a substantial sum of guaranteed money in addition to a percentage of our ongoing harvest. However, you haven't shown the least inclination to working with us, whether possibly as a mole within your current group or directly working for us so that we can figure out how to redirect your system's attention away from us. We do not believe that you could remotely access your system and direct it away from us without alerting your employers. Your scruples do not appear to be for sale unless we apply additional, to-be-determined pressure.

"I will bid you *adieu,* for now, Dr. Johnson. I will talk more with you about your future in a few days."

There was silence on the other end of the phone. Kim got off the bed, walked through the open door to Beta still sitting at the bottom of the stairway. She handed him the phone and returned to the four walls of her temporary prison. A moment later, she heard Beta shuffling behind her and then the click of the lock.

Kim started to pace again, figuring out what she might have learned in this conversation with Omega. As she had already gathered, she hadn't learned anything new except that they were going to move her. *Just keep your cool*, she thought, *and wait for your opportunity*. Kim also knew that it was possible to apply more pressure on her, especially if Omega involved her family, and that was a frightening prospect. He had said that they wouldn't hurt her, but he didn't mention anybody else about whom she cared.

**Chapter 12**

Very early the next morning, Kim was startled awake with a loud knock on her door. Her room was still quite dark. The door opened; no lights were on in the basement, although light spilled down the stairs from above.

"Time to get up and get moving," Beta said. "We're leaving in fifteen minutes. Pack your clothes, use the toilet and let's get goin'."

Kim was still trying to wake up and make sense of her morning. Beta had left the door open, although the door at the top of the basement stairs was closed. She rolled out of bed, fumbled to turn on the light, dressed, and washed her face. She didn't have many clothes or toiletries to pack into her daypack, so she was ready to go in ten minutes. She sat on the edge of her bed, still trying to wake up, and waited for her next orders.

A few minutes later, the basement lights switched on from above, someone came down the stairs and a silhouetted man stood in the doorway.

"Time to go, Dr. Johnson." It was Alpha's voice and his body profile, but there was something different, Kim thought. He wasn't wearing his hood! Since he was backlit, she couldn't make out too many features other than that Alpha had close-cropped hair.

"Alpha, you're not wearing your hood," Kim noted. "What's up with that?"

"Even though you saw me the other night, we won't be needing them anymore, not where we're going. Let's move out."

Kim picked up her pack, walked past Alpha, and up the stairs. She felt a bit suspicious that Alpha wasn't wearing his hood and the meaning of *we won't need them anymore, not where we're going*. The first thought that came to her mind was that he wouldn't need it anymore because they were going to kill her; not a comforting way to start the day.

Kim emerged from the basement and into the kitchen, above

the room where they had kept her; a living area was to her left. The door through which she tried to escape two nights ago was in front of her, hanging open. Another man was in the kitchen, also not wearing a hood, and Kim surmised that it was Beta. She didn't realize that she had stopped at the top of the stairs to take all of this in; there was a gentle nudge in the small of her back from Alpha to move on. Kim sort of stumbled to her right, into the kitchen, and just stood there, a bit confused, trying to figure out what was going on and why Alpha and Beta had reduced the level of secrecy.

Kim finally got her first good look at both Alpha and Beta in the kitchen light. They were both busy, gathering a couple of sacks of groceries, a green duffel bag filled with something, and a couple of full trash bags. Alpha and Beta looked similar, like they could almost be brothers. Both were well-muscled with thick necks and a little over six feet tall. Both had short, brown hair with flecks of gray. These two guys reminded her of men who had played football or rugby or had been in the military or all the above. Her earlier thought was that they might be ex-military, so this was not surprising to her. Their movement was efficient; they knew their roles and what they were doing. Their eyes were attentive, keeping watch on her while they gathered their gear.

They weren't paying much attention to her, and Kim started to think that this might be her moment to run. The thought was coursing through her mind more strongly now, but she couldn't get her feet to move. There was little distance between them now; if she did try to bolt, one or both would be on her in a moment. Alpha and Beta looked like gym rats, and Kim was no sprinter. The men held the physical advantages while Kim hoped that she had the mental edge. How and when that was going to help her, though, she didn't have a clue.

A few moments later, she could see vehicle headlights glaring through the windows, and a van drove into the driveway that was on the side of the house, just outside the door. The men moved towards the door and van, and then Alpha realized that they both couldn't go outside at the same time and leave Kim alone. He moved closer to Kim, getting between her and the outside door, while Beta carried groceries to the van. Kim could hear the van doors open and Beta grunted a bit as he loaded the sacks. As Beta opened the kitchen door, Alpha grabbed a load and carried it to the van while Beta watched Kim. When

Alpha returned, Beta walked into the darkened living room and picked up a couple of large, military-style backpacks. He grunted and strained as he stood, so he put one of the packs down and then carried the first to the back door.

"Are you sure we have enough gear for this trip?" Beta said sarcastically. Alpha just gave him a little smile and watched him pass by on his way to the van.

When Beta returned, Alpha picked up the second backpack. He let out his own grunt, and Beta just chuckled at him and shot a look of knowing at Alpha. There was a tight connection between these two, Kim thought. Alpha loaded his pack into the van and returned.

Speaking to Beta, he said, "You take Dr. Johnson to the van, secure her and sit tight. I'm going downstairs and clean up." Kim started to move towards the door, and this caused Beta to jump.

"It's OK," she said. "I'm not leaving without you two. Let's head on out." Beta grasped her by the elbow and led her to the van.

This morning was the first time that Kim had smelled fresh air in several days – *how many?* She had lost count of the days, at least for the moment. Kim looked and saw that the morning twilight was nicely silhouetting the hills to the east. It was wonderful to feel the morning's cool air on her face; she had missed that feeling. It was still dark, and she couldn't make out any more of her surroundings or the house. Haphazard streetlights glowed to the west. Inside the van, Kim glumly wedged into the third-row seat, her little knapsack beside her. Beta asked her to put on her seat belts, which she did, and he stood in the side door to the van, blocking any possibility of escape. She let out a little sigh of exasperation, of frustration, of not knowing what was going on. Next, he looped a long zip tie around her ankles, snug but not tight. Looking around, Kim saw the backpacks behind her, along with the groceries. The duffel bag was in the seat in front of her. The van's motor wasn't running, but the dashboard lights were on and glowing around the driver's head. The driver appeared to be a woman or at least had curly, long hair pulled back in a ponytail, and was peering down and scrolling through their phone. Yes, it was just a typical morning if you're a kidnapper, nothing special.

About fifteen minutes later, Alpha exited the house and gave the door a tug shut. He opened the back of the van and stowed a broom, dustpan, and another garbage bag. These people seemed to be thorough, Kim thought. She hadn't thought to try to leave any clues behind, and if she had, it likely would have been pointless. At that moment, Kim was kicking herself. She hadn't thought of creating any kind of a breadcrumb trail that someone might follow, in part because she hadn't realized they'd be leaving so early. But then, Alpha and Beta hadn't given her anything useful for such a possibility. They had collected her few food scraps, and she hadn't left any trash behind in the basement. Maybe she wasn't as smart of a hostage as she thought — even more reason to be glum on this new, beautiful morning.

Beta sat on the bench seat in front of her, and Alpha took the passenger seat next to the driver.

"Let's roll," Alpha said, and they were off without another word.

After about a half-hour of driving, Kim still had no good idea where she was. She had a feeling that she was still in the Bay Area, but that was all she could guess. Nothing looked familiar, even as the morning light brightened. The general geography – the rolling hills to the east was her main clue – made her think that she was east of the bay and heading south because the sun was on her left, but that was the best she could guess. Eventually, she saw a highway sign for San José, and she was feeling a bit better about knowing her location. Not that it was going to help her in any obvious way, but it was a tiny bit of information.

Beta unexpectedly turned to face her. She thought that he was a good-looking, rugged man, but she wouldn't be interested even if the situation had been different.

"I just want to be clear that as we're driving today and making stops, you're not to do anything to bring attention to yourself, do you understand?"

Kim just nodded, *yes*. She knew that she didn't have any other choice regarding an overt answer, even if, deep down, she might feel differently.

Beta continued. "We'll be driving for a few hours; I'm not certain how long. In a bit, we'll make a stop for breakfast. I'll be here in the van with you at all times."

There was no threat in his voice, just a straightforward presentation of fact; this is the way it is, no questions.

The van's back windows were darkened, but Kim could look out and gather some details. They were generally heading south-southeast on a multilane interstate. Even if she wanted to try to wave and signal for help, it was the morning rush hour, and the other drivers had their eyes on the road trying to get to their desks, shops, and schools. She was feeling a bit forlorn to be out in public but not seen by anyone. *Kind of a metaphor for typical city life*, she thought to herself, *like how I behave when walking down the sidewalk or driving on the freeway.*

After ninety minutes or so, the driver took an exit and pulled into the lot of a large truck stop. She parked on the outskirts of the lot, nowhere near any other vehicle or building. *Yep*, Kim thought to herself, *not a whole lot of chances of being seen way out here.* Alpha and the woman got out of the van and clicked the electric door locks. Beta sat in front of Kim, paying her no attention. He was busy checking social media on his phone and scanning the news. There was nothing that Kim could see that gave away his identity.

After about ten minutes, Alpha and the driver returned, carrying a couple of sacks and a tray of drinks. Once in the van, Alpha turned to Beta and handed him a cup of hot coffee and a cup of iced coffee. Beta gave the iced coffee to Kim. *I guess they don't want me to boil them alive*, she thought to herself. *At least I'll get my daily dose of caffeine.* A moment later, Alpha gave Beta a warm, inviting sausage and egg biscuit, and he sat it on the duffel bag. Next, Alpha's and Beta's bucket brigade handed Kim a glass of orange juice, a banana, and a lemon danish. The scent of Beta's biscuit caused her to drool just a bit, but Kim figured she was better off with what they gave her since she had exercised so little the past few days. She usually jogged three or four miles every other day, but the pacing in the room in which they had held her wasn't the same.

They were soon back on the freeway, and a few minutes later they exited near Gilroy – at least that's what the sign said. She had noticed that farm fields extended all around them, but she hadn't fully taken it all in while she focused on her breakfast and traffic. The driver headed eastward through acres and acres of what? *Probably garlic and other vegetables*, she thought. *I should get out more often and discover more of California, preferably on my own, without these escorts.* The road was narrower now, and there was more slowing and accelerating for traffic. It was good that she had already finished her orange juice and much of her iced coffee because she didn't want to spill any.

The van slowed, following a long line of cars led in a morning parade by a tractor pulling a large trailer. The van driver, like most of the other drivers, Kim figured, was irritated to be crawling through these agricultural lands. After a quarter mile, the tractor pulled off into a field, and the line of vehicles slowly picked up speed. A few minutes later and they wound around and through hills and gained a bit of elevation. The driver did have a flair for taking the corners a bit faster than necessary, which caused Kim to sway back and forth in her seat. Kim enjoyed the views out of the window; they were so different from her neighborhood in San Francisco and better than her basement dungeon. She enjoyed seeing the trees, the hillsides covered with grass and bushes, and the infrequent home. Kim wondered what it was like to live in a rural area. She had always been a city girl, first in the Chicago suburbs growing up and the city for college, then at Cal Tech in Pasadena, and now in San Francisco. She didn't get out enough, she knew. Kim hoped to change that about her life if – *when* – she got out of this situation.

After thirty or forty minutes of sloshing back and forth in her seat, a large lake or reservoir appeared on the right side of the van. There were boats out enjoying the morning, some with anglers, others with people relaxing and enjoying a beautiful summer morning. Kim felt sorry for herself, sad that she wasn't out on the lake, making a great day of it. *OK*, she thought to herself, *snap out of it — chin up. Take a deep breath. I'll be out of this someday soon, I hope.*

Shortly, they left the hills, and the vast Central Valley opened before them. There was just acre after acre after acre of farmland. Next up was Los Banos. Kim's Spanish was pretty weak, but she started to chuckle to herself. Shortly, she said, mainly to Alpha, but also to Beta and the driver, "That coffee and OJ have gone right through me; I need to use the lady's room. Could we please make a stop? I know that you'll be watching me, following me – I understand. I won't run – promise." She meant it, but she didn't.

Alpha gave out a little sigh, a bit of frustration, but his mood seemed to improve quickly. Kim thought that he might have been thinking the same thing. He pointed to a truck stop on the edge of town, and the driver pulled in. Alpha was in luck this morning! Next to the truck stop was a construction site with a port-a-potty; the driver made her way over to it without being told. There was a smile on the driver's and Alpha's faces. Kim had not been thinking of this kind of a toilet, but she realized that this was the best she could expect. Alpha got out of the van first and used the port-a-potty. When he finished, the driver and Beta made the more civilized choice and headed into the truck stop.

Alpha cut the zip tie around Kim's ankles, helped to untangle her from the seat belts, and then followed her to the john. Inside, the odor of ammonia and excrement were overwhelming. She couldn't remember the last time that she'd been in a toilet as foul as this one. She quickly did her duty and burst out the door, gulping for air, hands on her knees. Alpha laughed at her while he guided her back to the van. Several minutes later, the driver and Beta returned to the truck, and Alpha told them about Kim's adventure as he replaced the zip tie around her ankles. Everyone was laughing now, except Kim, but she eventually started to grin. She didn't feel the desire to be agreeable, but she realized that she needed to put on a friendly face to gain a few style points with the boys. The more agreeable that she seemed outwardly, the better her chances in the long term, she reasoned.

They were off again, driving eastward through endless green fields of vegetables. Kim had no idea where they were taking her. Sitting in the corner of the room where they had kept her for the past several days, she had imagined several scenarios, many ugly, but none of them involved driving through the Central Valley. Kim had no idea that the roads here were so straight and boring. She was happy to live in San Francisco when compared to this view. In the distance, Kim could make out the foothills rising on the eastern side of the valley, backed by the hazy Sierras. Maybe there's a remote cabin in the hills or mountains that's my next prison, she thought, complete with manacles on the wall. *How gruesome*, she thought. So much for the power of positive thinking.

Chapter 13

When Kim disappeared her employer and teammates noticed. Working from home and being away from the office wasn't unusual for Kim, but she always let her team know when and where she'd be working. Working from home meant dealing with non-secure issues like employee reviews, reading journals, catching up on non-secure emails, or just relaxing after putting in way too many hours in the office. Kim hadn't logged into her computer or any other digital work device on the day of her disappearance. Her employer knew this was unusual behavior as she was usually very prompt and courteous about her work routine and about letting people know when she'd be working or not. The last anyone on her team knew, Kim was supposed to be working either from home or in the office until her vacation in a few days. Her employers could track her movements through her cellphone. They knew that she had taken her usual walk for coffee and more and returned home. Their typical efforts to contact her went unanswered. There was just an unusual, suspicious amount of silence emanating from Kim. All that they knew was that Kim had left her home that morning and returned. Her security cameras were on the fritz, too, which heightened concerns.

A car drove past Kim's home several times that afternoon, looking for signs of life, and the driver saw nothing of interest. In the early evening, a van returned and thermally scanned the house. Her appliances were running, and there were three people in her home, two larger figures and a third smaller figure. That raised additional concerns, as Kim had unexplained company. Maybe she was entertaining guests, but, if so, then why hadn't she been on her computer or answered her phone? The security team decided that an intervention would be best, given what they knew, and likely after sunset to minimize being seen. They positioned a car down the street from her home to keep watch.

An hour later, a team assembled and readied to quietly enter Kim's home. When the team tried to contact the agent who was watching Kim's home, there was more silence. Another agent was sent to walk by the car watching Kim's house and could see the driver lying on his side in the front seat. There were no apparent signs of foul play, but it was difficult to see in the fading light; the walker continued, passing Kim's quiet house on the other side of the street. Given the situation and their concerns, the team quickly descended on Kim's house, found it empty, and reported back on the vacant house and the unconscious agent watching her home.

Special Agent Andrews was not in a good mood. He let out a loud sigh of frustration. His day had gone from bad to worse. And his night was not going to be any better.

Andrews had worried that something like this might happen when staff were permitted to work from home during the COVID pandemic. Since the pandemic had ended, his worries had diminished but were not eliminated. Staff weren't remotely working nearly as much, but they still worked from home more than he liked. One of his worst fears had come to pass, it seemed.

Andrews assembled a larger team of agents to look for Dr. Johnson. They searched the internet for clues, listened to police frequencies, made discrete inquiries, and just kept their eyes open. Their job was to search for Kim without letting anyone know that she was missing. The people who had taken Kim had done an outstanding job, very professional. They left no fingerprints. Andrews' team found no DNA other than Kim's around the house. No one had used Kim's computers, so there were no digital fingerprints. If he was a betting person and wasn't aware of Kim's outstanding record, Andrews thought that it might be some kind of an inside job, but there was nothing to indicate that route. He was flummoxed, but that's the way he frequently felt at the beginning of a new case.

Andrews' team checked aircraft manifests and flight plans for clues in the surrounding airports and found nothing. No suspicious car rentals that they couldn't trace to legitimate people. Kim and her presumed captors had disappeared, and this wasn't good at all. She was too valuable to have simply vanished. Since agents had seen thermal images of three people in her home that evening, he knew that she was not alone and likely hadn't gone somewhere of her own volition.

Special Agent Andrews was settling in for a long search and he expected the situation to test his patience. He let out another sigh of frustration and took a deep breath. He knew that he needed to have an open, flexible mind and to calm himself. Composure was the key here. Andrews knew he needed to maintain control and manage the many frustrations he would face – for how long, he didn't know.

Over the following twenty-four hours, nothing of substance appeared regarding Kim's disappearance. There were no physical clues to be found. Monitoring landlines and cell phones didn't provide any clear clues. There were a few leads on which his team followed up, but nothing developed.

Recognizing that Kim's field of work was 'special,' Andrews sought assistance from sources that he didn't typically need to pursue. He interviewed her team and immediate supervisor and then her supervisor's supervisor over secure lines. He had trained to work with and for clandestine groups, but that didn't make it any less frustrating. On the one hand, these agencies' functions were on a need-to-know basis. On the other hand, he still had no real idea of who he was seeking from what they would tell him. The many potential people or groups that Kim could have irritated were substantial, primarily international, and all were well secluded. Her agency followed up to see if they could detect any unusual traffic or patterns that could explain who was involved or where to find Kim, but that was another dead end. There was no indication that Kim had accessed files for which she wasn't authorized, nor was there any sign that she'd been copying files, especially in large quantities.

A day later, there was the slightest of breaks that one of Andrews' more talented agents stumbled upon, knowing that they were up against some very sophisticated and likely well-financed operatives. While monitoring traditional communication lines had been fruitless and exhausting - no cell phone signals could be triangulated to Dr. Johnson's home for the day she went missing - there was one odd blip of information that might lead somewhere. The agent had been chasing satellite telephone frequencies in the greater Bay area. There were hundreds of different satellite phones in the region, mainly for legitimate and secure purposes. Satphone monitoring had been going on for years since it was over the open airwaves, and there wasn't much variation in usage patterns. There were stable satphone activity hot spots in the Bay area, mainly around the financial district, foreign consulates and lines of traffic down the major highways and streets. Much of the time, users scrambled their signals, but the underlying carrier signals were present. Andrews' people weren't spying, *per se*, as they never knew what was said, but they could still monitor the carrier signals. On the day of Kim's disappearance, there were signs of satphone signals emanating from near and in her home, which was unusual. There were at least two different satphones being used near Kim's home. The triangulation was weak, but the calls were from her neighborhood—finally, the slightest piece of information. Andrews had the agent dig deeper into this avenue.

After another day of viewing and parsing the satphone activity records against past patterns and GPS data, the agent found three new and unique activity spikes that might be promising. In the early evening, Andrews sent three different agents to check the buildings from which they thought signals radiated. Those buildings' IR thermal scans found signs of life in two of them, one in Oakland and the other in Milpitas, but no obvious satellite phone transmissions.

Later that evening, Field Agent Anglin was assigned to check on the two possible hits and drove by the first address. Her infrared thermal scans found three people at the building, a two-story condo in Oakland. Everything about this location seemed normal.

After searching databases for who lived there, what they did, and more, Field Agent Anglin decided to check on the condo in person. She parked a block away, walked to the building, and pushed the intercom button. Anglin identified herself as a concerned social worker seeking information on a distant relative of the owner, and the owner let Anglin in. Carefully walking up the stairs, not knowing what scene she might encounter, she prepared herself for the worst. Anglin was greeted by an effusive but curious older Asian man when the door opened, just as her research had told her to expect. Entering the condo, she found the other two members of the man's family – his wife and her visiting sister – and she relaxed. Kim wasn't here, and this was a dead end. Anglin briefly continued her ruse and apologized for having mixed up the family names that she was seeking.

Anglin headed to the next address, a house in the hills east of Milpitas. It was getting late, and she was tired. She drove south from Oakland on I-680 a little faster than the speed limit but this was California. Anglin had her cruise control set, mind wandering here and there about her current case. Database searches didn't reveal much, except that the house belonged to a couple who spent most of their time living in Germany. There was a truck in front of her, cruising along like she was. Suddenly, the muffler dropped off the vehicle and into her path, flying sparks lighting the freeway. Anglin swerved to avoid the muffler but bounced over it with the left wheels of her car. Her swerving took her into the path of a small truck on her right that was close by and even though the driver was paying attention, there wasn't time to avoid Anglin's swerving. Anglin hit the little truck on her passenger side and bounced off, continuing and slowing on the 680. They were both able to maintain control and safely make their way to the right shoulder. Field Agent Anglin jumped out of her car with traffic whizzing past to check on the other driver; he was a bit dazed, confused, overwhelmed, and overly apologetic. Anglin explained that it wasn't his fault, that she had swerved to avoid the muffler.

Anglin called the California Highway Patrol, explained the situation, and a cruiser was dispatched, along with a couple of tow trucks. She also called Andrews' office and left a message with one of his lieutenants about what she had discovered at the first address and that she'd follow up on the second hit in the morning.

The first thing the following morning, Field Agent Anglin was again on her way to Milpitas without any drama. An hour later, she sat in front of the house. The thermal scanner wasn't picking up any apparent signals other than warm spots from the hot water chimney and refrigerator compressor. Anglin knocked on the front door and waited. No response. She knocked again. After the second time, Anglin walked around the house. There was nothing remarkable, nothing unusual, no signs that the house was occupied. An empty trash can sat next to the side of the house. The grass had been mowed, but not for a week or two. She could peek through the kitchen window, and the house was practically bare. There were a card table and two plastic patio chairs in the kitchen – that was all that she saw. She was about to write this stop off as a waste of time when she recalled that satphone transmissions pointed to this address and that the day before, thermal imaging noted two people in the house. There were no other houses nearby that might be confused with this location.

Anglin called the agent who had checked on the house the previous day, and the agent confirmed that it was the same house and that the scans had picked up a couple of people sitting and walking around. Anglin contacted Andrews' office. Utilizing her training and experience and recognizing the exigent circumstances, she requested a search warrant. When Andrews' people wanted a warrant, they were usually granted and quickly.

While she sat in her car and watched, there was no activity in or near the house. It took a bit of time, but Anglin received the warrant. She again knocked on the door and announced who she was. Nothing happened. With a bit of effort, Anglin forced the front door open. If this was a hideout of some type, it certainly was far away from anything else and not well secured.

The house was spotless, which was surprising and inconsistent with the idea that a couple of people had been here the day before. She scoured the kitchen, living room, bathroom, and bedrooms – nothing. There was no furniture except the kitchen table and chairs. Next, Anglin went down into the basement. There was another small bedroom here, with a small mattress on a metal frame but no sheets or blankets. Nearby was the laundry area and another toilet. Water puddled in a utility sink, which was odd if the house had been unoccupied. This clue was about the only sign that anyone might have been in here for the past several weeks. The washing machine was musty and hadn't been used in months she figured. Anglin returned to the small basement bedroom, looked for clues, but nothing jumped out at her. Again, this room was as spotless as the rest of the house – almost.

Field Agent Anglin found it unusual that this room had a bed, but the upstairs bedrooms were barren. She also thought it unusual that there were no dust bunnies under the bed, but given how clean she'd found the house, no big deal. But it appeared that someone had done their best to sanitize the house since there was seemingly nothing to indicate that anyone had recently been there. If the house had been left unattended for weeks or months, then she figured that there should a mustier odor, dust bunnies, dead insects, spider webs. Then something caught her eye, just barely. On the metal frame of the head of the bed, some hair had snagged – black, curly hair. Interesting, she thought, since the database said that the owners were German, older, and had blonde and gray hair. She took a photo of the bed, the setting, and a closeup of the snagged hair. Anglin took a small envelope from her pocket, plucked the few strands of hair from the bed and put them into the envelope. She hoped the forensics team could make something useful of this tidbit. It's the only thing anyone had to go on.

After she left the basement bedroom, Anglin again looked over the basement area and then worked her way back upstairs to the kitchen. Yes, it was rather remarkable, she thought, that this house is practically spotless.

On her way back to the city, Anglin checked in with Andrews' office and noted her concerns and the lack of obvious signs that anyone had recently been in the house.

When she returned to the office, Anglin dropped off the hair sample and chain of custody paperwork with the lab and went down the street for lunch. Thirty minutes later, Special Agent Andrews excitedly tracked her down in the diner. He told her that the results were preliminary, but the DNA in the hair samples had a very high likelihood of being from Dr. Johnson based on a match from her personnel file. Finally, a possible break!

Andrews didn't have much more to go on, but he now figured that Dr. Johnson was not dead and that she had not been spirited away on an aircraft or ship – at least not yet. One possibility was that Dr. Johnson had chosen to disappear and take her secrets with her to someone who might pay her more. If that was the case, then why had her hair likely been found in a remote, bare house? *If I was going to go work for a competitor, I'd hope that they stash me in a nice hotel,* reasoned Andrews. It was more likely that she was someone's hostage, someone who was interested in or negatively affected by her work. Johnson hadn't reported any stalkers to the police or her supervisors, so a manic pursuer wasn't likely. Presuming that she was still alive led him to believe that she had some value because of the secrets she held, and her captors might be holding her for a ransom or were hoping to turn her to their side. Again, presuming that she'd been kidnapped, the people who had taken Dr. Johnson seemed to be more sophisticated than typical criminals, there was a team of them involved to pull something like this off so cleanly, and they likely had explicitly targeted her for her work. That's about all that Andrews could presume from the situation, which wasn't comforting, and he knew that he was making a case that she'd been captured with a minimum of information.

Chapter 14

Fred checked the time on his phone and found that it was only about 9:00 pm; he'd barely slept, and it seemed that this storm was going to keep him awake for some time. He laid there, listening to the wind pick up, startled by the blinding flashes of lightning through his thin tent walls, and the thunder echoing off the surrounding peaks. His tent flapped in the wind and strained the guy lines. One of his stakes pulled loose, and the flapping was worse.

And then, the weather died down. Not quickly, but over about thirty minutes, the storm moved to the east. It skirted to the north of his camp, he thought. He felt bad for everyone else in tents to the north of him, but he was thankful that maybe, just maybe, he'd avoided the worst of the storm. He was tired enough that he was asleep before the cold wind died down.

Fred's right shoulder was stiff and sore when he awoke. He had slept so deeply that he hadn't moved around much, and now he was paying for it. He made up for the lack of sleep earlier last night by catching a few extra winks this morning. Other than his shoulder, he was feeling perky, and that was a good sign. When he inched his way out of the tent, the morning light was well over the peaks to his east. Fred made his tea and oatmeal, cleaned up and packed, and was on the trail by 8:00 a.m., a personal record for a slow start on this trip. Before leaving camp, Fred thought to send a message to Asta to reassure her about the storm.

37.20544; -118.69105; Worst of the storm missed me. Maybe a long day today – I'll see. Luv!

Within an hour, Fred was atop Alpine Col, looking back at last night's home. He felt invigorated to be on the trail – climbing, working, sweating, and making progress. He looked out to the north and saw much of the terrain he hoped to cross before making camp tonight. The next landmark beneath him was Goethe Lake, followed by Humphries Basin. He could make out the cleft that marked French Canyon, and he figured he'd be there by lunchtime. Eight to ten miles in the distance, he could see the profile of the peaks that he would traverse via French Pass but had no idea where to find it. He'd stop for the night somewhere north of French Pass. It would be a long day after a late start, so he knew he needed to get going.

Fred carefully picked his route down the north face of Alpine Col and skirted Goethe Lake on its north shore less than an hour later. There wasn't a well-defined trail here and lots of talus, so the going was slow. After about an hour, he was at the north end of Muriel Lake, and the walking was more straightforward – less talus and more solid granite. He was moving relatively fast now and quite pleased. He had to slow for Piute Creek, which was still running high from last night's storm. This creek was his first water crossing of the trip, which was a benefit of having most of his journey being at higher altitudes. He slipped off his boots and wool socks, put on his trail shoes, and then side-stepped across the creek. It took him more time to change shoes than to cross the stream, but he preferred walking in dry footwear, especially on a long day. After that, he was off again at a nice clip. Moments after leaving the creek, he was crossing Piute Pass Trail and continuing his way northward. After being confined by Mount Goethe and Muriel Peak, it felt fantastic to be wandering through the expanse of Humphreys Basin! There was a nice, cool breeze blowing against his face, the sun wasn't too hot yet, and he was feeling good. The storm had left some wetter areas that squished when he walked through them, and he could feel his socks getting wet and cool. Oh well.

Less than an hour after crossing Piute Creek, Fred ambled up Puppet Pass. It wasn't a substantial obstacle, but it was a landmark by which he could mark progress. He was back into scree and talus on the north side of the pass for a short way before enjoying more of the fast, solid granite. It felt good to be almost flying this morning!

He worked his way between Paris Lake and Puppet Lake and then carefully made his way below timberline, down into French Canyon.

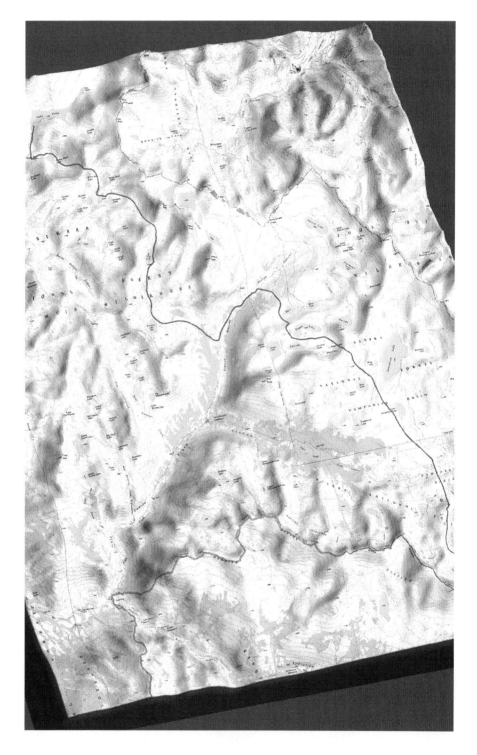

Fred headed downhill for a little over a mile and found his next land-mark, the faint trail leading through the forest to Merriam Lake. He was thankful for his GPS and maps because he didn't know if he would have found the faint path without them. The shade was good along French Creek, and this was one of the better, cooler places that he'd find for lunch and to refill his water, so he dropped his pack. The gurgle of French Creek was a pleasant diversion compared with spend-ing so much of the past few days above tree line listening to mostly silence except for last night's fireworks. He had made good time this morning and was pleased with himself, but he recognized that much of his walking had been relatively flat or downhill. That was to change this afternoon, he knew.

Fred was soon clambering his way up to Merriam Lake with a bel-ly that was a little too full. The afternoon warmed. The air temperature never really got hot up here, but the sun was intense from late morn-ing until late afternoon. While he had made good time in the morn-ing, he expected that his pace would slow this afternoon as he spent more time climbing and the temps increased. He stayed to the north and east of Merriam Lake's outlet stream as best he could so that he didn't have to slow to change shoes. Soon, the forest thinned, and the grade smoothed out. It took him about an hour to get to the lake, with his clothes drenched in sweat. He now bushwhacked across smooth granite slabs, still heading northward. The going was a bit easier now, with the granite slabs and being above treeline, and he had a good view in front of him. It was easier to see boulders and other small obstacles and avoid them while he kept his eyes up, looking toward La Salle Lake when he could see it. About an hour after passing Merriam Lake, he was sitting on La Salle's shore and looking up at Feather Pass. He felt the miles that he had already covered; it was the daily struggle. After water and dried fruit, he moved and picked his way amongst rocks and boulders. Compared to other passes, the south side of Feather Pass was relatively smooth. He'd have to see how smooth it was on the north side, though.

After forty-five minutes of humping up the slabs, he took in the views on the pass. Fred always enjoyed looking from where he had come, feeling satisfied with making progress and accomplishing some-thing. He also enjoyed looking at where he was going, the excitement of the unknown. Fred had studied this route and the maps so much over the previous winter that it wasn't exactly unknown, but now it was real. When he looked forward on the trail, he had a better sense of the accuracy of his expectations. Usually, his expectations were easier than reality. Viewing the route on maps and Google Earth did not make the expectations real because there was no wind, smells, and sweat. Studying for his trips did not provide the satisfaction of what he now felt; studying just left him anticipating and wondering if he would be sufficiently prepared. Knocking off these obstacles helped him realize that he was usually well prepared, and the wind and the scents it carried were the icing on the cake.

Everything in front was pretty much light-colored granite. There were a few lakes in his viewshed, along with the expanse of rock and mountain profiles. He still wasn't entirely sure how much farther he'd go today. Now that he'd made this last high obstacle, he was feeling better. Fred felt that he had another couple of hours of hiking that he could make today, which would make for his longest day yet. A more extended day helped him to keep on schedule and maybe get a little ahead – a plan that was dictated by his food supply, more than any-thing.

Getting off Feather Pass wasn't as tricky as some passes. There were boulders, rocks, and tiny clefts to avoid, but this was easier than negotiating talus slopes. He soon found himself traipsing among the bears – Bear Paw Lake, Ursa Lake, Big Bear Lake, Black Bear Lake, and then White Bear Lake. Fred had only encountered one bear in all his backpacking, and he was pretty thankful for that. It had been sitting in a modest puddle, staying cool, relaxing and lazily eating grasses. It was of no harm to him and nor he to it. He had seen plenty of black, brown, and grizzly bears from the safety of his car while traveling in the West, Canada, and Alaska, and he wanted to keep it that way. Final-ly, he was on White Bear Pass and looked back on Feather Pass, where he had been maybe an hour before. He was making decent time this afternoon and content with this progress. There were a couple of more bears in front of him – Brown Bear Lake and tiny Teddy Bear Lake – and beyond that, he could see Mt. Hilgard. At its base and just out of view was where he figured he'd make camp for the night. If he didn't stop there, then it would take more miles than he felt like covering before he got to the next decent campsite. Scrambling down the north side of White Bear Pass, he soon skirted the last of the ursine lakes and less than an hour later hiked up the outlet stream from beautiful, desolate Lake Italy.

As he walked upstream, he noticed a couple of tents along the creek. Nearby were a couple of men, eating their supper. He gave them a cheery wave and a smile, and they grumpily returned the salutations. This afternoon was one of the few times that he'd seen anybody since he picked up his resupply at Parcher's Resort, so that was slightly thrilling. It also meant that his trail might be getting more crowded, but he doubted that since he was taking the road less traveled.

Fred found the rock shelters at Lake Italy unoccupied, so he took the one closest to the lake. He first filtered some water to slake his thirst, put up his tent, and filled it with his sleeping pad and quilt. Fred still had a couple of hours before sunset and wanted to rest for a few moments and recall the great day he just had. According to his calculations, he had made sixteen miles this day, by far his longest day. Pretty darn good for a middle-aged guy, Fred thought! He was about on schedule, he figured, and maybe ahead of schedule, which was nice. Not accounting for the terrain, Fred felt that he'd be able to hike a mile or two farther each day as he became stronger and better acclimated. He was pleased with himself and looking forward to more! He might even make it home sooner than he had planned!

Fred turned on the satellite transceiver, expecting a message and wanting to send one, too.

To Fred: *Hope you had a good day today. Had our own rainstorm last night, but we didn't get wet. XOXO*

He just grinned and was sort of looking forward to being safe under a roof again.

37.35465; -118.81506; @ L. Italy. Good, long day today. Happy, content. Luv 2 u all!

He fired up the stove and just sat there, taking in the expanse of Lake Italy before him while he ate supper. Fred was hungrier than he had thought, so it was good to get some nourishment into him. Besides being hungry, he was also tired. It had been a long day, and he was still recovering a bit from his lack of sleep because of the storm last night. He headed toward his tent and figured he'd probably be asleep a little early tonight. The sun set over the mountains to his west, and twilight was here.

Fred sat in the vestibule of his tiny tent, taking off his shoes. He took a gander downstream to see what his neighbors were doing. He could make out the guys who were camping along the outlet stream from Lake Italy, and it looked like there might be a third person there now. There was something about how they carried themselves that made him think that they were very tired, irritated and not having a good time. One of the people looked slightly animated, pointing and maybe ordering the other two around. He could make out that they were talking, but had no clue about their conversation. It looked like they were hitting the sack, too. Despite the distraction his neighbors provided, he was soon fast asleep.

Chapter 15

Lost in thought, Kim hadn't realized that they were now driving southeast on a different but equally straight and boring freeway. A few minutes later and they were off the highway and passing the northern suburbs of Madera. *Never heard of this town before,* she thought to herself. After skirting Madera's suburbs, they were again on a straight, flat, boring road, heading east through vegetable croplands. *Maybe they're just trying to bore me into giving up my secrets,* and she just chuckled at herself under her breath.

Moments later, there was a minor change in the topography. They were climbing ever so slightly. The chaparral of the foothills replaced farmlands. This country was more interesting, more open, less orderly, but Kim was still puzzled about where they were going. The driver seemed to have relaxed while driving through the farmland. She had maintained a steady speed and didn't seem to be as bothered now by slower drivers or farm vehicles. The driver's mood perked up as they approached the mountains, which meant to Kim that they were either getting closer to the destination, or she enjoyed the mountains or both.

The driver hadn't said a word all morning, at least in Kim's presence, but now she turned to Alpha with a pleasant smile and told him that she had grown up near here, in a small town just to the south. She said it felt good to be back here and out of the city. The driver also said to Alpha, and looking at Beta in the rear view mirror, that they should have a good time over the next several days.

What the hell does that mean? Kim thought to herself. She took a deep breath as she realized she had no idea what to make of it. She had no idea what was going on and remembering again that she was just a pawn in someone's game. *Just let it go,* she said to herself, *and keep your cool.* Kim took another deep breath and closed her eyes, calming herself, thinking about visiting her family in Chicago, giving them great big hugs, and eating a scrumptious meal in her parents' backyard with everyone.

The van pulled off at a convenience store, and Alpha got out. Maybe fifteen minutes later, he was back, plastic bags of groceries hanging from his thick arms. There was a solid look to this man when he walked. His t-shirt stretched across his pecs, biceps popping just a bit. He looked like a soldier, with his short hair and sunglasses keeping anyone from seeing his eyes. Yep, they had something planned for her, likely something similar to their training. Since Kim hadn't been in the army or anything like that, she had no idea what to imagine.

They were back on the road a few minutes later. The drive was slower, the roads narrower, and it was tougher to see around corners for oncoming traffic. They were most definitely climbing, generally tending eastward. Kim still had no idea where they were going. The only reasonable guess that she could make was that there was a mountain cabin up here. That made a lot of sense. Get her away from civilization and snooping eyes. Take her someplace so remote that if she screamed, no one would hear her. Or take her someplace remote, kill her and bury her. Omega had said something to the effect that they weren't going to harm her, so killing her didn't make sense. She guessed that there must be thousands of remote cabins up here, and it would be easy to secure her in a basement or outbuilding for as long as they needed, one with designer shackles. More comforting thoughts, she said to herself.

They were still driving, still climbing. The forest was thicker now. Kim noticed that the temperature was becoming a bit cooler. Yep, climbing into the mountains. More bends and turns in the road. The higher they drove, the slower it seemed their forward progress. The driver was reasonably careful, not taking any risks, not speeding. Kim figured that she didn't want to have an accident or get stopped by the highway patrol. Very considerate of her, Kim snidely figured.

They drove, climbed, and twisted through a forest tunnel. The afternoon light filtered through the trees. *This could be such a great day up here*, Kim sighed, *without these three yahoos*. She was close to crying now, but she wouldn't let herself. Her insides were practically shaking, and she was doing everything that she could not to let it show. Another little village. More happy tourists. A ski area rested for the summer.

Another mountain lake. Cabins. Funky little restaurants. No more freedom.

The van slowed and then stopped. It was summer road construction season here, and a work crew was resurfacing the highway. They waited in line for their turn on the single lane. Beta turned and looked at Kim, gave her the look of "don't try anything funny." Kim looked behind the van, but all she could see was the grill of a dump truck. Beta laid his arm on the back of his seat, looking like he was ready to grab her arms if she tried to wave. They moved soon and passed the flagger, a friendly-looking, well-tanned, gray-haired woman in a fluorescent vest and orange helmet who smiled and waved at everybody as they passed by. *This is so unfair*, Kim tersely thought. She was so close to screaming, so close to exploding – and yet, she forlornly knew it would do her no good.

There was a resort on her right side, another opportunity for rescue that she was passing by. Cars whizzed by, going in the opposite direction, paying her no never mind, just as she would have done if she drove her car up here. Soon, the van slowed and turned right onto a slightly narrower road. Still climbing, fewer vehicles, lots of forest, rocks, boulders, nature. *This cabin must be really remote.*

After several more minutes of climbing, a hairpin turn, and more climbing, they were now on an even narrower road. There was a parking area alongside the route, filled with cars. People were out hiking, walking, enjoying the sunshine, enjoying their freedom. The pavement changed from concrete to worn, narrow blacktop. When another vehicle approached from uphill, the van driver pulled to the side to let them pass. These roads almost reminded her of San Francisco, except this road was crowded by rocks and trees rather than shoulder-to-shoulder homes and tightly parked cars nudged up against the curbs. The forest thinned some, and the trees were not as tall as they had been when they first drove into the mountains. The driver moved at a slow, steady pace, watching for rocks and oncoming traffic. She seemed more alert now, on the edge of her seat, craning to look around corners. The van's engine strained a bit from the grade, load, and altitude.

Driving past a ranger station, Kim wanted to wave at the hikers who rested there, but she kept her hands in her lap. The view opened even more - fewer and shorter trees, more smooth, white rock. *It is pretty up here, in a rustic sort of way.* They turned left onto a different road, even narrower if that was possible. Up and over mounds of rock, scattered trees. She saw numerous cars and a couple of buildings ahead in the distance. *Maybe that's where we're going, but I figured there'd be fewer people.* They came to a sign and a turnoff for Mono Hot Springs – general store, café, post office, camping, cabins, hot mineral baths – and drove higher into the forest.

The driver moved very slowly now, especially compared to the four-wheel-drive cars and trucks that practically zoomed by them. The driver said that she had grown up in the foothills, Kim recalled, but maybe she was now more of a city girl than a country girl. In all her years in California, Kim had never been this deep into the forests and mountains, never so remote. If there was a cabin up here and she had the chance to scream, it wouldn't make any difference.

The van turned onto a gravel side road. This road was much rougher, and the passengers and cargo bounced around. There was no road at one point, just smooth rock to climb that was a path to the next section of gravel. The van's motor strained, and the driver seemed to be encouraging the van, wanting to spur it along. Alpha and Beta were quietly sitting, not bothered by the jouncing. The driver kept going, and then there was a loud scrape from beneath the van. The driver let out a *whoopsie!* and kept going. At a fork in the road, she hesitated and took a left. After another hundred yards, the road ended.

"Well, this isn't where we want to be," she said.

Alpha looked down at his phone. Kim figured he must be consulting his GPS.

"Yep," he said, "We should have taken a right back there at the fork."

The driver looked around, picked a spot where she could back up and turn around, and then headed back down the side road. Back at the fork, the turn was so tight and the van so long that she couldn't easily turn to the left. After some maneuvering, they were back on the narrow, bumpy road. A jeep was coming down the road, and the van driver pulled to the side. There was barely room for the two vehicles side-by-side, and everyone in the van looked out the left windows to see if the jeep made it without scraping – it just cleared them. More crawling over rock scarred by the underside of cars that shouldn't have come up here.

Kim had the feeling that if they drove too close to the right side of the road, they wouldn't stop rolling until they were back in the Central Valley.

While the driver wrestled the steering wheel, she looked at Alpha and said, "You know, if I puncture the oil pan on this thing, we're screwed." Alpha just nodded his head in agreement, eyes forward.

After fifteen minutes more of scrambled kidneys, they came to a small reservoir and a dead end. Several cars were parked nearby, but Kim could see no people.

"This is it," Alpha said, "the correct end of the road." He got out of the van and stood up in the doorway so that he could get a better look around. Kim had no idea what he was looking for – the cabin, maybe?

He eased himself back down into the van and looked at the driver. "Sorry to do this to you, but let's go back to that dead end where we turned around. We can pull off there and have a bit more privacy. I didn't really see any other decent places to pull off of the road." He pointed back the way that they had come. Kim thought, *why do we need more privacy?* She took a deep breath, held it for a moment, and then let it gush out. She felt a bit light-headed.

The driver let out a bit of a sigh, shook her head and then swung the van around and followed Alpha's pointing fingers.

"Yeah, I know the way," she said with a bit of irritation in her voice.

After one last bit of bouncing and scraping, the van was back at the intersection of the first dead end. The van lurched to the right and again onto the side path that was maybe a hundred yards off the main route. At the end of the trail was a clearing and the small turnaround where they'd been thirty minutes before.

Alpha announced, "This looks good. We'll make this our home for the night."

Kim just looked at Alpha, then Beta, and then the driver. Her brow was knit, and more than a little bit of incredulity in her eyes. "What do you mean by *our home for the night?*" she asked.

"This is it, our beautiful mountain retreat for the night," Alpha said with a growing grin. Beta grinned, too. The driver maintained a neutral attitude.

Kim just looked at Alpha, hands on her hips, jaw dropped. "You've *got* to be kidding me," she said.

"Nope. No kidding. This is it. We're going to camp here for the night. We'll have a beautiful sunset, it appears. It should be pleasantly cool and a clear sky. There'll be millions of stars in the sky tonight. We have all the camping gear we need in the back of the van. We brought lots of food and a couple of jugs of water for tonight. We're set. It'll be wonderful."

Kim just sat there, confused, dejected, bewildered. "I'm a city girl. I've never been camping before in my life."

Kim's confession caused Alpha and Beta to grin even more broadly.

Beta broke in, "Well, there's a first time for everything, now isn't there?"

**Chapter 16**

Alpha moved to the back of the van and opened the doors. He pulled out one backpack and then the other and handed one to Beta. They looked around the clearing near the truck before selecting a mostly flat, sandy area. While Alpha started unpacking, Beta returned to the van.

Inside the van, Beta cut the zip tie around Kim's ankles and then secured a new tie around each of her ankles – loosely, but not so loose that she could slip them over her feet. Next, he tied those two zip ties together with a third zip tie. This way, Kim could move her feet and clumsily walk but not go too far too fast.

"Dr. Johnson, I don't want you getting any ideas about going for an evening stroll, OK? I'd prefer that you stay close to us so that we can keep an eye on you. If you'd rather, though, we could tie you up inside the van. It's your choice."

Kim grumpily shuffled her way to the other end of the clearing and loudly flopped herself on a large, irregular rock. She put her elbows on her knees and then her chin in her hands. "This is the worst first date ever," she said.

Alpha and Beta howled with laughter. Kim gave them a little smirk of a smile and shook her head, but inwardly was upset as well as pleased with herself that she didn't seem to be giving them any clues regarding her desired intentions. She figured that they knew that she'd try to escape if they gave her a decent chance, but they were doing their best to make the prospects uninviting. Kim felt that she was sending them signals that she was going along with them, which was not how she felt. *Yep,* she thought, *gotta get me outta here.*

Returning to their backpacks, Alpha and Beta pulled out a couple of cylindrical packages that landed with a clanking thud on the ground, followed by some folded plastic.

"These will be our home for tonight, these tents. It would be better for you, ma'am, if you watched and learned how to put one up."

Kim looked at Alpha, then Beta, trying to decipher their meaning. "What do you mean *I should learn how to put up a tent?*"

Kim could tell that Alpha was trying to contain himself, trying not to give out too much information.

"Well," he said, "you should look at this as an adventure, a learning opportunity, a time to develop new life skills." He said this as he pulled the tents out of their bags while Beta spread plastic sheets over the ground.

"I've heard and read about camping before," Kim replied, "and don't believe that it's my cup of tea. The closest I've come to camping was going to cabins in northern Wisconsin with my parents and brother and sisters or to science camps in Michigan. At science camp, we slept in small, smelly cabins and ate our meals in a rustic cafeteria."

Alpha and Beta spread the tents over the plastic sheets, inserted poles through the tent sleeves, tossed out stakes, and generally got everything ready. About ten minutes after they started, they flexed the poles to put up the tents and staked them into the sandy soil, occasionally having to move a stake because of buried rocks.

"See, Dr. Johnson, it's not that hard. Even a computer scientist could do it," cackled Beta. Alpha was almost laughing himself silly, bent over and turning red in the face. A moment later, he was gasping for breath but still laughing. Alpha calmed himself, looked upward, took a few deep breaths, hands on his hips, and then one last deep breath before relaxing a bit.

"We're something like eight thousand feet higher than we were this morning. That much altitude change over such a short period can be rough on a person," Alpha stated.

Kim had driven through the mountains before and remembered getting out to view beautiful vistas, playing tag with her brother in a roadside parking lot in Colorado, and then suddenly gasping for air. Yes, she had felt the effects of altitude before, but it had been a long, long time ago.

The men pulled out more fabric sausages from their backpacks, and Kim could only guess that they were sleeping bags and something else. *Ah, sleeping pads*, she figured, *of course*. The sleeping bags were pulled out and fluffed over the tents. Alpha gave everyone one of the smaller packs and showed Kim and the driver how to open them and pull out the sleeping pads. He showed them how to unfurl the pads and then find the black knob that was the valve. Twisting the valve open, Alpha blew air into the pad and then pinched it off. He stopped for a moment to catch his breath and then repeated the process. He nodded to Kim and the driver to do the same, and they fumbled with the sacks, pads, and valves. Beta and Alpha had their pads blown up in maybe five minutes, but they were red in the face and winded. The driver and Kim took their time. They were much less proficient; after maybe ten minutes, their sleeping pads were ready.

Beta took his pad and Alpha's and slid them into one of the dull green tents. He then took Kim's pad and started to take the driver's pad when she pulled it back from him.

"Nothing personal, Dr. Johnson, but I'll be sleeping in the van," the driver announced.

Kim wasn't hurt. It made her feel better. She'd rather have some quiet and alone time in this new setting than share it with a stranger, especially a stranger who was a part of her kidnapping.

Beta pulled more gear out of the backpacks, but not much of it was familiar to Kim. She sat on her rock, slightly curious but trying not to show it. She thought to herself again, *if I'm going to get out of here, I need to pay attention, learn, and act when the time is right.*

Beta took things apart and then put them back together in a different way. Kim finally figured out that he must be putting a small stove together, with some kind of a fuel tank on the bottom. Another small sack held some small cooking pots, and he went to the back of the van and poured water from a jug and into a pot. Returning to the stove, he twisted a knob, and the stove hissed. Pushing a button or something that she couldn't see, the stove gave a little *whoosh,* and a yellow flame quickly turned into a blue jet. After placing the pot of water above the flame, he sat back, adjusted the flame to his satisfaction, and then looked around.

Looking at Kim, Beta said, "I'm making some pasta for supper. Since there are four of us, it's going to take a couple of times for me to boil enough water so that I can make enough pasta for all of us." Kim had made pasta before, hundreds of times, but never in the great outdoors like this. She was curious, at heart, and followed along fairly well. Beta pulled out a couple of bags of pasta from a sack, along with bags of precooked chicken, spaghetti sauce, and some cheese. *Ah,* Kim thought to herself, *I see what the chef is doing.*

The sun sank lower in the west. It was still an hour or two before sunset, but Kim began to feel a bit of a chill. "May I go to the van and get a jacket out of my pack or would one of you like to get my pack for me?" she said.

The driver, who had been sitting around and seemingly not paying attention, got up, found Kim's pack in the back seat, and then walked it over to her. Kim rummaged around in her pack, found her fleece jacket and put it on. *Now,* she thought to herself, *I'm finally using my fleece for its intended purpose, rather than looking city stylish with it.* She grinned a bit at herself.

After the water boiled, Beta poured it into a bag of pasta and then repeated the process. The pasta hydrated in maybe fifteen minutes, but Beta waited until the second batch of pasta was ready before finishing the meal. He poured the extra water off the pasta and then combined it with chicken, sauce and cheese in the sack.

"Supper's ready, everyone," he said. Kim didn't know what to do; she just sat there on her rock, waiting for more direction, watching Alpha and Beta. She figured that the driver had been camping before, but the driver wasn't taking the initiative. Alpha and Beta grabbed odd utensils like Kim had seen at fast-food restaurants. *Sporks,* she thought to herself, then got up, found one for herself, and handed the last one to the driver.

Standing there, Kim tried to figure out what was next. The men took one of the pasta and chicken pouches and sat down near each other, taking turns eating. Kim was taken aback.

"Wait a minute. You expect me to… to… to share supper with her?" Kim said, pointing to the driver.

"Well, yeah, that's the way it works out here," Alpha responded dryly, with a bit of a grin on his face. He always enjoyed taking greenhorns camping for their first time, and this situation was no different. "Each of these pouches is enough for a couple of people to eat, and this way, we have fewer dishes to wash."

"Unbelievable," Kim sputtered. She grabbed the other pouch of pasta, fumbled with how to carefully hold the hot bag – almost spilling it – and then gingerly scooped a portion out. Kim gladly ate, being a bit hungry, but didn't want to let on that she appreciated the food. After taking another bite from the pouch, she handed it to the driver. The driver was not at all revolted like Kim and calmly scooped out a couple of mouthfuls for herself before giving it back to Kim.

While this was going on, Beta retreated to the back of the van, filled water bottles for them, and found some fruit and candy bars. He distributed these to everyone and resumed his supping with Alpha.

Kim had eaten outdoors numerous times, but this was more *au naturel* than she had ever experienced. She took the proffered water bottle, fruit, and candy after she had passed the pasta to the driver again. When the pasta pouch came back to Kim, it was nearly empty. Kim scowled at the driver, who just shrugged and said, "Ya snooze, ya lose girl. Out here, it's the survival of the fit, and you're showing yourself to be fresh meat."

After that admonishment, Kim sulked. She was so far out of her element. Where was her kitchen, her dining room, her big soft bed when she wanted them most?

The good news, Kim soon realized, is that with so few dishes used to make supper, there weren't a whole lot of dishes to clean – just the sporks rinsed with boiling water. Well, there was one perk for camping that she had never known.

The sun dipped below the tops of the trees, and Kim was glad she was wearing her coat. She sat back on her rock, watching and learning. Her captors took their sleeping bags and threw them into their tents, and then one of them did the same for Kim and then threw the last sleeping bag inside the van for the driver. She didn't know what time it was, exactly, but based on how she'd been living her quiet life a few days ago. Kim figured it was getting close to eight o'clock.

Everyone was sort of sitting around, relaxing, taking in the day, enjoying the last moments of daylight. Alpha rummaged in the backpacks and pulled out a couple of headlamps, giving one to Beta and keeping the other for himself. Kim felt slightly miffed that she didn't get a light. The guys checked to make sure that their lights worked and then flicked them off.

They all heard the slamming of car doors in the distance and then an engine turning over. Someone had come back from hiking and gotten in their car somewhere nearby. Even if Kim had wanted, she knew that whoever it was wouldn't hear her over the crunch of their tires, their conversation, and whatever else was going on in their vehicle. She sunk into herself for a moment.

Sitting there, feeling bad for herself, Kim perked up for a moment. Something had come to her to snap her out of her torpor.

"So, Alpha, Beta. What are you doing with me tomorrow or the day after tomorrow? I don't understand why we're up here. Is there a secret hideout or a cabin or something that you're taking me to? What's the game plan?" Kim sat on the edge of her rock, seriously curious, seeking information, certainty about her future.

"Well...," Alpha started. He glanced at Beta, who didn't reveal anything. "We thought about letting you in on the plan tonight, but we've... rather, I've... decided that it would better to wait until the morning."

At this, Beta grunted a deep, knowing, approving chuckle.

"Well, that doesn't tell me anything," Kim retorted. "Can't you tell me something more? I don't understand what's going on, why we're doing any of this."

Alpha looked up, scanning the sky. Venus was the only bright light in the sky, the sun having set several minutes ago.

"No, ma'am, it'll wait until the morning," Alpha replied. "We have another long day ahead of us tomorrow, and I suggest that you get some shuteye. But, the reason that we're doing this is to keep you away from civilization, prying eyes and the internet."

Kim sighed, sat up, and threw back her shoulders, signaling that she wasn't satisfied with the answer she had received. In the waning light, she could sense that Alpha was looking at her, trying to find his words so that he didn't reveal too much.

"Dr. Johnson, you have your pack of clothes, a sleeping bag, and pad. If you need, our driver will escort you away from camp, and you can pee or whatever. Then, I'd like you to crawl into the tent and go to bed. And, before I zipper your tent closed, I want you to hand me your running shoes."

Kim just looked at Alpha for a moment, letting this sink in. She hadn't thought of trying to run away during the night, but it made sense why he wanted her shoes. Exasperated, she looked at the driver and said, "Let's go," and started shuffling away from the camp in her zip-tie shackles. The driver jumped up, not fully ready for her new responsibilities, and followed Kim several hundred feet into the sparse trees.

When they returned, the driver headed towards the van, got in, and shut the door behind her. The dome light came on, which threw a faint glow across the camp. Kim searched for the tent's opening with her fingers, found it, and unzipped it. The sleeping bag and pad laid on the floor. There was plenty of room if you're used to a coffin. Before she crawled in, she picked up her pack of clothes and set it inside the tent. She found it awkward getting into the tent. She hadn't crept into a small, enclosed space like this since, *when?* Childhood? Making a tent with a blanket and table in her parents' living room, she supposed. Once inside, she sat on her butt and took off her shoes. After handing them to Alpha, she heard him say, "Thank you."

She crawled deeper into the tent and tried to figure out how to orient her pad and sleeping bag. Once they were configured, she spent some time thinking about leaving her clothes on or taking them off. She decided to leave them on, especially since it was impossible to get her pants off over the zip ties. While all of this was going on, she heard someone, Alpha presumably, zipping her tent and driving another stake into the ground at the front of her tent to better secure the opening, she figured.

She had slept in sleeping bags at friend's homes in her childhood, but this was the first time in twenty, thirty years. She unzipped the bag, slid in, and zipped it back up. Laying there, she was uncomfortable in her clothes and the bag, it all being so unfamiliar to her, so she pulled herself out. Sniffing the bag, she realized that it had been some time since it had enjoyed fresh air. She next laid on her bag, then rolled to her side and then to her other side. She missed her pillow and then figured out that she could use her coat and knapsack as a makeshift pillow. The light from the van blinked off; the driver must be trying to sleep. Feeling a bit more comfortable, she could also hear the guys next door, going through their sleeping bag contortions and quietly talking about things that she couldn't make out. She laid there, contemplating the day, considering whatever it was that tomorrow might bring.

She soon heard snoring from her neighbors but felt slightly agitated about everything, especially about sleeping outdoors in a tent like she'd never done before. From somewhere in the distance, she heard an owl. That was a new experience for her, almost thrilling. It gave her a bit of hope; someone lived, thrived out here, so maybe she could, too. An owl was a symbol of wisdom, and she needed to be calm and wise if she was going to get out of this predicament. She slid back into her sleeping bag and slowly nodded off, mind trying not to race considering what tomorrow might bring.

Chapter 17

Kim was half asleep, trying to make out where she was, the odd sounds she was hearing, and why her hips and shoulders hurt so much. Blinking her eyes, it came to her: she had slept in a tent, in the outdoors, for the first time in her life. She could hear the muffled sounds of the guys moving around in their tent, unzipping it, and getting out with various grunts. Kim laid there, snuggled inside this musty sleeping bag, not wanting to make a sound like she might be. She soon heard the *whoosh click pop shoosh* of the stove lighting, and then it's hiss.

Kim rolled onto her back and then stretched this way and that way. Her shoulders and hips were stiff and sore. The zip ties had gnawed at her skin through her socks during the night and had kept her from moving her legs as much as she wanted. Sleeping out here was different from being in her bed, which she dearly missed right now. Kim's sleeping pad had lost some air during the night, and parts of her had been resting on the cold, hard ground – that's why her hips and shoulders were complaining this morning. Another outdoor skill she realized she needed to learn was to seal the sleeping pad's valve better.

She started to extricate herself from her tangle of clothes and sleeping bag, unzipping it further and further, making enough noise that she knew that Alpha and Beta knew she was awake. Her hair must be a real mess, and she needed to pee. Sitting up and looking around for her shoes, Kim remembered Alpha took them from her before she went to sleep. Speaking to the outside world, she asked to have her shoes returned. A moment later, someone slipped her shoes under the front edge of the tent, and she scooted to retrieve them.

Slowly, stiffly, she emerged from the tent on her hands and knees. Kim could now give a dour good morning glare to Alpha and Beta. They both grinned, sort of understanding what she was experiencing. Without asking permission, she said, "I'm going over there behind some trees to pee. I couldn't run away right now if you tried to shoo me away." There was a guffaw from the men, and she stumbled her way through the trees

Returning to camp, she was grateful when Beta handed her a cup of coffee. She took it and used it to warm her hands while she blew on it to cool it a bit. Sitting on her rock, butt cold, eyes still puffy, she tried to take in the world. The sun was just coming up over the mountain behind her, and Alpha and Beta were basking in its warmth and quietly talking, a map spread at their feet. *Where are we driving today?* she wondered.

Kim croaked, "Is there anything to eat? Or should I waddle out for donuts?"

Alpha and Beta gave her another grin, and Beta made a move towards the stove. "I hope you like oatmeal," he said. Like she had a choice. Soon, Alpha handed a spork and a second mug filled with warm, gooey, apple-and-cinnamon flavored mush to Kim. Several sarcastic thoughts came to her mind, but she kept them to herself.

"So, couldn't trust me with the boiling water, huh?" she asked. Alpha and Beta gave her a knowing look.

She was feeling warmer and waking more. The more she moved, the less that her aches and pains hurt. The sunlight was now on her back and felt glorious. It wasn't as cold here as she had first thought; she was getting used to it. Rubbing her eyes with her fingers, her focus on the world improved. Kim was usually perky when she awoke, but this was not her typical morning. Looking over at the van, she could see that the windows were fogged over from the driver's condensed breathing. Soon, a fuzzy head popped up in the truck, messy hair and all, swathed in a sleeping bag. Kim felt better to know that she wasn't the only unkempt woman on the side of the mountain this morning.

Kim was finally feeling that her personality was again infusing her corporeal body. She stretched some more to work out the morning kinks, stood up, bent over to stretch her back, and groaned. It had been some time since it had taken her so long to wake up, but Kim was getting there. Almost like having a hangover, but without the headache, she thought.

After one last big yawn, she said, "OK, gents, you told me last night that you'd tell where we're driving today, what the plan is. I'd like to hear more so that I can pick out which dress to wear."

Alpha gathered himself, grinned a bit, started to speak, and then didn't. Kim could tell that he was enjoying himself, but she didn't yet know why.

"Well, Dr. Johnson, before we get into all of that, we need to pack up camp. Could you please stuff your sleeping bag into its sack and let the air out of the sleeping pad? We'll show you how to roll and fold the sleeping pad after it's deflated. Then we'll take down the tents. I need to give the driver her coffee and oatmeal and stow away the cooking gear."

Alpha's response was not the answer that Kim wanted to hear, but she gave a little sigh, slowly got up while stretching, and crawled into her tent and sat on the pad. How in the world was she supposed to get this sleeping bag into the small sack? She zipped the bag and then pushed it into the pouch, and it spilled out. She could hear that Alpha and Beta had already gotten their sleeping bags packed and listened to the long *whoosh* as their sleeping pads collapsed. She gave up struggling with her stuffing and found the sleeping pad's valve and twisted it, releasing the air. Shortly, her butt was on the hard ground, and she could feel the cold seeping through.

Kim slithered out of the tent and then pulled the half-packed sleeping bag out behind her. She held it up, irritated, so that Beta could see her failure. He grinned and then showed her how to push everything deeply into the sack with several deft moves.

"Oh, you make it look so easy," Kim said. Ah, her sarcasm was warming with her body.

"That's the easy one. Next, we have to fold and roll the sleeping pad and tent, and each of them is tougher. Let's get to it," Beta said.

Kim dragged the limp sleeping pad from her tent and handed it to Beta. He almost gave it back to her and realized that she didn't know what she was doing. He showed her how to roll and fold the pad to get the air out and then re-roll and refold it. The sleeping pad snuggly fit into its little sack.

"The tent," Beta said, "packs like the sleeping pad after we remove the stakes and poles and then let out all of the air. Alpha and I will show you how to pack our tent, and then I'll help you with your tent. These are good skills to know," he said with a wink and a smile.

Kim just gave him a side-eye. *What does that mean, good skills to know?*

"By the way," he said, "we're counting the stakes and making certain that they get properly stowed. We don't want any of them disappearing into your pockets, now do we?"

The first tent was soon down, flattened, rolled, and packed. Kim removed the stakes from the tent in which she had slept and set them in a prominent spot, and then she slipped out the poles. She thought that a stake would make a decent weapon, but she'd have to stab these guys dozens of times to take them down, and there wouldn't be time for that before being jumped by the other one. As he said, Beta helped Kim to pack her tent. Alpha and Beta put all the gear into the backpacks and checked on the driver. Pretty much everything seemed to be packed away.

Kim sat on 'her' rock, the sun warming her back, her knapsack at her feet, taking everything in, and was still puzzled about the plan for the day.

"OH, HELL TO THE NO!" Kim started yelling. She had just figured out their plan. *"THERE'S NO FUCKING WAY I'M GOING BACKPACKING! JUST KILL ME HERE AND NOW!"*

Alpha and Beta had been bent over the packs, making adjustments. They slowly straightened, looked at Kim, looked at each other, and started grinning. The driver was smiling, too.

"By golly," Alpha said, "she is one smart computer scientist. She figured it out all on her own. Now we don't have to tell her about today's plans after all, and we can get on the trail sooner."

Alpha, Beta, and the driver were trying their best not to laugh, to maintain control of the situation. Kim's eyes were darting around, looking for her escape. There was none. Her shoulders tightened, and she was fuming.

"Look, Dr. Johnson, we've been told that you need to be 'isolated' from the world for a few days. Omega and others are working on the next steps of their plan. Someone figured out we were keeping you in that house, and we got out just ahead of them. Omega asked us where there was a safe place to isolate you. We were both in the army ten years ago, deployed to the mountains of Afghanistan. We suggested to Omega that we all go on a 'wee wander' for a few days where we can escape the eyes and ears of your many interested friends. He thought it was as good of an idea as any, so here we are."

Kim just rolled her eyes. "You have got to be kidding me," she said. "This is the craziest kidnapping ever. This is the worst first date ever! How do you guys think up this kind of crap?"

After a moment of silence, she said, "Last night was my first time sleeping outdoors. How do you think I'm going to survive backpacking?"

"Don't worry. We'll take good care of you – lots of exercise and good, clean mountain air. We're certain that you'll enjoy your wilderness vacation better than sitting in a dingy basement bedroom," Alpha replied.

"*WILDERNESS VACATION?*" Kim sputtered and shook her head in disgust.

Alpha grinned and replied, "Yes, this is your chance to get away from the city, from your work for a few days. You should look at this as a digital detoxification. At least, that's how Omega is hoping it turns out." With this, Beta was turning red, his laugh spilling through his nose.

"I don't find this the least bit funny or amusing," Kim snapped. "Goddammit! What if I don't want to go? What if I just sit here and throw a tantrum?"

"We anticipated that possibility," Beta chimed in. "Let's just say that it would be better for your physical and mental health if you joined us on this holiday." Beta's statement was the first time either of them had really threatened Kim, and she didn't quite know how to respond.

Kim narrowed her eyes, hoping to pierce holes through Alpha and Beta. "So, for my mental health, could you please give me some more details about this so-called 'holiday'?" she said icily. "If I was feeling a little overwhelmed before, then I'm definitely overwhelmed now."

"Well, as we said," started Alpha, "Omega wants you thoroughly isolated from the digital world for several days. That's so that it's easier for you to stay lost from your searchers, and there are fewer possibilities for you to get into any digital mischief. Out here is the perfect place for that! No computers and no cellphones!

"We plan to backpack from the trailhead that you saw last evening by the reservoir and work our way up and over the Sierras. Our wonderful driver will meet us on the other side in a few days. Hopefully, by then, Omega and his team will have their next steps ironed out."

Kim gave him a look that could melt steel. She was seething. She wanted to let her anger out, but she didn't know how. Kim was feeling a lot of different emotions at the moment, none of them good or healthy.

Slowly and carefully, so that less venom might escape with her words, Kim asked, "How long is this up and over trip? How many days? How many miles? What else should I know? And get these damn zip ties off of my ankles!"

Beta walked over to Kim and cut the zip ties off with his knife. "Well, that's why we were looking over the map this morning, to re-acquaint ourselves with the route. We're guessing that it's about twenty-five miles. If it was just Alpha and me, we could easily make this trip in two days and possibly one. But, since you're a woman and a nerd, we're guessing that it's going to be three or four days."

Kim was seeing red now. She couldn't remember the last time she was so mad. She stood up, hands on her hips, stretched her legs, and looked like she was about to bolt. Beta was taken aback, scooted away from Kim and held his hands in a defensive stance.

"*A woman? A nerd?* Are you saying that I'm not as capable as you? That you're so damn superior because you're men or because you've been in the military?" Oh, she was hot now.

Beta backed further away from Kim, watching her so that he didn't get kicked.

Alpha was feeling a bit defensive. "Well, yes, ma'am, that's about who we see it. You said that this is your first-time camping, your first time outdoors like this. And you're just not as strong and well trained as us. So, we're trying to plan appropriately. Besides, Omega doesn't seem to be in any hurry for you to return to civilization."

Kim paced near her rock, trying to figure out what to do. She had no answers. She was overwhelmed, over her head, and way pissed off. She looked at Alpha and Beta, shook her head, and pursed her lips. With all this anger, she might be able to outrun these two, but where would that get her? Tired and lost is all that she could figure. She couldn't run back the way that they had come because that was the obvious way out, and they'd probably find her. She didn't have food or water. She had enough sense to know east and west but wasn't sure how long it would take her to get to a highway or town. Again, she was stuck and without an apparent escape. Yeah, she might escape but she didn't know if she'd survive. The only way to survive seemed to be to go with Alpha and Beta and buy a few more days of thinking and hoped-for opportunities.

Again, she muttered, "This is the worst fuckin' first date ever." Kim picked up her knapsack and started marching to the road, to the trailhead. She stopped, turned around, and looked at Alpha and Beta, daggers coming out of her eyes. "Are you two coming or not? I won't be a kidnapping victim if you don't catch up quickly, and then you'll have to tell Omega how I left you behind." And she was off again.

Alpha and Beta grabbed their heavy packs and threw them over their shoulders, grunting and scrambling to catch up to Kim. Already out of breath, Alpha looked back at the driver and yelled, "We'll see you in a few days. We'll keep in contact."

Kim's holiday to hell had begun.

Chapter 18

Since Kim was quite perturbed – to put it mildly – she set a torrid pace. Alpha and Beta tried to catch up to her, yelled for her to slow down and wait for them. *Not happenin'*, she thought to herself.

After about thirty minutes, Kim made it to the Bear Creek Diversion Dam where they had turned around last evening. She didn't know which direction she was supposed to go from here, didn't know where to find the trail, except deeper into the wilderness. Several trucks and jeeps were parked uphill from her, so she guessed that the trail started up there. The guys moved as quickly as they could to catch up to her, deeply panting. They always had her in sight and could drop their packs at any time if they really needed to run after her. She decided that she'd wait for them, after all.

When they caught up to her, both were breathing deeply, and sweat beaded on their foreheads.

"Just hold up," gasped Alpha. All three of them stood in the parking area. The guys leaned over, hands on their thighs, catching their breath. Inwardly, Kim was proud of herself, but her face was expressionless. They had barely started and she was getting to them, taking some of their power for herself.

"So, here are the rules," Alpha said. He was starting to talk again and had to take a deep breath before proceeding. Finally, it looked like he was getting his wind back, and he spoke.

"Beta or I will walk in front of you and the other behind you so that we keep you in sight at all times. If you need to make a stop, just ask. We'll stop every thirty to sixty minutes for a break and drink of water, maybe some snacks to keep our energy up. And whoever is in front will set the pace, not you. Any questions?"

Kim looked at him, pursed her lips, squinted her eyes, and tersely said, "Which way? Lead on." Yes, there was an edge to her voice.

Alpha pointed uphill, and then she spotted a dark, wooden sign. They started walking to where Alpha indicated with Kim in her assigned position. As they got closer, she could read "Bear Creek Trail, John Muir Wilderness, Sierra National Forest, US Forest Service." As usual, she still had no idea where she was in California. Everything was new for her on this trip. The trail wound through modest-sized pine trees, well-spaced, and presumably along Bear Creek, which flowed to their right. Kim didn't feel that the trail was particularly steep or strenuous, especially when compared to San Francisco's hills that she frequently walked and ran. The most significant difference for her was the altitude. She could feel a bit of tightness in her chest and was very thankful she wasn't carrying big packs like Alpha and Beta.

The morning sun was in her eyes, flashing through the trees. She followed Beta and kept a decent distance behind him. Kim could hear Alpha behind her, the plod of his boots on the trail and an occasional scuff. As far as she was concerned, Beta set a very comfortable pace. She had her eyes up and enjoyed the views. Kim especially relished being outdoors after being kept in the basement cell in the house. When she walked and ran around San Francisco, she always had a plan, a goal to meet. Here, she didn't have to think about anything, didn't have to get home for a conference call, didn't have a coding problem in her head or a project deadline. *Well,* she reminded herself, *yes, I do need to think about escaping, but I need to take all of this in so that I'm as prepared as I can be.* Kim breathed, plotted, and inwardly enjoyed herself, and there was a hint of a smile on her face. *Best not to let on that I'm not as upset as I was an hour ago.*

A trail bisected their trail, and they continued up the hill. In the morning chill, Kim grew warmer, pulled off her jacket, and stuffed it into her pack without slowing. It felt so good to stretch her legs, to get her heart pounding a bit. She guessed it was before mid-morning, but not too much. They had taken their time getting around this morning. She thought to herself, doing basic math problems in her head as she often did. *If we have to go twenty-five miles over three to four days, then that's only six to eight miles a day — easy peasy! Maybe this backpacking stuff won't be so bad.*

Kim was looking around, taking in the sights, when Beta called for a break. Along the side of the trail was a fallen tree and, after removing their packs, they all sat on it. Kim gently set her backpack down while Alpha and Beta practically dropped their bags. She could see that both had sweated through their shirts. Kim felt a glow where her knapsack rested on her back and that was about it. Alpha handed her a liter water bottle, and she took a couple of sips. When she tried to hand it back to him, he told her to keep it in her pack. *Ah, trying to lighten his load.* Kim just grinned. Alpha and Beta had hoses snaking from their packs and sucked on those.

They sat there for a bit longer, and Kim started to get a chill and wanted to move on. She was beginning to make some motions to go when Beta told her to relax. He had just started to breathe normally, and he was going to enjoy it for a few more minutes.

Just to be annoying, to get in their heads, Kim asked, "So, how far do you think we've gone? A couple of miles?"

Beta just looked at her glumly and then threw a glance at Alpha. "If we're lucky," he said, "maybe we've gone a mile at the most." There was no smile on his face, just a look of strain.

Inwardly, Kim smiled. *Maybe this trip won't be as bad for me as it is for them.*

Finally, the guys hefted their packs, and they were all off again. Kim enjoyed herself as much as a kidnapping victim could. The basic curiosity that had always been one of her hallmarks lead her eyes. She wished that she knew more about the trees and rocks and their names, but she enjoyed the exploration. It was a wonderful reprieve from sitting in her cell, trying to figure out her future. She now knew that she'd be out here for a few days, moving, taking it all in. She wasn't worried about being killed or tortured, at least not for the near term. The adventure that she'd not been enjoying the past several days was becoming more tolerable, at least until they got to the other side of the mountains.

Bear Creek spilled over a waterfall, and Kim loved it. Without thinking, she stopped for a moment to take it in, and Alpha almost ran her over. He hadn't seen her stop because he had his head down as he plodded up the mountain. He gave her a bit of a push, and they were moving again.

Kim felt lighter than she had felt since the kidnapping started. She couldn't explain it. And she didn't want to reveal it to her involuntary companions. They might do or say something to bring her down or force her to carry more of the gear. She was quite content with her small knapsack; there wasn't much room left in it to take anything. She guessed that her pack weighed less than ten pounds, and she was thankful.

Kim walked on while Alpha and Beta trudged. Maybe a half hour later, Alpha called for another break. They found another log on which to sit. Kim sat, stretched, and relaxed. She felt that her face was likely showing how much she enjoyed this walk, but Kim tried to keep her look as neutral as possible. It was maybe mid-morning now, she guessed. Kim felt that if she were alone with her pack, she'd be walking faster. She thought that she looked better than either Alpha or Beta. Sweat dripped off their faces, down their soaked shirts. The guys took long tugs of water, let it slide down their throats, and then drank more. They also pulled out something that looked like old shoe leather and offered it to Kim.

"What's this?" she asked while she took what they offered and looked closely at it before putting a bit into her mouth. She enjoyed the sweet, salty taste, although the chewing was tough.

"Beef jerky," said Alpha. "It's a good source of protein and relatively lightweight. It's easy to carry and doesn't spoil easily."

"I never had this before, but I like it." Kim savored the snack, savored the moment of being out here in the wilderness. Bear Creek still flowed by and over rocks, adding background music to their trip. Alpha offered her more jerky and she took it.

This stop was a bit longer than the first. Kim felt that if she wanted, she really could make a good run for it from here. Alpha and Beta weren't looking nearly as good as Kim felt. But, again, if she was able to run back to the trailhead, then what? How would she get back to civilization from there while avoiding these two, what with no food or water? Maybe she just needed to take a risk, go for it and hope for the best.

To keep herself busy, Kim decided to try and pick up Alpha's backpack. She could slide it across the ground and lift it onto its butt, but she could hardly budge it off the ground.

"Wow," she said, "you're carrying some serious packs here. I'm glad I'm not you two!" She said this with a bit of snark in her voice, trying to get a dig in at Alpha and Beta. They just gave her a sullen look. She was ruffling their feathers and loved it!

Eventually, Alpha said that it was time to get going. It seemed to Kim that the guys were slightly less willing to put on their packs again, but maybe she imagined it.

They continued up Bear Creek Valley with the soothing sounds of the stream; at least Kim found the creek's gurgling to be soothing. Reading their faces, she didn't think that the guys were feeling quite as soothed as her.

In front of them, three backpackers giddily marched down the trail. Alpha quietly told Kim to be calm and quiet. As the three young adults approached, Kim could see that they seemed to be all smiles. They were moving downhill on a beautiful morning at an incredible pace, arms swinging, presumably heading back to their truck waiting for them at the trailhead. The young bucks gave a hearty "Good morning!" to Kim's group and continued. Kim didn't say anything, but she guessed that she was the only one who smiled at the young men.

Their morning continued like this for a few hours. Every half hour or so, they'd stop, drop their packs, Alpha and Beta would groan and drip, slurp water and grab a snack. Kim would sit, look out over the forest and mountainside. She could hardly contain her smile, she knew, and it seemed like the guys were getting irritated. Kim didn't do anything to rub in her better attitude, knowing that she had the emotional high ground for now. She didn't want to overplay her hand just yet. Nor did she want to forget how she had gotten here. The landscape unfolded before them, and Kim enjoyed it as much as she could, given her circumstances. Pine trees, rocks of all shapes and sizes, the soft soil, pine cones, birds, bird calls, the murmur of Bear Creek, waterfalls and cataracts, beautiful green and turquoise pools of calm water. She had never experienced the calming effects of the wilderness quite like this, and she was as content as a kidnapping victim could be – relaxed but on edge, if that's possible.

Eventually, they stopped for lunch. Alpha and Beta pulled out fruit, some type of lunch meat, pita bread, cheese, nuts, and raisins. For as tired as they looked, they didn't devour their lunch like Kim thought they would.

After eating most of their lunch, Alpha said to Beta, "Let's not have both of us fall asleep here. One of us needs to stay awake." Hearing this, Kim realized that they were more tired than she had thought. Beta pointed at himself to indicate that he'd stay awake. A few minutes later, leaning against his pack for a cushion, Kim heard Alpha snoring. She didn't feel at all like napping and was content to sit back and relax with her eyes closed, listening to the sounds of the creek, wind in the trees, and the birds.

Her mind wandered, taking in the sights and sounds, thinking about what was ahead, thinking about another night in the tent, thinking about escaping.

Shit! she thought to herself. *If I had timed it right, I could have run back downhill and gotten to the trailhead just about when those backpackers got back there! They could have helped me to escape! Damn! Damn! Damn!* Sitting there, she shook her head and mentally kicked herself, frustrated with not thinking quickly enough.

Yeah, why haven't I been planning on how to escape from a bizarre kidnapping like this for the past several years? She smirked at herself, annoyed, but gave herself a break, knowing that you can't anticipate everything in life. Kim also knew that she had to be on the lookout for escape opportunities out here that would look different from being in the house or the van.

It was probably half an hour later, and Beta nudged Alpha to wake him and said, "We should get going." Alpha groaned as he moved, possibly as stiff as Kim had been when she had awoken this morning. He rolled over, looking a bit grumpy, trying to encourage his body to rise for more torture.

The afternoon was similar to the morning, only windier, warmer and brighter light. Kim sipped from her water bottle more frequently but otherwise was fine. Beta pulled out a water filter and pumped water from Bear Creek to fill the hydration packs and Kim's bottle during a mid-afternoon stop. The fresh cold water tasted terrific!

The sun was still reasonably high in the west, Kim thought, when Beta said they would stop and make camp. Bear Creek was nearby, smaller than it had been in the morning. They were in sort of a clearing; the sun was far enough in the west that the pine trees provided some decent shade. Alpha and Beta started the process of making camp – pulling out tents, sleeping bags, and sleeping pads, unfurling everything, blowing up the pads, and setting up the tents. Kim helped this time after watching the process yesterday. Once everything was ready, Beta said that it was his turn for a nap. Alpha tied Kim's ankles together, and she laid in her tent, relaxing to the sounds of nature and snoring.

An hour or so later, Kim awoke, realizing that she also had fallen asleep. If her goal was to escape, she wasn't doing a very good job. Alpha had gathered more water and had it ready to make supper. When Beta awoke, he started the stove and set water to boil. Unlike last night, though, supper was removed from large, tough-looking plastic containers. Kim was puzzled, having not seen anything like this before.

"OK, I have to ask, have to have you educate me, but what are those plastic jugs you're both carrying?"

A little perkier now, Beta grinned at Kim and said, "These are bear canisters. We carry our food in them so that the bears can't get at it. They're heavy suckers, but they serve a purpose. They also make decent camp stools up here. Tonight, we'll set them away from camp, just in case bears do smell us."

"Wait, there are bears up here?" Kim asked. "I hadn't thought about that before."

"Yep, we're in bear country. We're not very likely to see any, though," said Alpha. "You're much more likely to see a bear on the state flag than up here." That comment made Beta chuckle!

Soon, Beta had the water boiling, and he prepared dehydrated spaghetti to sumptuously serve at the Bear Creek Café, along with fruit and nuts. This night was special because they each got their own package of pasta and didn't have to share.

After starting her spaghetti, Kim asked, "Do you have some wine in those backpacks? Maybe a nice red?"

Alpha just grunted in response.

"So, I don't get it," continued Kim. "You two said you were in the Army and served in the mountains of Afghanistan. If that's the case, why does it seem that you had a difficult time today? We went how far today, like ten miles?"

Alpha sat up straighter, maybe a bit peeved with the implication of Kim's question. He relaxed a bit, stroked his chin, and let out a big sigh.

"Yes," he started, "we didn't perform as well as expected today. I've been thinking about it this afternoon and at supper. Here are my thoughts. Beta might have different or additional ideas.

"First, it's been ten years since we were in Afghanistan, in the mountains there. Second, we work out and train, but we haven't been preparing for situations like this. Today was not the type of situation that we typically consider in the gym. When we planned your kidnapping, a backpacking trip in the mountains wasn't on our minds. This backpacking trip came to mind when Omega told us to find a way to hide you away for several days. We should have put more thought into backpacking as an option before plowing ahead with it.

"Third, our packs are really heavy as you figured out for yourself. Ten years ago, we could carry ninety-pound packs all day. I didn't think about how I've gotten soft over the years and packed similarly to how we packed a decade ago. Never gave it a second thought. We're also carrying some special 'just in case' gear that adds some weight. And another reason is that we're carrying gear and food for you, too. We're not carrying ninety pounds, but we're well above seventy, and that's too much for us. Anything else, Beta?"

"Well, yeah, one more thing. The altitude. For all our training, we didn't train for climbing from sea level to seven, eight, nine thousand feet so quickly. That's a major change in altitude and might be one of the toughest factors. We're just not getting as much oxygen as our bodies need. And, for all our training, these big muscles are great for fighting, lifting, and intimidating, but they need more oxygen than if we were more normal-sized mortals. Big muscles make more heat, and it's tougher for us to cool off. Backpacking is a situation where we'd be better off with smaller muscles that use less oxygen."

"I'd thought about that earlier," Alpha responded, "but forgot to include it in my list. I must be lightheaded." That brought a smile to both of their faces.

"One last thing," Alpha started, "I think that we might have gone only six to eight miles today. I was way off in my belief that we could have gone further. We started later than I had hoped and took more breaks than I expected."

Kim asked, "Wait, that's all the farther you think we went? Wow! I knew that we were moving slowly, but not that slowly. So, do you think that it will get easier for you now?" She hoped so because she didn't want to carry any of the gear.

"Well, yes and no," thought Beta. "We'll acclimate to the altitude over time, but maybe not quickly enough. It would normally take a week or more to acclimate to these altitudes decently. We're not likely to get much stronger or have better endurance soon enough, either. The only little thing that I can think of is that we'll be losing some weight because of the food we eat."

"I have an idea," Alpha interjected, "for losing some weight, but I'll hold off on letting you know until tomorrow morning after I sleep on it."

That left Kim wondering and concerned. She hoped that Alpha's plan wasn't to lose her.

Kim decided to pitch in, collect the trash from supper, and put it into a garbage bag, which then went into one of the bear canisters. She was feeling magnanimous, took everyone's sporks, and washed them with leftover hot water.

She didn't want to feel that she was nice, but she needed to keep busy to keep her mind off this horrible situation and to build a façade of niceness for the guys. She didn't know how to play this game. Alpha and Beta had played this game before, it seemed, whether in Afghanistan or working for Omega. They had the advantage, but that didn't mean that they wouldn't slip up.

Kim was typically a pleasant enough person at heart, but she'd never been in a situation like this. She was scared of what her future held, what would happen once they reached the other side of the mountains. Shoot, maybe she wouldn't make it to the other side of the Sierras and they'd bury her in the wilderness where no one would find her. At the same time, Kim didn't want to be ruled by her fear and knew that the calmer she was, the more that she could put her fear aside, the better that she could think, reason and plan. Whenever she let go of her fear for a moment, like when she had enjoyed the vistas earlier today or collected trash and washed the sporks, she'd then snap back to reality and ask herself why she was so nice, why was she 'enjoying' herself, and where that was getting her. It was a perplexing conundrum, being sort of in control of her emotions some moments and then letting her emotions control her in other moments. *There must be a happy medium here*, Kim thought to herself, *a happy medium that includes planning an escape.*

Maybe she was just going to drive herself crazy, they'd have to carry her out of here, and she'd be a pliant, limp rag doll who'd do anything that they wanted. If that was the case, then Kim hoped that she would lose her mind sufficiently that she couldn't be a helpful computer scientist for Omega nor remember how she got into this mess. Unfortunately or not, though, she was feeling too much of her emotions at the moment to believe that she was going to somehow become unstable. Yes, she was feeling emotional, but not unstable. Kim didn't quite feel overwhelmed, but she also certainly didn't feel in control. She needed to be with this stress, acknowledge it, and hope that she'd be ready to act if – *when!* - an opportunity presented itself, like the one that she'd maybe missed earlier today.

Kim sat down near the tents and realized that it was getting dark. The sun was setting in the west, over the Central Valley and Bay Area – home. She felt a bit homesick for just a moment. Leaning back on a rock, she could look up to the dimming sky and make out Venus and a few stars. She also noticed that the clouds were thickening to the north, looking sort of ominous. The trees and mountains occluded her view, but Kim thought there were hints of lightning flashes giving the clouds some interesting highlights. She yawned and realized that she was more tired than she had felt she should be. Maybe Kim hadn't slept as well as she thought she did last night; perhaps she worked harder today than she knew. The emotional stress of her situation took a toll on her, too, even though she didn't want to admit it.

Whatever the reason, she crawled into her tent and dutifully left her shoes outside. She heard someone collect them a few minutes later, followed by a "Thank you, ma'am."

Kim hunkered into her sleeping bag and laid there, unsettled, scared, and annoyed, but also reliving the better parts of the day – the creek, wind, birds, beautiful views. She could feel herself starting to nod off, serenaded by snoring and some low rumbling – *maybe the wind?* she thought.

Chapter 19

Sound asleep, Kim dreamt of horses chasing her. She could hear the pounding of their hooves as she ran down the streets of San Francisco. A crack of thunder shook her out of her slumber.

It was pouring rain and sounded like she was on the inside of a drum. She felt around the sleeping bag and tent to see if anything was wet. There was hardly any water inside – just a few, stray droplets. She pulled the sleeping bag over her head and tightly curled into a fetal position, listening to Mother Nature do her best to keep her awake. When lightning flashed, it was sometimes so bright that she could see it through the tent wall and sleeping bag. Kim wasn't so cold that she needed to bury herself in her bag, but she just doing the seemingly common-sense thing to try to protect herself with what little she had to defend herself from the elements.

The pounding gave way to a gentler thrum, and she was able to relax some. She felt around the tent some more, and it seemed like there was some rain blowing under the edges of the tent, maybe splashing up, but nothing flowing into her cocoon. She was content, loosened, stretched the tightened ball that she had become, and then curled up again but more relaxed. So far, she had slept well. She made sure to close the sleeping pad valve before she had turned in, and it seemed to be holding. She figured that she had only slept a few hours and wasn't feeling any stiff or sore spots – yet.

Since she had never been camping before, she had never experienced a rainstorm like this. She had imagined in the past that it must be terrible to be in a tent during a storm, that she'd be cold and sopping wet. That was the furthest from the truth, she found. In fact, after the initial pounding, the sound of the rain falling on the tent fabric was quite soothing. Feeling better that she wouldn't die in this moment, she unwound and even started to enjoy it. Before long, she was into an even deeper, more relaxing sleep.

Now, she was again awake. Something had intruded on her sleep. She could hear the guys next door tossing and turning, grumbling, and then the zipper of their tent opening.

"Yeah, I'll check it out," came a voice.

"What's going on?" Kim asked.

"We've got water leaking in our tent, and everything's wet. I'm going to dig a trench around our tent and see if I can divert the water. I also want to check to see if the creek is rising, in case we're too close, but I think we're fine. Do you have any rain getting into your tent?" Kim thought that it was Alpha's voice, muffled by the tent and raindrops.

"No, I'm fairly dry in here," she responded.

She heard squishy boot steps clomping around, and the sound of maybe a heavy branch being used to scratch and plow the soil nearby. Flashes from the headlamp were flying all around the camp as Alpha dug. These antics went on for several minutes, and then the boots walked away.

"The creek is coming up, but we're fine. We're plenty far away, as I figured. Is there water still flowing into the tent?"

A voice that must have been Beta's said, "We're too wet for me to tell if the flow has stopped. Does it look like your trenches are working?"

"Yeah, it looks like they're doing the job. I'm coming back inside."

Kim could hear the *zeeep* of the zipper as Alpha opened the tent and struggled to get in.

"Ah, man, you're flipping water everywhere!" That must be Beta complaining, she thought.

"Sorry, dude, but it's not going to make a whole lot of difference."

Kim snuggled deeply into her bag, glad that she was warm and dry, enjoying the white noise of the rain on the tent. She could hear the guys struggling with their flooding, trying to get comfortable, moving gear out of wet spots, grunting, whining. She quietly smiled to herself; *karma's a bitch*, she thought.

The guys eventually settled down, but she didn't hear snoring coming from their tent. Soon, she didn't hear anything as she was soundly sleeping.

Later in the night, the guys woke her again. She could hear muttering, the tent's zipper, and more scratching. She rolled over and tried to ignore them, tried not to enjoy her comparative comfort too much without giggling. If it was raining at all now, it was light. Before long, she zonked out.

Kim laid in her bag, in the tent, and blinked her eyes. Buried in her cocoon, the inside of the tent was becoming lighter. The rain had stopped. Lifting her head out of the bag, she could hear Bear Creek; it sounded almost angry now, crashing down the mountainside. There were a few bird songs, but it seemed that the world was more subdued this morning than yesterday morning. Her hips and shoulders weren't as stiff and sore, but she could certainly feel her shoulders, legs, and feet today after yesterday's hiking and climbing, and not in a good way. She needed to stretch some this morning, that was certain. Under the creek's rough splashing sounds, she could hear one and then a second wave of rhythmic snoring, almost in unison.

She was thinking about how easy it might be to escape right now. The guys were likely so tired, so dead to the world that they wouldn't hear her leave the tent. However, there was the issue of not having shoes and her ankles being tied together with the zip ties, bringing Kim back to reality. It would be tough to quietly find her shoes and then just start stumbling downhill to wherever.

Laying there for longer and longer, maybe dozing a bit and enjoying the rhythm of the creek, Kim tried her best to keep her bladder in check. She knew that she'd have to give in at some point but hoped that the guys would awaken before worse came to worse. Finally, she couldn't take it anymore. And, frankly, Kim didn't really care if she woke her tormentors. She pulled herself out of her bag, scooched to the front of the tent, unzipped the door, and flung it back. The outside world was gray; fog and mist hung in the air, everything damp. Drips fell from pine needles. There was no noticeable wind. She was able to peek out and see the other tent. It sat there motionless but not silent.

"Guys? *Guys?* I need my shoes so that I can pee. Or you could just throw them to me, go back to sleep, and I'll take care of myself and then be on my merry way."

She could hear the *sooshing* of fabric rubbing against fabric, grumbling, coughing, and general discontent.

"You get 'em for her. I got out last night and dug the trench. It's your turn to be useful." Ah, that must be Alpha's cheery voice, she thought.

After a bit of struggling, grunting, and more *sooshing*, the other tent started to open. Beta stuck his sorry-looking head out. He practically scowled at Kim when he turned her way. He tried to throw her shoes to her, but they landed in some mud in front of her tent. Now she was the one who scowled.

"Hey, I need some toilet paper, too. A woman's gotta do what a woman's gotta do."

There was grumbling, the sound of someone digging through a backpack, likely a soggy one, and the tent opened again. A plastic bag of toilet paper flew her way, landing in the vestibule of her tent.

Kim gave a cheerful "Thank you!" and heard grunting in response.

After getting her shoes on, Kim picked her way around camp, taking shortened steps in her plastic shackles, seeing how the world had changed overnight. There were small puddles here and there, along with flow lines where water had drained. She could see the little trench uphill of the guys' tent and how water had likely found a way into their tent. Kim had unknowingly set her tent on a slight mound, but enough that it had remained relatively dry. A sly, satisfied smile spread across her face; there also was hint of indifferent reckoning in her smile.

After doing what a woman had to do, she returned to the camp. There was no dry place to sit, so she just stood there, taking in the dark, dank morning. *Quite a change from last night*, she thought, *almost eery.* She heard snoring coming from the guys' tent but figured it was just Alpha. Kim had no idea what time it was. The sun wasn't peeking through the clouds. A gray, non-directional light surrounded her. She hobbled over and checked Bear Creek. It was flowing torridly, had risen substantially and was not clear like yesterday.

Standing there Kim realized how much the ties hurt her ankles. She had likely strained against them during the night and tottering around camp was just digging into her skin more. She sat on a cold, damp rock to relieve some of the pressure on sores. She looked at the marks on her legs – red, slightly indented, but not seriously injured. Her socks saved her from the brunt of the possible damage. Trying to escape with shackles like these would be difficult, slow, and painful. She'd have to find a way to cut the zip ties off, likely without a knife.

Tired of waiting, tired of being but not playing the victim, Kim spoke to the silent tent. "So, what's the plan today, guys? Are you going to make breakfast? I'm hungry."

Silence.

"Guys? Did you hear me? I'm hungry, cold, my ankles hurt from these zip ties, and I'm pissed off because I'm not at home, where I want to be."

A moment later, there was audible grunting, *sooshing* of fabric, and finally, a groan.

"I've been dead to the world, Dr. Johnson. I'm not doing too well this morning. Beta and I need to check in with each other and figure out what's going on. We'll be out in a few minutes. We've been watching you through the tent flap and listening to you walk around."

Kim's butt was cold and damp from sitting on the rock. Her pants would eventually dry, and it wasn't that cool out here that she was going to get too cold, but she wasn't comfortable. Kim heard Alpha and Beta murmuring in their tent but couldn't make out what they were saying. She also could make out their lumpy figures through their tent flap. She sat there, took in the morning, and enjoyed the sounds of the rushing creek, despite all the difficulties she faced.

After several more minutes, the guys' tent fluttered a bit. There was movement inside, and then the netting unzipped and flew back. Sock-covered feet stuck out, hands searching for boots in the vestibule, and then the boots were tied to the feet. Beta crawled out and pulled his backpack out. Kim could see wet spots on it, and it was dripping from the bottom when he lifted it. *Wow, they really must have gotten soaked in there.*

Beta sort of looked like death warmed over. Kim could tell he was hurting. He lurched around camp, trying to loosen tight muscles. He bent over and couldn't come close to touching his toes. His eyes were red, and there were bags under his eyes. Kim thought to herself, *yeah, I think that I could outrun him right now if I weren't sorta lame.*

After watching the Beta cripple show for a few minutes, Kim spotted Alpha starting to exit the tent. She didn't think it possible, but Alpha looked even worse. As he stood up straight, he squatted down, elbows on knees, holding his head. Alpha stumbled over to the rock on which Kim was sitting and clumsily sat beside her. This was the closest either of them had allowed themselves to get to Kim and she was surprised. For all the competence these two had shown when they had first captured her, their current state was quite a shock.

"Guys, you're a couple of really sorry-looking criminals right now. What odds would you give me if I tried to escape?"

Alpha didn't move and just sat there with his head in his hands. Beta looked at her, and the best that he could offer was a grimace.

"OK then, well, I'm leaving." Kim made a half-hearted attempt to get up, and Alpha reached out and grabbed her wrist. He held her tightly but didn't hurt her. He wasn't worried about her going too far with her ankles bound.

"Look," Alpha said weakly without looking up, "last night was not one of the best nights of my life. Aside from the lightning and thunder, the storm kept us awake, sort of a flashback to firefights in Afghanistan. Almost everything in our tent is wet, which made for difficult and uncomfortable sleeping. I'm stiff and sore from carrying too heavy of a pack. When I could sleep, I was waking up, gasping for air. Lastly, I have a raging headache. I feel like a bus hit me."

Beta looked at Kim and said, "I'm in about the same boat, except my headache is tolerable. I'm going to pull out the stove and boil water for breakfast."

Kim's forehead wrinkled a bit and she asked, inquiringly, "So, you two have a bit of PTSD from your time in Afghanistan?"

Alpha looked at Beta and Beta at Alpha. Slowly, Alpha shook his head, yes. It was quite the sight to watch these two, Kim found. They were slow, stumbling, disabled, and generally pitiful. She thought about offering to help them make breakfast, but she decided to sit since she was the kidnappee. It took nearly an hour for them to get the water boiling and breakfast out. The fog started to lift, and the sun was trying to poke through gray clouds, but just barely. Kim was bored, particularly after being so active yesterday. She had expected to be moving again today, to do something to keep herself busy.

Finally, there was coffee and oatmeal to share. Kim took hers and staggered to the creek for more exciting entertainment. She sat there, entranced by the flowing water, enjoying the scenery, but not the situation. After finishing her oatmeal, she filled her cup with stream water, wiped out the oatmeal remnants, wiped down her spork, and threw her wash water up the bank. Bear Creek was clearing a bit, but still quite turbid.

Back near the guys, she asked, "So, what's the plan for today? You guys are slow getting out of the tent this morning and not looking too good."

Alpha slowly, carefully nodded. "Beta, you tell her. My head hurts too much."

Beta tried to straighten himself to appear more authoritative than he was feeling, but he wasn't convincing. "We're probably going to spend the day here, Dr. Johnson. As you said, we're in too poor of shape to try to push on. If the sun comes out, then we'll dry our gear as best we can. Hopefully, we'll feel better tomorrow morning. If not, then we might have to head back the way we came. Our trip is not working out as we had planned."

Kim looked at them for a moment, first taking in Beta, then looking at the woeful, slumping Alpha on the rock and then shaking her head. She was surprised at what a difference had come over these two in the last day or so. They had seemed so gung-ho the night that they all camped near the trailhead, and now they were almost laughable. Kim felt the slightest bit of empathy for them just as she would for anyone else who was hurting, but she wasn't going to do anything to help them feel better.

"Look, I don't know what all is going on with you two. I can understand your muscle aches and pains because I'm feeling it, too, and I hope for your sakes that you have some ibuprofen or something like that."

"We've already taken ibuprofen. I felt it starting to kick in, but it's not helping a whole lot," Alpha offered.

"So, what should I do for now?" Kim asked.

"For now," Beta said, "we're going to have you get back into your tent and give me your shoes. Alpha is going to try to sleep some while I stand watch out here and try to loosen my sore muscles and help our gear to dry."

Kim just rolled her eyes. Now she was being confined in an even smaller cell than before. She did as they told her, wobbled to her tent, plopped her butt down just inside, and took off her shoes. She didn't make an effort to hand them to Beta. He can bend over and get them himself, maybe suffer a bit, for all she cared.

In her tent, flap open, she saw Beta lumber over and haltingly bend over for her shoes. It took him several groans and half attempts, but he finally snagged her shoes and slowly stood up. After stretching his back a bit, Beta moved away from Kim's line of sight, but she could hear that he was sitting on her rock. Alpha lumbered to their tent and slowly worked his way in, accompanied by his own grunts and groans.

Kim laid back, hands folded behind her head, and tried to entertain herself. She could hear Bear Creek, an occasional bird, and rising wind in the trees. Kim draped her sleeping bag over her for a bit of warmth. Even though she had slept much better than the guys, her last night's sleep had been interrupted several times, and it wasn't long before Kim was lightly sleeping.

It was probably late morning, and the tent was warming. Kim awoke, surprised that she had fallen asleep and that she had slept so long. She crawled to the front of her tent and caught Beta's attention. For whatever reason, Kim was sort of trying to be respectful and let Alpha sleep if he needed – old habits die hard. She pointed to her feet, asking for her shoes without words. Beta understood and but shook his head no. Kim gave him a very annoyed look of *what the hell?* Oh well, Kim thought. After she was out of the tent, barefoot, picking her way over rocks, sticks, and pine cones, she looked around camp to find it surrounded by drying gear. It looked like an ugly yard sale or the aftermath of a tornado. There were clothes and a sleeping bag on trees, branches, rocks, and whatever else might support a wet garment. Kim chuckled a bit and rolled her eyes at Beta. Beta smiled and shrugged his shoulders.

She went to him and whispered, "*Lunch?*" Beta headed to the edge of the clearing and picked up the bear canisters. He opened them and rummaged around, finding jerky, dried fruit, nuts, and some chocolate bars. They'd been pretty much silent through all of this, and Kim motioned for him to sit by her over by the creek.

They started nibbling on this and that, not saying a word. Finally, Kim said to Beta, "Why?"

"Why what? Why did we take you hostage?"

"No, I've already heard Omega's perverted rationale for kidnapping me, and I don't understand it. What I want to know is, why are you two involved in this?"

"That's a good question," started Beta. "I guess that when you spend years in the military like we did, you're good at it, and that's all that you know, then you want to continue. There's a rush that goes with combat situations but surrounding those bursts of action are long periods of boredom, training, preparation, and more boredom. In our case, when we decided to leave the service, it was hard for us to fit into civilian society. We tried college for a couple of years and then found nine-to-five jobs, but it just didn't feel the same, wasn't as exciting, wasn't fulfilling. We found special 'consulting opportunities' for people with our training and experience through friends of friends. Our first job was fairly simple, straight forward, nothing illegal or anything, but the people who hired us liked our work ethic and style. We got references from that, and then more work. For the most part, we've hired out as sort of mercenaries, heavy security, and worked outside of the country some. We have hardly ever fired weapons and haven't killed anyone.

"We get plenty of time to be with our families. Yes, I know it might surprise you, but we are normal in every other way. I have a great wife and two daughters in LA; Alpha's married to a wonderful woman and has a son and daughter in Michigan. In a way, we're a lot like you. We're selling our services and talents to the highest bidder. It's just that our work might sometimes not fit within society's goals and laws. Does that help? Does that make sense?"

"Yes, it helps. I don't know if it makes sense to me yet, or if it ever will, but I sort of understand. I look at people with whom I grew up or went to college, and they have all different kinds of lives and careers. Some of the ways that people I know make money seem shaky or illegal. Other friends, I look at them and think how could they do what they do and feel good about themselves? But I also suspect that some of my friends would look at me and my work and have ethical qualms, if they knew what I did and whom I work for, even though I don't. Ethics are one thing, but my job is legal while yours isn't, so that's what puzzles me. I don't think of myself as some paragon of righteousness. I enjoy what I do, I'm good at it, it pays well, it's exhilarating, and it gives me the time and freedom to travel and do other things that I en-

joy. So, yeah, maybe I'm not so different from you, but I feel that I am. At least, until the other day, I haven't been looking over my shoulder, wondering if someone was after me. I also want to say that I appreciate how you two have treated me – respectfully, decently, even if it is a kidnapping."

"Well, ma'am, thank you for the compliment – I guess. That's why we get the roles that we do, ones that are less dirty than you might expect. Maybe if we took more risks or were more forceful, lethal in our ways, we might make more money, but it's not who we are. In this situation, Omega has been very specific that he wants you treated well. It's our job to secure and isolate you and keep you safe. We thought that we could quietly keep you in the house for a longer period, but someone was snooping around and we felt that we had to get out of there fast. So now, we're trying to shepherd you, against your will, over these mountains. I sincerely do not know what you do, what it is that has you mixed up in Omega's world, nor do I know what he does or what his plans are for you. We've never met him but have worked with him and his group on a couple of previous contracts. I just know that he's satisfied with how we're treating you, but not with how this situation is unfolding. I believe that he hoped it was somehow going to be easier with you."

While they sat by Bear Creek, Alpha trudged up behind them, looking a bit better and finding his own rock. He scooped up some stream water, washed his face, and slicked back his hair. He seemed to be moving better now, too. He had found the bear canisters and brought some food down to the stream, also.

"So, have you two figured out our next steps?" Alpha asked. "I've greatly enjoyed my beauty sleep. I'm stunned how difficult these past twelve hours or so have been for me."

"Dr. Johnson and I were waxing philosophically, discussing the meaning of life, that's all," Beta said with a smile.

"To be clear, I was asking how you two got into this line of work. From there, it fell into a sort of philosophical discussion," Kim said.

"Ah. But, have you figured out the more immediate issues of the next few days?" inquired Alpha.

"No, I was waiting to check in with you," said Beta. "I'm trying to keep Dr. Johnson in the dark, keep her off guard."

"Actually," Kim responded, "I was thinking of just grabbing my pack and heading down the hill and let you two continue, so you don't need to worry about me. Just cut these shackles off, give me my shoes, and we'll call it square."

Beta just grinned. "You know, for a hostage, you sure are funny. You have a weird sense of humor. I know that on the inside, you must be more fearful than what you're showing, but you hide it pretty well."

Kim grinned at the compliment but didn't reveal anything else. "Well, I figure that I've sort of had a few opportunities to try to escape, like this morning, but I also feel that I'd make things worse for me. I'm way out of my element here, and I can't very easily travel with my ankles bound like this, can I? Even if I could walk away, then what? In my way of thinking, I'm better off going along to get along unless you start seriously threatening me. Maybe you'll make a mistake with me after we get on the other side of the mountains. We'll see." She gave them a sly grin, hoping that her words were as misleading as intended.

"How's the gear drying, Beta? I checked on a couple of things, and they seemed to be drying well. My sleeping bag is still wet, but it's no longer dripping. I'm going to hang it up on a tree limb before I eat something."

"I think that as the sun comes out this afternoon, stuff will mostly dry, especially if the wind comes up some more," Beta replied. "And how's your headache?"

"I'm feeling better, but it's still a low-grade pain. I was gasping for breath a few times while I was trying to sleep," Alpha replied.

"It's good to hear you're improving. Do you think that you'll be good to go tomorrow morning?" Beta asked.

Alpha shrugged his shoulders and then shook his head affirmatively, but he wasn't entirely convincing. Next, he checked clothes and gear and laid his sleeping bag out to dry and motioned for Beta to take a rest while he ate lunch. Kim stayed at the creek, pondered life, and threw stones in the river. Every time that she looked back to camp, Alpha had her in view.

Kim knew that she had most of the afternoon yet to do nothing, so she decided to grab the few dirty clothes that she had and rinse them out in the creek. This chore took her longer than she expected, partly because of her shortened steps but also because she drew it out as much as she could since there was nothing else to do. She hung her clothes out to dry and retired to her tent to rest.

A couple of hours later, Kim was surprised to find herself waking. She couldn't remember the last time that she had taken two naps in a day! Mountain life was possibly agreeing with her. After crawling out of her tent, barefoot still, she saw Alpha sitting nearby with a small sat phone beside him. Ah, she thought, that makes sense as a way to stay in contact with Omega and others.

"So, any news from the outside world?" she asked.

"Nothing special. Omega is content with our progress. No hurry. He still doesn't have a clear plan on how to proceed with you. He's considering the possibility of somehow moving you closer to him and his group, but that would take some effort and logistics."

Kim took this news without outward reaction, but inside she was still confused and more scared, hoping for a chance to escape but not finding one. And, the thought of being even more deeply hidden away from her normal world, to wherever Omega worked, was not at all pleasing.

The sun was out in full force, and it was a warm and pleasant afternoon. She checked her clothes and found that most of them were dry enough to pack away. Beta emerged from the guys' tent and saw what Kim was doing, and he did the same with his dry gear. All three of them lounged around, not showing much energy or initiative, enjoying the sun and views. At least, Kim enjoyed the sun and views as best she could, given the bizarre circumstances.

The guys got around to making supper a little earlier than might be expected, and no one complained. On the menu tonight was dehydrated rice and sausage, cheese and crackers, dried fruit, nuts, and all the water you could drink. After they finished supper, Alpha and Beta checked their remaining drying clothes and gear and were satisfied. It was starting to cool, so Kim asked for her shoes, and Alpha gave them to her. It felt good to have them back on, to have her feet and legs warming. The soles of her feet hadn't been exposed to so much rock and sand in a long time and couldn't figure if it felt good or if she might have overdone it today by being barefoot so much.

Despite everyone sleeping so much during the day, they all headed for their sleeping bags before the sun was down. Kim set her shoes outside of her tent, and a little while later, a big hand took them to the guys' tent for the night. She laid there, enjoying the soothing sounds of Bear Creek, the last few birds of the night, and a coyote's howl. She had never heard a coyote before, so there was a new experience, a new thrill, and one that spread a slight smile on her face as she fell asleep.

**Chapter 20**

The next morning arrived cool, and Kim was awake before the guys. She had heard some noise from their tent during the night but didn't pay any attention.

"Alpha, Beta, are you awake? I need my shoes."

There was some muffled grumbling, the *sooshing* of fabric, a zipper, and then her shoes plopped near the front of her tent. Beta looked at her with a look of death warmed over. He just sat in the vestibule of his tent and motioned for her go to do whatever it was she needed to do, although he was having similar thoughts but couldn't work up the energy. He sat there and watched to make certain that she didn't stray too far.

After shuffling away with her ankles still bound by zip ties and doing what she needed to do, she stood around, hands jammed into her pockets to keep warm. The sun was still behind the mountains to the east, but the sky was pinking up. *It's a gorgeous morning!*, she thought. She could even see stars shining and the faintest sliver of the moon. She enjoyed the morning quiet, interspersed with the occasional early bird songs.

She was colder than she thought and tried to jump in place without falling, but the shackles were cutting into her ankles. Finally, she couldn't wait any longer.

"Guys, are you getting up soon? Can I make some coffee or something warm?

More grumbling, more *shooshing*, and a few moments later, a spork and cup flew her way.

"You know where to find the bear canisters. Help yourself. We're still hurting some, so please keep it quiet if you can." Kim didn't know which muffled voice it was that had said that.

"Well, maybe I'll just start heading back down the hill," she said.

"*PLEASE* don't do that. You've been such a great hostage – so far."

"You two are pitiful. If you just give me the stove, I could toast you to a crisp and put you out of your misery," Kim chided. She shuffled off, filtered water and recovered the bear canisters. A few minutes later, Beta was out of the tent, slightly better than the morning before. He had the stove and fuel with him and started warming the water that Kim brought back to camp. Within twenty minutes, Kim was drinking coffee and eating oatmeal, along with some dried fruit. Beta made a cup of coffee for Alpha and set it near the tent flap.

"Alpha is still hurting a lot this morning. He has a bad headache again and had difficulty breathing last night. I'm hurting, too, but not nearly as badly." Beta poured himself some hot water and made coffee, and then got to his oatmeal. The sun was now over the Sierra Crest, and the morning was warming nicely.

After finishing his cereal, Beta took Alpha his breakfast. Alpha crawled to the front of the tent, stuck his feet out, and ate and drank in the doorway. He looked worse than Beta, with bloodshot eyes, and he seemed about ten years older than yesterday. After eating most of his breakfast, he was looking better but not by a whole lot.

"So, guys, what's the plan?" Kim asked.

"Well, after I figure out if I'm still alive, we'll break camp and head on up the trail. But I'm not in any hurry," said Alpha weakly.

Kim asked him, "Have you had any ibuprofen lately?"

"Yep, just before I ate breakfast, that's why I need some time to get my motor running," Alpha replied.

Kim relaxed, knowing that there was no hurry this morning, so she sat by Bear Creek and enjoyed its rhythm. The water was much clearer this morning, similar to how wonderful it looked before yesterday's storm. Downstream, Kim saw a fawn peek out from across the creek, through some shrubs, and take a drink while keeping an eye on her. She had never seen anything like this and quietly sat there in awe. The sun was on her back, and she was feeling warm enough to unzip her light jacket.

After another thirty minutes or so, Alpha was out of his tent, stretching and blinking at the bright sunlight. He stood in the sun for a few moments, eyes closed, allowing the warmth to penetrate and heal him. Slowly, he walked over to Beta and sat on the rock with him. Kim could see them huddled in conversation, but the creek was too loud for her to make out their discussion.

Kim sat and thought more about escaping and how she might do it. She still had no good ideas. Opportunities were presenting themselves, sort of, but she didn't know what she would do once she took off, especially since she couldn't move too fast. If she took off, she'd have to stop somewhere and figure out a way to cut off the hard plastic zip ties – without a knife. Maybe she could find a sharp rock to rub against them to cut them so that her feet would be free. If Kim made it back down to the trailhead, then what? What was the likelihood that someone would be there to help her? Not much, given that they had only seen a handful of people the past couple of days. So, if no one is there to help me, then how do I help myself? And what were the guys carrying in their packs that made them so heavy? They likely had a weapon if they felt the need to force their views on her or someone else. Kim also wondered whether the guys were carrying electronic devices that might help them find her if she took off. Many unknowns, a few opportunities to leave that she might have missed, and her survival was on the line.

Kim realized that she needed to be more proactive in her efforts. Some thoughts came to her yesterday while lying in the tent, but nothing clear was forming in her mind. *If I'm going to survive on my own, I need food, water, and shelter.* From what she could tell, water likely wouldn't be an issue. Even if she didn't have a filter, she'd gladly drink the relatively clean water from a stream like Bear Creek. Kim also knew she couldn't just up and take a tent and sleeping bag with her. She had no place to carry them in her small pack. But she could pilfer some food from the bear canisters and put it into her knapsack. It wouldn't be a lot, but she could likely survive a few days longer than if she didn't have any food.

With these thoughts, she left the creek and went back to her tent. The opened bear canisters were nearby, but they'd notice if she took more than a few snacks out of them. She took her sleeping bag and pad from the tent and set them on the rock next to the canisters with her knapsack at her feet, slowly packing her sleeping gear. While the guys weren't looking, she grabbed a few items and tossed them into her pack. She continued to steal and stuff until she felt that she had enough food in her bag to get by, but not so much that it would be noticeable. She was feeling pleased with herself, retaking the initiative.

The guys saw that Kim was packing, and they begrudgingly started to pack too, going through the same motions as Kim. They loaded all three sleeping bags, pads, and both tents in their packs as before. But, to Kim's surprise, they started to pull out some of their clothes and gear and sorted them into a couple of different piles each. Finally, they packed one pile of clothes and left the other pile to sit. They next took the bear canisters, rummaged around to find trash bags, and then filled the trash bags with the food from the bear canisters.

"OK," Kim said, "I don't understand what you're doing. I'm confused."

Beta looked at her with sort of a grin but also a look of defeat. "We decided that our packs are too heavy, so we're dropping some of our clothes and the bear canisters. We figure that we each could easily lose ten pounds that we're carrying this way. We're hoping that it makes the hiking easier for us because we're still not feeling great."

Kim nodded her understanding, then shook her head. "So, you're confirming that you're a couple of wimps after all?" There was a sly grin on her face.

She didn't wait for an answer and finished the little packing she had to do. Kim's clothes were snug in her bag now, sitting on top of the food she'd stolen, but it wasn't apparent that she was carrying more in it. She was pleased with herself and waited for the guys to finish their packing.

By midmorning, the guys had sorted themselves out. They lodged the clothes and bear canisters behind some boulders, so they wouldn't be quite so evident if someone came along right behind them. Even so, when they hoisted their packs onto their shoulders, they both groaned and wobbled around. The last thing that Beta did was to cut the zip ties from Kim's legs.

"Sure doesn't feel much lighter," Alpha growled. "It's still going to be a long day. Let's head out. I'll go first, Beta bring up the rear." He was off, very slowly. Before he went too far, he stopped and turned around to talk with Kim.

"In twenty or thirty minutes, we're joining a major trail. We expect that we'll see more people, so we'd appreciate it if you stayed quiet.

Understand?"

Kim nodded her head *yes* feeling a bit discouraged that they'd be watching her again. She grabbed her pack, quickly threw it on her back, and followed Alpha. She could hear Beta behind her, struggling those first few steps, searching for his stride.

As she started heading up the Bear Creek Trail, Kim thought about being quiet, not asking for help, the pros and cons. So far, the guys hadn't threatened her. They were bigger than her and could outrun her in a sprint. Over a distance, she felt that she could outrun them, but it would be tough to get a good lead on them when they were so close. They likely had knives and other weapons within easy reach. If they ran into a few backpackers, then there's a reasonable chance that Alpha and Beta could take them on and make their lives difficult and worse. *Was her life more important than someone else's life? Worth more than two or three other lives??? A large group of people would possibly work in her favor, except how large is 'large'? Six? Eight? No one else out here was likely carrying weapons nor knew how to use them as well as Alpha and Beta.* Kim just sighed to herself, still not knowing what to do. Maybe someone in a larger group could escape and get help, but what would happen to her and anyone else in the meantime?? *There are still no easy answers*, she glumly thought to herself.

The trail was similar to what they had experienced a couple of days ago – Bear Creek on the right, a gentle uphill grade, and a mix of trees and smooth, open granite faces. Kim felt good to be moving again, and she was delighted with how she was feeling and the sights she was seeing. It felt good to have the shackles off and stretch her legs. She felt a slight bit of empathy watching Alpha lumber in front of her and could hear Beta puffing behind. As usual, they stopped every half hour or so. At the first stop, the guys' shirts were damp, and by the third stop, they had soaked their shirts with sweat.

They were soon at the trail junction. Kim saw a brown wooden sign with arrows pointing in both directions: John Muir Trail/Pacific Crest Trail. As Alpha had told her, they took a right turn after finishing the Bear Creek Trail. The new trail mostly leveled out here, and all three of them were hiking a little better and ever so slightly faster. A short time later, they passed the first people that they had seen in a couple of days, a young, fit-looking couple who were sitting by the side of the trail for a break with water and snacks. Alpha and Beta gave a curt "Hi" to the couple, and Kim just nodded. The couple looked tired, disheveled and a bit beat but had such bright smiles on their faces. Kim was impressed and intrigued. *Wow, people enjoy this stuff, huh?* she thought to herself. She wished that she was enjoying it more.

Maybe ten minutes later, they were passed by four young studs. It seemed like they were moving twice as fast as Kim, Alpha, and Beta. Their packs looked to be less than half of the size of the guys' loads. Kim thought that her captors had made more mistakes on this outing than she could imagine, even with her being so ignorant of backpacking norms. The young guys were talking, laughing, and didn't have a care in the world, while Alpha and Beta seemed to be struggling under the weight of their packs, their lack of conditioning, and whatever else Kim couldn't know. Kim felt more at ease out here and was starting to nurture the slightest bit of desire to come back someday – without her current escorts. The thought of signaling these guys crossed her mind, but they were now gone, and she saw no opening that didn't get someone else hurt.

After an hour or so of this trail and seeing a few more people, but no group greater than the four young guys they had earlier seen, Alpha checked his maps. Speaking to Beta, he said, "Our turnoff should be up here on the left in another five or ten minutes. We can stop for lunch sometime after that turn."

Sure enough, there was a trail that headed off to the left, and they took it. The three were climbing again, the grade more noticeable. The past hour or so had been relatively flat without significant climbs or descents. Maybe thirty minutes later, they came to a beautiful open meadow, and Kim was entranced. The sun beat down on them now, but the views opened, and there were fewer and fewer trees. They stopped, dropped their packs, found some cool, pleasant shade next to the trail and meadow, and sat for lunch. When they had eaten their fill, Kim told the guys that she would wander across the field to the stream and wash up. They didn't stop her and watched Kim walk away. Beta followed her while Alpha sat in the shade. Beta made sure to make noise so that Kim would realize she wasn't alone.

This stream was different from Bear Creek, along which they had camped for a couple of nights. While Bear Creek had been loud and kinetic, this stream, near the meadow, was slow, quiet, even bucolic. Kim saw fish – *trout?* – lazing in the current and watched them dart when she startled them. She found a sandy bank, took off her shoes and soaked her feet. It had been a long time since Kim had pushed herself – or been pushed – so far out of her comfort zone she realized, and she was surprised by how well she was getting on. It was so quiet and peaceful here, and the views were stunning. The mountains were rising around her now like she hadn't yet experienced. There was a gentle breeze through the trees that sighed as it passed. Kim would have enjoyed this dream much more if it wasn't a nightmare.

After reveling in her perceived solitude for longer than she expected, Kim heard a whistle and turned to see Alpha waving at her to come back and Beta sitting in the shade on the edge of the meadow. After pulling on her shoes, she walked back by Beta, and he followed her back to the trail. Alpha had taken off, slowly trudging up the trail in a haggard manner.

After donning their packs, Beta and Kim soon caught up with Alpha. Kim slowed to talk with Alpha, while Beta meandered upward, but kept them within earshot.

"How are you feeling?" she asked. She didn't want to be nice, but it was against her nature to be uncaring.

"My headache is as bad as ever, and I'm short of breath. I think, I hope," he gasped, "that I'll be fine as long as I walk slowly," Alpha said. "Besides, it's not like I could go fast if I wanted." Kim gave him a little smile and kept on walking. She could hear Alpha struggling behind her, gasping more and stopping to catch his breath. *Yea, I could probably easily ditch him right now,* she thought.

The more Kim walked, the more comfortable she became. Again, it felt wonderful to be moving, to be in the fresh air, to work up a sweat, and, most of all, to take in the gorgeous views. While Kim had been in the mountains before, she had been driving or hiking. This time was much more intimate, she thought, without expecting to head back to civilization in a few hours. But Kim knew it would be nicer to go home and be rid of the problems that had rained down on her these past several days. The more she walked, the more the wilderness opened before her and the more that she opened to the wilderness. She made her way above treeline, with the creek in which she had soaked her feet just to her right. *This view is breathtaking*, she thought! *I have to come back someday to enjoy this with less stress and a fresh eye.*

As she climbed, Kim realized that the altitude was causing her some issues, too. She was slowing and breathing harder but maintaining a steady, moderate pace. She figured that if she were to start running now, it wouldn't be too long until she'd have to stop to catch her breath. She doubted whether she could outrun Beta and didn't have the energy to find out.

Just ahead, she could see Beta waiting for her. Alpha was struggling a good five minutes behind, wanting to keep up but not able. When Kim got to Beta, he told her that they'd wait for Alpha in part because he wanted to make sure that he didn't get lost. The trail was fainter here, but it was still a trail, so there wasn't much chance of Alpha going astray. Kim figured that Beta was watching after his friend, making sure that he would make it. It had been an hour or two since lunch and they were all feeling a bit tired. Even though it had been a short day of hiking and not as difficult as the first day, Alpha and Beta weren't moving too fast in part because of the higher altitude and generally feeling poorly.

When Alpha arrived, he took a break. Beta told Alpha, "From the map, it looks like there's a decent place for us to camp not too much farther up. I'm hoping it's a mile or so, but less than another hour. I don't see any good reason for us to keep pushing ourselves at this altitude. It might be a little early to stop when we get there, but tomorrow we'll have to hike about as far as we did today to meet the driver. Better yet, tomorrow will be mostly downhill!"

Alpha grinned at the news and waved for Beta and Kim to keep going without him. "That sounds good to me. You go on ahead and start making camp or relax. I'll be along in a bit. Don't worry about me," he said. Alpha was quite red in the face, dripping with sweat and breathing was a chore for him.

Thirty minutes or so later, Kim and Beta stood near the mouth of a beautiful mountain lake. Kim felt enthralled with how starkly beautiful it was here! For the most part, all she could see were the lake, rock, and mountains. There were hardly any trees and mostly just low shrubs and bushes for vegetation. Everything around her looked so simple and yet so complex. The more she looked, the more details she took in. She wanted to sing *The hills are alive, with the sound of music,* but couldn't bring herself to express that much pleasure in front of one of her captors. There were so many conflicts between all that she was feeling right now – surrounded by stunning beauty while a crime victim. Rather than sing, she smiled and sighed.

On their way towards the lake, Beta noticed some decent camping spots along the stream. After they walked back downhill a bit, Beta chose an open area for their camp, on a site of sand, gravel, and hummocks of vegetation, with the stream burbling nearby. He shrugged off his backpack and groaned. Alpha would have to be blind not to see them here.

Beta carried Kim's tent and gear; he removed it from his pack and handed it to her before he flopped down. He made no effort to help her set up her tent, and that was fine with her. She was getting the hang of this camping stuff, and if she was going to get out of this situation, she needed to be as independent and competent as possible. She laid out the ground cloth and tent and set it up to face the east – into the sunrise and away from the afternoon sun. She had learned from listening to the guys that it was good to lay her sleeping bag to air out over the tent; maybe she could get bake out some of the mustiness in the intense afternoon sun. The breeze through this saddle felt great on her warm skin. The wind had a long run over the lake – this big, beautiful, turquoise lake. Again, she thought, this view is so raw and yet so spectacular, so mesmerizing. She shook her head, pulling herself back into the distressing reality of her situation.

After her tent was up and sleeping bag freshening, Beta called her over. "I know that you don't like it, but it's time to hobble you." Kim just made a disgruntled sigh when she saw the zip ties in his hand. A moment later, she was clearly captive. Kim trundled to the stream, making sure that Beta saw her and kept her in view. She sat there and absorbed as much of the scenery as possible. It was a beautiful sunny afternoon and a nice breeze. The sun was hot on her skin and shirt. She slid off her shoes and carefully waded in the cool, clear stream. The cold caused her to inhale slightly, but she quickly grew used to it and appreciated the contrasts. Upstream, she could make out the trail on this side of the creek that they'd take tomorrow, as well as a faint trail on the other side. Back on the bank, she was able to lay back on a rock, her forearms protecting her eyes while she kept her feet in the water. Laying here was the closest to nirvana that she had been in a long time. Too quickly, she remembered that she wasn't here by choice but force. Kim was tired of all these conflicting emotions that welled through.

She hadn't given them much attention before, but Kim sat up, with Beta behind her, and looked closely at the zip ties and remembered using them around her home to hold some of her plants up on poles. These ties were similar, except larger and thicker. She could pull the zip ties tighter if she wanted but couldn't loosen them – that was by design. *Frustrating as hell!* she thought to herself and laid back down.

She hadn't been there too long before she could hear some noise coming from behind her. Alpha seemed to fall into camp on his last legs. From a distance, he did not look at all good. Beta helped him take his pack off, got him some water to drink, and dug out a snack for him from one of the packs. Kim wanted to be more empathetic, but it was tough for her in this situation, so she decided it was best to keep her distance and enjoy the gurgling stream.

After lying for a good long time, Kim realized that it would be better to use her time to return to camp and wash herself and her smelly clothes. It was easy to do so near the stream, and she did her best to relish the cold water. She felt refreshed to have washed up but still felt a bit grimy. She couldn't wait to take a proper and hot shower sometime soon, maybe in a day or two, if she was permitted. She was certainly going to try to force the issue, that's for sure!

While her few clothes dried on rocks and shrubs, she shuttled over to the tents and her captors. Alpha looked slightly better, but he was just lying there with his eyes closed, forearm resting across his eyes. Beta saw Kim walk up and gave her a bit of nod as a greeting.

"So, what's up, guys? Have you made dinner reservations for the three for us tonight?"

Alpha slowly moved his arm and opened one eye, looked around to locate her, and found her. Next, the other eye wavered and then opened. Neither of his eyes had much in the way of signs of life. He had his shirt unbuttoned, splayed on a rock. His skin color looked off; parts of him looked sunburned, while skin that his clothes had been covering looked dull.

"How are you feeling?" Kim asked.

"Like hell," he said. "I still have a headache. I'm short of breath, slightly nauseous. I felt better this morning, but today's hiking and climbing really took it out of me. I'm hoping I feel better when we get to lower altitudes tomorrow. In the meantime, I'm mostly drinking water and eating ibuprofen. My appetite is shot."

Kim scrunched up her face. She found that she did feel the slightest bit of empathy after all. She was still quite human in this inhumane situation. They weren't going to rob her of her humanity, but she also didn't feel the need to display it.

Beta piped up, "I'm going to start warming water for supper in a bit and try to get him to eat something and get some energy in him. I'm worried about him, but I also figure that he'll be better tomorrow, like he said. We should be able to meet the driver by early afternoon, I hope."

"I better check in with her," Alpha said. After a quick gasp, "to make certain that we're all on the same page." He slowly rolled over, reached for his pack, and started coughing from the exertion. Kim didn't think that he sounded too healthy, either. After he had rummaged around in an exterior pocket of his pack, he pulled out the sat phone and just looked at it, seemingly trying to remember how to work it.

Kim's compassion got the better of her. She walked over to Alpha and placed her hand on his forehead and then on hers. She thought that his skin temp was about the same as hers, so she figured he didn't have a fever. Whatever his ills were outside of her area of expertise.

"So, what's going on with you? Do you have any idea?" she asked.

"Oh, yeah, I'm fairly certain that it's altitude sickness," Alpha replied. "Several days ago, we were in San Francisco and the Bay Area, near sea level. Then, boom, seventy-two hours ago, we camped at the trailhead at seventy-five hundred feet. The past couple of days, we climbed to nine thousand feet. Right now, we're over eleven thousand feet. My body isn't adapting quickly enough to the change in altitude, the lack of oxygen in the air, and all the exertion. I've been short of breath at altitude before but never felt this bad. For some people, that's a tough but doable ascent to altitude, but it's been too much for me. I've made some relatively quick ascents in the past, but not this time, I guess. It's another sign of how poor of shape I'm in for this environment and my age."

"So, you'll be fine once we get to a lower elevation?" Kim asked.

"Yeah, the best thing would be to go down right now, but I just can't move. It'll just be a struggle for maybe one more day. I should be fine – I hope," Alpha saying this almost convincingly.

After catching his breath again, Alpha said, "Once we get to the trailhead on the other side, the driver should take us down several thousand feet and I'll be much better off." The exertion of just speaking caused him to gasp again and he winced as he tried to breathe. Kim could easily read the pain in his face.

"I've felt short of breath if I overexert myself and have caught myself gasping for breath a few times, but I haven't had any other issues," Kim said. "I guess I should consider myself lucky."

Beta forced a weak grin on his face. "I've been feeling the altitude, too, but not nearly as bad as Alpha. The altitude affects everyone differently, and he's got it pretty bad this time. When we were in Afghanistan, we'd climb up and down the mountains day after day, carrying loads and weapons. We're just not that young and fit anymore."

Kim walked away, concerned but also confused with how cavalier Alpha seemed to be about his health. *Men,* she thought, *too much testosterone and not enough brains.* Flippantly, she said to the guys, "If you want, I can walk down the trail and get Alpha some help."

With this, Alpha groaned, and Beta grinned a bit.

After a deep breath, Alpha responded, "Thank you for your kind offer, Dr. Johnson, but I think I'll be fine. Just another day of this, and I'll be better." Alpha closed his eyes and recommenced his suffering.

Kim muddled her way over to check on her clothes, and they were nearly dry. Rather than go back, she sat on a rock, watched fish flit about a calm pool, and took in the sunlit mountains – she enjoyed the stark beauty and warm colors of this place. Kim heard Alpha on the phone, checking in with someone, while Beta gathered water from the stream and started the stove. Kim was pleasantly warm sitting in the waning sun and quite content that she had her health.

While eating supper, Beta noticed a backpacker coming up the trail from the west and told Kim to get into her tent. She wasn't happy about the order but did as they told her. She could hear the backpacker approach with his crunching boots, and he said a pleasant *good evening* to the guys, which they returned. It sounded to her like he had slowed but kept on walking. After his footsteps faded away, Beta told her that she could come out but to stay down and not bring any attention to herself. She was more than slightly peeved about these warnings from Beta but better understood when she saw that the visitor was setting up camp near the lake, in an area of some rock openings that she had spotted with Beta when they arrived in the afternoon.

After supper, Kim returned to her rock and took in the light show as the tawny mountains changed color from yellow to orange and then pink. Again, she found herself almost smiling, almost enjoying the moment despite her whole situation. It was so beautiful here, wonderfully desolate and quiet. She could easily imagine returning under better circumstances and sharing this world with friends. She looked over at the other camper from time to time but didn't do anything to attract attention to herself. She knew that the guys, especially Beta, very closely watched her, especially with someone nearby. She avoided making eye contact with the other backpacker and didn't even know if he knew that she was there. As she had pondered at the start of their hiking today, she knew that this one guy wasn't going to be able to rescue her unless he was well-armed. His pack was half the size of Alpha's and Beta's packs, so she wasn't expecting him to be carrying a weapon or to be able to save her, especially since he had no idea of her situation. And he was older and much more slender than Alpha and Beta. At a remote location like this, they'd likely kill the stranger as anything, she figured, even if Beta had said that they were friendly kidnappers. They had told her that they were to treat her decently but didn't mention that they'd extend that courtesy to anyone else.

Just in time to break up Kim's brief quiet moment, Beta hollered at her, loud enough so that she could hear him over the din of the stream. "Time to get into the tent and hit the sack! We're dead tired, which means that you're tired, too!"

After returning to her tent and shedding her shoes for Beta, she started to feel sorry for herself again, feeling a bit hopeless. Someone was nearby who might be able to save her – if he only knew. If she tried to get to the other camper or shout out, that would only mean there would be two hostages. Or maybe still one hostage and a fresh corpse. By tomorrow this time, she'd be back in a more familiar form of captivity with her future as murky as ever. She had no idea how she might get out of this situation, how she might save herself. And, if she didn't save herself, she had no idea of what her near future held. She was stuck and didn't know her way out, which was pretty much how she'd been feeling for the past week or so.

Chapter 21

Fred was deeply asleep. His dreams were of Asta and the kids, being here in the mountains, enjoying his family, floating on a lake. Suddenly, Asta was yelling, screaming at him – *what's going on?*

It wasn't Asta yelling. It was someone else, coming from outside his dreams. Pulling himself from his slumber, half awake, he realized the yelling was probably coming from the backpackers who were nearby. Then, he heard them very clearly: *BEAR!!!*

Fred was awake now. He jerked up, but his sore muscles knocked him back down for a moment. Unzipping his tent flap and pulling it aside, he could see lights moving wildly near the camp downhill, this way and that, seeming to be heading away from Lake Italy, downstream. That made him feel a bit better; at least they weren't herding trouble his way. He tied on his shoes, grabbed his jacket, and crawled out of his tent in his thermal underwear. His headlamp was in his coat pocket, but he didn't turn it on since his eyes were accustomed to the dark.

It was too dark for Fred to run, but he quickly made it to the other backpackers. He started yelling to get their attention to not scare them by approaching them too fast or quietly. A light pointed his way but then pointed back to where it had been. It seemed to Fred that the other campers were running after the bear, maybe to scare it away. Not knowing what he could do to help, he stood near the two tents and waited in the cold night air. There was no need for him to go chasing after a bear, after trouble, in his underwear – not his problem.

He had no idea what time it was. It was a clear, moonless night. Had he been asleep for an hour or six hours? Fred wasn't feeling groggy, but he knew that he hadn't had a whole night of sleep. Stomping his feet to stay warm, he wished that he had brought his gloves. It seemed like the other campers were still chasing the bear, so Fred went back to his camp, pulled out his gloves, and put on his pants. He was slightly warmer now and worked his way back down to the other camp.

After maybe ten minutes, he saw a light beam bobbing its way back to this camp. The light was no longer moving frantically, just bouncing along as if someone was walking behind or under it. The beam raised and caught Fred, so the camper knew that someone else was now in their camp. When he could hear the crunch of footsteps, Fred called out: "Did you have a bear in camp? Are you OK?"

The light responded grumpily, "Yeah, we had a bear. Damn thing dragged off one of our backpacks. My buddy is still chasing it. I'm hurting from the altitude and couldn't keep up. I'm hoping that he'll be able to get the pack back, or we're in trouble."

"Oh, man, I'm sorry to hear that. I heard you yelling, and it took me a moment to wake up and get down here," Fred responded. "Is there anything that I can do for you? Any help that you need? By the way, my name's Fred."

The light flashed off, and it took a moment for Fred's eyes to adjust.

The man said, "Oh, thank you very much for your offer, but I think that we'll be fine. We appreciate you coming over here to check up on us."

Fred pulled his phone from his pants – it was 4:30. He shook his head, realizing that it was too late for him to get back to sleep.

"Well, I'm heading back to my tent and make a slow breakfast. If you need anything, just let me know. I hope that your buddy recovers his backpack."

"Thanks, dude, we appreciate it. Yes, if we need your help, we'll come up and see you."

Fred turned and walked in the dark back to his campsite. He took his time making breakfast and loading since it was still reasonably dark. He'd be able to get packed and be on the trail much earlier than he had wanted, especially after yesterday's long hike. *Oh well, that's the way it goes*, Fred thought to himself.

One of the benefits of being up so early was the opportunity to enjoy the slowly evolving light show that was sunrise. The darkness gave way to lightening blues, oranges, yellows and whites that doubled with their reflections in the lake. It was a spectacular morning despite being awakened so early. By the time the sun first peeked over the eastern horizon, Fred was packed and heading out.

He backtracked to check on the other campers. There were now the two men in the camp, looking a bit befuddled. At their feet was a well-mangled backpack, with clothes and food spilling out. The men looked up at Fred in the dim morning light, sort of welcoming him to their bit of misery.

"Well, it looks like you recovered your pack. That's good," Fred said. "Did you lose anything?"

Fred couldn't tell which of the men he had spoken to an hour ago, it had been so dark. Eventually, one of the men said in a grumpy voice: "We're still taking inventory. It looks like the bear got off with some of our food, but that's about it. There might be some clothing that fell out, too. The bear tore up the backpack pretty good, but we can use it to continue our trip. Besides, we'll be out later today. We're heading down to the Pine Creek Trailhead. Thanks for checking up on us – we appreciate it." The voice sounded like that of the man with whom Fred had spoken. The second guy was silent, but he was sitting there and shaking his head. Was he freaked out or something else?

"Well, I'm glad everything is OK. So, were you using a bear canister? I don't think the Forest Service requires them in this area, but they're a great idea." Fred inquired.

"No, we felt overloaded, so we left bear canisters behind. I guess we learned our lesson, huh? We're lucky it wasn't worse than it was because we had the packs sitting just outside of our tents."

"Yeah," Fred replied, "I guess you were lucky. I'm surprised that a bear came up this high – that seems to me to be unusual. It must have picked up a strong scent from your backpacks. Since you seem to be fine, then I'm taking off. I have a long day ahead of me. Good luck getting down the mountain. You'll have a story to tell your families!"

Fred waved goodbye, and the two men returned the wave, although not with any pleasure, which wasn't surprising. Walking back upstream a bit, he crossed the Lake Italy outlet stream, Hilgard Branch. He was fortunate to find enough rocks above the flowing water that he could cross and stay dry. On the other side, there was a faint trail, possibly from deer or some other animals, but more likely the rare backpacker who came this way, crossing over rocks, sandy soils, and ground-hugging plants. Not much grew at this altitude. It was a beautiful morning! Clear and cool, sunrise reflecting off the lake to his right. His route took him along the west side of Lake Italy and then the north side, over low rises of talus and sometimes closer to the shore. After a mile or so, he climbed a draw that took him pretty much eastward, heading toward Gabbot Pass, the next obstacle. He looked back, and the morning sun was lighting the lake and creating an incredible scene. He felt it was going to be a great day in the Sierras!

The draw varied between damp, sandy soil, small- to medium-sized rocks, tundra grasses, and small, low flowers. It was a gentle climb and an excellent way to start the morning. He was warming now and knew that he'd be sweating hard by the time he made it to the pass. His head was down as it usually was while he hiked cross country, watching for minor obstacles on which he could trip or turn an ankle.

Suddenly, to his side, he heard a *psssst!* Turning a bit and looking, he suddenly jumped. *"JESUS! You scared the shit outta me!"* Fred yelled.

Sitting behind a large rock was a woman, looking cold, with a knapsack and no shoes. He stood there for a moment, trying to gather his wits and figure out what the hell was going on.

"I'm sorry, but keep it down, please. Could you do me a favor and help me?" the woman quietly said.

"Uh, I suppose so. What are you doing out here alone and with so little gear?" Fred asked. He had a very quizzical look on his face, not certain at all about this woman or her situation. *You have to be crazy to be out here and dressed like this,* he thought to himself.

"Well, I'm in a sticky situation. I'll gladly explain. But, while I explain, could you, like, sit here on the rock and not look at me? Like, look back toward the lake to not give me away?"

"Sure, I guess." Fred was puzzled and curious, because he'd never run into a damsel in distress in the middle of nowhere. Fred walked to the rock, took off his pack, sat down, and faced the lake. The woman sort of sat behind him, and he could see her out of the corner of his eye — just in case.

"OK, you've got my full attention, as if I had a choice," said Fred.

"Well, it's like this. Those two guys who you saw camping near you last night? They kidnapped me maybe a week ago; I don't know, I've lost track of time. Oh, and by the way, my name's Kim."

"It's nice to meet you, Kim. My name's Fred. So, I thought that

I saw three people at that camp last night, so you're the third person, right?"

"Yes," Kim replied. "I was the third. I've been looking for an opportunity to escape. When the bear surprised us this morning, I decided that it was as good of a time as any to get out of there. I was half awake when I heard something being dragged, along with some huffing or grunting sounds. I didn't think anything of it in the moment, being sort of groggy. Then I heard the guys' tent unzip and couldn't figure out why I hadn't heard the zipping sound before. About that time, one of them was shining their flashlight around and startled the bear. I think that it was Beta who screamed *BEAR!* and that's when the chaos began.

"I unzipped my tent and peeked out in time to see Alpha and Beta chasing after the bear and their lights bouncing all over. When they ran off after the bear, they forgot about me. I've been playing the part of the good hostage and hoping for an opportunity to escape. It didn't seem like there was going to be any better of a chance, especially since we were supposed to be picked up today on the trailhead, heading on down the trail we were on, to the east."

"OK, I'm following along. Part of your story lines up with what they were telling me this morning. But, more importantly, where are your shoes?"

"They took my shoes at night and at other times when they wanted me to stay near their camp and not run away. Their thinking must have been that I wouldn't go too far if I was barefoot. But I was getting desperate and so ran – *er*, stumbled – away during the bear chaos.

"When I was sitting by the stream last night, I thought that I could see a trail on this side of the lake. When they started yelling at the bear and chasing it in the dark, I peeked out of my tent and realized that it was a good time to leave, that it might be my last, best chance. I checked their tent for my shoes but couldn't find them. So, I just took off in my socks, crossed the stream, and followed the shoreline. Oh, and maybe you haven't noticed yet, but my ankles are bound together, making my morning walk difficult and slow. My ankles are hurting a fair bit now. I got this far when the sun started coming up, so I figured I'd hide behind these rocks and try to get the zip ties off. I didn't want them to see me in the morning light, and I thought that I might be able to see them from here, to see what they're doing. I figure that they'll assume that I've either gone back to the west from the way we came, which makes the most sense or that I'll head east along the other side of the lake on the trail we were on, heading down to the other side of the mountains to where we are supposed to meet their driver today. There are only two of them, so maybe one will head west and the other east to look for me, so this side of the lake seems like it's the least likely for them to go. That's the best that I've been able to come up with, anyway."

Fred thought for a moment, taking in all this new information, trying to understand what he had stepped into now. He also looked back at Kim to confirm her shackles – yep, there they were. He could see that she had been trying to saw through them with a rock between her legs. "So back up for a moment. Are you worth a lot of money, is that it? Did they kidnap you for a ransom or something?"

"They took me hostage because my work interferes with what their boss's organization is doing. It's a long story. I don't know who they are, though, nor do I exactly know what I've done to upset them – but I've got a pretty good guess. They thought that their problems would disappear if they got me out of the way, but that's not happening. They kept me in a remote house for a few days, but I guess that someone nearly caught up with them. Their next idea was to bring me up here, to get me away from civilization; they figured that it would be less likely that anyone would find me up here, and they seem to be right. I've hardly seen anybody for the past few days. I'm thankful that you came by so soon after I escaped. I thought that after I got the zip ties off, I'd head west to the other, more heavily traveled trail and hope to run into someone to help me."

Fred kept on digesting all this new information, trying to fit the pieces together, trying to make sense of it all. "So, let me get this straight. These guys kidnapped you because you're damaging their work, right? So, are they the bad guys, or are you? I'm not clear."

"Oh, no! I'm the good guy, *er*, good gal. I'll gladly tell you more about my work later, but I'm hoping that you can help me to get someplace safe so that I, or we, can call the police."

Fred took a deep breath and let out a sigh. He was silent, thinking about the options, considering whether this woman was telling the truth and what kind of trouble he was in now. He rummaged in a pocket on his pack, feeling around for his knife, which his fingers finally found. He took it out and carefully handed it to Kim, who was extremely grateful. It took only a moment for her to cut away the zip ties and free her ankles.

"Oh, that feels so much better," she said. Kim stretched her legs this way and that so that she could feel and stretch her sore muscles. She rubbed her ankles and checked the damage under her socks. The skin was raw, especially on the outside of her ankles.

"We need to treat those wounds so that they don't get infected," Fred said. "They don't look too bad now, but it doesn't take much out here to make life miserable." Now he was feeling around for his little first aid kit. He pulled out a small tube of antibiotic cream and handed it to Kim, along with a few bandages.

"Use the antibiotic sparingly because that's all that I've got. Once those wounds dry, you should be OK, I hope. Do you have any other injuries that need attention?"

"No," she said, "I'm in better shape than I was expecting to be a few days ago, other than these wounds on my ankles. I was doing better than Alpha and Beta – the altitude was taking a toll on them, and they were carrying much heavier packs."

Fred let this all sink in, let out a sigh, and shook his head. He sat there, the cool rock under his butt, considering all the new variables in his adventure. He also realized that in addition to keeping sight of the woman behind him, he also needed to be looking across Lake Italy for signs of the two men, who might now looking his way.

"Well," he finally said, "it seems to me that you're fortunate or else I'm extremely naïve, or maybe both. This trail that you followed is not much of a trail. Few people come this way. Most hikers stay on that main trail over there, on the south side of the lake, the Lake Italy trail. I'm mostly backpacking cross-country, south to north, and avoiding the main trails. There might be someone else come by here n another day, or it might be a week – who knows. Anyway, if you're expecting me to help you, then I hope you've had more time to think about how I'm supposed to do that."

"Oh, I've thought about it, especially as I saw you walking this way," said Kim, "but I don't really know what to do. I've been excited seeing you and hoping for help! This is the first time I've been back-packing in my life, and I didn't come prepared for it. In fact, I'd never been camping before. The guys were carrying most of my camping gear. I have a water bottle, a bit of food, and the clothes they told me to bring when they took me from my home in San Francisco. I know that I'm in the Sierras, but that's about all. I was hoping that I could either head up and over this mountain to escape them or, like I said, wait and head back to the trail we were on. But, if I get back on the trail, I'm guessing that they'll be looking for me, maybe bring in oth-er people, and have people watching at the trailheads. So, that's why I thought I'd be better off getting onto the north side of this lake and maybe hike over the mountain to a town or something, or maybe run into someone like you who could help me."

Fred blew out a big breath. "Well, we do have a predicament, don't we? We have a lot of little problems facing us, from what I can tell. I need to think about this some more. I have the beginning of a plan, but not much of one. I'm going to eat a snack and drink some water while I think. Do you need anything to eat or drink?"

Kim shook her head, no. "I'm a little hungry because I took off before breakfast, but I decided that I'd better ration my food because I didn't know how long I'd be out here."

"Yeah, that makes sense. Knowing what I know and what I think might happen over the next few days, then I'd better not have a snack either. I just had a good breakfast less than an hour ago."

They sat there for a few minutes, lost in thought, Fred sipping his water, looking out over this beautiful vista that had gotten very com-plicated and sort of dark. He started to say something and then pulled back, thinking some more. After maybe five minutes, Fred spoke.

"So, here's what I'm thinking. I need to help you get out of your 'sticky situation.' That's going to be more difficult than you're think-ing, though. I agree that these two will most likely be looking for you along the Lake Italy Trail or back along the main trail that goes north and south through the Sierras – the John Muir Trail and Pacific Crest Trail. You're best off avoiding those main trails and staying on these more lightly used trails or just going cross country. One of the prob-lems, though, is that if you cross over these mountains behind us, then there's no civilization for quite a distance."

Fred paused for a moment to let his thoughts sink in.

"My first thought was that I'd like to walk back to their camp, to where I camped last night. I'd like to check them out, try to figure out what they're thinking, how they're going to go about looking for you, but I just don't see a good way to do it and don't know that it would make a whole lot of difference. I don't think that there's anything useful that they'll reveal to me. When I spoke with them this morning, one of them did all the talking and he didn't mention anything about a third person. If he didn't say anything then, I don't know why he'd mention you if I went back. For the moment, at least, the best thing for us to do is to hunker down behind this rock and just watch 'em to see what they do. What do you think about that?"

"Well, it sounds like the beginning of a plan to me," Kim replied. "I don't think that the bit of information that you might gather is worth the risk of exposing yourself to them again. They might get suspicious, and I don't know what they might do to you. I don't see that the bit of information that they might share is worth the risk to you."

Fred shook his head in agreement, gathered his pack, stowed it behind the rock, and joined Kim. She had her back against the rock, sitting in a bit of shadow, while he sat facing her and peering over it, watching for any movement from the kidnappers. Alpha and Beta were too far downstream for Fred to see their camp from here, and that was fine by him. He figured that he'd easily see them before they might see him, especially since he knew where to look and he was sitting still.

Fred was lost in thought, his mind scrambling to think about how the next few days might unfold in their favor – or not. There were so many new issues for him to consider, new possibilities of getting into trouble. Life on the trail is relatively simple but challenging – get up in the morning, pack and eat; walk, eat and drink; walk, eat, and drink some more; deal with mosquitoes, rain, and sun; stay healthy; find camp, make camp, clean, eat, sleep; repeat. When he had backpacked with his family, he felt the added responsibility to watch out for everyone else. He now had that type of responsibility and more since Kim had never been backpacking before. There was also the new liability of having someone looking for them, possibly with weapons and likely with unpleasant consequences if found. One thing about being on the trail like this is that you need to be flexible because you never know when an obstacle would arise – an injury, slipping on snow or a bad storm, for example. For all the possible difficulties that Fred had imagined and prepared for, running into a kidnapping victim hadn't entered his calculus before. None of the articles that he'd read about other backpackers' terrifying experiences mentioned kidnapping victims. Worrying would accurately describe Fred's active mood now.

Kim, on the other hand, was elated! She wore a big grin and she was feeling very relieved, at least for the moment – a pleasant feeling that she hadn't felt since going for a morning walk several days ago. She was away from Alpha and Beta. Someone had luckily stumbled upon her, and he seemed capable of getting her away from her nightmare and back to civilization and safety. For someone that she'd just met, she put a lot of hope and faith in Fred. In a happy place now, she was comfortable giving Fred mental and emotional space to think and feel, especially since she was over her head out here in the wilderness. She figured that if the tables were turned, she'd be thinking and worried, even overwhelmed with the new responsibilities and the change in plans. She may not be a great people person, but she was sufficiently aware that this was a moment to leave Fred be until he was ready to speak. She could see him unconsciously pulling at grass, rolling rocks in his fingers, fumbling with his water bottle, hear him sighing, and occasionally looking over her stone backrest for signs of life at the Lake Italy outlet. Kim's mind was churning, too, in a happier place, of course, but also thinking about how to stay safe and out of sight for the next few days.

Finally, Fred let out a big sigh and looked straight at Kim. His smile contorted into an odd grin that she read as curiosity, interest, and acceptance of a new responsibility thrust upon him. She could read the angst in his face and knew that she had put him in a difficult spot. Kim also could see the twinkle in his eyes that said he was invested in this situation no matter what, he was on her team and that he had her best interests at heart. She found it strange, in her mind, how she was such a poor people person, and yet she felt that she was reading Fred so well and felt good about it. She could sense that he was getting ready to talk and that he would when he was ready. Kim gave him a friendly smile, a smile that said, *thank you for helping, I appreciate you, and everything will work out fine.*

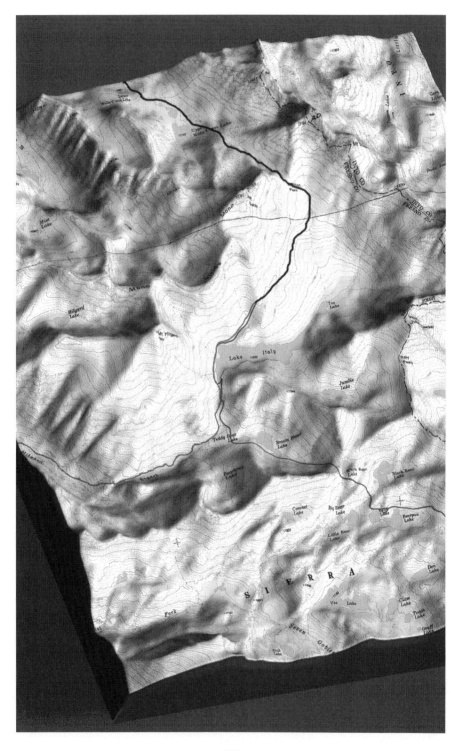

Fred shook his head to get out of his mind and back into Kim's world, followed by another big sigh. He opened his mouth as if to speak, but he didn't. He was attentively looking beyond Kim, across the lake.

"What? What's up?" She was looking across the lake, too, trying to discern whatever it was that had captured Fred's attention. Now she saw it! A lone figure was hiking, backpacking eastward on the far shore of the lake.

"Well, isn't that interesting," Fred said. Kim looked puzzled, and then it slowly dawned on her why this view was so interesting. Kim scooched away from the rock and turned to face Lake Italy so that she could better watch Alpha's or Beta's hiking.

"Yes," Fred started, "if you're going backpacking with a buddy, wouldn't you think that you'd both continue together? Instead, it looks like they've separated, with one heading towards Pine Creek Trailhead. I'm guessing that the other guy is heading back the way you came up here, from the west."

Kim smiled a bit. "So, do you believe me now?" she asked.

"Oh, it certainly makes your case stronger," he said. Fred was smiling. "I thought that maybe you were overdoing it by faking the zip ties, but I guess not."

Kim grabbed a few pebbles and sand and tossed it at him in jest, a wry smile on her face. "You're a jerk, you know that? Here I had you up on a pedestal, my new hero."

"Hey, did I ever say that I didn't believe you?" Fred was smiling broadly, a glint in his eyes.

"Look, I never doubted you," Fred said. "That's not what's been on my mind. I just want to sit here until he's out of sight. I don't want to move; I don't want to draw attention to us. He might have binoculars or something, just in case. He should be out of sight in a few more minutes." They quietly sat there, watching the backpacker head farther and farther east.

Fred continued. "There's a lot we need to talk about. Like, I want to hear more about who you are and how you got into this predicament. But, what's on the top of my mind is how to get you – and me – someplace safe."

Alpha pulled out the sat phone and pushed the button to call Omega. He was not looking forward to this conversation.

"Yes, this is Omega. What is it? We're in the middle of a meeting to figure out what to do with Dr. Johnson."

"Bad news, sir. Our guest has disappeared."

"What do you mean *disappeared*? This not what we want to hear."

"Well, sir, we had a bear come into our camp this morning while it was still dark. While Beta and I were scaring it away and recovering the backpack that it took, she walked off. We started to search for her immediately, but it was dark. After the sun came up, we searched further for her, but no luck. Beta is heading back down the trail we came up, and I'm continuing forward in the direction we were going to meet the driver later today. That's all that we can figure to do. If we find her, I'll call you as soon as I can; Beta doesn't have a sat phone with him, so he's out of communication until we can figure something out. I'm going to be thinking more about this problem and how to resolve it while heading down the trail today."

"Is that all, Alpha?"

"Yes, sir. I sincerely apologize for our screw-up. We're busting our butts right now to fix this problem."

The line went quiet. Alpha was glad that the call had been short and direct. He grabbed his pack and headed east on the Lake Italy Trail, walking quickly, keeping his eyes open for signs of Dr. Johnson. While he walked, he called the driver to let her know about the new situation, to be ready for anything and to ask her to arrange for someone to pick up Beta at the Bear Creek Trailhead.

Chapter 22

Fred sat for a minute, thinking more, and looking at Kim. "We have several different issues that are going to make our lives difficult over the next few days but not impossible. The first thing you obviously need is shoes. I'm wearing my hiking shoes, but I carry a pair of shoes for around camp. That's the best that I can do for you. They're too large for you, but hopefully, an extra pair or two of socks will help with how they fit. They'll probably feel loose and sloppy, and we'll have to watch for blisters, especially on your heels and toes.

"Another issue is that I just want to sit here for a bit longer. We can't see if anyone is still across the lake, so let's just sit tight in case someone is watching. When we go, we'll walk as closely together as reasonable so that it might look like one person from a distance.

"The third issue is food. You have some, and I typically carry enough food to get me from one resupply point to the next, plus an extra day's worth of food, just in case. I guess that I'm carrying about enough food for one person for four days – maybe a little more. I'll check my maps later, but we should be about three days from Mammoth. The way that I figure it, we're short of food, which is no surprise. I brought a fly rod, so I hope that I can catch some trout. I've been eating some fresh fish along the way, but not counting on it. Now, we'll have to count on it."

He sat there a moment longer, pondering their situation, and then dug into his pack for his camp shoes. As expected, they were a few sizes too large for Kim. Fred fished out a pair of his thick hiking socks and gave them to her. Her feet were slightly loose in the shoes. She'd be fine on level terrain but sliding in the shoes while walking uphill and downhill could be an issue.

"You'll need to be careful while walking. You're likely to trip over the toe of these shoes as if you were wearing clown shoes. Your footing won't be secure because of your feet sliding in the shoes, so just take your time. I'd rather us be safe and slow."

Fred was still sitting, still thinking. "I forgot! I never asked you how you're feeling, how healthy you are, other than the abrasions from the zip ties. Did they mistreat you or hurt you in any way?

"No, I'm feeling pretty good," Kim gladly offered. "I'm probably healthier than those two. They were very respectful for being the bad guys. They fed me decently. My biggest issue is that my feet and ankles are sore from shuffling around in my socks to get away from them this morning. I think that I sort of stubbed my toes a few times, but no major damage."

"OK, that's good information to have. You'll have to let me know if we walk too fast, if your feet are sore, or you're developing blisters, and so on. All you have to do is ask my wife – I'm no mind reader."

Kim grinned at this and tied the shoes as tightly as possible. She was ready to go, and Fred pulled on his pack.

"When we start hiking, at least until we get over that next ridge up there, it would be best if you could walk so that I'm between you and the lake so that if they're watching, they're likely to assume that it's a backpacker climbing this ridge. Once we get over the crest, no one should be able to see us from the lake, but we'll check. Ready to go?"

Kim shook her head *yes* and fell into her place leading Fred. He kept one hand on her hip, to keep the distance between them tight. They took a leisurely, hesitant pace as Kim got used to the shoes and got a sense of how much her feet might be hurting. After a hundred yards or so, she told him that her feet were feeling fine for now and that the shoes were reasonable; she also felt great not to wear shackles. They kept the same pace but were taking it more confidently now. A few minutes later and they were on top of the ridge, moving farther north. Unfortunately, someone could still see them if they looked up from the Lake Italy Trail, so Kim and Fred continued to walk in tandem. They both would look back to the trail from time to time to see if they could make out anyone across the lake, but nothing caught their eyes.

They continued like this for more than an hour. As Kim and Fred got further away from Lake Italy, they felt better, but they couldn't know if anyone had spotted them. They eventually walked over a small rise that shielded them from view along the Lake Italy Trail and could walk more freely. The last scramble up Gabbot Pass was challenging, but Fred kept Kim in front of him as closely as possible, not knowing her skills, abilities, or comfort level. They were moving slowly, taking a few steps, and stopping to catch their breath. He could tell that her feet were sliding some in his shoes and worried about her heels and blisters. When they crested the pass, Fred kept them going a little further so that they could rest out of view of Lake Italy.

When they stopped, took off their packs, sat, and caught their breath, Kim was ecstatic. Her face radiated joy! Her reaction was not quite what Fred had been expecting, so he was pleasantly surprised. Kim loved the spectacular view from up here and loved that she had accomplished her first big climb up a tall mountain pass. Most of all, though, Kim could feel the tension drain from her, the tension that she didn't realize she was carrying. Kim was freer than she had been in a week despite being in the middle of nowhere, far away from civilization. She felt safe here and now, on top of a remote mountain pass and hadn't felt this comfortable in a week. Kim was grinning from ear to ear and then started sobbing with tears of joy. Fred didn't know why she was crying, felt concerned, and went to sit by her. Kim snuggled up to him, and he put his arm around her shoulders and held her for a moment. Looking up at him, big, wet tears in her eyes and wearing a big smile, she simply said, "thank you!" Fred caught on now, smiled too, and gave her another hug.

They sat there for a few minutes, Kim enjoying her freedom and the moment. Fred said, "I don't mean to burst your bubble, but we still need to be watchful to see if anyone is following us. I've been scanning the Lake Italy Trail to see if anyone is hiking westward on it just in case someone saw us and they're coming after us. So far, so good. But that doesn't mean that someone didn't spot us while climbing and watching from above Lake Italy on its southeast side. We need to keep looking over our shoulders, at least through tonight.

"Also, it's going to be tougher getting down the other side of this pass than it was coming up, at least for the first few hundred yards because it's steeper. You need to watch your step, watch that you don't catch the toes of those oversized shoes on rocks. It might be easier for you to sidestep down the mountain at first, at least until the terrain becomes less steep. Just take your time, and we'll be down in an hour or so. There's no hurry," Fred said. "There are some lakes down there that we can't see yet; we'll stop there for lunch and to check on your feet."

The initial descent, the first steps, from the pass weren't difficult, but about fifteen minutes later, Kim realized that the second step was steeper and trickier. She made it down fine, took her time and side-stepped as Fred suggested, and had a big smile on her face when they made it to Lower Mills Creek Lake. Kim dropped her pack and turned a full circle, slowly taking in all the vast scenery that she could.

"This is just so beautiful!" she exclaimed to Fred. "In fact, it's even more beautiful because I'm away from Alpha and Beta!"

Fred caught up to her and wore his own big smile. He was very thankful that she enjoyed the trip – so far – and hoped that she would continue to do so. Digging into his pack, he found some snacks and his water filter. They ate and drank in respectful silence, Fred trying to understand what Kim had recently been through, not wanting to force her to talk if she didn't want to. But, since there was no one else with whom to speak, his curiosity got the best of him.

"So, let me get this straight. You were kidnapped, kept in a house for a few days, and then brought out here to keep you away from civilization, right? I have too many questions for you, and we have plenty of time to get through all of them. What's most important to me right now, though, is your health and how you've fared over these past few days up here. You said that you've never been backpacking, but you sure are enjoying yourself."

Kim smiled a bit and took her time to give a thoughtful answer. "Yes, this is my first-time backpacking. The guys served in the military in the Afghanistan mountains, maybe a decade ago. Their general plan was to get me someplace away from computers, the internet, and civilization for a few days, to hide me away, while their boss – he calls himself Omega – could figure out what to do with me for the longer term. Alpha and Beta were carrying these massive backpacks, especially when compared to your pack. When they were in Afghanistan, they said they carried ninety-pound packs, and they thought they were just as capable today. Their loads were too much for them, I guess. They struggled with their packs plus the altitude. Alpha and Beta – especially Alpha – complained about headaches and general aches and pains from the packs. We got hit by a storm the night before last, and they decided to take a day off to dry out their gear and maybe feel better. Alpha and Beta moved slowly the whole time, it seemed to me. I've been doing pretty well because my little knapsack only weighs a few pounds, and I'm in decent shape. I jog in San Francisco and feel that I'm reasonably healthy. My biggest issue was walking over sharp and uneven rocks in my running shoes. My feet are a little sore, but other than that, I'm fine. The altitude hasn't been as hard on me as it was on Alpha and Beta for some reason, and they fed me decently. I've been short of breath several times, but no headaches or anything like that. Seriously, I'm feeling pretty good, considering how far out of my routine I am.

"Mentally and emotionally, I'm feeling terrific now since I'm no longer their captive. I know that we still have a lot more of a trek before us, but I feel a whole lot better being with you than with them. I seriously have never been out in the mountains like this, and I love it! I know that might sound odd, but I've never been in the wilderness like this. I've done many things in my life, but camping wasn't one of them, and I haven't hiked much outside of the cities in which I've lived. Is that the kind of stuff you wanted to know about me?"

Fred took in what Kim had said before responding. "Yeah, I guess so. While I'm getting to know you, I'm most interested in your health and well-being. You seem to be in good physical health, and your spirits sure seem to be a lot higher than mine would be if I'd been kidnapped and then taken into an extraordinary, demanding environment. I want to know these things about you so that I can be most helpful to you. I don't want to push you too hard, and I don't want to hurt you so that we get through these next few days and get you back safe and sound. But we also have severe limits on how much time we can spend out here because of the amount of food we're carrying.

"Now that your health seems fine enough, can you please tell me more about why you think they kidnapped you?"

Kim took a deep breath and thought for a moment. "It's difficult to explain, so you'll have to follow along and trust me. I'm a Ph.D. computer scientist, and I work mostly on issues involving hackers and cybersecurity. Over the past few years, I've developed a different way to spot, track, and neutralize some of these computer threats. Many people think that I'm brilliant, but I'm not really, at least in my mind. Many 'discoveries' are just old tools that someone packages differently, and that's what I've done. I took some existing security tools and repackaged them and gave them a little more power and precision."

Fred took this in, listening but not hearing enough to understand. "Who do you work for?" he asked.

"Well, my employer would prefer me not to say," was Kim's dry response.

Fred heard that message after a moment. After a pause he said, "When I lived in Washington, DC, many years ago, I played on a co-ed rec volleyball team. One of the players was a wonderful person, and she was an awesome passer! One time after a game, we were all drinking at a bar, and I asked her where she worked and she just sort of blew off my question. That annoyed me a bit, so I asked her a second time and a bit more forcefully. She gave me pretty much the same response that you just gave me, and it took a moment for it to sink in. I never asked her about it again." He finished this last comment with a wink.

"Good," said Kim, "so you understand." She gave Fred a wink back. "Anyway, I've been developing this suite of tools that work together to reduce cybercrimes. We're still sort of testing it, and I'm not certain how well it's working. When you try to prevent something from happening, it's hard to tell if it works – it's difficult to prove a negative. But I'm now getting the feeling that it's working well based on Omega's reaction."

"How does it work?" Fred's curiosity was getting to him, being the inquisitive guy that he was.

"I can't tell you. If I did, I'd have to kill you." Kim said this with a solemn look on her face.

Fred sat there for a moment, perplexed, eyes growing wide, maybe a bit scared. Kim started smiling and said, "Gotcha!"

Fred gave her a mild scowl and said, "Now who's the jerk?" and they both chuckled. "I'll tell you what. When we start walking, you look over your shoulder for your kidnappers while I keep an eye on you!"

Kim smiled and started telling him her story. "It's not that magical of a system, to be honest. Again, we're packaging old tools in a new way and using very powerful computers. Computer hackers and cybercriminals are human, just like you and me. The hackers and criminals talk about what's working and what's not. When they identify a weakness to break into a computer system, word gets around the hacking community, and more people target the same flaws. They also are intelligent, lazy, or both, and they share code snippets and packages that are currently working well for them.

"Using a statistical analysis as one part of the larger package, the system figures out what hacking methods are popular and what's not and uses that popularity to try more appropriate countermeasures as well as focus on the likely targets. We're just trying to focus our limited computer tools where we think they'll have the most impact. This part of the system looks at the current ways that people are breaking into computers and uses that information to predict how and where someone will next try to get into other computer systems. We all do this in whatever work we do – we tend to repeatedly use the same tools until we realize that it doesn't work, and then we move onto a different tool until we overuse it and move on again.

"Our system – I direct a team of really great computer scientists and statisticians – also looks at critical current trends, what's considered valuable and therefore most likely to be a target. A few years ago, digital currencies were hot and they still are. Last year, coronavirus research was hot. And these cybercriminals are always looking to get into infrastructure computers either to shut down systems or simply obtain a ransom for data. So, the tool has a trend analyzer to focus computer security resources on those hot topics. Banks, markets, and financial institutions always get a lot of attention from hackers and cybercriminals, but industrial and medical research labs creating the next gee-whiz tool or disease cures also draw attention.

"And, since computer languages and codes use similar basic logical operations, the system looks for the code patterns in the malware that create these malicious logical operations and the type of computer security systems that are vulnerable to these malicious logical operations. We also watch for emails that contain malware links and code. Another part of the package scans for obscure types of computer languages, where an experienced programmer might use an odd language to avoid detection or confuse possible fixes. There's also an element in this part of the system that checks on internet traffic patterns and routing, and especially those servers from which most of the malware and ransomware is coming from, and then focuses on traffic from those specific servers and IP addresses that seem to send out the most malware. Cybercriminals constantly change the way they route their tools, mixing it up so that it's harder to track them. It's another statistical parsing tool – the popular codes, functions, servers, and addresses get attention first. That part of the tool can then suggest the appropriate countermeasure to neutralize those codes and routes.

"The last part of the system is sort of an artificial intelligence umbrella layer that takes all of the information to learn and predict subsequent threats. That was the weakest part of the system, I thought, because I haven't figured out how well it's doing. It's learning and responding at a faster rate than we can keep up. It's practically impossible to measure computer hacks that the system has prevented. In that way, we've been sort of flying blind, not knowing how well we are doing or not.

"To summarize, all we've done is to create a better mousetrap in the world of computer security. We could detect some trends when we got the system up and running in total and were tweaking it. We saw some downward trends in hacker activity and success, but we couldn't know if it was our system or if something else was going on. For example, when we first turned the system on about eighteen months ago, hackers changed their methods, maybe every one to three months. When I last checked the statistics, it seemed that the hackers were changing their ways every two to four weeks. It makes it more difficult and expensive to change methods more frequently, so we think that their success rates and stealing declined. Their return on investment declined markedly, we thought.

"We backed up this thinking by looking at bank profits, stock prices, and ransomware attacks, adjusted for various broad financial factors like economic growth. Financial institutions don't like to report how much money they might be losing to hackers and the like, but they still need to report losses to the government. We can also watch the stock prices of financial institutions and see their quarterly financial reports. Adjusting for typical economic factors, we think banks are losing less money – a lot less money – because they're more profitable than they were a couple of years ago, with all other factors held even. We also feel that fewer ransomware attacks are occurring, which leads to higher profits and productivity. Again, we have no firm numbers, we're reading between the lines of these various financial reports, but we think that global finance firms have 'lost' close to fifty billion dollars less over the past year when compared to earlier years. That's real money that's not going to nefarious purposes, and the hackers behind those losses aren't happy.

"Lastly, though, I've not told you all the details or been fully transparent, as all of this is secret, hush hush.

"The bad news seems to be that 'they' figured out that I'm behind this system. The bad guys and gals must have a lot of resources behind them because they found me and disabled the high-tech security system at my house so that they could kidnap me. I don't know how they did it, but I hope my people are on top of it! My employer reluctantly let some of us work from home, but not on these high-level, secure projects during the pandemic and required better security systems in our homes. We failed on our security because we thought we were well hidden behind layers of computer systems that we didn't know anyone could track us. We seem to have gotten complacent ourselves.

"Our team is still in place, I believe, and the system we created should still be working. I've moved onto different projects and have been maintaining and monitoring this system, and watching the financial data that we're following for clues of success. I think that's what is upsetting Omega's group because it seems that their thinking was that if they got me out of the way or intimidated me, they'd be working well again. I'm isolated, in their terms, but the system is still working and stifling their efforts. They were trying to figure out their next steps to neutralize our tool and what to do with me – until I escaped.

"Wow, what a story!" Fred exclaimed. "A lot of it is over my head. It's about as clear as mud to me! I understand enough to appreciate how much you all have irritated them and kept them from stealing as much as in the past. It must be a big blow to whoever is behind all of this hacking."

Fred sat there for several more minutes, taking in this information. After a bit, he spoke up. "So, you're more valuable to these hackers than I imagined. When you said that they'd kidnapped you, I thought that somehow you worth a ransom of a few million dollars or something like that because you or a family member were very wealthy.

You're much more valuable than that!

"So, do you think that you have another four or five hours of hiking in you for today? The next hour or two will be relatively easy, but we'll have a slow, tough climb after that. Oh, and one more thing," Fred started. "What kind of bounty do you suppose this Omega is offering for you?"

Kim picked up a small stick and playfully threw it at him. "I'm feeling fine," Kim said. "If I start flagging, I'll let you know. I suspect that you'll be able to read it in me, too. Are we ready to head out again?"

With a smile, Fred looked out over the landscape and pointed out their route. "Yep. We're going to head down this gentle valley and then make our way into a deeper valley. We'll come up on the other side over there, and that's where it will get tougher. I'm hoping that we can make it into that valley on the other side and find a campsite for the night. If you're good with that, then let's hit the trail!"

Kim picked up her pack and was off in a flash. *Yep, she's feeling good*, he thought. *We'll see how she does later this afternoon.* He didn't try to keep up with her, knowing that he was carrying a heavier load. He just shouted out directions if she needed them and let her take the lead. If she didn't know where to go, Kim stopped and waited for Fred to point with his hiking pole or tell her which way he thought they should go. *It's easier hiking with her than with my kids*, he thought. *I guess I'll have a story to tell when I get home!*

**Chapter 23**

After a couple of hours or so, they worked their way down to Mono Creek and started heading upstream on the trail. A few minutes later, Fred called a halt. "It's time for a break. This shady spot is a good place to stop, get some water, and relax for a bit. The rest of the afternoon will be uphill and tough."

They were sitting on rocks beside the creek while Fred filtered water for them. Kim was taking in the views and feeling pretty good after all that she had been through this day.

"You know, you've been gracious, asked about me, and helped me. But I don't know anything about you! You could be some crazy wilderness man for all I know!" she said jestfully.

Fred sat on the rock, smiling, filtering, and pouring water into bottles. He looked up at her and then looked downstream, off in the distance. "Well, I'm someone who likes to backpack, to get out into the wilderness and escape civilization. Back home, I have a wife and three kids – a daughter and two sons. I expect that they miss me; I sure miss them. But I feel the need to get away by myself every year to have my 'me' time. I work as an environmental consultant, and it can get stressful at times, working with clients to help them deal with the messes they've made or complying with changes in the regulations. I'd like to think that I'm a relatively normal, typical guy.

"A couple of years ago, I was here and backpacked the John Muir Trail with my younger son. It was the trip of a lifetime! That trail is down this stream a few miles, and it's a lot busier. It sounds like you were on it for a bit yesterday, so maybe you know what I mean. That's one reason I'm on a different route this summer, to avoid some traffic. Three years ago, I was out here on my first attempt on the JMT with both of my sons and a nephew. We had an earlier start that year, and there was too much snow. We ended up bailing out that year because it was too tough for us. That's part of the reason completing the JMT with my son was so special. Again, I'm just a normal guy who likes to be outdoors."

"How long have you been out here on this trip?" she asked.

"Let's see. I think that this is my tenth day. I started about a hundred miles south of here. The first couple of days were tough as they were mostly uphill; it was a climb of five thousand feet, and I was still getting into shape and acclimating. Since then, it's been a pretty good trip except for that small storm a few nights ago. I had a bit of wet gear but nothing serious. I stopped for a resupply a few days ago, too. Other than the storm, it's been a pretty uneventful trip until I picked up a hitchhiker." Fred grinned at this last comment and Kim smiled, too.

For now, Kim was satisfied with what she'd heard from Fred. She knew that there was a lot more to him and that it might take her some time to open him. "You're an introvert, aren't you?"

Fred grew a big smile and said, "Now, what made you think that?"

Fred had another thought come to him. "So, you're telling me that these bad guys are after you, and there's lots of computer security stuff involved. I send a satellite text message to my wife every night. What do you think about that?"

Kim sat for a moment, thinking, and then her eyes got wide. "Oh, it would be best if you didn't mention anything about me just yet. Those things aren't secure at all; they aren't secure from snooping. If I wanted, I very likely could get into the messages that those things send, and if I can do that then whoever is after me can get to them. Now that you mention it, since they know I've taken off, if I were them, I'd be watching for satellite text messages, satellite phone calls, and cell phone calls from the Sierras to see if anyone has come across a lost computer scientist. Those messages send latitude and longitude information, so it wouldn't take much to track us down."

"OK, got it," said Fred. "That makes sense. There's no need to let anyone know that you've been found and give away our location. I'll change up my messaging so that my wife doesn't become concerned and so that we're a bit less predictable."

After taking a last big swig of water, Fred pronounced that they'd better get going, and they hit the trail again.

As expected, the rest of the afternoon was tough. It was hotter now that they were at a lower altitude and climbing. After another hour or so, Fred could see that Kim was sometimes tripping over the toes of her clown shoes, so he tried to get her to slow down and take more frequent breaks. Kim worked up a good sweat this afternoon; Fred could see it rolling down her forehead and cheeks.

"You're doing great for being a noob!" he told her, and she smiled weakly. She appreciated the compliment, especially since she was tiring now.

"OK, I told you that I would let you know if I was 'flagging,' and now I'm pretty close to 'flagged,'" she huffed.

"The trail is sort of leveling off, it's not climbing so steeply now, and we have maybe another thirty minutes to go to get to the place I was hoping we'd make it for the night – Laurel Lake."

"Good! I'm ready for a hot shower and a large steak and fries," she said with a big grin. She kept marching on, head down, slower than earlier in the day, and occasionally looking at the fantastic valley they were climbing. She'd stop, take a look around her, catch her breath, soak in the scenery, and then put her head down and go on for another five minutes or so. *I'm so tired and sore, but this is so beautiful!* she thought to herself.

Finally, they crested a rise, and there was a small lake in front of them, surrounded on three sides by spectacular granite walls. Fred put his pack aside and started to make camp. Kim dropped her bag and flopped onto a small patch of cool, soft, green grass. She just laid there, looking up at the sky, thankful to be away from Alpha, Beta, Omega, and whoever else was responsible. Moments later, she was fast asleep.

Fred put up his little one-person tent, inflated his sleeping pad, and laid his quilt across the tent to air out. He'd had a long day, too: getting up early for the bear's visit; being found by Kim; and, backpacking ten miles or so. There was still much to do if they were to eat and be somewhat comfortable for the night. He realized that with only the single sleeping pad, someone – that is, him – would be sleeping on the ground, so he had placed the tent on the softest soil that he could find and tried to find some dry pine needles to place under the tent and cushion his bed.

He now had his little fly rod out, hoping for some fish for dinner. Laurel Lake was small and shallow, and he wasn't feeling optimistic about trout tonight, but he'd still try. Thirty minutes later, Fred was thankful to have three modest trout onshore and cleaned. He decided to cook the trout on a hot slab of thin granite, so he started a small fire and placed his granite griddle over the fire when it was burning well. Fred figured he was breaking Forest Service regulations since he wasn't supposed to build a fire at this altitude, but since he was short of food and working to help save Kim, he hoped the Feds might cut him some slack. Besides, as he smiled to himself, if a ranger showed up now and wanted to ticket him, that was just fine by Fred because the ranger could help get them out of this mess. While the trout slowly cooked on his makeshift griddle, Fred boiled water to rehydrate rice and pulled out some dried fruit, nuts, and cheese. When the trout had about cooked, he gently awoke Kim.

"Hey, Sleeping Beauty. Supper's ready. It's being served tonight on the finest table in town."

Kim's eyes fluttered open, and she laid there for a moment, trying to figure out where she was, what was going on. She finally started coming back to reality and rolled over on her side, taking in the basin in which they found themselves. The west side of the bowl was now in shadow, and she would soon be in a cool shade herself. Rubbing her eyes and sitting up, she was mostly awake now, although she could feel sore muscles.

Wandering over to where Fred sat, he handed her his spork. She had a big smile on her face now as the presentation of supper was unlike anything she'd ever enjoyed! The trout were perfectly cooked and surrounded by rice on the granite slab, with dried apples and bananas artfully placed around. Two bottles of water were nearby.

"My lady, your feast is ready," Fred said with a bit of flair. "You'll find a vintage white wine in your goblet there."

"This is unbelievable! I didn't know that it was possible to have a gourmet meal out here. I'm very impressed," she said. "Maybe we're not going to go hungry after all."

She tucked into the trout and rice – it tasted heavenly! Kim passed the spork to Fred, and she nibbled on bits of fruit and drank her water. She enjoyed the food and ambiance, as well as the company.

"This is the finest outdoor dining experience I've ever had. I'll never forget this moment! Thank you so much for taking such good care of me. I sincerely appreciate it."

Now, there was a tear in Kim's eye, and Fred was totally confused for a moment and then recalled that she had cried earlier in the day. She held up a hand to signal that everything was fine, not to worry. At this moment, Kim was finally relaxing from all the tension that she'd been carrying. Kim was away from her captors, had caught up on a bit of sleep, was eating well this evening, and she was in one of the most beautiful settings in which she'd ever found herself. Kim tried to explain to Fred that she was overwhelmed in so many ways; Fred understood and felt thankful for his part in her relief.

"I do have some bad news, though," he said. "Since I cooked, you have to do the dishes."

Kim was smiling again and laughing. "Yes, sir. I understand. My only question is, what do I do with the fish bones?"

"Oh, we'll gather them up as best we can and throw them as far out into the lake as possible. We'll also move the cooking rock well away from camp, maybe throw it into the lake too, so that odors don't attract bears.

"That reminds me. I was thinking today while we were walking. I didn't think about this earlier, but you said that the bear in your camp this morning took one of the guy's backpacks. Were they carrying food in bear canisters or their backpacks? I thought that they told me that they left their bear canisters behind or something like that."

"Well, that was one of their mistakes, I think. Yesterday morning, just before we left camp, Alpha decided that they were carrying too much gear, too much weight, and he started getting rid of some stuff. He set aside several pieces of clothing and their bear canisters and hid them behind some rocks. I didn't think much of it at the time and hadn't thought of it until now since you brought it up."

"Most of the bear problems in the Sierras," Fred started, "tend to be closer to the areas where people congregate, like Yosemite Valley. People see bears up here with some frequency, but they're seldom a problem because the backpackers secure their food and run them off before they cause any real problems. Also, bears don't typically come up this high, but that doesn't mean they won't come up here. Still, sometimes people let their guard down, do something stupid, or both, and these things happen. The only time that I've seen a bear out here, it was quietly sitting in a big puddle of water happily eating grass and sedges that were growing there. Our trail passed about twenty-five feet from it, and we quietly, respectfully watched it for a bit before backing away."

"Wow! That must have been an amazing experience," Kim exclaimed.

"Yes, it was. It helps to put you in your place, that we're just a piece of Nature out here and not the dominant species like we are in the cities. I've seen bear in the wild all over the US – California, Wyoming, Montana, Alaska, Virginia – but nearly always, I was in a vehicle and not in danger."

Kim pondered these bear issues for a moment. "So, how do you not get scared of bears out here? I've been out here three days, and a bear stole a backpack, so it seems my luck isn't as good as yours."

"Well," Fred thought, "I tend to think like a deer. Deer live out here all the time. It's their home, surrounded by all this beauty – and predators. They also deal with the elements year-round. They are watchful for predators and everything, but they still go on with their lives, too. Before I go on these trips, I think about bears, particularly if I'm heading to places where grizzlies roam, like my trips to Wyoming. Once I'm out here, though, I'm busy hiking and taking care of myself. All this beauty surrounds me. So, I'm either too busy with other little, mundane things to think about bears, or else I'm so entranced by the grandeur that I don't think of them. But they're always in the back of my mind. I don't let my guard down, but I don't let it impede my enjoying all of this beauty."

Kim's smile grew as she thought about what he had just said, taking it into herself.

"If I were to run into a bear up close, then maybe my attitude would change. I seriously have no desire to see a bear up close, especially a hungry bear, so I work hard to maintain good camp hygiene," Fred said.

Kim enjoyed Fred's down-to-earth attitude about being out here in the wild.

Fred smiled, knowing that he was entertaining Kim, and continued. "The sun will be getting low in another hour or so, and it's going to start cooling off soon. If you want to clean up in the lake, then you'd better do it now. I'll clean up after you."

Kim looked at him, a bit confused. "So, how do you suggest that I 'clean up'? I'm waiting for my hot shower here."

Fred grinned and said, "It's pretty easy, although not necessarily pleasant. I have a little bottle of soap. You put a drop of the soap onto a wet cloth and wash away – that's about it. Then, rinse the cloth out and wipe yourself down again. I have a little cloth bucket that I use to carry water so that you can rinse the cloth out without getting soap in the lake. We wash away from the lakes and streams so that we keep those trout happy. Oh, and make certain that you check for blisters or chafing and let me know if you have problems. You've already seen my little first aid kit, and we can fix you up."

Kim hadn't washed since yesterday, sweated a lot more today, and had to talk herself into another cold bath. She walked away from camp and found a slightly secluded spot and washed as best she could. The water was cold and exhilarating – after she got used to it. Kim discovered that she enjoyed it more than she expected, except for exposing her skin to the mosquitoes. Insects hadn't been much of a problem before, but they were quite a nuisance near the lake.

While Kim was off for her adventure in cold bathing, Fred sent a message home.

To Fred: *We're good on this end. Hope that you had a good day. It's hot & muggy here; I'd rather be with you in the mtns! XOXO A*

To Asta: *37.45974; -118.85943; Long day here. Up early, many miles. Sort of on schedule. Fresh trout for supper! Luv 2 u all!*

After washing and returning to camp, Kim smiled, refreshed, and gave Fred the soap, cloth, and bucket.

"One more thing about being out here," he started and looked up and all around. "You'll find that backpackers tend to have much less regard for dignity and privacy – their own and others. I'll try my best to protect your privacy, but don't be surprised if others don't feel the same way." He gave her a wink and walked away.

Kim sat there, smiling to herself. *I got really lucky today.*

After Fred washed, he sat near the lake with Kim, swatting mosquitoes and taking in the peace and quiet before returning to camp. "So, Kim, I have more good news, and I have more bad news," he said.

She sat there looking at him, forehead knitted, looking concerned. "OK, whatever it is, we've dealt with a lot today; I guess that we'll deal with whatever else life throws at us. What's up?"

Fred sat there for a moment, very serious in the waning light. Venus was just starting to glimmer, and it would be dark soon. After letting the gravity of the moment set in sufficiently, he said, "Well, you didn't pack very well, and we only have one sleeping pad, quilt, and one tiny tent. We need to make some decisions about which rock you'll be sleeping on tonight."

Kim sat there, confused, slightly stunned, not knowing what to say. That's when Fred started laughing so hard at how seriously she was taking the news! He was rolling on his side, laughing hysterically, and she finally had to chuckle at herself.

"You know, what I said before is true – you really are a jerk!" Now she was laughing hard, too!

After they settled down, Fred said, "In all seriousness, we're going to have to be snuggle buddies if we're going to get through the night. I've carried an emergency space blanket in the past, mostly when I'm packing with my family, or had extra-large plastic bags that I can use for protection. But, when it's just me out here, I cut out some of these things. You'll need to put on a couple of layers of clothes, and I'm going to do the same. I have a stocking cap that you can wear to keep your head warm. My puffy coat has a hood, so I'll use that to keep my head warm. I have a couple of pairs of gloves, so you take one pair. I'll use my backpack and your knapsack as a sleeping pad, and you can take the inflatable sleeping pad. I'm hoping that we can snuggle and spoon enough to keep warm. The quilt might slip off one of us from time to time, so we'll just have to put modesty aside and make the most of it."

Kim had a wry smile on her face now, after having her leg pulled. "I sort of figured that that's how the sleeping arrangements would be tonight, but I was hoping that you'd pull something more luxurious out of your pack. Oh well!"

"Well," Fred continued, "there was a method to my madness because that's why I wanted you to wash up so that it might be more pleasant for my nose."

"Yes, you really are a jerk! How does your wife put up with you?" Kim was beside herself, laughing at Fred!

"She doesn't have much choice anymore. We've been married for too long. She cut the tags off a long time ago."

They sat there for a while longer, taking in the views, the sunset and thinking about all they'd been through over this very long day. They talked about Kim's escape and watched to the south for signs of anyone following them. Fortunately, they had a pretty good idea that they were alone here at Laurel Lake.

A bit later, Fred set about doing his best to make a comfortable bed for himself with the two packs and spare clothes. His sleeping arrangement would likely keep him reasonably warm, but he didn't know how well he would sleep; he figured his back and hips would be hurting in the morning. If it was like a typical night of sleeping while backpacking, he'd be out like a light.

Kim stayed outside the tent and enjoyed the evening's light show as the western wall of their natural amphitheater turned from yellow to pink as the sky darkened and stars appeared. She was enjoying the moment and could feel sleep calling despite her nap.

Eventually, Fred called her into the tent. It was a tight fit. They would both be pushing against the walls. Fred said, "At home, I sleep on the right side, and my wife is on the left, so that's the way it'll be tonight."

Kim just said, "Yes, sir!" and they both smiled in the inky darkness.

"In all seriousness," Fred said, "if you get cold or something else comes up for you, please, please wake me up if you need, and we'll see what we can work out. I hope that we'll both be able to keep our feet in the quilt to keep them warm, but our upper bodies will be cool, and that's why we'll need to snuggle and spoon."

Kim understood and took her place on the left side, on the sleeping pad. It was a tight fit, but they'd make it work. They didn't have much choice. It had been a long time since she'd slept with anyone else, so it was going to take a little getting used to for her. She stuffed some of her clothing into the tent bag to make a small pillow and laid on her side. Fred snuggled up against her, his arm over her waist. *Yes, this is*

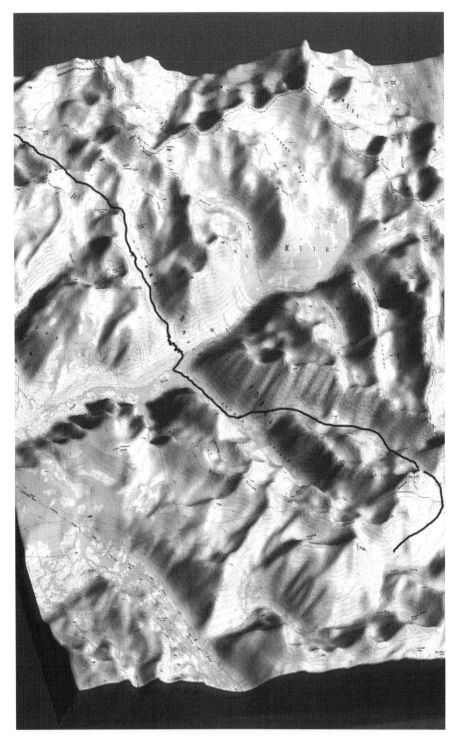

going to be an intimate and awkward night for me, she thought.

They laid there, spooning and warm. Kim's mind was racing over all the changes that she'd experienced over the past week or so, particularly today. For all that she'd been through lately, she had a smile on her face and warmth in her soul. Kim laid there, taking it all in and appreciating the good luck that had befallen her today.

In a slight whisper, she said, "Fred, I want to tell you again how much I appreciate you taking care of me and rescuing me. I don't know how I'll ever repay your kindness."

Fred's answer came in the form of a twitch and then a snore – he was gone and hadn't heard a thing she'd said. Kim just smiled again at her good luck, squeezed his hand for a moment, and closed her eyes. Her last thought before falling asleep was, *Obviously, he's tremendously worked up about sleeping with a strange woman.*

Alpha put in another call to Omega on the sat phone.

"Sir, no signs of Dr. Johnson on the east side. The driver received a call from Beta and the colleague who picked him up, and he didn't see her on the return route on the west side. Nobody that either of us spoke to mentioned seeing a woman of her description."

There was silence on the other end of the phone and then a sigh. "What else have you considered while you were hiking today?"

"Well, I think that we should set up a network of people to watch the major trailheads on either side of the Sierras. I'm going to start looking at maps now that I'm getting reception from the Owens Valley to see what that's going to take. Beta will coordinate the west side of the Sierras, and I'll coordinate the east side. We have contacts that we can call for a situation like this, so I think that we'll be OK. Everyone should have cellphone reception, and we'll distribute a photograph and description as soon as we get additional people in position. Beta and I will stay at these two trailheads for the time being because we think that's where she's most likely to show up in the next day or so. The additional people we'll post north and south of here. Most of the major trailheads are to the north of here, so that will be another emphasis.

That's about all that I can think of for now. What do you think?"

"Alpha, that's your field of expertise; I'll leave it to you, but I don't have anything further to add. I have people on this end who are aware of our problem and seeing if they can offer suggestions. We're monitoring communication lines to see if Dr. Johnson somehow makes a call or signals for help. So far, it seems like she's keeping her head down in the mountains, maybe she's lost, so she's not causing any additional problems on our end. But we want to find her and keep her alive so that she can undo the damage that she's causing us. Anything else?"

"No, sir. I'll get on it and contact you again tomorrow."

**Chapter 24**

Kim and Fred awoke early the next morning. The first glow of golden morning peered over the peaks to the east, lighting the tent ever so little. Neither was in a particularly jovial mood. Last night had been less-than-comfortable for them. They had both tossed and turned, trying to keep the parts of themselves that weren't under the quilt warm. Fred was an extra order of magnitude stiff this morning since his cobbled-together sleeping pad wasn't very soft or insulated. His left hip had laid on a buckle or something for too long that left him with a particularly tender spot, sort of like a hip pointer. His hips and back were as sore as they'd ever felt in the morning on a backpacking trip. There wasn't enough room to really stretch in the tiny tent with the both of them in there. Finally, figuring that Kim was awake, he whispered a quiet *excuse me* and crawled over Kim as gently as possible while trying to contain his groans of pain.

Quietly, as hunkered down in the quilt as she could get, Kim said, "So that's it, huh? Sort of a dine and dash thing with you? No *good morning?* No, *how are you this beautiful morning?*"

Fred sat in the tent's vestibule and pulled on his cold, stiff boots; this was one of his least favorite things to do in the morning. He turned in the barely lit tent, looked at her with a scowl, and turned it into a fake smile. "Better now?"

"Yes, much better, sunshine. Go pee or whatever you need to do while I stay warm. Also, I'll take my coffee with one teaspoon of sugar and cream."

Fred rolled out of the tent onto his hands and knees, gathered himself and slowly unfolded to nearly his full height. He grabbed his lower back after a sharp spasm, then slightly bent over and slowly stretched out. When his back was ready, Fred reached his arms up and stood on his tiptoes. He stood there for a moment, seeing how his body might work, collected his thoughts, oriented himself to the world that he'd left last night. He lightly rubbed his left hip to try to reduce the pain.

"Sorry, ma'am, but there's no coffee at this café, just hot tea. I'll start it when I get back." He clomped off to water a tree.

When he returned, he heard mumbling from the tent. "What do you mean no coffee? I'm leaving a poor review for the service and quality of this bed and breakfast. The view is great, but you should turn the heat up a bit higher."

Fred just shook his head and smiled. "I come out here to be alone and have some quality time in the wilderness, and I end up picking up a snarky lady who doesn't appreciate how lucky she is." Now, they both smiled.

In a few minutes, the water was boiling and tea steeping. Fred gathered fruit, cheese, nuts, and granola from the bear canister for breakfast.

"Fred's mountain bed & breakfast is now serving. However, we don't serve breakfast in bed here, so you'll have to wiggle out of your cocoon. Better yet, bring the quilt with you to keep warm."

Kim peered a sleepy eye out the tent, let her head flop onto her makeshift pillow, groaned, and sat up.

"You're looking mighty fine this morning, my dear," Fred offered in the pale, pre-dawn light. "Those bags under your eyes are very becoming of you."

Kim sneered as she pulled on Fred's camp shoes. She had nearly as much difficulty as Fred in raising her body to vertical. A few of her vertebrae audibly popped when she stretched, and Kim had a satisfied grin on her face. With the quilt over her shoulders, she made her way to breakfast. She couldn't quite bring herself to sit on a cold rock, so she stood next to Fred as they passed the hot cup of tea back and forth.

Fred looked at Kim, sized her up, and then proceeded to goad her some more. "For someone who I figure is ten, fifteen years younger than me, you're acting more my age this morning. In fact, I'm not even acting my age this morning, I'm so tired and sore. I hope that I'll sleep better tonight."

"Well, that was one of the poorer night's sleeps of my life, too," she started. "I don't know that I've ever slept with someone who snores as much as you do! Remind me not to marry someone who snores."

"Maybe we should trade sleeping pads tonight, and maybe I wouldn't snore as much then," Fred suggested. "Pine needles and duff can make a halfway decent cushion, but there's not a whole lot of that at this altitude, above tree line."

Kim stood there, warming her hands on the teacup, considering her options.

Fred continued, "You have a bit more padding than me so that it might be more comfortable for you." He had his head down, plucking a feather from his puffy jacket, and tried not to laugh at her.

Kim decided that it would be better to take a moment for some silence rather than the bait. She wasn't yet awake enough to successfully engage in this kind of banter. She turned to face the eastern horizon that was more than a thousand feet above. There was just a sliver of a new moon showing above the peaks and still some stars out as the sky lightened. To the west, she could see more stars.

"What time is it?" she asked.

Fred checked his phone. "It's about 5:30. If we were on flat land, the sun would be up in about ten minutes, but it's hidden behind the mountains for another hour or so. One of the best ways to get warm in the morning is to get packing. Fortunately, there's not much for the two of us to pack."

Kim enjoyed the morning's changing light and the reflection off the lake. Trout would rise to pick off insects at the surface every so often, leaving expanding rings. *Peaceful but cold.* Stomping her feet helped wake her body, but the sound startled something in the trees, causing Kim to jump and look. Fred sat and watched Kim as her eyes grew wide, then turned to watch a deer scamper away, and then he turned back to smile at her. Kim gave a bit of a crooked grin, trying to signal that she wasn't so scared after all.

Again, facing the east, Kim continued to take in the grand morning. She loved how the world changed so much and looked so different depending upon the time of day. The sky was turning from pinks and oranges to light blue in the east, and the western face of the bowl was catching some colorful morning sun and making their world lighter. The tea and food warmed her, along with some gentle pacing to get her blood flowing.

She turned to face Fred. He looked up at her, waiting to hear what was on her mind. "If I wander into that little stand of trees over there, do you think any more wild animals are going to jump out and scare me?"

Fred smiled when he heard this; he replied, "I don't think so. Sasquatch is on summer vacation, so we don't have to worry about him."

Kim shot him a look of concern and then saw that he was trying to hide a smile. "OK, smart-aleck, I'm going to take care of my feminine needs. If you'll kindly share some of your toilet paper with me, I'll be on my way."

Fred sat there, thought about it for a moment, furrowed his brow a bit, and said, "Well, that's going to be a bit of a problem. I don't carry toilet paper with me when I'm in the backcountry."

Kim just looked at him, defiantly. "What do you mean you don't carry toilet paper?"

"Just what I said. I don't bring toilet paper. I have a little trowel that I use to dig a cathole, that's it."

"*ARE YOU KIDDING ME?!?*" Kim was practically screaming. The echoes reverberated off the mountains, coming back to taunt her again and again.

"You have no toilet paper?" she asked again in a more composed voice. "Even the kidnappers brought toilet paper! What kind of an uncivilized uncouth are you, anyway?"

Fred sat there, giving some attention to the cup of tea in his warm hands, not saying anything. Finally, he pontificated. "It's like this. I've seen too many little white toilet paper 'prayer flags' sticking out of the ground that backpackers leave in odd places, and they detract from my enjoyment of Nature. There's no real need for toilet paper out here because there are plenty of rocks, leaves, and pine cones to make do. My ancestors, and I'm guessing yours, too, didn't have toilet paper. They got by just fine on corn cobs and the like. I'm confident you'll survive, too."

Kim let out a huff and knew that there was no point in discussing this any further. If there was no toilet paper, then there was no toilet paper. "Fine, then. Where's your trowel so that I can be a *proper* Nature girl?

Fred looked up and over to the tent and pointed to his backpack. "It's stuck in the outer pocket, there on top, so that it's ready for use at any time." He quickly pulled the mug up to his mouth to not reveal the big grin on his face.

"I want you to remember, dear woman, that which doesn't kill you, makes you stronger. Except for bears – they'll kill you." Fred was trying so hard to keep from laughing at her.

Kim marched over to the backpack, slung the quilt over the tent, plucked the trowel from its pocket, and then briskly walked off into the dark woods. Fred heartily enjoyed his quiet time while Kim was away.

Several minutes later, Kim returned to camp, straightening her pants, jacket, and hair. Looking at her, Fred called out, "Wait a minute! Did you flush?"

Kim stopped, turned around, and caught herself in the act. Taking a deep breath, she slowly turned and stomped back to camp. "Yes," she said, "it is now confirmed that you are a BIG JERK! This is the worst first date EVER!!!"

Fred didn't know what that meant, but he was howling! He nearly fell off his rock, he was laughing so much, and then Kim joined in. "One of the best things about taking a noob camping is all of the fun that you can have with them," he said, tears welling in his eyes. Kim just shook her head, knowing that she was the butt of his jokes.

When the frivolity died down, they set about cleaning and finishing packing. Kim took the initiative, stuffed the quilt into its sack, and deflated and packed the sleeping pad. While she was doing this, Fred took down the tent, shook it out, and packed it away. The stove was next to be packed, followed by filling their water bottles.

Fred checked in with Kim about her feet and whether she had any blisters. "I'm pretty good," she answered, "but my heels felt tender yesterday."

"Well, let's put some tape over your heels and see if we can avoid blisters. Today's distance will likely be shorter than yesterday, but it will still be a long day."

After taping Kim's heels and finishing packing, Fred called Kim over to sit on the rock with him. He had some papers in his hands. "When I was planning this trip over the winter, I printed these maps to bring with me just in case my phone dies. I want to use them to show you what I'm thinking.

"First, this is Lake Italy. That's where we camped the night before last, and this spot on the map is about where we met nearly twenty-four hours ago. We went up and over Gabbot Pass, ate lunch here at Lower Mills Creek Lake, rested at Mono Creek, and we spent last night here at Laurel Lake." He gave her a moment to take this all in. She shook her head yes, silently urging him to continue.

"If we had gone east or west from Lake Italy when we first met, then there was a good chance that your buddies could have caught up to us, or other backpackers would have seen us, and they could have been alerted that you were ahead of them." Kim grimaced at this comment about her 'buddies' but let it go.

"At the time, I thought that we were better off continuing northward because it seemed like it was the least likely direction for you to go if you were alone. Since there are two of them and they had three or more directions to choose from, it seemed like the best choice, and so far, it seems to have worked out.

"Also, when we were at Mono Creek for our rest break, we were at another decision point. I was less conscious of the choice then, but looking at this map now, it was the best choice. If we had gone downstream and west, we would have been back to civilization at Vermilion Valley Resort, but someone could have easily been waiting for you. We don't know if someone would be there, but so far, you're still safe. Similarly, we could have gone upstream and eastward and exited at Rock Creek Lake, but it's another obvious point for you to get out. If I am them and they have as many resources available to them as you suggest, then your best bet for safely getting out of this situation is to keep your head down and keep them guessing for as long as reasonable.

"While I was making supper last night, I figured one of two bad things could have happened to us in the past day. One, they could have spotted us while we were hiking and followed us. Or, two, they could have spotted us and then sent out an aircraft to check up on us. As far as I know, neither of those things has happened – *yet* – but I'm still crossing my fingers."

Continuing, Fred said, "When I look at this as a game – which it's not – but if it was, then I want to consider our strengths and weaknesses and theirs. Your captors seem to have lots of resources available and seem to be quite able to track you down. We have no idea how many people they have out here looking for you now, right? There could be someone waiting and watching at all these exit points, as far as I know. If they have weapons and vehicles, we wouldn't have many options. Our strength, I hope, is that we know this wilderness better than them and can navigate it more easily."

Kim shook her head in agreement with Fred and understood his logic. "Go on," she said, "I like what I hear from you, valiant knight."

Fred blushed a bit and continued. "So, here's what I'm proposing – well, very strongly suggesting. My planned route was to continue northward from here and hike to Reds Meadow, here," pointing at a different map section that he laid above the other map that they'd been considering. "At Reds, I'm supposed to pick up a resupply bucket, but that's not likely going to happen now, at least not as easily. I believe that we should continue on about the same route but somehow exit to the town of Mammoth Lakes, here on the east side of the Sierras, near Reds Meadow. There are many different trailheads in that area, and it would be challenging for your adversaries to cover all those points. Everything funnels into Mammoth Lakes, but if we can hitch a ride or something rather than walk into town, then we can very likely get to the police or sheriff without being seen. We're about two easy days from Mammoth. How does that sound to you?"

Fred sat up and gave Kim some space to consider his proposal. She was running her fingers over the maps from this point to that, thinking about what he had suggested. After a moment, she, too, sat up and smiled.

"Ya know, Fred, as a computer scientist, I like your logical thinking. If I didn't have you here or your food, and I had some sense of direction, yes, I may have wandered back to civilization by the easiest path. I would have gone downhill, followed a stream downward, once I felt that I had left Alpha and Beta behind. But I like how you're looking at this problem, looking at it from all sides and considering our – er, your – strengths. I also think that the longer that we're out here, then the more frantic they get. We might even hear about them looking for me from some other backpacker. I doubt that they'd stop looking for me, but it seems like the advantages build in our favor the longer we're out here."

"Yeah, I think that you're right that the advantages grow for us over time," Fred responded. "However, our food supply is the limiting factor, so we can't stay out too long. By my reckoning, we had about two days of food yesterday, and we'll be down to one day of food tonight or tomorrow morning. The trout helped – a lot.

"What I think that we should do is to continue north. The first thing that we need to do is tackle this pass in front of us, especially before it gets too warm. In an hour or so, we'll be up there," he said, pointing up and to the north to Bighorn Pass. "Less than an hour later, there's a second pass, but we won't have to climb as much. After that, hiking should be easy for several hours. We'll then descend into Tully Hole – the mosquitoes are typically bad there! – and then an hour-long, hot climb. Just after we finish that climb, we'll stop for the night at Virginia Lake – it's gorgeous! I'm hoping that I can catch some more trout there, too.

"The last thing that I want to tell you is that once we reach Tully Hole this afternoon, we'll be back on the John Muir Trail. We'll see other backpackers, unlike the past day and next few hours. When we run into people, we should act like a couple, husband and wife, girlfriend/ boyfriend, so that people aren't suspicious. Again, if I'm your captors, I might put the word out on the trail that there's a lost woman and ask finders to call a particular number. Does that make sense? Any suggestions?"

Kim sat back and digested everything that she had recently heard. "I think you're right," she finally said. "Our main advantage out here is *you*. You know this territory better, and the plan that you're suggesting makes a lot of sense. Alpha, Beta and whomever else might have the resources to search for us, but they haven't studied this area like you. From everything that I know and what you've told me, my best chance is to try to slip through to safety at Mammoth Lakes. I don't know how that will happen, but we still have a day or two to think about it. Besides, it doesn't sound like we'll starve for another few days. Let's get going!"

With that, Kim gave Fred a friendly nudge with her shoulder. She stopped and thought about it for a second. Then, she took him by the shoulders, gave him a big hug, and didn't let go quickly. "I tried to tell you last night about how thankful I am for meeting you, but you were already snoring, so I'm saying it again."

Fred turned away so that Kim couldn't see him blushing.

Chapter 25

After Kim escaped, Omega's staff worked overtime to find clues through intercepted phone calls, text messages, emails, and satellite text messages. Omega had people available worldwide, in various specialties, and he could readily find additional help if needed. His group's resources and skills were able to pry into almost any communications systems that they wanted. That was one of the benefits of working on the dark side of the internet. Omega's people still had the problem of sifting through millions of messages, trying to find the needle in the haystack.

Alpha and Beta called their mercenary friends and contracted with them to get to the Sierras and watch for Kim at various trailheads and even put some people out on the trails. They had pretty much unlimited resources available to them, courtesy of Omega and company.

A mercenary contact picked up Beta at the Bear Creek Trailhead and brought him a sat phone to talk with Alpha and be ready for whatever might come. Beta had his contact drop him off near Vermilion Valley Ranch, appearing to arrive as if he was any other backpacker who sauntered in off the trail. He spent his time sitting around the fire pit or on the porch, acting like he was reading a book or just relaxing, but intently listening in on conversations, hoping to overhear stories of a stray hiker or backpacker.

Alpha spent a night at the Pine Creek Trailhead with the slim hope that Kim would fall into his lap. The next day he was in Bishop, coordinating everyone as best he could, positioning people at trailheads, and ensuring that everyone had whatever communications and other gear they needed. It was frustrating but necessary work if Alpha hoped to recapture Kim. His reputation was on the line; he also didn't know what Omega might have in store for him if he failed.

As for Omega, he had been in plenty of difficult situations before. One of the reasons that he was good at his job was because he was usually relatively calm. He had learned that this was the best way to manage the nearly constant chaos around him. He had learned that chaos could be his companion and knew how to handle it for his benefit. In many situations, chaos created a cover. In this situation, there wasn't so much chaos as there was an absence of it. No word on Dr. Johnson or her whereabouts, so Omega was more stressed than usual. He wasn't as familiar with the relative quiet that this situation brought him.

Omega was a good manager and delegated tasks well but didn't tell staff any more than they needed to get their work done. He typically took on coordinating everything and compiling the information to achieve his goals. The less that staff knew, the less they could deduce on their own, share with others or otherwise undermine him. He also was aware that with everything funneling upward to him with little context, it also created blind spots and weaknesses for his staff, but that was a risk he usually felt he could take. This time, this situation, he thought it better to let staff know that they were looking for a lost woman in the Sierras, who had been backpacking, where she had become lost and a few other details. He didn't let anyone know that she had become lost because she was escaping from his kidnappers. Searching for a lost person wasn't one of his staffs' typical tasks, so he felt it was better to be slightly more open with the hope that it would lead to something. Most of his team found it an unusual information request based on previous experience with Omega. Still, they took it seriously, recognizing that a life was at risk.

Today, luck was with Omega, partly because he was more forthcoming about his information needs. He was extremely fortunate to work with some talented, skillful – and very well-paid – people. Selling one's soul doesn't come cheaply if you're the buyer, although not all of the staff knew how much of themselves they were selling. Several people working for Omega were adept at monitoring various, seemingly secure, communications channels and searching for rare breadcrumbs that might lead them to, in this case, a lost backpacker. One of Omega's protégé's also was more familiar with monitoring environmental information channels to help with various projects. Awareness of local weather conditions had allowed Omega to hide earlier projects behind Nature's chaos or use storms to enable his team to slip in and out of situations with less likelihood of being detected.

In this case, unbeknownst to him, he had staff available who were also outdoors people and had a sense of how hikers, skiers, and backpackers think and behave. They could better focus their searches than if they had not been familiar with these pursuits that Omega didn't understand as well. Omega was good at what he did – relieving businesses and governments of their assets – but being an outdoorsman was not one of his strengths.

The supervisor in charge of the communications specialists contacted Omega to let him know that one of his staffers might be onto something. Other staffers had nicknamed this analyst *Mal'chik Prirody* because of his outdoor interests and adventures. Omega hastily arranged a video conference with the supervisor and Prirody, hoping that there might be a helpful lead. The supervisor allowed Prirody the rare opportunity to directly address Omega and share his findings.

Prirody realized how the basic information he'd received might help him figure out what had become of the lost backpacker. The woman had gone missing from a camp just downstream from Lake Italy in the Sierra Nevada Mountains after a bear encounter while accompanied by a couple of other backpackers. A third person had camped nearby the night before and offered assistance just after the bear was in their camp. During earlier operations, Prirody had used satellite photos to help his supervisor create visual layouts for a few projects, so he was aware of the capabilities and maintained accounts with several different remote sensing services. He had access to satellite images of reasonably decent quality on a nearly daily basis for just about anywhere in the world. Knowing the day that the backpacker had gone missing and the location, he found a couple of overhead images of the Lake Italy area. He could make out the Lake Italy Trail in the corner of one morning image but nothing else of interest. A late afternoon image showed three small rectangles that hadn't been there in the morning – a greenish object surrounded by rocks near the mouth of the lake and two bluish objects just downstream. *Tents.* He couldn't see any other distinguishing features in the images, but it was something. Prirody assumed that the blue tents belonged to the people he was following, including the missing backpacker, and the green tent was for the backpacker who tried to help.

Prirody asked for help from his coworkers who had been gathering satellite text messages, phone calls, text messages, and email traffic. He asked: *had they found any messages from the vicinity of Lake Italy the day that the backpacker disappeared or the day before?* After checking the geo coordinates of the pilfered satellite text messages from those couple of days in the Sierras, they found one message that originated from there and several other messages within a few kilometers. *I might be on to something!* he thought. He asked for these messages, their geo coordinates, and unique identifiers. The message from near Lake Italy had essentially the same geo coordinate as the green tent. Maybe it was just a coincidence, and maybe not.

For his next data request, Prirody asked for all the messages sent by a single user based on their meta data, the one who might be using the green tent. He shortly received a list of dozens of messages from that user – from remote mountainous and desert locations in various parts of the United States over the past few years. Messages that said *I miss you, wish you were here, I'm tired today, the scenery is spectacular, it's cold and rainy,* and so on. Prirody was most interested in the most recent messages and their geo coordinates. He loaded these message coordinates into his GIS system and pinpointed the locations on a map of the Sierras. The points formed sort of a zigzag line as he expected, but they did show someone traveling south to north through the spine of the Sierras who messaged on a reasonably regular basis – just about every evening.

Prirody returned to the satellite imagery and pulled photos from the Sierras over the same date range as the text messages he tracked. He couldn't find decent images for every day he wanted, but he could gather good pictures for most days. The geo coordinates of the satellite text messages aligned well with a green rectangle that appeared in a couple of the photos. There were ten text messages that he could track on his GIS system, and two of the satellite images showed a rectangular greenish object at practically the same location. The most recent text message came from several kilometers north of Lake Italy but didn't mention anything about finding a backpacker, just that the backpacker had gone many miles that day and eaten trout for supper.

Lastly, Prirody asked his coworkers to create a file of all satellite text messages for two hundred kilometers north and south of Lake Italy over the past couple of weeks. He loaded the geo coordinates of these hundreds of messages into his GIS. There was a strong pattern of messages coming from a main line through the Sierras, with a smattering of points outside of this corridor, mostly leading to and from the main trail. The main line followed a path labeled *"John Muir Trail/ Pacific Crest Trail"* on his maps. The messages from the green tent texter were clearly separated from most of the other message locations. In fact, there were only a few other messages from similar vicinities as the green tent texter over the whole fortnight, and they were separated by kilometers and days from the green tent's location when the messages of interest were sent.

Prirody gathered, summarized, and presented his findings to his supervisor, along with his modest conclusions – if no one had found the backpacker so far and reported about her, then there was a reasonable chance she had been found by and joined the green tent texter. Another major option was that she was still lost. It wasn't much to go on, but it was something, Prirody told him. It was enough in the supervisor's opinion to contact Omega.

It was an odd video call for Prirody. He had never spoken with Omega before, barely knew who he was except that he was the group's leader, and he found it disconcerting to address a blank screen. After listening to Prirody's analysis and viewing his GIS images, Omega asked a few questions and then one particular question. Prirody responded that he felt that the green tent texter was heading north toward a resort area called Mammoth Lakes and would be there in a day or two. Omega sincerely thanked him for his efforts, offered thanks for the whole of the supervisor's team efforts, and concluded the video call.

Breathing a small, hesitant sigh of hope, Omega forwarded Prirody's GIS image files to Alpha and then called him.

"Alpha here. What's up, sir?"

"We have a lead. I just forwarded the information to you. The bottom line is that an analyst here has co-located satellite text messages from an individual backpacking in the Sierras with satellite photos of the area. He thinks it's the same person who camped near you the night before Dr. Johnson escaped. And, that person is likely headed north to Mammoth Lakes."

"Well, OK, that's new information, but I don't see how it's helpful, sir. We haven't had any luck finding her on the trails or trailheads, nor does it seem that anyone has heard anything about her."

"Alpha, here's the critical point. I only revealed to our analysts that we're looking for a lost backpacker who went missing near Lake Italy. I did not tell anyone else that she wasn't wearing shoes and that her ankles were bound when she escaped."

"Wait, sir, so let me work through this new information. We've been looking at the situation like this. If Dr. Johnson went east or west on the Lake Italy Trail, we likely would have run into her because she couldn't move too fast, at least initially. But she would have figured that those were the most obvious routes for her to escape and the easiest for us to find her. We've been guessing that Dr. Johnson also figured that we might search for her on the Lake Italy Trail but eventually give up and head down to get more help. No matter which way she went, we've been assuming that she would stop and cut through the zip ties with rocks or something, which would take some time, and then she'd be moving faster after that, but still not wearing shoes. If anyone found her, the lack of shoes would be apparent, and people would be talking about that detail, as well as her being a kidnapping victim.

"If Dr. Johnson took off to the south, then she needed to climb a rise that wouldn't get her anywhere, and she would have to come down and still work her way east or west to get to help. We should have seen her at the trailheads, or someone should have found her on the trails. The news of her being found should have spread – if she has been found or gotten back to civilization.

"Now, that other backpacker. We didn't talk much with him because we didn't want to let on to anything. But we watched him cross the stream and take off along the north side of Lake Italy, heading to who knows where, but he had to know where he was going. We thought there was a slight possibility that Dr. Johnson could have crossed the stream to escape, so we crossed the creek and looked for wet footprints after he left, but we only saw his prints. If she did cross the stream, we were there too long after she left – any signs of her wet footprints dried up in the morning sun.

"Since there were only the two of us, we had to make a choice and assumed that even though it was the most obvious way for her to take off staying on the Lake Italy Trail was the only way that she knew that she'd have a decent chance of being found by someone else or getting to a trailhead for help. She had no experience in the mountains, at least that's what she told us. When we checked the area maps, we figured that if she took off across the stream and away from our camp, she was taking a helluva risk because she didn't know what she was getting into, sort of similar to heading up the mountain to the south. No matter which direction she went after escaping, if we didn't find her on the trail, then we figured that she'd wait until we left and then come on down to one of the trailheads on the east or west side a day or two later.

"Damn! What I hear makes sense. I mean, Dr. Johnson may still be out there, waiting to come down the trail we were on, one direction or the other, but she doesn't know the area, doesn't have maps, and she'd have to be cold and hungry. If that backpacker ran into her, then she'd have a lot more options. We thought that was a possibility, but the least likely. We didn't follow him because it would be obvious that we were following him, and we told him that we were hiking out to the east. We also thought about sending someone back into the mountains to try to follow that backpacker, but we had no idea where he was heading, so we felt that it wasn't likely that we'd find him and doubtful that it would get us anywhere. If your people can track him, then that's a big help. But it would explain why we haven't heard anything about anyone finding a lost backpacker. *Shit, shit, shit!*"

Omega was silent as Alpha spoke, letting him work through it all. Omega had come to a similar conclusion.

"OK, sir, I'm going to keep thinking about this new intel and check what you sent to me. But I figure that I'm headed to Mammoth Lakes to set up a post and focus our people and efforts there. We'll keep some of our people to the south of there, at the trailheads and the like, just in case. This new information makes a lot of sense."

"Thank you, Alpha. Your understanding of the information is similar to mine, which is why I shared it with you so quickly. Keep me informed of your progress. Also, listen: from what I can gather, you two made the same decisions that I would have made with the available information. Don't kick yourself over this news; just focus on finding her."

That was the end of the conversation.

Alpha's mind was racing again, but he felt better and called Beta to share the intel. He packed and headed to Mammoth Lakes with a clearer mission, waiting to be joined by Beta and others.

**Chapter 26**

Even though they had awoken early, Kim and Fred took their time getting out of camp. There was no hurry today as they had put a fair amount of distance between themselves and Kim's captors yesterday, they hoped. The morning sun was already well above the eastern ridge, and they had shed clothes before starting. Within a few minutes after leaving camp, they scrambled up the south side of Bighorn Pass through loose rocks that made footing difficult.

"Yep," Fred said, "just another stroll in the park," while catching his breath.

The only response Fred received was a grunt from Kim. They were both busy watching their steps, checking for shifty talus, sliding downhill a bit, but slowly gaining on the obstacle. It may have been morning and cool, but they had already broken a good sweat. A few minutes later, they were on top of the pass and enjoyed beautiful views to the east and west.

After catching her breath, Kim started to leave. Fred gave a holler and called her back.

"We don't have any photos of the two of us enjoying ourselves out here! Let's take a selfie!" Fred exclaimed.

Kim stopped, turned around, grinned, and came back to capture a moment in time, a moment of freedom and accomplishment.

"I'll proudly display this on my wall at home, along with all of my other backcountry photos with my family," Fred announced. "It'll be a conversation starter, for sure!"

"Just make certain to send me the file when we finish, so I can better share with my parents the story of my knight in stinking armor." They both laughed at her description of Fred.

The traverse on the north side of the pass was much more comfortable than the climb from Laurel Lake. They stayed above Ross Finch Lake and kept on a reasonably level route to the next pass. Hiking along the western flank of the mountainside was tough on their ankles, but it was better to take this route than all the way down to the lake and back up. It wasn't long before they were on the next pass.

Kim crested first and slowed but didn't stop since they hadn't exerted themselves as much as going over the last pass. With no warning, Fred gave out a big yell of *YIPPEE!* that startled Kim.

"What was that for?" she asked.

"This is Shout of Relief Pass, and I'm shouting my relief!" he said with a big grin.

"Oh, great. More dad jokes. Just what we need up here."

From far away came another yell. Someone else was out here enjoying the moment, too, responding to Fred.

"See, someone out there likes me," he said with a big grin.

"Yeah, or else we're being tracked, and you just gave away our location," Kim dryly responded.

"Oooh! I hadn't thought about that, but I'm not too worried. We're so remote now that they'd have to be really desperate to be coming after you."

Kim shot him a slight glare. "I don't think that was a compliment, so I'm just going to let it go."

Fred's response was just a grin.

The next couple of hours were pleasant and downhill. The walking was easy. After a tough first half of the morning, it was nice to relax and sort of coast. There was a pleasant breeze at their back, a few clouds in the sky – it was a great day to be out here and soaking everything in. Everything was before them, no surprises in the landscape, just a wide-open vista. Coming off Shout of Relief pass, they stayed to the east of Tully Lake and picked up the McGee Pass Trail. It was nice to be on a path and not bushwhacking so much. Beyond Horse Heaven, but before they made it to Tully Hole, Fred suggested that they stop for lunch. He hoped that there would be fewer mosquitoes here above Fish Creek than down near Tully Hole.

They found a shady spot well off the trail where no one could see them, and if there were any mosquitoes here, the wind helped to keep them at bay. Kim felt much better than a day ago as she put distance between herself and her demons. They ate a small but decent lunch, conserving their limited food. Pointing to the northwest, across the valley, and through the trees, Fred said, "See those zig-zags going upward there? That's our next obstacle and probably our last obstacle for the day. It'll take us an hour to an hour and a half to get up there from here, and then not too far beyond that is Lake Virginia. It has a beautiful view and is very popular. Unless you want to keep on going, we'll camp there for the night. It'll be an early stop for us, but it will give me a chance, hopefully, to catch more trout for supper."

"How much farther is it to Mammoth Lakes?" Kim asked.

"Well, like I said this morning, it's another good day or so to get to Mammoth beyond Lake Virginia. I'm trying to balance how you're feeling and the possibility of you developing a few blisters against our food supply. We're tight on food, but not too tight. You're not complaining about blisters, right?"

Kim shook her head no and continued to listen.

"When we get to Lake Virginia, let's find a secluded, shady spot. I'm expecting that we'll start seeing backpackers, and I don't want them to notice you if your bad guys have put the word out that you're missing. I mean, if there's a reward for your capture, I want to claim it for myself!" With this comment, Fred chuckled. Kim picked up a pine cone and tossed it hard at him, catching him in his calf.

After settling himself, Fred continued. "I want to tell you that I still don't have a great plan on how to get you safely into Mammoth. I'm guessing that our best bet will be to try to get into town while it's dark, but I don't know. At night, we're less likely to be able to hitch a ride into town, but it's not so far that we couldn't walk. If we come down in daylight, we have no idea who might be watching. There's a tall ridge between our route and Mammoth. We'll have to hike over it somewhere, I forget where, and that ridge tends to block cellphone signals if I remember right. We should be able to call the police or sheriff when we crest the ridge."

Kim thought about this for a moment. "You know, I'm a little leery of making a cell phone call. Omega and his group could very easily intercept it with the right equipment. Like you said this morning, there are several routes into town, and it would be easy to set up a device to monitor calls, track us, and maybe get to us before the authorities. We need to think about this more, and we have the time. If you used your phone to make a call, for example, I'm guessing that it would be safer to leave your cell phone off afterward so nobody can track us. There are lots of variables and unknowns here, at least from my perspective."

Fred considered what she had said and nodded his agreement. "Backpackers have a value system that's called 'leave no trace,' and that's especially true with your situation. We don't need to give anyone any hints that you're alive, healthy, and slowly moving back toward civilization someplace. We just need to lay low for the next twenty-four hours or so, not be obvious on the trail, and keep our heads down, especially you." He laid back and closed his eyes, thinking more about their situation and how to make it work in their favor.

Kim nudged his foot. "Hey, sleepyhead, should we get back to work?"

Fred blinked his eyes, trying to figure out where he was. "What do you mean, *sleepyhead?*"

"You fell asleep. You've been out for like an hour – I don't know how long. Since you didn't seem to be in a hurry today and since we slept so poorly last night, I let you sleep. I've been enjoying the shade, cool breezes, and trying to think more about getting back safely. I've been resting, too, but didn't fall asleep."

"Hmmm. It's time to get back on the trail. We have a couple of hours to go yet, maybe less, but it's going to be hot and tough going up the trail to Lake Virginia."

Fred stretched his tight muscles. His butt was sore now from sitting on the cool, hard ground, and the spot on his left hip was tight, and it took him some time to get back onto his feet and his pack on his back.

"Let's go, old man! We're burning daylight!"

Ten minutes later, they were in a swarm of mosquitoes in Tully Hole, the nastiest Fred encountered this trip. They got through the worst of it as quickly as they could and then started huffing uphill on the north side of Fish Creek. The sun was as intense and brutal as expected. The good news is that they had their backs to it some of the time. Compared to where they'd been hiking, it was also relatively humid here. They were bathing in sweat within a few minutes. They'd trudge a hundred yards or so, stop for a rest and a sip of water, swat a few lingering mosquitoes, and then start again. The higher they went, the more tired they were, but the mosquitoes were fewer and fewer. At one stop, Fred told Kim that on his first couple of days of his trip, he had climbed nearly five thousand feet on a trail sort of like this, and that was five times more than they'd be doing now.

"I'm impressed and exhausted for both of us," was Kim's comment, between snatches of breath. "I'm pretty pooped already, and I'm not carrying as much as you."

"The one advantage I may have is that I'm more acclimated than you. Even so, it'll be nice to get on top in another twenty minutes or so. We'll make it, I know we will, but it sometimes seems like quite a struggle to tackle these long, steep climbs, and this one's humid, too."

The grade eventually reduced, the breeze picked up, and the air was slightly cooler and drier. Kim and Fred made one last stop to survey where they had hiked today. Fred pointed out the knob where they had eaten lunch and then kept his hand rising until he pointed at Shout of Relief Pass.

"We're pretty awesome, aren't we?" Kim said with a big grin on her sweat-drenched face.

"Now, if I remember right, Lake Virginia is just over this rise, or maybe a bit further, but it's not too far from here." Fred's memory was pretty good because the lake was just a short walk away.

"Most of the foot traffic is on the north and east sides of the lake. I'm guessing that most people will be camping on the north side where it's open and the view there is great toward the west. I'd suggest we head off to the lake's west side and try to be a bit more secluded. I can fish from there, and we should be able to find a decent place to camp." Kim agreed with Fred's suggestions, and they rounded the north end of the lake a few minutes later.

"When my son and I came through here a couple of years ago, there was a big fire a few miles west of Reds Meadow. The smoke here really hampered the view. It's so much more impressive this year!"

On the west side of Lake Virginia, they found a quiet spot with some shade, dropped their packs, and flopped on some large, flat rocks for a few minutes, until their shirts were cool and dry, and they shivered just a bit.

"Can I put the tent up tonight?" Kim asked. "I want to learn more about these outdoor skills so that I can be just like my hero." She said this with a sweet, exaggerated smile and batted her eyelashes.

Fred just rolled his eyes at her and dug the ground cloth and tent out of his pack. "It looks like there are several good possibilities for places to put the tent. My suggestion is to locate the tent where you think that ground will drain well if it rains, and the rainwater won't flow into the tent. I also look for shade and a good view. But maybe you're a better exterior decorator than me, so have it."

Kim picked a good spot that had a bit of shade now and would be even more in the shade as the sun moved westward. She struggled a bit getting the tent laid out and the stakes set in the rocky soil, but she got it done.

"OK, now I need the sleeping pad and quilt."

Fred had already pulled them out of his pack, so he lazily pointed to the pad and quilt from his angle of repose. Kim walked over, picked them up, pulled the quilt out of its stuff sack, and threw the bag on Fred, who had his eyes closed. He barely moved in response.

Kim laid the quilt over the tent to let it air out and blew up the sleeping pad. She was light-headed by the time she finished and realized that she still had a way to go to become well acclimated.

"So, now what, my savior?" She enjoyed giving Fred a hard time and felt pretty good since today had been shorter, and they were stopping earlier.

"Well, if we're going to have trout with supper, I'd better pull out the fly rod and get to it. While it's still warm and sunny out, you might want to clean up and wash your clothes."

"Oooh, that's a good idea. I have salt stains on my shirt I was sweating so much today. I don't think that I've ever done that before," Kim said.

"Yeah, it's easy to do up here. You work hard, sweat hard, and the dry air sucks all of the moisture out of you and your wet clothes." Fred checked his shirt for stains, and there they were.

After putting his rod together, Fred walked down to the lake to see if he could get them some protein. He was back in camp a few minutes later.

"Hey, Kim! You know what? There's a nice shallow cove just down the bank here. The water might be ever so slightly warmer there, and the cove is slightly protected from views to the north. Here's something for you to consider. Since you said that you've never really been in the wilderness before, then I'm guessing you probably haven't been skinny dipping, either. You might want to wander down to that little cove, get in the water with your clothes on, rinse them out, take them off, and lay them on the shore to dry. No one can see you well from the north and west, and I'm going to head north from here where you'll have your privacy and where I can watch for visitors. It's up to you, but if you're going to be a real woodswoman, then there's another experience for you."

She looked at Fred, a bit puzzled at first, quizzical, and then started to grin. "I'll tell you what," she said, "I'll walk on down there while you walk away, and I'll think about it real hard."

"There ya go," said Fred. "Hopefully, I can catch three or four trout, and that should give you lots of time to luxuriate in the sauna." He walked off in the direction that they had come thirty, forty minutes ago.

Kim felt frisky in an outdoorsy way. She had never swum naked outdoors like this; yes, she had jumped the fence at the swimming pool a couple of nights when she was a teenager and goofing around with friends, but never in broad daylight. Near the water's edge, Kim found a rock on which to sit, took off her shoes – Fred's shoes, she reminded herself again – and socks. Stepping into the water, she found that it was pleasantly cool but not cold. The farther from shore she walked and the deeper, the colder the water became. The cold water was more like what she had expected, and she was able to find a happy medium about knee-deep in the lake. Just for grins Kim turned to face out into the lake and dived. She came up, whooping! The chilly water was refreshing! Kim had no idea how clean she would be afterward, but she knew that she'd feel better.

Back on shore, she grabbed her socks and sloshed back into the lake. She rubbed them furiously and their appearance only slightly improved. The water that drained from them was cloudier than the lake, so she was making a difference. She was back in the deeper water after draping her damp socks on a warm rock in the sunlight and took another plunge. She was ready for the shock this time, but it didn't hit her as hard. She was getting used to this and enjoying it! Closer to shore again, and her shirt came off. She wrung it out and laid it across a nearby bush. Next, her pants were drifting in the water and then wrung out. *Skinny dipping is pretty good, after all!*

After laying her pants out, she was back in the water and scanning all around her. She figured Fred was to the north but couldn't see him. A tent was going up farther north, near the lake's inlet, and some backpackers were on the east side and heading away. *What the heck!* A moment later, she was naked and gleeful! She hadn't felt such a release, so much freedom since she was a child. After another dive, she stood in the shallows and let the water drain off. The warmth of the sun on her skin was divine. Kim sat down in the water and used her hands to rub off the grit and grime and ran her fingers through her wet mop of hair.

Sitting in the shallows, Kim took in the bright sky, lake, trees, mountains – and life. She felt so wonderful now, feeling more relaxed, joyful, and content than she'd felt in years. Reality returned to her, reminding her that she wasn't here of her own volition but because of Omega and crew. Kim let go of all of that and basked in the moment, head back, eyes closed, sitting on the sandy bottom, warmish water flowing with cool around her legs, ankles, and feet, and skin glowing. Kim loved the contrasts of sensations she felt.

After a few moments of soaking this all in, she realized the sun was rather intense and getting a little too warm on the parts of her that weren't in the water. She'd been still for some time now. As she started to come back to reality, she felt something nibbling at her feet and opened her eyes – little fingerlings caused her to squeal and pull back. She laughed at herself now, beyond happy!

A moment later, she still was laughing at herself! *Yes, I'm a noob!* She had come down to the lake to clean up and wash her clothes. She hadn't brought any clean, dry clothes with her. *OK, if I'm a woodswoman now and we're not supposed to be so modest, then I'll have to make do.* She shimmied into her damp underwear, worked it into place, and gathered the rest of her clothes. Fred's shoes slopped on her feet, but she wasn't going far. Back in camp, she was thankful to find that Fred hadn't returned. She found her clean clothes and changed. It felt so good to be clean and wearing dry clothes.

A half hour later, Fred returned to camp with a big smile and four trout just as she finished hanging her clothes on low-hanging tree limbs. Her smile was even bigger than his; she positively glowed!

"Well?" he asked. "Was the water pleasant?"

"Oh, Fred!" she exclaimed, "That was a wonderful experience! It felt so good, and I felt so free! Maybe it's too soon, but I want to get back out here someday, sometime. I've been exposed to so many new things these past few days, and it's so much better than I ever imagined. Most of my friends and family are city people and haven't been out in the wilderness like this, so no one ever really asked me to get out. Here I had to go and get myself kidnapped to find something new to enjoy!"

Fred grinned from ear to ear for her. One of his favorite things was to share the wilderness, freedom, and beauty with someone who hadn't experienced it before. At the moment, he felt like he had one of his kids with him for their first time out in the wild, and it made him smile even more.

"I'm very, very glad that you're enjoying your time out here. I just want to remind you that, other than being kidnapped and dragged here by Alpha and Beta, you've had mostly great conditions. A few nights ago, when a storm came through, I didn't sleep as well I wanted. And my first couple of days on this trip, mostly climbing all day and being winded and dead tired – that was not fun. But you usually have more good days than bad out here, and the bad days help you to appreciate the good days."

Turning to his backpack, he pulled out the stove and his pot. "These fish aren't going to cook themselves tonight, so I'm going to sort of poach them. We're not supposed to have fires up here, and we'll make out just fine. I'm guessing that supper should be ready within an hour, so just relax some more."

"Wait a minute!" Kim said. "Before I relax, can you show me how you fix the trout? I want another woodswoman lesson."

They moved well away from camp, down by the lake, and Fred showed Kim how to clean the trout. She was a bit squeamish, watching Fred gut the first fish. On the third trout, she took charge and did a pretty good job of cleaning it. Fred gave her the fourth trout and just sat back. By the time she finished, it was apparent which two trout she had cleaned, but they were fine and ready for their meal.

Fred fired up the stove and got to making supper. Kim sat nearby, tried not to think too much, and just savor the moment, but she was still fairly deep in thought.

"So, I was considering Mammoth Lakes and how we get me to

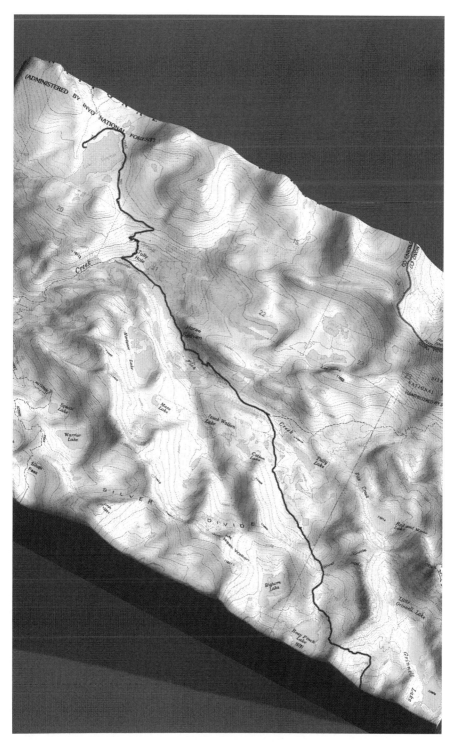

the authorities," Kim started. "You've talked about a couple of your thoughts. I wondered, though, what if you went to Mammoth alone and left me hidden in the woods someplace. You bring the authorities back to where I'm hiding. It sounds like about as good of a plan as any other. What do you think?"

"Yeah, I thought of that before, while we were walking this morning. I didn't bring it up because I just don't like the idea of leaving you alone out here. I can't say why I feel that way other than it just goes against my ethics about the buddy system in difficult situations. If I set those feelings aside, then I think that it's about as good of an idea as any other that we've floated, but none of these thoughts, these plans jump out at me as being great. They're all about the same degree of good in my mind. I'm hoping that something else comes to you or me before we get to Mammoth or run out of food."

"I understand what you're saying," she replied, "but if a better idea doesn't come up, then I'm game for that one. I'll permit you to abandon me, as long as you promise to come back."

Fred just answered with a smile and a nod while he cooked.

Supper wasn't quite as good as the night before, but it was OK. "I'll give this meal three stars," Kim said. "Last night got five stars, though."

"When you're up here, have had a long day, and are hungry, just about anything goes down nicely," he said.

After supper, they sat by the lake, watched the sun go down, reflecting the mountains on the lake and the wave rings made by rising trout. There was a pleasant, comfortable silence between them – sharing the quiet, solitude, and company.

Fred had brought his satellite device with him and was thinking about sending a message home. Kim looked over his shoulder because she hadn't seen one before this trip and wanted to understand.

"You know," she said, "since we're so close to town, I think that it would be better to not turn that thing on, just in case someone is watching, listening in. From what you showed me on the map, it's now easier to find us, especially now when we're on the main trail and we might have nosy neighbors."

"Yeah, you're probably right," he responded with a sigh. "I miss my wife and family, but I'll be able to call her in a couple of days and explain everything. She'll likely be a little worried, but she won't go ballistic until I haven't checked in after two or three days." He tucked the transmitter away in his coat.

Suddenly, Fred gave a little start, raised his eyebrows, and looked at Kim. "You know, if you're going to be a real woodswoman out here and maybe, just maybe, a long-distance backpacker, then you need a trail name to be complete."

"Uh, I didn't know that there was a requirement to have a trail name. Since I'm such a city girl, the only city names we have are *darling, girlfriend, dear, sweetheart* – names like that are generic, valley girl names. What are you talking about?"

"I don't know how it all started, but it's sort of one of the rights of passage up here. Usually, you're given your name by your trail mates because of some quirk of yours, a mistake you make, a habit, where you're from, things like that."

Kim thought about this for a moment and reflected. "So, what's your trail name? Have you been out here enough to deserve one?"

"My preferred trail name is Timber Wolf since I like to be out here alone, and I'm an introvert. However, my son gave the trail name of Slow Poke. When my nephew was with us out here a few years ago, we gave him the trail name of Redwood because he's tall, and he seemed to sunburn every other day." Fred let out a chuckle thinking about these names.

"OK, Timber Wolf, have you thought of a trail name for me, then?" Kim was quite curious.

"Well, yes, but you have to want to adopt it to make it stick. So, I was thinking of something like Brown Bear."

Kim was taken aback and quizzically raised her eyebrows, trying to make sense of the appellation. Finally, she spoke.

"OK, you're going to have to explain that one to me because I don't get it. Don't you think that it might be more than a bit racist?" At this moment, she was rubbing the black skin on her forearm, maybe a little put off and giving him a bit of the evil eye.

"Yeah, I was afraid you might have that reaction but hear me out. I mean it in the best possible way!" Fred was a bit defensive, but he had thought about this enough that he wasn't too worried.

"You see," he continued, "one of the reasons that I like the trail name of Timber Wolf is because it's sort of my spirit animal. I've always felt that way, and one day in college, some friends and I were talking, and one of them said that she thought my spirit animal was a wolf, so that's where it comes from.

"In your case, it has nothing to do with your skin color even though it's easy to see why you – and I – reacted that way when it came to me. I thought of black bear or brown bear because you're enjoying yourself out here and have been so remarkably comfortable. But the other thing that brought it to mind is because it was a bear that may have saved your life. If it wasn't for the bear that found its way into your camp with Alpha and Beta, who knows what might have happened to you. Maybe the bear is your spirit animal, and that bear knew you were in trouble. It figured out a way to distract the guys so that you could slip away. That's how I think about it."

Kim's face softened, and she a smile spread across her face. "I see how you got there now, and that makes sense. Nice save!"

"Well, either that or the bear was just hungry, like you're eating my food," Fred said with a deadpan voice and quickly received a jab in the ribs.

"OK, well, maybe your trail name is something on the order of Timber Jerk," Kim said sarcastically.

Fred smiled, pleased with himself, comfortable here and enjoying this moment, making memories. While they talked, the sun had set to the west, and the sky glowed with the typical radiant pinks, oranges, and deep blues. He looked up at the sky and pointed to the beautiful colors. "Well, maybe we could call you Pink Bear instead."

"I think I'll stick with something like Brown Bear, thank you very much. Besides, I think that my spirit animal is tougher than your spirit animal." She grinned again.

"Well, how 'bout Teddy Bear, then, since you're growing comfortable out here and enjoying yourself. You know, you have it both ways – tough and nice."

Kim thought it over for a moment. Finally, she sat up, a big grin on her face. "I like that new trail name – I'll take it!"

They sat in the evening quiet, taking in the last bits of daylights, darkening pink and orange rays spreading from the western horizon.

"There's something else I want to ask you," Kim said. "Why do you come out here? What's the draw for you?"

"Oooh, that's a good question," responded Fred. He sat back and thought for a moment.

"Well, as you surmised and I said, I'm an introvert, so I enjoy being alone. Another reason is that there are so many rewards out here – along with the risks. I put so much effort into planning a trip like this, from studying maps and routes to planning my meals and sending out resupply packages. And, the physical effort out here is huge, as you've experienced. So, there are a lot of costs. But I see sights that few other people get to enjoy, and I have so many special memories from being out in the wilderness, whether the mountains or the desert. At the end of a long day, I'm tired and oh so grateful. I love my quiet time first thing in the morning and the last thing at night, taking in the changing light. For me, being out here in the wilderness is magical and sublime."

Across Kim's face, a large, warm, knowing smile grew, and she let Fred's words sink in. "After being out here these past couple of days with you and experiencing it from your perspective, the wilderness is growing on me, too." Now it was Fred's turn to smile.

Fred yawned and stretched. "OK, Teddy Bear, I'm ready to hit the sack. I'm bushed. I didn't sleep well last night, and the nap today was helpful, but not enough. And I don't know how long tomorrow will be." He put his hand on her shoulder, used it to help get himself up and groaned while he rose, and then extended his hand to help her stand. "After you set the tent up, I spread it out a bit more so that it's a bit wider tonight and, hopefully, slightly more room and more comfortable, but it's lower now. We'll see."

Fred sat on a rock outside the tent, pulled on more clothes and added padding for him on the tent floor. They were soon snuggling as best they could under the quilt crafted for one person, Fred on the backpacks and Kim on the pad. And, like the night before, Fred was quickly asleep.

Chapter 27

Fred was dreaming, sound asleep, off in his pleasant, peaceful world. But it didn't last long. Someone was shaking him, pushing him, talking him out of a happy place.

"Fred, wake up! It's raining – like, raining hard! Water's leaking into the tent!"

Kim was the reason he was awake now. Well, the pouring rain was the real reason; Kim was just the one who delivered the message. The heavy thrumming on the tent delivered the same message.

A little grumpily, Fred tried to roll over, but Kim blocked him on his left side. He rolled to his right, and his forearm landed in a puddle of water. *That'll get your attention every time.* He tried to sit up a bit, but the roof of the tent was almost on top of him, weighed down by the deluge.

"Well, shit," he frustratedly murmured. He found his tiny flashlight and scanned around to try to see how bad it was. The tent was lying low, and he had to move it out of the way to find the edges. He didn't like what he saw – the water was flowing in from near their heads and slowly coursing toward their feet. A moment later, he felt a damp area on his hip, where he'd been laying on the backpacks.

He laid back down and let out a big sigh. "Well, this is what happens when I forget to check the weather forecast. It wouldn't have made any difference. It still would have rained. And, when it pours like this, you just hope for the best. Unfortunately, this isn't the best."

Checking the time on his phone, he found that it was a little after ten; they'd only been asleep for a couple of hours at the most. He wanted to glimpse out and see how bad it looked but knew better. It was too dark, and he'd only let in more water. The beating of the rain grew louder and then was loudly thrashing the tent. The temperature seemed like it dropped a good twenty degrees since they'd turned in. The wind picked up and was lashing everything. He just laid there, taking it all in. This was a wild storm, maybe the craziest he'd ever experienced while in the mountains.

Fred rolled over and hugged Kim. He had to raise his voice to be heard over the din of the rain pounding the tent. "We'll be alright, but it could be a long, long night. Usually, the first wave of a mountain storm is the worst, and then it will slacken. The major issue is that everything is getting wet, it's uncomfortable, and it's going to be even more difficult to sleep."

Kim's sarcastic response was spot on: "No shit, Sherlock."

The initial torrent let up some, but it was still pouring. Fred rechecked the time, and a long hour had passed. The combination of the wind's stress on his tent and the shallow, wet sand caused the upwind tent stake to rip loose. The rain was now blowing under the tent, and the quilt was getting even wetter. Fred grabbed the flapping edge of the tent and stuffed it under Kim, which fixed the problem for now. The stress of the wind on the tent fabric caused another stake to loosen, and the tent flapped again, but less rain got inside. Fred figured it was time to collapse their shelter and hope for the best. He pulled down the hiking pole that held up his tent and gathered in the tent edges, tucking them around and under the two of them. His tent was a pretty good shelter now, not letting any more rain inside. He felt better about their situation but knew that condensation would soak everything if they had to spend the night wrapped like a Christmas present. Kim's body held down the upwind edge of the tent, his arm held the downwind edge, and he tucked the other two tent sides under their feet and heads. He could feel the cold rain pounding on the tent through his coat's hood. Oh, it was going to be a very long night.

Feeling for Kim, he found that she was about as wet as him, with damp spots on her jacket and pants. For the most part, they were relatively warm but very uncomfortable. Now that he had collapsed the tent and pulled the edges under them, the flow of water under them was just a trickle, but rainwater was still getting to them.

"Look," he said, "the best thing that we can do for now is to snuggle together and maintain our warmth. If we get too cold in these conditions, then we could be screwed. So, just cuddle, snuggle, and let me know if the rain or cold are getting to be too much for you. I know you're wet but try to keep the wet parts from getting cold."

The rain pelted down, lightning and thunder hammered the peaks, and Fred felt something like a drowned rat in their sopping cocoon. Yep, he was making another memory tonight, just not the kind that he wanted to make. Fred wasn't worried about them making it through the night. He was cold, wet, and miserable and assumed that Kim felt about the same. Wishing that he was home in his nice, warm bed beside Asta wasn't doing him any good. These thoughts were just making him more miserable. Looking at his phone again, he found that it was after 2:00 a.m. Yep, it was a long night. If he'd caught a wink of sleep yet since the storm started, he wasn't aware.

In his mind, Fred started to make alternate plans for the next day. If the rain stopped, maybe they could dry out and recover. Fred felt that they were better off taking it easy rather than forcing themselves to march on without yet knowing what the weather would be like when the sun came up even if their food supply was low. He laid there, listening to the rain on his collapsed shelter, wondering how Kim was doing. His wet spots didn't seem to get soggier, but he wasn't getting any warmer. The cold seeped into Fred's back and shoulders, and he was sore from holding onto the tent and laying on the wet backpacks and tent floor.

Fred wanted to roll over onto his right side since it seemed like he'd been the outside spoon with Kim for hours. He started to roll and then thought to ask Kim how she was holding up.

"I'm okay," she responded. "The last time that I had this much fun was pulling an all-nighter while coding a program. Except I'm cold, wet, and pretty fuckin' annoyed that there's no hot coffee."

"Yep, that sums it up pretty well," Fred said. He rolled over and dragged her with him. "If you want to roll back over or try to move in some other way, just let me know."

For whatever reason, Fred let out a deep, throaty scream – his way of trying to scare off the storm. Nope, it didn't work, and he just laid there and laughed at their predicament. Kim might have been scared, except she had felt Fred's chest expand, and she felt like screaming too. Fred knew that they were going to be okay – probably. He knew that they just needed to make it through the storm, however long it would last. Tonight's storm reminded him of his first day of this adventure, one step in front of the other. Except now, they weren't moving, weren't making progress, and they were cowering under a thin piece of fabric in a nasty storm. Just for grins, Fred screamed again, and Kim joined in this time.

They both started laughing at their predicament! *This is a crazy night!* Fred knew that their situation was difficult and uncomfortable, but he wasn't too fearful of getting colder. Again, he knew that he would have a lifelong memory that would help carry him through other difficult situations, but this memory was being forced upon them by Mother Nature.

Fred laid there, feeling around the tent floor on occasion, checking how much rainwater might be flowing through the tent. Sometimes he straightened out as much as he could because he was tired of curling in a fetal position with Kim; she'd do the same. When he first felt his arms and legs getting wet from the rainwater, he had pulled his rain jacket and pants under him. They had kept some parts of him from getting much wetter, but not all. Kim was drier since the sleeping pad protected her from getting as wet. Yep, this night is going from bad to worse. He fumbled around, accidentally elbowing Kim, trying to keep his wet spots from getting wetter, but he wasn't entirely successful

The wind wasn't quite so bad now, and he felt that he didn't need to hold down the edge of the tent. The rain was still coming down hard, and he felt cooler than he wanted. He rubbed his hands together under his piece of the quilt, flexed them, and stretched and rubbed his arms. A hot cup of cocoa would be fantastic right now, he thought, except that wasn't going to happen anytime soon. He remembered that he, too, had pulled an all-nighter once or twice in college, but they were nowhere nearly as bad as this night.

Maybe he was getting a bit delirious, but Fred started singing, anything to slightly entertain himself, bide some time, and keep his mood up.

Raindrops keep falling on my head... Too bad he couldn't remember more of the words. Maybe Burt Bacharach would be willing to trade places with him right now.

Beside him, Kim was giggling and shaking. *Well, at least I'm keeping her entertained,* he thought.

Ridin' the storm out, waitin' for the fallout... REO Speedwagon! He was keeping time by flexing his cold feet. His loud singing got his blood pumping, and Kim was laughing more.

Up next were Gene Kelly and Debbie Reynolds. *I'm singin' in the rain, just singin' in the rain! What a glorious feeling, I'm happy again!*

"Oh, bullshit that I'm happy again!" Kim yelled, and they both laughed.

Yep, definitely getting delirious. And now, for something completely different, let's hear it for Prince! *Never meant to cause you any sorrow, Never meant to cause you any pain, I only wanted to one time to see you laughing, I only wanted to see you in the purple rain. Purple rain.*

Kim had her head buried in Fred's back, laughing harder and harder. Maybe she was getting delirious, too.

They laid there, humming, singing, and laughing. Maybe Kim and Fred fell asleep – who knew for sure. They had no idea what time it was nor how long the storm pounded them.

Omega sent a message to Prirody, asking if there were any updates on his theory. In his response, Prirody told him that a storm obstructed the satellite's view of the Sierras, so he had no idea where the green tent texter might be now. That was discouraging, Omega thought.

But Prirody also wrote that this person had broken his pattern, which was interesting. There was no satellite message, no apparent contact from the green tent texter to his family for the past day or so. The family had written to him, wondering where he was, how he was doing, letting him know that a storm was coming, but it didn't appear that he had connected his satellite device to the messaging system. The lack of communication was unusual because this guy had written a message most every evening on this trip.

Interesting, thought Omega.

**Chapter 28**

Something pulled Fred out of his deep, troubled sleep. It was probably the pain and cold that he felt. He laid there, feeling the dampness in his clothing, and peeked open an eyelid from under his puffy coat's damp hood. There was a bit of light in the grey morning sky, tinted green by the tent. They had fallen asleep, thankfully, needfully. Behind, he could hear Kim faintly snoring, felt her gently twitching. He wanted to move but didn't want to wake her. His right hip was killing him, as was his right shoulder; he'd spent too long laying on his right side on the cold, damp backpacks and other gear. Fred could feel that his side was wet but not squishy.

The inside of the tent wall was dripping wet with condensation droplets and resting on top of them. Their clothing was wet on top from absorbing condensation and on the bottom from rainwater that had flowed into the tent when the storm began. It didn't really matter that the flow of rain into the tent had mostly stopped, they were still getting wet because of their breath condensing on the cold tent material. Fred wanted a cup of hot tea, hot cocoa, hot anything, right now. There was a light rain falling, occasionally interspersed by heavier plops dripping from the trees.

Gently and painfully rolling to his left, he was able to get Kim to move and relax her hold on him a bit. He let out a soft groan after relieving the pressure on his hip. Fred rolled and flexed his right shoulder, willing blood to flow through it and down his arm again. He laid there in his damp cocoon, the tent pressed against him, streaks of condensation just in front of his face.

The tent door was on Kim's side, and there wasn't any way that he could get out without waking her, so he just had to do it. He found his hiking pole and reset it to hold up the tent, with more condensation dripping onto them and flowing down the tent walls. Fred's puffy coat was soaking the condensation wherever he touched the tent fabric; he could feel it through his right sleeve. Kim stirred now, eyes fluttered, followed by a bit of a grimace.

Looking up at him, Kim said sourly, "Maybe I'm not so interested in this camping stuff after all. That was one of the worst nights of my life."

Fred grinned back at her. "Yep, that was a bad one, alright. I don't think that we will be moving too far today, so just take it easy and rest. We're going to spend most of the day letting everything dry out. I'm hungry, but we need to go easy on the food. I'm guessing that the lake is a bit murky, so I doubt that the fishing will too good, either. Our situation is a bit more difficult now, but we'll be fine."

He didn't really know if they'd be fine, but he wanted to put on a good face for Kim's sake. Fred knew that if worse came to worse, they were about a day's hike from Mammoth, so they'd survive. The next day or two were going to be tougher than he'd been hoping yesterday.

Fred crawled over Kim, dragging the tent fabric with him, unzipped the bug netting, and found his wet boots. These were the kind of mornings that no one enjoyed out here, but you still have to muddle through them. He inched his way out of the tent, cold, wet sand sticking to his palms. It didn't make any difference if he got any wetter. Pulling his raincoat across his shoulders and his down jacket helped to keep him a bit warmer, but he shuddered as his damp, wet clothes clung to him more tightly.

Ugly. That's pretty much how Fred felt and how he'd describe the dreary world around him. What a change from the beautiful pastel sunset that they'd enjoyed last night. *Oh, well.* He gave a shiver – it was still cold. He could see his foggy breath. He needed his gloves, too, which he found just above Kim's head. There wasn't any wind to speak of, just cold drizzle. *Ugly.*

Fred walked around, hoping to warm himself and generate enough heat to dry the clothes he wore. He straightened the tent, reset a couple of stakes, and pulled the lines taught, which would help it dry better, faster, when the sun came out. Down by the lake, the water wasn't as turbid as he had thought he'd find it, so that was good. He might be able to snag some fish later. Fred stretched, clapped his hands, and rubbed them together. His circulation was returning. His feet were cold and stiff, and stomping helped him to feel them.

Fred could see that someone had built a smoky fire to the north, likely with wet wood. The rising smoke gave a bit of character to an otherwise dreary morning. The curling smoke seemed to be about the only living thing out here. Everything else was calm, dull, grey. Clouds hung low, obscuring most of the peaks. It was almost eerily quiet since he was used to the nearly constant background noise of light wind through the trees and ridges. Fred could make out the morning sun trying to peep over the mountain tops, but the clouds weren't in a sharing mood.

Aside from a cup of hot tea, what he wanted was to crawl back into the tent and under the quilt, but he might have a fight on his hands trying to take it away from Kim. *Best to let her keep warm and rest for now*, he figured. The bear canister was where they had left it the night before, but the violence of the storm had knocked the stove and pot off the top. The stove soon sputtered to life, and water warmed. Fred removed his gloves and cupped his hands over the air rising from the stove, capturing as much warmth as he could.

Since Kim had the quilt, he got the first cup of hot tea. The warmth spread through his gloves and into his stiff hands. He wished that he could pour the water over his feet to warm them, but he also figured that the glow would spread throughout his body in due time. He found a couple of small granola bars in the canister, putting one in his pocket for Kim and eating the other one. The remaining rations were on the meager side.

The drizzle let up, and there was almost a break in the clouds, but that gap quickly filled. Fred could nearly make out a full circle of dull sun above the peaks and through the low-hanging veil, but no heat reached him through the clouds.

Yep, ugly.

The tea didn't taste like anything other than warmth, and he was okay with that. A piece of the granola bar was stuck in his teeth – he wanted every morsel of nutrition that he could get. A plop in the lake caught his attention – the fish were jumping and hopefully biting. That was encouraging. He was almost in a trance, it seemed, his slow, groggy mind wandering from one thing to another. He wasn't cold, but he wasn't close to being warm either. Fred shivered occasionally, and the uncontrolled movement caused him to feel his sore back, hips, and shoulders. He was tired and sore, and the world around him was dreary.

And ugly.

After finishing his tea, he checked on Kim to see if she was moving. Whispering, he tried to get her attention to see if she'd respond. Nothing. Hopefully, she was asleep and warm, and he'd leave her like that. She was out of sight, so that was an added benefit. Maybe he could work in a nap this afternoon.

Today was one of those *you take the good with the bad* kind of days. Fred's mind wandered over how to care for Kim and get her back to safety, how to occupy himself today, the needed drying of clothing and gear, fishing for food, and myriad other little details. He doubted that it was even 8:00 am yet. One thing about backpacking is that there wasn't a lot to do except walk and enjoy the scenery, and on days like this when he wasn't walking, he felt bored. A dull day in the mountains beats a boring day at home, though. Another memory made, stored for future appreciation.

Sitting by the lake on a cool rock, he slowly took in all the scenery he could, creating a mental panorama, pulling in little details that had previously escaped him. Fred could make out a light-yellow tent across the lake, almost hidden behind a bush, but no one stirred there. The hanging clouds reflected in the nearly still lake. There were three tents on the lake's north side, with the fire near one of them; the fire wasn't as smoky now. Another tent was set into the woods, away from the triad. Next to the fire, a lone figure sat, maybe enjoying morning coffee, huddled under a sleeping bag. Everyone, it seemed, was of a similar mind – rest, dry out, and hope for better weather to come soon. A couple of backpackers meandered down towards the lake off the slope to the northwest of the lake. They didn't look too spry this morning, but then no one probably felt good. They stopped for a moment, chatted with the sleeping bag-clad camper, and pointed to the south, the direction from which Kim and Fred had come the day before.

Fred couldn't take the boredom anymore, sitting around and doing essentially nothing. He quietly approached the tent and opened the flap and bug net. His knees created a divot in the wet sand; his pants would dry again. Kim was covered with the mostly dry quilt, a few wet spots on the edges that touched the tent floor. He reached over her and fumbled around, feeling for his fly rod, and some rope or twine that he knew were in a pocket of his wet backpack. *What the heck*, he thought, *just pull out the bags and hang them up already.* Fred didn't mean to drag the backpacks over her, but there wasn't much other way around it, the confines were so tight. Kim reacted to being brushed by the packs with a groan and rolled over to her side, face peeking out from under the quilt. She peered out at Fred, hat pulled low over her head, a look of disdain on her face. Fred smiled at her, pulled the quilt over her face, and backed out of the tent. Seeing her gave him a bit of tenderness, thinking of his own family when they had been camping in poor weather in the past.

He emptied the backpacks and hung them upside down from a tree; a few drops of water fell from them, but not much. It would take a warm sun and wind to dry them. Fred put up a clothesline with a piece of light rope and hung clothes as best he could, giving them space to breathe. They were plenty damp but not dripping, so that was encouraging.

Back at the spot where he'd fished the afternoon before, he scanned the lake, looking for signs of piscine life. The pale reflections from the lingering clouds kept him from making out much detail below the lake's surface. He tied a fly onto his rod and blew it dry, fluffing it so that it would lay on the lake's surface tension and hopefully attract the interest of their lunch.

He cast out the line, let the fly sit for a moment on the cloud's reflections, gave a little jiggle of the rod to induce some movement in the fly, and then snapped it back. He repeated this several times, his mind focused on his efforts, leaving the boredom behind. The camper with the fire to the north saw Fred and gave a good-morning wave; he returned the salute with this free hand.

How long this went on, Fred didn't know. He was in a zone, just him, the mirrored clouds, his fly, his empty mind, and his fatigue. He'd lost track of time. He was semi-focused, and the thought of fresh trout for an early lunch gave rise to a growl from his stomach. Being one with nature had its drawbacks. Nature was beautiful but also cruel and challenging. To be cool, damp, and hungry was not why he came out here. At this moment, he'd appreciate laying in a warm, dry bed, snuggling with Asta, without a care in the world. When he got home, he would appreciate it. Yep, it's still an ugly morning.

The casting continued, interspersed with occasional digestive grumbling. He was concerned that his growling stomach was so loud that it might scare away the fish. Another cloaked figure appeared by the fire to the north. Fred couldn't see his tent but assumed that Kim was still in her cocoon. He was growing tired of his failures, losing interest, trying to come up with another plan for food, and how to keep himself busy.

The sun peeked out from the clouds to the southeast, with beams moving their way across the lake and mountains, the reflection momentarily blinding him. Fred could feel a bit of joy rising in himself, the hope that conditions would improve, he'd be warm again, and clothing would dry. From behind him, Kim whispered – *"Hey, dude! I'm awake and out of the sack. What's for breakfast?"*

Fred turned and saw a disheveled Kim standing in a patch of trees. He couldn't tell if she was hiding because she didn't want to be seen by kidnappers or because she looked like she'd just gotten out of bed. He grinned at the sight of her, pulled in the fly, and retreated to the trees to talk with her.

"Good morning!" he exclaimed. He almost meant it. Kim gave him a half-hearted smile in return.

"Last night was one of the worst storms I've encountered when I've been camping. The storm wasn't the worst. It was being crowded in a tiny tent and not staying dry – that was the worst part. If we'd been in a bigger tent, each with a quilt and pad, the night would have been much more tolerable."

"I've had better nights, too," Kim responded, yawning, stretching, grimacing and grabbing her back.

"I feel like I've had pretty much a full night's sleep, but it wasn't a good sleep. So, what's for brunch? Eggs benedict maybe?" She smiled, knowing that Fred probably had similar dreams.

"Well, I can make you a cup of hot tea, and here's a granola bar. We need to watch our rations, especially since I don't think we'll be moving much today. My priority is to dry out as best we can. I'm trying to land some more trout. If I can come up with a decent haul, we'll be better off, and I'll feel better about our situation. If not, then we should probably keep moving toward Mammoth. There are another couple of lakes in the direction that we're going, so we could move, make camp, and I could fish some more."

As Fred started the stove and warmed water for Kim, more and more sunlight bled through the clouds. Looking up, he could see patches of blue. *This is a good sign,* he thought. After he poured the hot water and Kim warmed her hands on the cup, he checked the clothes. They were still damp in the folds but starting to dry where exposed. *More good news.* Looking at her, Fred saw a smile start to grow on her face, a calm coming over her as she warmed and became more alert.

"I'm heading back to try to catch some lunch and supper. Can you check the clothes and make certain they're drying, and pull out the quilt to dry? If anything else is damp or wet, it needs to be dried, too."

"Aye, aye, Captain!" was Kim's smiling response.

Fred returned to the spot where he'd spent a fruitless hour or so and decided to change it up. Nearby, there was a large rock jutting into Lake Virginia, and he could stand or sit on it. Fred felt a bit tired, so sitting was the better choice. The clouds were thinning, and he was happy to feel the sun's warmth creeping into his body. He figured his mood would improve now that he was warming and the sun made more frequent appearances. Seeing Kim's mood improve as she woke and warmed helped him, too.

After a few weak casts, Fred got back into his groove and was able to place his fly close to where he saw rings of wavelets expanding on the lake. With a sudden splash, his fly disappeared. A deft tug on his rod set the hook and he carefully brought in the trout. He felt better now; they'd at least have a small lunch. He laced a length of his light rope through the trout's gill and mouth, tied a knot to create a loop, placed his foot through the loop, and then gently placed the fish into the water. The fresher the trout, the better they taste!

The sun appeared more frequently from behind the clouds. Intermittent sun and shadow kept his body guessing as he loosened his jacket and then pulled it tighter. Luck found him again with a second, larger trout! This trout joined the first on his make-shift stringer. He found a nearby rock to hold his stringer in the water. He didn't want to lose the fish now; he'd be heartbroken and they'd be hungry.

After about sixty more minutes, Fred hooked four more trout. He felt much better now, expecting that they had enough food to narrowly make it through a recovery day here at Lake Virginia. He took his stringer of fish and gently and quickly carried them back to camp and then to their little cove. Kim watched him march by, a big smile on her face. He anchored the stringer in the water with a large rock, washed his hands, and proudly returned to camp.

"Good work, Captain!" Kim exclaimed. "I'm impressed. Maybe we'll survive after all," she said jestfully.

"Yeah, I think that we'll make it out of here, although I'm still not clear about how we'll get you safely into Mammoth. I was more immediately concerned with making it through another day and having enough to eat. I wasn't worried about making it out here; the question was how hungry we'd be getting out of here. It's only about ten miles to Mammoth from here, as the crow flies, but it's still a hike."

"I understand. Your priorities are the same as mine," Kim said.

"Um, can you entertain yourself for an hour or two?" Fred asked of Kim. "I'm dead tired and want to take a nap. I'd like to eat something, but if I can sleep, then I'll forget about that. Why don't you find yourself something to eat in the bear canister?"

"Yeah, sure. I'll just take a walk to the library and pick out a good book, too," Kim chided with a wink. "I've been watching you and feeling restless sitting here, so I'm going to walk south of here, along the lake, and away from our neighbors to the north. Sweet dreams!"

Now it was Kim's turn to wander with her mind and body. Before she left on her walk, she picked up the maps and carried them with her. She may not have a book, but she could read maps. Well away from camp, but with the tent in view, she found a sunlit boulder against which she could lean, warmth oozing into her back. Though she was hungry, the sun's energy filled her and kept the gnawing in her stomach somewhat at bay. Keeping her mind busy also helped her to avoid the pangs. She leaned back for a moment, eyes closed, and breathed in the fresh mountain air. And she smiled, remembering again that though she was uncomfortable, at least she was away from Omega, Alpha, and Beta.

Spreading the map in front of her on a flat stone, small rocks holding down the corners, she found the places that Fred had pointed out over the past few days: Lake Italy; Laurel Lake where they camped their first night together; and now, Lake Virginia. Up and to the left, she could see the village of Mammoth Lakes. Yes, it wasn't too far away, as Fred had said, at least when compared with how far they'd already come. They had made it this far; they'd make it the rest of the way. She also found Reds Meadow, where Fred had mentioned that he planned to pick up a resupply. Her fingers wandered over the various lines, symbols and colors, moving from Lake Virginia to Purple Lake, then Duck Lake, and on to Mammoth. Her finger circled back to Reds Meadow and then returned to Lake Virginia.

There were several possible ways to enter Mammoth. Omega's people couldn't possibly cover all the routes into town, could they? They didn't have to hike down Main Street or anything like that. Maybe they could split up and use Fred as a of diversion for her, maybe without putting him at risk. Her mind was in problem-solving mode now and feeling better. She was lost in her world, not paying attention to her hunger, sort of oblivious to being in the middle of nowhere. Kim was in a comfortable, familiar place now – her mind – and started to see and feel possibilities unfold before her. She looked north to the mountains and didn't see obstacles but opportunities. She was smiling now, coming back to the person whom she knew, retaking control.

She hadn't played the victim on this unplanned adventure, but she hadn't always been active either, mostly following along. Now, Kim felt inspired again. She had a better feel for her situation, how she'd gotten here, and how she might get out of it.

With a smile across her face, she laid back, warmth from the sun filling her. She rested her arm across her eyes to shield them from the sun. Her mind was churning, seeing different ways to solve the problem, different risks, and various opportunities. Kim felt better than she had in days because she was moving from kidnapping to escaping to surviving to rescue. A sense of lightness and calm welled up in her, and she smiled even more deeply.

A fly buzzed around her mouth, tickling her. She swatted it away and slowly opened her eyes. Her back, hips, and shoulders were sore now – she had fallen asleep. It was a deserved and needed nap. Her thoughts of finding a safe way into Mammoth returned, along with her smile. Slowly sitting up on her elbows, she arched her stiff back and found her center again. She had no idea how long she'd been out but wasn't concerned.

After gathering herself for a few minutes more, Kim folded the map and walked farther away from their camp, taking in the sights and sounds. Across the lake, she could make out backpackers on the move, mostly heading southward. It seemed like the two of them might be the only ones who were hunkering down today, but then, they were likely the only ones who double bunked and had a sleepless night.

When she returned to camp, she could see Fred still asleep in the tent. She figured that it was mid- to late afternoon. Their clothes were mostly dry, so Kim folded and put them into the backpacks, took down the clothesline, and stowed it. Now that she felt like she was retaking charge of her life, she felt her energy flow, wanted to move. She also knew that it was rather pointless to think about packing up camp and hiking for another hour or two, only to make camp again. Best to sit here, take it easy, breathe in the moment and strategize.

She was seriously thinking about waking Fred when she heard pitiful groans coming from the tent. A minute later, his feet stuck out through the flaps, searching for boots. Lastly, he rolled forward onto his hands and knees, crawled out of the tent, and crookedly raised himself, almost to full height. He was the one who now looked worse for wear, and Kim smiled at him. It was her turn to empathize with his painful looks.

While Fred worked out the kinks in his back, she took the knife, retrieved the fish, and cleaned them. It would be a long, slow process to cook all these trout, but well worth it. Besides, they weren't going anywhere until tomorrow morning.

After their hearty supper, they both felt much better, warmer and more alert. Kim and Fred weren't ecstatic but content, especially after what they'd been through the past day and more. They were reasonably well fed, dry, warm and rested. There was a buoyancy about them that they hadn't felt earlier in the day. Kim took advantage of their better spirits and asked Fred about how his thoughts had developed regarding getting her into Mammoth.

"Well," he said, "I feel like I'm at a bit of an impasse. I was sort of thinking about it this morning while you were sleeping, but my mind has been busier with fishing and sleeping since then. I still don't feel like I have a decent plan. What about you?"

"While you were napping, I pored over the maps and thought about it some more. I think that I have an outline of a plan," Kim excitedly said and then served up her thoughts as Fred smiled in the fading light.

Chapter 29

After another understandably less than restful night, Kim and Fred awoke to partly cloudy skies, a sliver of the moon peeking around the clouds. Kim was out of the tent first this morning, wandering away and then taking in the sunrise by the lake's shore. When she left, Fred rolled onto the sleeping pad and was soon deeply asleep.

Kim had been an astute enough observer and shortly had water boiling and tea ready. Sitting by the lake, the sun peeked through the clouds and around the rocky crags to the east of the lake and warmed her on the outside as the tea warmed her inside. She felt alone in the world at this moment, but not lonely. It was another beautiful morning! When the sun would hide behind a cloud, Kim could feel the chill in the air, but then she'd warm again when the sun broke free. To the north, she could make out three or four tents, and the lives in them stirred. Kim was thankful that she was in the morning sun and not still in shadows as they were.

Just as Kim's derrière felt sufficiently cooled by the rocks, grunting and groaning came from the tent. Fred dragged himself out, looked her way through squinted eyes, waved, and then wandered off behind the trees. When he returned and looked her way, Kim raised the cup and then turned it over – *time for a refill* – especially if Fred wanted his morning tea.

After retrieving the cup and filling it, Fred sat beside Kim, sharing her rays of sunshine. Kim noticed that Fred was a better backpacker than she, the noob, was as he was sitting on his gloves to keep his butt warm and slightly more comfortable. *So much to learn*, she thought.

"So, what are we doing today?" she asked.

"Well, I'm not in a hurry to get moving. Depending on what we do and how far we go, the day could be like a couple of days ago, before the storm, or a bit longer. We have enough food to get through today and a little bit more if we stretch it. I don't feel that we need to be near Mammoth until later in the day. We might be a bit hungry, but we're not going to starve. The trout last night made a big difference. I have to admit, though, that I am hungry and am trying to be comfortable with that feeling. I believe that I'll have enough energy so that we can make it into Mammoth or wherever today. Let's eat some of the nuts that are in the bear canister; they're full of fat and will keep us somewhat satisfied."

Kim talked while Fred retrieved the bear canister.

"I haven't come up with any better plans than what I shared with you last night for getting back to civilization," Kim volunteered.

"Me neither. I still like your general plan. The closer we get to Mammoth and Reds Meadow, the more people we're likely to see. That worries me if Alpha and Beta have put the word out that you're missing. The best thing we can do is to stick to what you suggested last night because that will, I hope, reduce the number of people we see, and we keep our options open. We'll be on the John Muir Trail for a few miles and then head north to Duck Lake. There's a trail into Mammoth from Duck Lake, so, yeah, we could try that, but I don't like the thought of walking into an unknown situation. As you said, I want to reduce the variables and do what we can to move the variables in our favor. We could go farther on the John Muir Trail and get to Reds Meadow, but we'll spend more time on the main trail with more people. The good thing is that it's easy to get from Reds down to Mammoth, but it's jam-packed and one of the more obvious places for them to be expecting you to come out in this region."

Kim sat there, nodded, and kept warming in the sun. "So, you don't want to leave me hidden somewhere and go get the sheriff?"

"No, I still don't. That's my least favorite option because I just don't like the idea of leaving you alone for too long. There must be good hiding places, and I doubt that anyone would find you, but it just doesn't feel right. Let's walk, get closer to Mammoth and see if there's anything else that we want to add to your plan."

By now, they'd eaten the nuts and drained the cup, and it was time to pack. Fred took the tent down while Kim stuffed the quilt and pad. The bear canister felt light, and Fred liked Kim's idea even more since they were running out of food.

An hour later, they stomped over the crest of the rise between Lake Virginia and Purple Lake. The outlet from Purple Lake was running high and strong, and they could see where the stream had recently flowed higher. Kim and Fred rounded the south side of Purple Lake and stopped for a break under a cluster of trees near where the trail rises away from the lake.

"My son, Will, and I camped here a couple of years ago. A woman named Rona, her son, Oscar, and their trail friend, a Korean woman whose name I don't recall, camped here with us. We ended up hiking the rest of the JMT with Oscar and the Korean woman. Rona traded off with her husband, Jason, at Muir Trail Ranch, and he finished the trip with Oscar. One of the best parts of being on a trail like this is finding new people and making friends. The introvert in me didn't anticipate that. I hadn't experienced anything like it on other backpacking trips where there are a lot fewer people on the trails and I backpack alone. Sort of like becoming your friend – we just fell into it."

Kim smiled warmly. "Well, I can't say that we *just fell into it.* I didn't give you much choice since I was in dire need of a rescue."

Fred sat there for a while longer before he said, "Well, if we don't get moving, then nobody will be getting rescued anytime soon. And we're not getting closer to more food by sitting here. I hate to tell you that my stomach is growling."

On the trail from Purple Lake to Duck Creek, Kim and Fred ran into a couple of young backpackers; actually, they heard the couple before they saw them. The backpackers stopped to ask about trail conditions on the JMT to the south. Fred told the couple that they had hardly been on the JMT and made up a story about coming in over Mc-Gee Pass and getting hit by the storm while they were at Lake Virginia, just in case they were curious about Kim. The couple didn't really show any particular interest in Kim and Fred other than gathering and sharing information. From their side, the couple told Fred that they'd been lucky to weather the storm and a recovery day at Reds Meadow. Worse news from them was that the storm had been strong enough to wash away the bridge over Duck Creek and that the trail had been temporarily rerouted up towards Duck Lake where it was safer to cross the creek. Fred thanked the couple for the information and bid them *happy trails!*

As the couple walked away, Fred looked at Kim and screwed up his face a bit. "Well, that's a minor kink in our plans. It sounds like we could be running into south-bound backpackers for longer than I'd

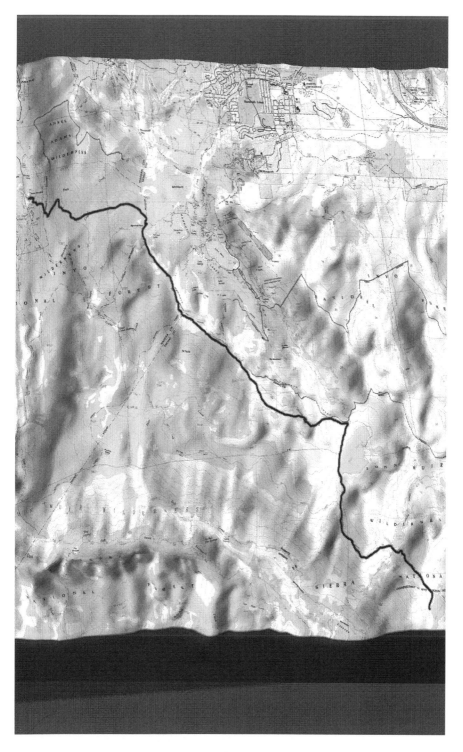

expected. As usual, we just have to adapt!"

Kim shrugged her shoulders, looked at Fred and said, "Isn't that pretty much what we've been doing for the past few days?" She gave him a knowing, thankful smile and headed northward on the trail.

It was maybe another hour before they got to the trail that took them to Duck Lake. They looked down over Duck Creek, where Fred could see fluorescent orange tape and signs directing backpackers towards Duck Lake. He remembered the small bridge over the creek when he passed through here two years ago, but he could only see the naked abutments and some of the damaged timbers that had been dragged downstream. Duck Creek was still running high, too.

"Like they told us, the storm took out the bridge over Duck Creek. That's too bad for the backpackers using this trail. And, as I said before, we need to watch for more people on the trail up to Duck Lake," Fred said. "I don't like it, but that's the way it is."

It took them maybe twenty minutes to climb the trail to Duck Lake. They saw some backpackers on the other side of Duck Creek who were slowly scrambling their way upstream, looking for a safe place to cross. At Duck Lake, they ran into a few packers crossing the creek where it was relatively shallow and safe as it flowed out of the lake.

Kim and Fred waited their turn to cross and watched where people stepped and checked how deep the water was on their legs. They took off their shoes, boots, and socks, stowed them on Fred's backpack, rolled up their pant legs and very slowly sidestepped across Duck Creek, holding each other's hand, while Fred held his hiking pole in his left hand, feeling his way across with it. It wasn't a difficult or scary crossing, but it was still annoying to get cold, wet feet. Fred wasn't a fan of crossing creeks barefoot, but he did it this time. The cobbles hurt his feet and he stubbed his toes a few times and Kim did likewise.

After checking and drying their feet and putting their socks and shoes back on, they continued on the trail around the lake. On the west side of Duck Lake, they found a secluded spot in some shrubs and Kim and Fred dropped their packs and stretched. "This is probably the best place for an early lunch that we're going to have, so let's eat a little something. And there's a whole big lake that we can drink."

As they sat and ate nuts, dried fruit, and jerky, Fred studied the map, looked up to think, peeked from the bushes to watch backpackers crossing the creek, and then went back to the map.

Fred pointed out the route, the lakes, and the ridge, and let out a heavy sigh. "So, let's kind of finalize your plan for today. Yea, we could try to walk into Mammoth from this trail when it gets dark, but like you, I'm not a fan of that approach. Let's go with your idea and hole up short of Reds and Mammoth. I'm guessing that we have another nine miles or so to get the area of our next camp that you suggested last night. That's a little more than I'd typically want to do in a normal afternoon, and especially now for an old and hungry Slow Poke, but it makes a lot more sense than stopping short of there or going into Mammoth or on to Reds."

"Yep. I'm sold. We'd better get going then, *Slow Poke*," and Kim pulled on her pack. She could see the trail winding up the side of the slope, and she was off. After Fred repacked, he was a few hundred yards behind.

The clouds kept the climb more than bearable. They were sweating but not as bad as the climb from Tully Hole a couple of days ago. Fred's load was lighter. This climb was more exposed but less humid and warm and with more breeze. When they reached the top of the ridge, they had an incredible vista of Duck Lake behind them and a basin with several lakes before them and red rocks beyond.

"So, it's sort of decision time; I just want to double-check with you," Fred said. "We can hike down here and have you at the trailhead in a few hours and likely into Mammoth by this evening. Or we stay to the west of the ridge and work our way north, like you suggested, working the variables in our favor."

Kim looked at him, looked down the valley at a possible rescue, food, and who knows what comfort and trouble, and then looked left to where she saw the trail rising slowly and disappearing into... *what?* She announced her decision by heading up the route to the west and not down into the basin.

"Ah, a woman after my own heart!" he exclaimed. "The road less traveled." And they were off again.

The view was desolate at this elevation, like how it had been on their first day and a half together. Eventually, the trail led to a steep decline that overlooked three ponds – the Deer Lakes. They stopped at the middle lake for a break and to gather water.

"I'm not certain, but this could be our last water until we make camp in a couple of hours, so drink up," Fred suggested. Kim drank what remained in her bottle and then filtered a liter of water and drank half of that. After topping off her bottle again, Fred did the same, and they were walking again.

The going now wasn't tough but it wasn't easy either. Kim and Fred were on the west side of the ridge and exposed to the sun when they weren't in the shadow of the occasional cloud. The footing was sufficient, frequently sandy, rocky, and loose. They had a grand view to the west and eventually were on the top of Mammoth Crest and able to look down into the basin to the east that they had passed up. After another forty minutes, the view to the east opened again. They could see cars down by Mary Lake but couldn't make out any people. Mammoth Lakes was in view farther behind. Kim felt a little desirous for the civilized world – a big burger, hot shower and a bed would feel good tonight.

From behind, Fred gave her a verbal nudge. "You are a strong outdoorswoman! Don't give in to the temptation of the soft life."

Kim turned, looked at Fred, and gave him a wan smile. "I promise not to tell your wife that you're a mind reader."

"Drat! My secret is out, at least with you. I still play ignorant with my wife. It's safer that way. If you look to the north, you'll see the ridge on the left and a lake to the right and down. That's McLeod Lake, and I'd like us to find a secluded spot near there to make camp, so it's not much farther and downhill!"

"So, where's Reds Meadow?" Kim scanned the horizon to the north and west.

"We can't see it from here, but we might be able to see it when we get a bit farther to the north in a few minutes."

At that next knob, they were able to look down but not quite see Reds. "I think that it's just beyond where the slope dips down over there. From where I'm suggesting we camp, it's maybe four miles. I wish we could be closer, but there's no easy water on the west side, and I'm afraid if we get too close to Reds, we could run into curious or dangerous people."

Pointing off to the northern horizon, he said, "See those sharp peaks there? If I'm reading my map correctly, those are the Minarets, and I'm supposed to be there in a few days." He looked wistfully to the north, realizing that there was a good chance he wouldn't make it beyond Reds this year. He smiled, also realizing that it was a much more eventful trip than he had planned.

A half-hour later, they had worked themselves into a nice little nook behind a couple of large boulders in the forest a few hundred feet uphill from McLeod Lake. Kim and Fred hadn't seen a soul since they'd left Duck Lake, so they felt that they were well concealed. Kim put up the tent and prepped camp while Fred wandered down to the lake for water. When he returned, he suggested that they both go back to the lake to clean, and he grabbed his soap and collapsible bucket.

At the lake, Kim hid in the woods while Fred dipped water for her. She washed up while Fred kept watch on the lake shore. While she was bathing, he saw a couple of people far across the lake, but that was it, making him feel better. Kim returned to camp while Fred cleaned up.

Back at camp, Fred boiled water to start supper.

"What's on the menu tonight, chef?" asked Kim.

"Tonight, will be one of my favorites. We'll be having carnitas, cheese, and chips, along with dried fruit and nuts. I make the meat at home and vacuum package it as *carnitas confitada*. It's nice to mix up these meals between store-bought freeze-dried, my homemade meals, and adding in fresh trout. I've eaten more trout than I expected, and I'm really ready for a change. Also, we really need the nutrition of a big meal since we haven't been eating enough the past few days and we hiked so much today."

Kim relaxed while Fred made supper. Her mind wandered to what the next day or two might bring. As much as Kim had learned to enjoy her time out here, she wanted to get back to a more normal life. Seeing Mammoth Lakes in the distance this afternoon made her feel thoughtfully for the little luxuries that she'd been missing. Tonight's camp spot was the least appealing that they'd made while she had been with Fred since trees surrounded them, and there wasn't much of a view.

"You know," she started, "I just realized that when I get back, I have to sell my house and move. Now that I've been outed by Omega and his crew, it won't be safe for me to go back there. It's a depressing realization because I like that house and neighborhood. I'll probably have to look at buying a condo so that I can have better security. It's just another big chore I'll have to manage. Maybe I'll just stay out here and avoid reality a bit longer." Kim's face showed the sadness she felt.

Fred stirred the pork while it warmed. "I've been in my house for fifteen years now and don't relish the idea of moving; all the packing, the little decisions, memories, things getting broken, discarding stuff you don't use anymore. I feel for you."

Kim responded, "I've been so wrapped up in my life and work in San Francisco and enjoying it so much that I've never really thought about where else I might want to live. I'll have to see how long the umbilicus from work might be, what they'll allow me. I'm guessing that once I get back, there will be a lot of finger-pointing and so on regarding lax security. Argh!"

"Well, now that you've been here for what, nearly a week, maybe you should consider being some kind of a hermit." Fred's sarcastic suggestion caused Kim's eyes to roll.

"Yeah," she said, "that's sort of what my social life feels like, so I'm already familiar with parts of the role."

Supper was ready, and they heaped hot spicy carnitas on tortillas and savored the taste of home.

"I liked the trout," Kim said between bites, "but it is nice to have so much more flavor. And the salt! My body has been craving that today!"

Fred's mouth was too full to talk, so he just grinned and nodded, juices dripping through his ratty beard and falling to the ground. Looking at him, Kim remarked that he'd need to go back to the lake to wash his face after supper, and they both laughed!

After supper, Fred could read Kim's face. Being nestled in the forest was not helping her mood, along with thoughts of house hunting and moving. "Hey, I have my phone. Can I show you photos of my trips and family?"

Kim looked at him and smiled. "Yes, please!"

Over the next half hour, Fred showed Kim photos of his wife, Asta, and kids; his backpacking trip earlier this summer to the Wind River Range; and several pictures from his John Muir Trail trip a couple of years ago, including a photo of Will and him standing on top of Mt.

Whitney at the end. Kim recognized his photo of Fred and Will standing near Purple Lake.

"Thank you so much for sharing those with me. I appreciate it. It looks like you have a wonderful family and lots of great memories," she said.

"Yes, just like you have with your family and travels, I bet," he said. "And, you and I are going to have some amazing stories to tell about this trip when we get back!"

After sitting quietly and listening to the sound of the wind through the trees, Fred decided it was time for him to get in the tent. "I'm likely going to get up and take off for Reds Meadow early tomorrow morning. That will leave more food for you because I'll be picking up my resupply, so I'll be fine. I figure that it's about two hours down to there, maybe a little more coming back, and I'll spend a few hours there to see if I can pick up any news on a missing woman in the Sierras. I'm off to bed. Make certain you turn the lights out before you come in!"

Kim gave him a friendly shove, and she was on her own. "Wait a minute," she called out. "Do you have earphones and music on your phone that I could listen to?"

"Sure," said Fred. "Just be certain to leave the phone in airplane mode so that we're not broadcasting our location to anyone just yet." He dug around in his pack and found his earphones and gave them and the phone to her. "There's a nice eclectic variety of music on there. Hopefully, you'll find something you like."

It was more pleasant than she had expected to be sitting alone in the forest, listening to the music, and breathing the pine-scented air. Kim just kind of spaced out, sitting deep in the woods, no spectacular view to enthrall her. Through the boughs, she could make out several stars and the glow of city lights from Mammoth. It pained her to think about selling her house and moving; she missed her family, her parents and hoped that she could make a trip to Chicago when this was all over. Then she started to remember the sunsets and sunrises over the past couple of days and found herself in a much warmer place.

Eventually, the duff under her keister became a little too cool and hard, and she felt it was likely time to go to bed. She wasn't tired, just tired of sitting as well as tired of not being home, being challenged in such a profound way. She turned off the music, removed the earphones, and Fred's snoring serenaded her. *Well, maybe I can stay out here a little longer*, she thought.

———————

Alpha called Omega to check-in.

"Bad news, sir. I've lost Beta. He went to this place called Reds Meadow yesterday. The plan was for him to hike south and keep his eyes open for Dr. Johnson since you suggested that she might be coming from that direction toward Mammoth. He acclimated better than me, so he was the better choice. We had a storm here a couple of nights ago, and he took off yesterday morning.

"He called on his sat phone that he was making progress, but the storm washed out a bridge over a creek. He said that he was going to cross it, and that's the last that I heard from him.

"I heard chatter on the scanner that a search and rescue team was called out to a location several miles south of Reds Meadow. They'd received an emergency message about someone being swept away in a flooded creek.

"I drove up to Reds Meadow to see if there was anything I could overhear there. Several backpackers talked about seeing a big guy trying to cross a creek, and a washed down log hit him, or he slipped or something. They haven't found the guy's body, but I'm guessing that it was Beta.

Omega let out an audible sigh. "I'm very sorry to hear this, Omega. I know that you two worked together on several projects for me and served in the military together. It's a tough loss, presuming that it's him."

"Thank you, sir; it means a lot. If I hear more about a body recovery, I'll let you know. He has a family, too, and I'll follow up with them after we resolve this problem."

Alpha continued: "Everything and everyone else are in place. I have people camping out and watching several different trailheads – four on the west side of the Sierras, three on the east side, plus five of us here in the Mammoth Lakes area, which has several trails converging here. We've also procured a few stingray devices so that we can collect cellphone information and feed that to your resources for processing. And, as I said, I've been monitoring the local radio frequencies."

"Good to hear, Alpha. Our analyst has lost track of the person who might be helping Dr. Johnson. Part of that is because of that storm – the satellites can't get visuals through the clouds. But he hasn't been checking in with his family like he was earlier in his trip. He may be minimizing communications at Dr. Johnson's suggestion, presuming she's with him. We don't know for certain if that's our primary target, but it's still a strong one. Check-in tomorrow or whenever something else breaks your way."

Chapter 30

Fred was up at first light. He very groggily and gently crawled over Kim, and she barely moved. Outside, it looked like it would be another beautiful day, and Fred hoped there would be progress towards getting Kim back to a more normal life. He had his backpack with him, a full water bottle, and a few other things, but that was about it. He'd repack the bear canister later today with the additional food while figuring out what to do tomorrow. Fred found his phone near Kim's head and grabbed it at the last moment.

A couple of hours later, he was at Reds Meadow. The trip down was pleasant and unremarkable. Fred would've made it faster, but he was really dragging this morning. The lack of food was catching up with him, particularly after yesterday's long hike. He was thankful for a relatively easy day today, as well the abundance of food here. Reds was just beginning to wake although the backpackers' campground had been sort of buzzing for some time. The Mulehouse Café was open, starting to serve hungry hikers. He was in no hurry to pick up his resupply, and hunger pangs gnawed at him worse than about any other time in his life.

Inside the café, the scents of cooking eggs, potatoes, and, of course, bacon enthralled him. Fred was now ravishingly hungry and found a small table for himself. There was only one other open table, so he felt fortunate. Maybe someone would want to join him, and that was fine by him.

A server approached his table, and he looked at the menu board for ideas. Everything looked so good! He settled on the #7 – eggs, potatoes, toast, and bacon – along with a cup of hot tea. Maybe he'd order a second breakfast later. Fred hadn't mentioned to Kim that there was café or store here because he didn't want to tempt her to come down. Before he left later today, he'd grab a couple of burgers and take them back to her – one for each of them. The service was quick, and his food was on the table before he knew it.

Before the server could walk away, Fred caught her attention. "Ma'am, when I was south of here, on the trail, there was word going around the backpackers that there was a woman who had become lost. Have you heard anything about her?"

The server gave Fred a quizzical look and shook her head no. "You're the first person to mention anything about a lost backpacker to me, although there were reports that a backpacker may have drowned a couple of days ago in Duck Creek," she said and went off to another table.

Fred relished his breakfast! He knew that he would have regretted backpacking on such a full stomach, at least for the first hour, but this well-deserved meal hit the spot. He hadn't had a hot meal cooked by someone else since he was at Parcher's Resort – eight days ago? So much had happened since then that Fred couldn't quite work out how long he'd been out.

An older man entered the café; he was wearing jeans, a denim jacket and cowboy hat, so it was a pretty good bet that he wasn't a backpacker. He made eye contact with the server, and she nodded at Fred. Now, that had Fred's attention, and the man made his way to Fred's table. He made a quick hand signal that he wanted a cup of coffee, too.

At the table, the man looked at Fred and said, "Good mornin'! May I join you?"

Fred said, "Of course!" but he was also curious why he was getting special attention that no one else seemed to be getting.

The man sat down across from Fred and set his hat on the table. "My name is Bill, Bill Shepherd, and I'm the manager here at Reds Meadow. And you would be?"

"My name is Fred. I've been out backpacking the Sierra High Route the past ten days or so. I have a resupply to pick up here and I'm enjoying the café's wonderful breakfast. It's great to have someone do the cooking for me."

Bill grinned, and a moment later, his coffee arrived. "Thank you. We like hearing that."

Bill continued: "I get to chat with a few of our guests when they pass through or rent cabins, mostly when they come into the store or I'll be out in the yard, and someone will have a question. I don't usually make a point of checking in with specific guests, but you're an exception.

"Marilyn, our server, called me and said you'd heard something about a lost backpacker south of here. We haven't heard anything of that sort. We make it our business to keep our guests safe and happy, even if they haven't been here yet. If there's word about a lost backpacker and I don't know about it, then there's a good chance that the Forest Service or Park Service rangers don't know about her either. So, could you tell me more so that I might contact the proper authorities if appropriate? There's already a lot of buzz around here because a backpacker likely drowned a couple of days ago, so this might be a new situation that needs our attention."

Involving a new, unknown person was a wrinkle that Fred hadn't anticipated. For a moment, he was perplexed and didn't know quite know how to proceed. He knew that he couldn't, wouldn't continue with the story of a lost backpacker, but he had to think carefully about divulging information about Kim. The café was loud with clanking forks, dishes, and cups, but Fred didn't want to be overheard by anyone, especially if there were eavesdroppers he couldn't trust.

Fred had finished most of his breakfast, except the toast and tea. "I'll tell ya what. Let's go outside and have our chat. I'll fill you in there while I finish."

After Fred paid, he walked out and found Bill sitting on a bench, keeping his hands warm around his cup of coffee, and sat beside him.

Fred began: "I came through here a couple of years ago while backpacking with my son on the JMT. I liked it here, especially the food, but it was nice to get back to semi-civilization for a night, and the staff was all so good to us. I hope that most backpackers are appreciative of what you all do, and it seems like the staff treats everyone well, which I hope is mutually reflective of the backpackers and how they treat you all."

Bill was a patient man who enjoyed listening to backpackers' stories, and he was thankful for the kind words of appreciation, but that's not what had piqued his interest. He started to speak up, but Fred asked for patience with a little wave of his hand.

"I know that's not why you want to see me. I'm trying to set the table to share with you a problem that I have and how I need to trust you about this."

Bill gave a polite nod, looked at his coffee, and then up at Fred. "OK, you have my attention, and I'll do the best for you that I can, but I'm not making any promises since I don't know your problem. Please, go on."

Over the next several minutes, Fred laid out how he had happened upon Kim, how she had been kidnapped, brought to the Sierras, and then escaped. Fred didn't provide all the details, but he gave enough so that Bill could gather the nature of the situation. And Fred told him that he didn't know what he could say or do to help Bill believe him.

"Well, this is quite the unusual, unique situation," Bill said. "We hear about lost hikers with some frequency, sick, injured, and inexperienced backpackers and many other happenings, but we've never had a kidnapping, that's for sure." Bill sat there with Fred, both trying to figure out what to do from here.

Fred continued. "My new friend came up with a plan a couple of days ago to get her into town. We don't know, but we fully expect that the people who kidnapped her are looking for her, so we're very cautious about how to get into town to avoid detection."

Backpackers wandered around, laughed, joked, and made conversation. Some of the packers were heading out, while others were still sleepily dragging themselves into the café or checking out the store. No one gave Fred or Bill a second thought, mainly since they were both much older than most guests.

Bill finally spoke. "I don't mean to be disrespectful or anything, but this is not a situation that we could deal with well." Fred raised his eyebrows and nodded his head to signal his understanding and confusion about dealing with Kim's problem. Bill looked around at all the activity, wheels spinning in his mind.

Bill gave Fred a puzzled look. "Ya know, why haven't you just called 911 or something like that? Since you haven't, I'm guessing there's a good reason."

"Yes, there is a good reason, we think. The details are too much to go into, but we're very concerned that the kidnappers will intercept our phone call, whether it's a landline or cell phone. My new companion expects that someone is monitoring your phone lines since Reds Meadow is in the middle of the backpackers' highway. She's in a high-tech situation that's way over my head, and she has good reason to believe they can listen in to just about any communication system they want.

"We've been cautious so far. For example, I've kept my cell phone off or in airplane mode since we got close to Mammoth for fear that we might be tracked. I also have one of those satellite texting devices and have limited my use of it, just in case. My wife is probably worried since she hasn't heard from me as often."

"Well, if it's over your head, then it's over my head, too," said Bill, as they sat on the bench, taking in the sights, and continued to ponder.

"Here's another idea, the next logical thought, I hope," said Bill. "What if you take the bus down to Mammoth and speak to the police yourself? The bus runs every forty-five minutes or so now and every thirty minutes starting later this morning. You could go to town, do your thing with the police or sheriff, and be back later today. How 'bout that?"

"Well, that's a good idea," Fred said, "and I've already given that possibility some thought. Once I got into town, though, I'd have to make my way to the police or sheriff, and that's going to chew up more time. I suppose I could take a taxi or something to get around town. My main concern is leaving her out there for too long. I left her with the idea that I'd be back by early to mid-afternoon, so that idea would likely make me later than that. It's not a bad idea, but it's the best one so far, short of us just walking into town."

They sat there, thinking more, considering the possibilities. Bill's eyes wandered around, and he had another idea.

"Missy!" he called out. A young woman in jeans and fleece was walking toward the general store, stopped, and looked around. She looked around, saw Bill, and Bill waved for her to come over.

"Missy, this here's Fred, and he has a predicament, and there's a way that you might help him. When are you heading into Mammoth to pick up supplies and stop at the Post Office?"

After shaking Fred's hand and exchanging greetings, she stood back and thought. "Well, I was planning on leaving in about an hour for my daily run into town. Does he need a ride into town for something special?"

"Here's what I'm thinking," looking more at Fred than Missy. "Fred, what if you write a message and Missy could deliver it to the police station and maybe wait around to see how they react. If your story holds up, then Missy here should get a fairly rapid response, and she'd be able to call back here to me. Maybe she could leave a little earlier than normal, too. That way, you'd get a response from the police sooner and maybe be able to get back to your friend by later this morning or early afternoon rather than waiting 'til later this afternoon. Whaddya think about that?"

Fred's eyebrows were up, and he had a smile on his face. "You know, that sounds like a good plan. It gets me in contact with the authorities, and it doesn't burden you all any more than needed. As you said, this isn't your typical problem. You don't have to believe me, I don't have to tell you too much, and it's up to me to make my case to the authorities. I'd appreciate it if we could go that route!"

Missy just shrugged her shoulders and said, "Fine by me. I don't know what's going on, but I'm always willing to lend a hand. What else do you need from me then?"

Bill said, "Let me get some Reds Meadow letterhead, an envelope, and a pen for Fred. You can sit at one of the picnic tables and write what you need. Missy, could you check in with Fred from time to time and then head into town with his message?"

Missy shook her head, yes. "I'm heading into the general store to get the supplies list, so I'll check on you again later, Fred." She smiled, wheeled around and headed off.

Now Fred was smiling. A plan was sort of coming together, maybe a bit haphazardly, but it was coming together. "Thank you, Bill! I, *er we*, really appreciate this!" Fred shook his hand again, and Bill headed off to get the stationery for Fred.

Fred was now deep in thought, trying to figure out what to say, how to seem credible, what to write about Kim so that they'd know she was legitimate, how to signal the authorities discretely, and how to share Kim's rescue plan. A few minutes later, Bill returned with the pen and paper and left Fred to write his message.

After a few mental false starts, Fred started writing:

Dear Mammoth Lakes Police:

My name is Fred Bortz, and I have cared for a woman who claims to be Dr. Kim Johnson for the past few days in the Sierras. She says that she was kidnapped in San Francisco more than a week ago. My wife is Asta, and her cellphone number is…

After Fred finished his message, he reread it, made a few edits, folded the piece of paper, and put it into the envelope. He wrote *Mammoth Lakes Police* on the outside and wrote down his cellphone number.

Missy stopped by a few minutes later, and Fred handed her the envelope. "So, I just want you to know that I'm sorry about all the secrecy here, but a woman's life is at stake. The reason that I'm sending this message down with you is that I'm worried about someone intercepting my cell phone calls – it's that weird of a situation. If you get a good response from the police, could you please call Bill and give him some simple message that they found my story plausible? If I don't hear from you, then I need to figure out what kind of mess I've gotten myself into and how to walk into Mammoth with this woman. Oh, and I have a photo of the woman and me on my phone – can I transfer that image to you to show to the police?"

Missy smiled and shrugged her shoulders. "Yea, I don't understand what's going on, but I understand that it's hush-hush. Let me open my phone so that you can send the photo to me."

A minute later, Kim and Fred's selfie on top of Bighorn Pass was on Missy's phone. "I'm leaving now, and it'll take me about forty-five minutes to get to town. I doubt that I'll be in contact for at least an hour, so hang tight."

"Thanks for the info; I appreciate it," Fred said. "I can pick up my resupply and maybe some other little things. I – we – sincerely appreciate your help, Missy!"

Missy gave him a little wave and walked away toward the parking lot.

Fred stood there for a moment, collecting his thoughts, trying to think of how to occupy himself other than the general store and his resupply bucket. He felt good that he seemed to be making progress for Kim, more than he had expected. Looking around, he saw the shower house and knew what he should do.

After his shower, Fred picked up his resupply bucket and had a snack at the store. He was sitting in the morning sun, thinking about his and Kim's next moves, what the possibilities were, what he'd do if the police didn't believe him, and so on. It was difficult for him to be patient in these moments. He was second-guessing himself, asking if he'd done the right thing by involving Bill and Missy. Even though it felt longer, only a couple of hours had passed, and he was beginning to think that maybe he'd put too much faith in Kim. So much to think about, so much riding on it. A few minutes later, Bill walked up and sat beside him.

"So, I just got a call from town, from the police chief. Missy is continuing with her chores, and the chief said that Missy received a very warm reception in town – if you get my drift – and the chief will here in forty-five minutes or less. That's all she said, so I don't know what else is going on, but I hope that you'll wait around here a bit longer. Go cool your heels in the Mulehouse – tell 'em that your lunch is on me." With a parting smile and a pat on Fred's relieved and curious back, Bill was off to tend to his more normal chores.

Chapter 31

Missy walked into the Mammoth Lakes Police Department a bit hesitantly. She'd only been here once before, and that was to pick up a friend who'd had an unscheduled meeting with the police concerning his drinking and driving issues. Missy looked around for a moment before she found a uniformed officer sitting behind the front desk. No one else was around, so she had this woman's full attention.

"Excuse me, ma'am, I work up at Reds Meadow. We have a guest who seems to have some issue that he believes is important to the authorities. He asked me to deliver this message," handing the officer the envelope, "and to share this photo with the police." Missy opened her phone and shared the photo with the officer.

With Missy's cell phone sitting on the counter, the officer opened the envelope and respectfully read Fred's letter. Missy tried to read the officer's face and didn't think that this woman would be a good poker player. The officer looked at Missy and asked her to take a seat in the waiting area. "Oh," she said, "do you mind if I leave your phone here on the desk for a moment?" Missy told her it was fine by her and went to sit down.

The officer retreated to a phone, dialed, and quietly spoke.

"Chief, this Collins."

"Yes, Collins, what is it? I'm driving to the monthly tourism luncheon."

"Chief, you remember that high-level bulletin you mentioned a few days ago about a kidnapped computer scientist? You should get back here ASAP. I think lunchtime is over."

Ten minutes later, Chief Madison, Officer Collins, and Missy were in the Chief's office. Madison was on her office phone. She had dialed the phone number that appeared in the bulletin and then entered a pass code. Moments later, she heard a voice on the other end: "Yes, I'm listening."

"My name is Police Chief Julia Madison of the Mammoth Lakes

Police Department, Mammoth Lakes, California. We have reason to believe that the party you seek is nearby, but we have not completely verified this information, nor do we have this person under our supervision. We have a message from a third party saying that the person you seek is healthy and an image that we believe to be of the person of interest. Please advise. I will hold."

After several minutes of silence, a different voice came on the line: "Chief Madison, this Special Agent Andrews. I am the situation coordinator. Please send a copy of the message you received, as well as the photograph, to the link that appears in your secure email. Please do not send any images or files by text message or anything like that. We'll wait. Thank you. And please do not hang up."

Madison was scrambling for a scanner to copy the two-page letter. To Missy she said, "Ma'am, could you please transfer this image to my phone? We would greatly appreciate it. Collins, after she transfers the file, please escort Missy to the waiting area. And please wait there for me. Also, Missy, we'd appreciate it you would please leave your cellphone with us. Thank you."

As soon as the Chief had the image file on her phone, she connected her phone to her computer, transferred the image file, and then transferred it from there to the link provided, along with the scan of Fred's letter. And then she waited. In her years of police work, most of the time, she was in an exciting situation, it involved a suspect in the field, drunk or with a weapon. She couldn't recall a time that she'd been on the phone, keeping her emotions in check, being patient.

After several more minutes, Special Agent Andrews was again on the line. "Chief Madison, we have every reason to believe that this message is credible and that the victim is nearby. I will take command of the situation, but I very much need your assistance. I would ask that you please attempt to personally contact the messenger, Fred, thank him for everything that he has done and ask him to return to Reds Meadow tomorrow afternoon by about 3:00 PM with the victim. I'd rather that they come in sooner, but also understand that they're cautious, and it allows us more time to plan and prep. How long before you think that you'll contact him?"

"Well, it's about a forty-five-minute drive from here to Reds Meadow, but I can make it faster," said Chief Madison.

"No, that won't be necessary. We don't wish to draw any attention to this situation. I'd like you to please make a friendly visit to Reds Meadow. While you're driving, I'm going to do a bit more planning. I will call you on your cellphone with additional information while you're on your way. Also, could you please assign a plains clothes officer to be on watch at Reds Meadow? We have reason to believe that there are likely people in Mammoth Lakes and other locations on the borders of the Sierras who are watching and waiting for the victim.

"Also, please sequester the phone of the person who brought you the photograph. If you have any reason not to trust this person, please consider isolating them.

"I will be on a flight to Mammoth in the next couple of hours. If you could have someone meet me at the airport, I'd sincerely appreciate it. I will also have people scrambling immediately, but at this time, I do not know their needs, nor how they will travel.

"Lastly, I wish to remind you that this is a matter of national security. Silence is golden. Thank you, Chief Madison, and I'll be in contact soon."

The line was silent, and Madison took a deep breath. *Well, I guess that our pleasant little ski town might be getting some attention now.* She stepped out of her office, looked around, and saw Officer Collins. "Collins, could you please bring Missy in here for me? Thank you."

A moment later, Collins led Missy into the Chief's office, who turned to leave. "Collins, I want you to stay; you're a big part of this now."

Chief Madison then gave them a brief rundown of what she could and didn't tell them a whole lot. "Missy, I need to ask some favors of you. First, when you left Reds, were you given any more instructions, like what to do after you spoke with us?"

"Well, yeah. If this message was interesting to you all, I'm to call or text my boss and let him know. Otherwise, no news meant that this Fred guy could be on his way."

"OK, good. Your boss is Bill Shepherd, right?" Missy nodded yes, looking a bit frightened since she had no idea what mess she was in now.

Chief Madison continued. "Did you read this letter from this Fred guy or share the image he gave you with anyone?"

Missy took on a severe look and shook her head no. "No, ma'am, they asked me to keep this quiet, and that's what I've done. You and Officer Collins are the only two people I've spoken to."

"Good. I'm delighted to hear that." The Chief sat and thought for a moment. "Missy, what are you doing here in town? Do you need to go back to Reds?"

Missy looked at her, confused, and stammered, "Well, I have my town chores to do this morning. I need to pick up some bulk items at the grocery store for our café and general store, and then stop at the Post Office to pick up backpacker resupply buckets and packages."

Madison took this information in and thought for a moment. "Collins, you're an outdoors person, aren't you?"

"Yes, Chief, but just about all of us on staff here are outdoorsy because of all of the recreational opportunities. I'm not special," said Collins matter-of-factly.

"So, ladies, here's what I'd like to do. First, as I'm now relaying to you, this is a very sensitive matter. Do not share with anyone what you've seen or heard here today. Can you do that, Missy? No phone calls, no texts, no social media about this? Can you do that?"

Missy looked at her feet for a moment and said, "I don't know. I'm pretty active on social media, and there are so many interesting people to talk to at Reds. I'm someone who hasn't ever really been good about keeping secrets, to be honest."

The Chief just smiled. "That's OK. So, I'm going to make a very strong suggestion, and I don't want you to think of this as punishment. I'd like you to please stay here while Officer Collins goes home and changes into her outdoor clothes. When she returns, she'll accompany you on your errands and help you to pick up the supplies and packages at the Post Office. Collins, I want you also to arrange a nice hotel stay for Missy with room service privileges. Assign someone to stay with Missy. If you have family, roommates, or someone you need to check in with, Missy, please do that when you're with Officer Collins. After she sees that you're safely at the hotel or the other agent does that, I'd like to hold your phone here in the office until this situation blows over, likely in a day or two. Can we all do that?"

Missy and Collins both shook their heads yes, although Missy seemed confused and less willing.

Looking at Collins, the Chief asked, "Do we have Missy's phone?"

Collins shook her head no and pointed to Missy's back jeans pocket, and the Chief understood. "Missy, could you please give your phone to Officer Collins? I'd sincerely appreciate it. If you need to make a business or personal call, especially to check in with family and friends to let them know that you'll be indisposed for a day or two, that's fine. But, before you leave here, please give your phone to Collins. I know that you don't comprehend what's going on right now, but I sincerely appreciate your help and understanding. And to be perfectly honest, I don't fully understand what's going on. I'm flying blind but in my own way. Collins, please come out into the hall with me; Missy, please stay here until Officer Collins checks in with you in a few minutes."

Out in the hallway, the Chief let her guard down, pulled back her hair, and gave out a long, hard breath. "So, I need you to find an officer to watch Missy at the hotel; they don't need to be in the room with her 24/7, but they need to make certain that she doesn't leave, escape or have contact with anyone. Take the phone or phones from the room. Also, Missy needs to be isolated while she's here until you return. Go home and change and accompany Missy on her errands, then take her to whatever hotel you can find. You take her vehicle to Reds and plan on spending the night there somehow – camp out someplace, maybe sleep in the storage area behind the general store. I don't know anything else, but I'll be in contact and keep you apprised. The only other thing that I can tell you that I didn't say in front of Missy is that this is a national security matter. They're not telling me anything else, for now. The shit's hitting the fan, and we're in front of it. Clear?"

Collins nodded yes, a slight twinkle of excitement in her eye.

"I'm calling Bill Shepherd right now, and then I'm driving to Reds Meadow. I'm supposed to receive additional direction from the Feds while I'm on my way up there. Are we good to go?"

Officer Collins gave the Chief a confident smile and turned to find an officer to watch Missy.

Chief Madison went to a quiet office, called Reds Meadow, and asked to speak with Bill Shepherd. A moment later, she heard, "Bill Shepherd, Reds Meadow, how may I help you?"

"Hello, Mr. Shepherd, this is Police Chief Julia Madison down in Mammoth Lakes. I have a package to deliver to one of your guests, and

I don't want to arrive unannounced. Will you be there in about forty-five minutes or so? I'd appreciate it."

On the other end of the line, Bill took a deep breath and sort of understood the cryptic meaning behind the message. He hadn't expected to receive this call. "Uh, sure, I'll be here. We'll have a fresh cup of coffee ready for you. See you in forty-five."

Driving to Reds, Julia was wondering what the hell was going on in her quiet little town. Sure, we have parties, drunks, too many crazy people, but this might be a whole 'nother level of crazy. *This is why I left LA, to get away from this shit.*

She felt her phone vibrate on her lap. *Unknown number* is what the screen read. She answered, anyway.

"Chief, this is Andrews. We're on a secure line, correct?"

"Yes, sir, this is a secure phone, courtesy of the Feds."

"Good. Sometimes, it comes in useful, like this time. We're still formulating our plan, as you might expect. I still want your Mr. Bortz and Dr. Johnson to meet me tomorrow by, what time did I say, 4:00 PM?"

"No, sir, you said 3:00 PM when we first spoke."

"Ah, thank you. Yes, I will meet our guests by 3:00 PM at Reds Meadow, along with your plainclothes officer. Dr. Johnson had a pretty good plan in mind, and we're going to follow through with what she suggested – to a point. If anything changes in the meantime, then Mr. Bortz should send an emergency message, and we'll ad-lib. Clear?"

"Yes, sir. If I need to get ahold of you, how do I do that? What time is your flight arriving?"

"Ah, good questions. I'll text you my direct cellphone number, and I'll text flight info when I have it. Are we good for now?"

"Yes, and I look forward to meeting you. I feel that we're on top of this and have the situation as controlled as we can," Chief Madison replied.

"Good. Frankly, I can't say that any of us has this situation under control. There are too many balls being juggled by too many people for me to feel comfortable. In a situation like this, the only thing that I can do is trust that everyone does the right thing, does what they think is best. I'll see you in a few hours." And he hung up.

Well, she thought, *he's a good agent. He gets his point across succinctly and gets on with business. No wasted motion in that man. He obviously doesn't work with the public a whole lot.*

Fifteen minutes later, Chief Madison was in the circle at Reds Meadow, quietly parking in an open spot and gently wandering over to the open area between the general store and Mulehouse Café. As usual, when she was in uniform and walked into a crowd of strangers, especially among younger people, they all stared at her, and the conversations reduced to whispers. Now was not one of the times she enjoyed wearing her uniform, but that's the way it was.

A face that looked familiar approached her and extended his hand. After a brief and friendly handshake, the man said, "Chief Madison, I'm Bill Shepherd, the manager here at Reds. Let's take a seat and talk through things."

"Mr. Shepherd," Madison quietly said, "if you and Mr. Bortz could meet me over in the backpacker's campground, I'd appreciate it. I'm trying to reduce the number of prying eyes, and I'm too obvious here. Over there, I'll still stick out, but there'll be fewer eyes and ears, I hope."

Maybe fifteen minutes later, they were all gathered at a campground picnic table. There weren't as many people here, and that was fine by Chief Madison. Most of the campers were relaxing or napping. Fred and Bill were sitting at the picnic table when she arrived, and they stood to greet the Chief.

"Fred, this is our local Police Chief, Julia Madison. I've met her a few times at town events and tourism meetings. She's a good person. And I frankly don't know why she's here, but I can guess." Bill and Chief Madison sat on one side of the table, and Fred was on the other side.

"Thank you for allowing me to visit you in your office, Mr. Bortz," as her hands swept around the forest. "May I please call you Fred?"

Fred nodded his head affirmatively, eyebrows knit with concern and curiosity.

"I'll get straight to it. I don't know what's going on, but you're bringing all kinds of attention down on my quiet little vacation town. Oh, and Bill, mum's the word.

"So, yes, I don't know what's going on. Fred, I read your message, but it doesn't tell me the whole situation. We received a bulletin a few days ago to be on the lookout for a kidnapped woman who meets the description you noted. The photograph you sent along with Missy was very helpful. It helped to confirm her identity. We passed your message and the picture to the proper authorities.

"Oh, I apologize for changing the subject on you, but Bill, your employee, Missy, we've been asked to isolate her, for the time being, just to keep her from talking or communicating with anyone else. She reluctantly agreed to my suggestion. Missy won't be back until this situation blows over, but one of my officers, Collins, will bring your truck back with the supplies and mail. She'll stay at Reds through this situation, to keep watch. Collins will be armed and have communications gear with her. I've asked her to dress as a hiker, a guest, so that she can blend in. If you could arrange a central but stealthy location for her to bed down, I'd appreciate it. Anyway, where was I? Oh yes!

"So, Fred, the basic plan you wrote in your message, Dr. Johnson's plan, is the working plan, although the agent in charge has made some modifications and more details need to be worked out. All you're supposed to do is to return to Reds tomorrow by 3:00 PM. You are not to set off your emergency beacon unless absolutely necessary, nor are you to turn on your cellphone. That's about it. It would be preferable if you're here well before 3:00, but it's up to you two. Officer Collins will be here as a lookout and protection, as I just mentioned. She saw the photograph of you and Dr. Johnson, so if a middle-aged, fit, sandy-haired woman in hiking clothes and a bit of limp chats you up, then that's likely her. Allow her to approach you and make the first contact. Her first name is Beth, so please don't address her as Officer Collins. She knows your names, so she has been told to identify herself by discretely addressing you without your prompting her. You'll also be meeting Special Agent Andrews here, but I have not received a description of him; he is the Federal agent in charge of this whole situation. I'm hoping that I can connect him and Officer Collins via cellphone before he arrives, but I don't know."

Fred looked at her, pleased and pleasantly surprised that they were running with Kim's plan. Bill just looked at the two of them blankly, like, *what the hell is going on?*

"So, gentleman, at this time, I don't know anything else, at least nothing that I can share with you. This is one of the wildest situations that I've encountered since I arrived in Mammoth as well as in my whole career. It's not why I moved here, but I'm guessing that it's one of the reasons they hired me, just in case of possible weird situations. Fred, if I never see you again, it will be my pleasure," she said with a wink and polite grin, "but I'm guessing that we'll be meeting up tomorrow. Oh, and just to settle your curiosity, that's about all that I know for now. Special Agent Andrews should arrive in Mammoth in the next few hours, take over and tell me more. And, frankly, I'm glad to let him have at it."

She looked at Fred and Bill. They all sort of shrugged and raised their eyebrows, like, *we understand, but we don't understand.* No more questions. They all knew their roles, to be quiet and carry on. Chief Julia reached out and warmly shook their hands. "Thanks, guys!" she said. "If you need me, you know how to contact me, but we need to keep this quiet."

And, looking specifically to Fred, she said, "Please give my regards to Dr. Johnson and let her know that everything will turn out fine. She's been in good hands for the past several days, and it's going to get better over the next few days." She calmly walked to her patrol vehicle and slowly drove away, drawing as little attention as she could.

Bill and Fred stood there, looked at each other, and started walking back to the café and general store. Bill spoke first.

"Well, I have no idea what's going on. Ignorance is bliss, so I'm going to carry on in my bliss and welcome Officer Collins when she comes back with our supplies and mail. I guess that I'll be seeing you by mid-afternoon tomorrow."

Fred smiled and walked along with him. "You know, I'm feeling more ignorant myself lately. Kim told me a lot, but it feels like I'm in a whole lot deeper than I thought."

Back in the yard between the café and store, Bill and Fred shook hands. "I'll see you tomorrow, Fred. Remember, this is a family resort, and we prefer to keep the excitement level down to a dull roar." Bill winked and smiled at him and walked into the store to continue his chores while Fred headed back to the café for a takeout supper and then hike back to his secret camper.

Chapter 32

Fred took a couple of hours getting to their camp. Walking uphill with a heavier load was tougher than coming down this morning, but he also felt a lot better after satisfying the hunger he'd carried for the past couple of days. He had been looking over his shoulder ever since he crested the ridge and felt that he was alone. When he had the boulders in sight and thought that he was close enough that he didn't have to shout, he called out, "Hi Honey! I'm home!"

Kim cautiously peered from around the boulders and then grinned. "Am I glad to see you! I haven't been this bored since I don't know when."

In his best Elmer Fudd voice, "And, I caught me a wabbit!" followed by Elmer's characteristic laugh.

Kim just shook her head, not knowing what that meant, but she caught the Elmer Fudd reference. A moment later, Fred pulled his resupply food out of his backpack, preceded by two takeout containers with double cheeseburgers. The burgers were barely warm, but Kim devoured hers and had such a grateful and satisfied look on her face. The fries were soft, but they went down quickly, too.

"Fred, my man, you are quite the trail chef! That was the best meal I've had in a long, long time, and I'm not usually much of a burger eater."

"Yeah," Fred started, "I apologize for not telling you that there's a café down there, but I was afraid that if I did, you'd be less willing to stay here all day."

"Apology accepted and logic understood." She gave him a playful punch in the shoulder, followed by a belch. They both laughed hysterically!

"Yep, you've become an outdoors woman now," Fred replied. "I have seriously degraded you.

"So, Kim, I have news from the outside world to share with you.

Tomorrow will be an interesting day for us; I just don't know how it's going to be interesting, though. We just have to hike to Reds Meadow and be there by 3:00 pm. That's it. We have a date with a new friend of yours, Special Agent Andrews." Kim was taking this in stride, waiting to learn more.

Fred just let that statement hang there and tried to ignore Kim's curiosity. Her face was saying *OK, get on with it*, but he enjoyed the tense moment he had created for her. Finally, she couldn't take it anymore.

"And...?" she said.

"Well, that's about it. Here's the full story, though. When I was at Reds, I tried to discretely inquire whether there had been any reports of a lost hiker woman. The bad news is that I wasn't as discrete as I hoped and set off some alarms there. The manager, Bill Shepherd, visited me. I made a calculated decision to trust him and told him that I need help.

"Speaking with Mr. Shepherd, we decided the best thing for me to do was to write a message, and one of his staffers delivered it to the Mammoth Lakes Police. Oh, and she took the selfie image of the two of us for more corroboration. I don't know what happened after that, but it appears that we struck a nerve. I guess that we'll find out more tomorrow. In the message, I wrote about your plan to get out of here. The Mammoth Lakes Police Chief visited and told me that they were going to run with much of the plan you suggested."

For a moment, Fred sat there, sort of beaming, proud with himself that he might have stumbled into a solution. Kim was trying to take this all in and make sense of it.

"So, let's back up a minute," she started. "We just have to get up and hike nonchalantly down to Reds Meadow, like nothing happened, like we're a happy backpacker couple out for a stroll? That sounds a little too simple."

Fred went into more detail about the message and what he had written in it. How he had introduced himself, noted that Kim was with him and safe, and gave his wife's phone number as a confirmatory contact, and then explained Kim's plan.

"OK," she said, "they went for it! That's good news. I'm not certain what they're going to do and what's changed, but I have some ideas. It does make more sense to get us out of the way, reduce our

travel, and the likelihood of being seen out here. There'll be more people at Reds, possibly Omega's people, but hopefully, we can figure out
a way to hide there. It sounds like my knight in stinking armor came
through for me big time!"

Fred blushed. "Aw, shucks, ma'am, t'ain't nothin' a typical man of
honor wouldn't have done for a damsel in distress." Again, they both
laughed.

Continuing, Fred said, "So, we're not really in any hurry. When we
get to Reds, a police officer in hiking clothes is supposed to be watching for us, as well as for any bad guys, just in case. Then at 3:00 pm or
so, Special Agent Andrews arrives. I don't know what happens after
that, but I'm guessing that you'll be out of the proverbial and actual
wilderness."

Kim was thinking about all of this, and then a bit of concern
came across her face. "I have just one question, though. It sounds
like we have a pretty good plan and that sharing it with the authorities
should lead to me getting out of here. My next question is: what if
my plan goes all to hell? What if someone at Reds or in town slips up,
and the word gets out that I'm up here. Then what? I'm not trying to
second guess myself but just want to be prepared."

Fred looked at her respectfully. "I was thinking about that, too,
while I was hiking back up here. I have a backup plan; actually, it's more
of an escape route. I sincerely believe that we have to trust everyone
around us in life until they prove that we shouldn't trust them. The
more time that I spend with someone, the more that I trust them. In
this case, we are dealing with many strangers, but many of these people
are strangers with authority. I didn't tell anyone where we're camping,
and I don't think that anyone followed on my way back. If your plan
doesn't appear to be working out, then we bail on it, head back into the
wilderness, and we'll find a different way back to civilization and safety.
We now have enough food to last several more days out here if worse
comes to worse."

Kim gave him a questioning look but also a glimpse of confi-
dence. "Guess what, Timber Wolf? I guess that I trust you – so far,"
followed with a smile and a wink. Timber Wolf returned her smile.

"Look, I know that it's not that late," Fred said, "and there's a bit
of light out, but I'd like to walk back up to the ridge and just look at

the stars. I'm a little tired, but I haven't really spent any time on my trip checking out constellations, in part because I'm so tired at night. I've had a long day, and tomorrow could be long, but there's no hurry to get moving tomorrow morning and the hiking should be relatively easy. So, if you'd like to join me, you're more than welcome! I snagged a ratty blanket from the hiker box at Reds, so we could sit or lay on it up there, and I'll use it tonight to hopefully sleep better."

"I'd love to join you!" was Kim's enthusiastic response. "I've seen the stars while we've been out here in the wilderness, but I've been hitting the sack early, too. I don't get to see too many stars in the city, so this will be a treat."

Fifteen minutes later, Kim and Fred sprawled along the top of the Mammoth Crest where they had looked over Mammoth Lakes and Reds Meadow the day before There were a few lights in the vicinity of Reds, but Mammoth Lakes was brightly glowing. They could make out the silhouette of the mountains to the north and south, with the last bit of evening light helping to provide some relief. To the west, the glowing night lights of the coastal cities gave the horizon some character along with the setting sun. Fred pointed out the Big and Little Dippers, Cassiopeia, and Scorpio, amongst many constellations. Kim was impressed, and Fred just shrugged. "It's just who I am and the things that I enjoy, just like you have your interests."

They sat and laid up there talking for about an hour, talking about returning to their everyday lives and having a sense of life returning to the mundane. Sometimes they didn't speak and just took in the cosmos, feeling even smaller than the wilderness made them feel. Eventually, they stumbled their way back down the mountainside to their camp, tripping and slipping, laughing at their missteps.

As he retired, Fred again regretted not sending a message to Asta. It was now two nights in a row that he hadn't texted home, and he didn't check for messages either. But he didn't want to reveal their location to her, especially if someone might be listening in. He hoped that the authorities would contact her and let her know that he was OK – but in danger.

_**Chapter 33**

The sense of relief they felt helped Kim and Fred to sleep better that night. They made no effort to get up early, to get on with life. Not waking up terribly hungry also felt good. It was nice to have an easy day, and they enjoyed themselves, and they had plenty of food for an excellent, filling breakfast.

Once they did get going, Fred took a stroll down to the lake for water and to wash his face. He couldn't see anyone else around, so he waved to Kim to come out of the woods and wash up, too. They both took in the morning with a fresh sense of meaning and purpose. Today was their last day together in the wilderness, and it was a spectacular morning, a great start to the day. They felt lighter than they'd felt the past several days, almost giddy.

They boiled water for tea and oatmeal and took turns eating and drinking. While one ate, the other packed. They even enjoyed some extra chocolates for breakfast since Fred had another chance to resupply again at Reds or in town. Even taking their time, they were ready by 8:00 am. There was no hurry in their steps, no fast intentions. They took their time, and the walking was easy, even pleasant in the cool morning air, full of added energy from their food and renewed outlook. They took off their packs and soaked in the morning sun and the gorgeous vistas from Mammoth Crest. The wind had come up and blew strong in their faces.

Looking down on Mammoth Lakes, they were almost wistful knowing that they'd be there by tonight, they figured, and with so little effort on their part. Their adventure was coming to a fitful end.

By late morning, they waltzed into Reds Meadow. Kim was almost beside herself to be back in some semblance of civilization, to be around other people again. They decided that the best thing for them was to find a place to sit, off to the side, where they could as easily observe as be observed. There were a few straggling backpackers still trying to get on the trail at this late hour. Most people seemed to be enjoying a lazy zero-day, just laying around, glued to their phones, showering, and doing laundry. People acted normally, without a care in the world. No one chased after them; everyone here was just chasing their dreams.

It felt odd for Kim to be sitting on a bench, something hard and flat with back support. She'd been sitting on rocks for these past several days, and it was such a contrast to feel her usual old self. Most of all, she was looking forward to a hot shower and clean cotton sheets!

A woman stepped out of the general store, headed down the stairs with no particular urgency or direction, looking around and made eye contact with them. She halted, turned about, and went back into the store; when she came out, she carried a small daypack over her shoulder. She didn't walk directly toward them but took her time getting there. She had sandy hair and a baseball cap with a ponytail poking out the back, a brace on her knee, and she walked with a bit of a limp. Fred knew who he hoped this person would turn out to be, but he sat there patiently and tried to ignore her.

The woman approached Kim and Fred. They had left a spot for someone to sit on Fred's left; Kim was on his right side, between his body and the café, sort of protected. The woman had a smile on her face and politely asked, "Is this seat taken?"

Fred just shook his head no, and she sat down with a bit of a flop. She didn't say anything, just sat there soaking the morning with them.

She began: "It's a beautiful morning, isn't it? It's an exciting morning if you've been on the trail for a few days, out in the wilderness, hoping to catch up on the happenings in the world. I was hoping to meet a couple of weary travelers like yourselves out here today. Maybe you know them? Their names are Kim and Fred. And, by the way, my name's Beth."

Kim sat there, eyes forward, not revealing any emotion. That is, except for the bit of tearing in her eyes. Fred sat there and nodded, nonplussed, taking in what the day brought to him.

Finally, Fred said, "You don't say? A couple by the name of Kim and Fred, huh? That's sort of a coincidence because we're supposed to meet someone who looks a lot like you. I believe that she goes by the name of Beth. Yes, Beth Collins, if I correctly recall."

The three of them just sat there, watching the goings-on in the town center of Reds Meadow. They felt no threat and still had several hours before Special Agent Andrews arrived. Kim could feel herself relaxing. Just as days before, when she met Fred and could relax after escaping her kidnappers, she felt another wave of relief.

"So, Kim, I'd like you to know that you're in good hands now. You're safe. We need to keep you here and under wraps for a few more hours before Special Agent Andrews arrives."

Kim was silently weeping, and Fred put his arm around her while she cried on his shoulder. It didn't last long, but the release felt beautiful. Beth sat and warmly smiled at her, having a sense for what Kim was going through, and reached over Fred to briefly take Kim's hand and gave it a knowing squeeze.

"Most of the time," Beth started, "I have to deal with traffic tickets, drunk visitors, and the like. It's nice for me to be at the happy ending of your ordeal. If you two will excuse me a moment, I need to step away and make a quick phone call to the Chief. I'm not going far. My duty is to keep Kim in my sight at all times."

Beth walked away from everyone and pulled a cellphone from her pack. After talking for a few minutes, she returned to the bench. She politely looked at Fred, winked, and gave him a signal to move to the bench's left end, which he did. Beth sat in between them.

"Chief Madison is downright thrilled that you've decided to visit our little community. She's going to share the news with some of your other fans, Kim. She doesn't think that she'll be able to make it up here today but hopes to see you two in town later. In the meantime, I'm to provide you all the hospitality that we can muster here."

Kim had regained her composure and smiled at Beth. "Thank you very much. I sincerely appreciate it. Why aren't we heading into town now? Why are we waiting here?"

"Aw, good question. I wish that I had a good answer, but I'm mostly just playing my role as your security. I've been here since yesterday afternoon and have had limited contact with the Chief or anyone else. I read your plan that Fred laid out in his letter. I think that what's happening is your plan is being put into play, and we should lay low up here. If you went into town, it's more likely someone might spot you. I've been walking, limping around here, looking for visitors who don't seem to fit in. I can account for most everyone that's come and gone on the bus from town or in their cars, or that they're backpackers who are staying longer. It's not foolproof, obviously, and I'm still keeping watch. The manager, Bill Shepherd, is graciously allowing us to use one of the cottages that someone was renting. The folks who were using it left this morning, and the next guests shouldn't be here until later today. So, if you'll follow me, we'll get you out of sight."

Beth, Kim, and Fred walked north from the open area and around the corner of the café to a cabin on the side of the hill. When they got inside, Kim practically collapsed on the floor. She was feeling safer, more secure, and relieved.

"It's just the three of us here for a few hours, so feel free to spread out and relax. There's a shower if you want, which I suspect you do. While you're showering, I can get us some lunch and bring it back here. Kim, I'd just as soon that you stay here. Fred, you're free to walk around if you wish since no one is looking for you. But, Kim, before you get distracted, I need to perform some professional duties."

Kim looked at Beth, shrugged, and said, "OK. What do you need from me?"

"Well, the most important thing is that I want to check on your health and well-being. For example, were you injured or do you have any injuries, were you abused, things like that. Do you need medical attention for anything?"

Kim thought for a moment, nothing coming to her, and then she looked at Beth and practically shouted, "Yes!"

Beth was looking at her expectantly, giving her a safe space to unburden herself. "If you'd prefer that Fred leave, if it's too personal, I'm certain that he'll be glad to step out."

"No, no," Kim said, "that won't be necessary. You see, he's the one who abused me."

Fred was shocked. He had been quietly laying on the floor, relaxing on soft carpet, when this news blindsided him. He cocked his head to learn more about how he was in trouble.

"Yes, Fred's my abuser. He didn't bring toilet paper for his backpacking trip, and now I'm scarred for life."

Fred was nearly beside himself, first relaxing and then laughing his head off. Still horizontal on the floor, he just raised his arms, hands held side-by-side. "Here, Beth, you can just handcuff me here and now."

Kim and Fred laughed so hard while Beth grinned and tried to be professionally respectful. "Well," Beth said, "I have to side with Fred on this issue – that's not an offense, just offensive. But, in all seriousness, you're fine then? No injuries or abuses to speak of?"

Kim settled down, merely smiling. "I'm fine. Fred took wonderful care of me! I have a few blisters on my feet, and my feet are a bit sore, but other than that, I'm fine. Oh, and I'm hungry because I've never worked so physically hard in my life as these past few days. And I stink, so yes, I'm hitting the shower when you're done with me."

"Kim, if you want," started Fred, "I can take your clothes and wash them, too. Just give me what you want washed, and I'll throw them in with mine. I'm heading over to the laundry to wash some things if the other backpackers aren't using all of the machines."

Kim was now nearly ecstatic. A hot shower, clean clothes, and hot food – she couldn't ask for much more for the moment, other than to be fully free.

Beth and Kim gave Fred their lunch orders, and everyone got to their respective chores. Fred took the lunch orders to the Mulehouse Café while Beth stayed with Kim in the cabin. He returned to pick up his and Kim's dirty clothes and found a free washing machine. Between the two of them, they still didn't have a full load of dirty clothes for the washer. After getting detergent and quarters from the general store and starting the laundry, Fred stopped by the café to pick up their lunches. Kim was just stepping out of the bath when he returned, looking clean and refreshed, a smile on her face. She ate her burger in a more lady-like fashion today, didn't bolt it down like she had the night before, and didn't burp. She was returning to being civilized.

Before Fred took his shower, he changed the laundry from the washer to the dryer. After soaking in the shower for what seemed forever, he realized that he had more aching muscles and blisters on his feet than he knew. Fred always enjoyed that first shower after a backpacking trip, even though he'd just had one yesterday. However, it still felt weird to have this kind of seemingly decadent personal care when he expected that he'd be on the trail again tomorrow morning. Fred decided that he could live with himself and this particular guilt.

Chapter 34

It was mid-afternoon by the time they ate lunch and cleaned up. The laundry was dry, folded, and packed into Kim's and Fred's respective backpacks. Fred laid his tent and quilt over the porch railing to air out. The three of them were just sitting around, staring at each other, almost bored. For Fred, he hadn't sat this still doing nothing for a couple of weeks, since before his trip. Kim sat around bored the day before, but now she was bored on a comfy chair, with a cup of ice coffee alongside. She was almost feeling human again. They all made chit-chat. Beth was doing her best not to interrogate Kim, other than the basics like her health. She knew that she wasn't supposed to ask too much of Kim. That was Andrews' job in this sensitive situation, and he should be along any time.

The comfort was getting to Fred. He was again on the floor, splayed out, a pillow under his head. He was soon asleep and gently snoring. Kim just looked at him, cocked her head, and pointed at him. Quietly she said, "Beth, there's another form of abuse that I had to weather," and they both just smiled.

Beth still had her pack nearby and cellphone on her lap. Just before 3:00, she received a simple text from a number that she'd been given last night – "@ Reds." She got up, considered nudging Fred to wake him, and thought better of it. She whispered to Kim that the company had arrived, and she needed to walk out and look for their guest while also keeping an eye on the cabin.

A few minutes later, Beth returned with a clean-cut man carrying a small backpack. The backpack wasn't new, but it wasn't as well-worn as most of the packs around here. They walked into the cabin, and the man saw Fred lying on the floor. He gave Beth and Kim a look of concern that melted when he heard the supine body rattle.

The man strode across the cabin and extended his hand. "Dr. Johnson, I'm Special Agent Andrews. It's a pleasure, and relief, to finally meet you. I trust that you're healthy?"

The noise of the conversation caused Fred to stir. He opened his eyes, looked, and sat up. Andrews walked over and extended his hand down to Fred. "Dr. Bortz, I'm Special Agent Andrews. Thank you very, very much for taking care of Dr. Johnson and getting her to safety."

Kim looked down at Fred with a bit of revulsed surprise on her face. "*Dr. Bortz?* You never told me you were a Ph.D."

Fred just sat on the floor, still trying to make sense of the situation, and having several people around him, none of whom he had known a week ago. "Well, it wasn't the most important issue on my mind. I was more focused on getting you safely out of the wilderness." He smiled now and slowly made his way to his feet, sore muscles wanting him to rest longer.

Andrews started: "May I call you Kim?" looking at Kim and "Fred?" looking at Fred. Almost in unison, they said "Yes!" and were grinning at each other again, shaking their heads at each other.

Continuing, he said, "It seems that maybe you didn't have as difficult of a time out there as I feared."

At this point, Beth jumped in. "Well, Kim would like to press abuse charges since Fred didn't provide her with toilet paper out in the wilderness." They all laughed, the tension receding.

Once order was restored, Andrews properly identified himself and his agency to Kim, along with some sort of coded message to confirm his identity; Kim responded with her own coded message to Andrews. Fred listened, but it made no sense to him, and he knew that was intentional. Andrews looked at Kim and asked her to tell her story of the past ten days in her own words. She didn't go into all the details but gave a sufficient day-by-day accounting so that Andrews could understand. She told him about Alpha, Beta and Omega and their roles. Kim knew that there would be days of interrogation and questioning ahead to ensure that she was healthy and hadn't been compromised, but this wasn't the time or place for that.

Andrews didn't have many questions for her; he mostly listened and took in everything. At the moment, his highest priority was to get Kim and Fred safely out of this situation. Andrews had been there for about an hour, focusing on Kim and her needs and assessing the situation. He paused for a minute, thinking, looking around, and seemed satisfied with what he found.

"So, I need to make some phone calls and check in with staff," Andrews said. "If you'll please excuse me, it would be better if I had some privacy. There are too many ears outdoors, but I'm going to risk it rather than have Kim go outside. I'll just be sitting on the porch, looking like a working tourist."

There were a couple of Adirondack chairs out on the porch, and Andrews sank into one where he could still see into the cabin. Inside, Kim, Fred, and Beth felt relieved that this episode was coming to an end. Fred stared off through the windows, into the distance, looking at the mountains and vista, feeling out of place here, confined, expecting that he'd be back out there tomorrow. Kim watched Fred watch the mountains, smiled, and sensed what she thought he was thinking.

"So, Fred, chomping at the bit, rarin' to get back out there?" Kim asked.

"Yeah, I guess so," he said. "It's a weird feeling coming back to these creature comforts and then getting back on the trail. The pull of hot showers, clean clothes, hot food, and a bed are hard to overcome. In another couple of days, I'll be back into my groove, I guess."

After several minutes of talking with staff, enjoying the quiet and watching the antics of arriving backpackers, Andrews rejoined them in the cabin. He laid back on one of the beds, closed his eyes, and wiped his face. After opening his eyes and propping himself on his elbows, he looked at the others and simply said, "Yes, it's been a long twenty-four hours for me, too." Andrews smiled, knowing that he was not the one being sought.

"So, Kim, let's back up. I have several questions and not necessarily in any particular order. I'm just trying to understand a few more things. For example, how do you think these people got into your house, overcame the security system?"

"I don't know, sir. I went out for my normal morning walk and coffee. When I returned home, they were there and making themselves at home. They didn't tell me a whole lot."

"Please, call me Ed. I'm trying to relax, too, at least for another few hours. So, I'm guessing that the security lapse is on us. From every report that I've received, it looks like the security at your house was pretty good. We're still looking into that one."

"Well, that makes me feel better," Kim said. "I thought that I'd done something wrong, like not arming my security system when I left, but couldn't come up with anything."

"No, don't worry about that. We're still looking into it, but I haven't seen anything that makes me think you let your guard down, compromised the system, or anything like that. These people are just really, really, good, from what we can tell."

Ed looked around, took a very deep breath, and thought a bit more.

"The altitude is getting to me a bit," he continued. Looking at Beth, "I wish that I was more fit and acclimated before flying up here last night." Beth just smiled as she'd heard similar comments from flatlanders before.

"OK, Kim, another question," Ed continued. "You were abducted and then taken to a house. Do you know where you were? Did they say anything?"

Kim sat there, shaking her head no. "They kept me in a basement bedroom of a house for about three days, I think. We arrived in the dark of night and left in the dark of morning. When they took me from my home, they put a hood on me because they were trying to keep me clueless. The guys, Alpha and Beta, didn't reveal themselves until the morning that we left the safe house. Again, it was dark when we left, and my mind was racing. The next town that I remember is Gilroy. I think that's where we made a stop, but so much has happened that I need to sit down and write out a timeline as best I can."

Ed shook his head in understanding. "You were being held in a semi-rural house near Milpitas. We were able to do some tracking and checked out a couple of places. One of those places was a house that belonged to a couple who live in Germany, and they hadn't given any-one permission to be in the house. The house was practically spotless, but one of our agents found a couple of your hairs that snagged on the bed on which you were sleeping. We were able to test the hair against your biometric profile and had a pretty good feeling that you'd been there. We're not certain, but we think that we missed you by only a few hours."

Kim was taking all this new information in, piecing it together with her life. "Thanks for being on top of things and looking for me.

I figured that I'd be missed pretty quickly but had no idea if anyone would find me. And then, when they took me into the mountains, I figured that my chances of being found were going downhill fast."

"So, why do you think that they kept you and are still looking for you?" Ed paused for a moment. "I don't get it. No one received a ransom note; there has been no request for a trade of any type – people or information. There's just been this silence from whomever, and that was the frustrating and confounding part. We've been blindly playing on one side of a chessboard."

Kim reflected for a moment before she spoke. "To be frank, I'm not fully certain. A part of me thinks that they underestimated the computer program we developed. From my conversations with Omega and him trying to get me to work with them, I felt that they figured that their problems would reduce or disappear if they separated me from computers and these programs. That's why they were holding me in that house – they were waiting for their problems to go away. I suspect that the program focused on them even more since it had found something active and responsive. So, when their problems didn't diminish but maybe got worse, they felt an even stronger need to keep me isolated. They said something about having been found in the house where they kept me and that it wasn't safe anymore. Alpha and Beta thought that they were competent mountain soldiers from their time in Afghanistan, so that's why they brought me to the Sierras. But they were under prepared here. Their loads were too heavy, and they both had altitude sickness; at least, that was Fred's diagnosis."

"Yeah," chimed in Fred, "from what Kim told me, that were suffering from altitude sickness, acute mountain sickness, pretty badly, especially Alpha, I believe. Alpha's lucky he didn't get any worse and die. Another day or two out, or moving to higher altitudes, and it might have been tough for them."

Ed sat on the bed, shaking his head, trying to understand why people do the things they do. A moment later, he snapped out of it. "Well, on another note, so far, the day has gone well. Kim, I have to say that you came up with a pretty good plan. Sorry that we had to overrule you on some things, but I hope that you'll understand as I tell you more."

Kim just shrugged. "Hey, I have no pride of ownership. I'm just glad that I'm out of trouble and heading home."

Ed wore a grin, and he started again. "So, we liked your idea of signaling your presence in one place and then coming out in a different location. That was a smart move on your part, more intelligent than you know. What you didn't realize is that there are a whole lot of people in your corner trying to get you back safely, as well as several of Omega's people who'd like to find you first.

"As testosterone-driven as we tend to be in the security field, we're also learning – slowly – when to let go, listen, and learn. Until we heard from you through the Mammoth Lakes Police, we really had no idea where to look for you. These people are good and left very few clues, which is why we're still a bit flummoxed and upset with ourselves. The only thing that caught our attention the past few days is more satellite phone traffic from around the Sierras. There's always a backpacker or two who carry sat phones with them out into the wilderness here, but we saw a significant increase in signals from the edges of the Sierras, plus a few in the mountains. We were hoping that meant that you were in this area, but we had nothing else to go on and were hoping for a break.

Backing up a bit, Ed said, "We were able to track unusual satellite phone signals and that's what lead us to the house in Milpitas. But after that, these guys stopped using that sat phone. Next, we picked up on the greater than normal sat phone usage in the Sierras. Yesterday, when we found out that you actually were in the Sierras, our people re-examined the sat phone patterns from this area and we're confident that they're looking for you, Kim. In fact, much of the spike in sat phone traffic is now coming from the Mammoth Lakes area, so that's partly why we're being so careful. They're here, but we don't know exactly where they are. And, if we can track them on their sat phones and cell phones, then we're expecting that they can do the same to us."

"Anyway, your plan gave us a good outline with which to work. We believed that you and Fred knew these environs better than us, and so far, so good. And, most importantly, you two were very good about not leaving any breadcrumbs for anyone to find or follow. Once we knew what to look for, we found your faint trail, but that's after the fact. We were pretty certain that if we couldn't find it, no one else could find it either. And that seems to be true. So, good work, you two!"

"Whoa!" Kim said. "A lot of this was Fred's doing, too. I had a few ideas concerning communications, but there was a lot of practical wilderness thinking that was Fred's. Seriously, I know that I wouldn't have survived without him, or at least not been caught again. When I escaped, I had no idea where I was nor how to get out safely. In fact, it turns out that I was heading deeper into the wilderness when he stumbled on me. Fred deserves a medal, not me."

"Well, sorry to burst your bubble, Kim, but there won't be any medal for Fred. He'll have to be satisfied with the sincere gratitude of the people of the United States. This event never occurred, just to be clear. We'll deny it if you can find us, and good luck with that." Ed sat there, trying not to smile, comfortable in his mystery. Kim was trying to hide a smile, too.

"Thanks, you professional spooks. I love you, too," Fred said. They all laughed, in part recognizing the truth and in part a release of tension.

"Anyway, where was I? Oh yes. So, to back up and bring you all up to speed. You suggested that Fred, and maybe you too, Kim, hike to Duck Pass and maybe Duck Lake from wherever you camped. And where were you last night? We have no idea, no clue."

"Oh, we were just up and over Mammoth Crest, just uphill from McLeod Lake. It's like a two-hour hike from here to there," Kim said. This was her contribution since she was feeling more like an outdoorswoman now. Quietly, Fred smiled, thinking that she was a good student and hoping that he'd hear about her future wilderness adventures.

"OK, so you two were going to hike several miles back to Duck Pass and then Duck Lake and set off Fred's emergency beacon as a distress call this morning. Next, you'd text or call your wife, Fred, to let her know that the emergency signal wasn't for you and that you'd found an injured hiker. Your goal was to make someone who you expected to be listening in think that Fred found Kim at Duck Lake, and she needed a rescue there. Right? I mean, it seems like a pretty simple and straightforward deception, and I like it!"

"Yeah, that's pretty much what Kim came up with," Fred replied. "We tried to keep it fairly simple and figure out how to put some distance between us and whoever might be looking for us. When Kim and I were out in the mountains and talking, she cautioned me about leaving electronic footprints and not mention her in my nightly texts to my wife. That's the best that we could come up with, given the circumstances."

Ed sat there for a moment to let their logic sink in. "Well, we took your plan and modified it, as you know. We decided that for Kim's safety and yours, Fred, it was better to keep you two away from Duck Lake and Duck Pass and not change the part about you two coming down here to Reds Meadow. We didn't want to make things confusing, and, again, we liked the thinking behind your plan. When I received the copy of Fred's message to the Mammoth Lakes Police, I was able to put two and two together – I hoped. But I also knew that we needed to create an even bigger ruse and keep you two out of harm's way if these people are as good as we think they are.

"And, so that we're clear, as I said before, there are a lot more people than just me, Beth, and Chief Madison working on this situation. I flew up here late yesterday afternoon. At the same time, a semi-truck full of people and equipment drove up and got here late last night. When I first spoke with Chief Madison yesterday, I knew that I didn't want you two to put yourselves at risk any more than necessary, which is why I told her to have you meet me here today. But, starting with Kim's suggestion, we crafted a modified plan and worked on it through the night. On the one hand, it's a straightforward plan, and on the other, it's a very elegant plan – we hope. Time will tell. We've learned the KISS principle and how to make it work for us.

"Anyway, we decided that it was best to separate you two from the situation as much as we could for your safety, as well as to keep you from creating more problems for us – no disrespect intended. So, this morning, about 4:30 am, my team quietly dropped off two agents at the Duck Pass trailhead on the east side of Mammoth Crest. They hiked up and over the pass and on to Duck Lake and got there about 8:30 this morning. Our Field Agent Anglin could pass for you, Kim, and she's been on the case from the beginning.

"A couple of hours later, Anglin set off an emergency beacon. As Kim suggested to you, Fred, we have some impressive capabilities. We temporarily borrowed your satellite transceiver account and tied our satellite beacon into it. When the emergency signal went off, the world thought that it was you sending the distress signal, Fred.

"The agents then sent a satellite text from Duck Lake to your wife, Asta. She's in on this, too, Fred, so you owe her big time. 'You' explained to your wife that you'd found this dazed, dehydrated, Black woman with no shoes and infected feet. She couldn't move and you were caring for her at Duck Lake. You asked Asta to call the authorities in Mammoth and have them send a search-and-rescue team. That was the end of the message.

"Moments later, Asta called the Mammoth Lakes Police and told them about a lost Black woman and how her husband, Fred, was helping this woman; the woman needed rescue, couldn't walk, they were at Duck Lake, and so on. We had already primed the companies who receive these emergency beacon signals that there would be a 'test' this morning from somewhere in the US and that they should act as if it was real.

"The search and rescue team took off about noon, and we figured it would take them two to three hours to get to Duck Lake, which it did. The other thing is that the SAR team was not the local SAR team. Our people dressed to look like the SAR team, and the local SAR team assisted them in getting to the trailhead and direct them to Duck Lake. That also helps to keep the local SAR team available for other needs.

"The other big unknown in all of this was the capabilities and interest of the people who abducted Kim. Just like you two, we weren't certain they were still looking for her, but we figured they were, based on the spike in sat phone traffic. We also had no idea of their capabilities to monitor various types of communications traffic. We know our capabilities and assume that they are as capable, if not more so. And that's what you two did, too. I know that you've given a lot of credit to Fred for your rescue, but I believe that Kim has a much better idea of what's possible for intercepting communications than Fred."

Kim didn't say a word but was quietly beaming inside.

"So, Anglin and the other agent have been at Duck Lake awaiting their rescue this afternoon. They were 'rescued' about the same time that I got here – 3:00 pm. The other interesting thing is that a helicopter circled over Duck Lake maybe twenty minutes before the SAR team arrived. The SAR team saw it, too, shortly after they crossed over Duck Pass. And it wasn't a helicopter that anybody we know ordered up. Imagine that!" Ed said this last part with a sarcastic smile. "It seems that Kim is still a hot commodity."

"We have the FAA looking into the chopper details. It's a local helicopter out of Mammoth Lakes Airport. It circled a few times and appeared to be thinking about landing, but the winds up there threw it around a fair amount. The last anyone saw, it seemed to be heading back to the airport." Ed was grinning, enjoying the intrigue, the gamesmanship.

"So, we were smart, lucky, or both, right?" asked Fred.

Ed didn't say anything but gave them a look that said, *well played you two; I'm impressed.*

"For now, that's all that I know," Ed continued. "The SAR team is reporting in the typical information to their base that they have the victim, she's stabilized, and they're transporting her on horseback. They expect to be back to the trailhead about sundown. I want to be in Mammoth Lakes before the SAR team arrives. I don't want to be at the trailhead, just in town to better track this situation. At the same time, I feel better keeping Kim up here as long as reasonable because I believe she's slightly safer here. I'm guessing that we'll leave here at about 6:00 pm.

Ed finished with, "So, should we put in an order at the café for supper? My treat!"

Chapter 35

Alpha sat in his SUV and watched the traffic on Minaret Summit Road west of Mammoth Lakes. There were too many cars and trucks coming down the road to make him think that he would be able to see anything useful, to see Dr. Johnson openly sitting in a vehicle. Another team member, Gamma, watched the trailheads near Lake Mary, feeling similarly frustrated. Yesterday, Alpha had stayed around Lake Mary watching all day, and Gamma had been up here. They traded locations to try to keep fresh eyes and avoid boredom, but it wasn't working too well. A third person wandered around the village watching for Kim. When Alpha checked in with Omega last evening, he had told him that he felt three people trying to cover all the Mammoth areas wasn't enough, especially after the loss of Beta. Still, the most significant weakness was that they just couldn't see into the many vehicles coming into and out of town: too many opaque subjects and too few eyes.

A little after ten in the morning, Omega called Alpha on the sat phone. He stood outside, trying to loosen his stiff legs and back. "Good timing! I think we're in luck!" were Omega's first excited words. "Someone sent out an emergency distress signal about fifteen minutes ago in the Mammoth Lakes area. We got the GPS coordinates, and the signal came from a place called Duck Lake, south of there a few miles. Then, a few minutes later, a text message was sent by the same device. The message noted a Black woman with no shoes, dehydrated, hungry, and a request for a search and rescue team at Duck Lake. Our analyst, Prirody, thinks they're legitimate messages because they're coming from the same device that was sending earlier messages that he was tracking. Keep your scanner on but follow up on this lead. I think it's Dr. Johnson. I'll text you the coordinates and copy the satellite text message."

"Yes, sir!" Alpha said. "Finally, some good news. I'll let Gamma know because the trailhead that most easily reaches Duck Lake is near where he's watching. I'll also message other team members and see who can get here to help ASAP. We're on it, sir!"

What to do, what to do?? Alpha pulled out his maps and found Duck Lake again. It was a two- to four-hour hike to get there, he figured, so if he left now, he'd be there by early- to mid-afternoon. But *so what?* How was he going to get Dr. Johnson back to town if he was alone? Alpha needed some way to carry her, like a horse, but that would be obvious, and his horse skills were pretty poor. The world is on alert for an injured woman, so Alpha needed to get in there and out faster.

Still high on Minaret Summit Road, Alpha called Gamma on the cellphone and let him know of a likely sighting at Duck Lake, that the SAR team was being called in, and that it looked like the fastest way for the SAR team to get to Duck Lake was from the Lake Mary area where he was stationed, and to be alert. Next, he sent a text message to the other team members on the Sierras' east and west sides, asking them to converge on Mammoth Lakes. He realized that the people on the east side were the only ones likely to get here before the evening, but it would help.

Back inside the SUV, he turned up the scanner's volume and sat there trying to formulate his next steps. If the authorities activated the SAR team, he might have a few hours to get to Duck Lake ahead of them and hopefully get Dr. Johnson out of there. If she were as injured as it sounded like from what the emergency message said, then he wouldn't be able to manage to get her back to Mammoth, or anywhere, alone, especially if someone was watching over her. A moment later, the copy of the emergency text message arrived.

> *37.54519; -118.96842; The emergency beacon is not 4 me! I'm OK. Black woman, 35-40 y.o. Dehydrated, starved, no shoes, feet infected, incoherent. I found her a day ago, but she wouldn't let me request assistance. Call Mammoth Lakes authorities, request SAR at my location. I'm tending to her. Luv Fred*

Well, hot damn! thought Alpha. *My day is looking up!*

Still looking at his maps, Alpha saw that the Mammoth Lakes Airport was just east of town. He looked out to the horizon to his east to locate the airport, but foothills and Mammoth Mountain blocked his view. He searched on his phone for aircraft rentals and the like at Mammoth and found a sightseeing helicopter that worked out of the airport. *More good luck!* A moment later, he was talking with the tour company.

"Hello! My name is Dale Ford," Alpha said. "My brother and his girlfriend just sent out an emergency distress signal in the Sierras, at Duck Lake. Could you fly me there to check on them or even rescue them?"

The person on the other end of the phone took a moment to respond. "Well, normally, requests like that would go through the search and rescue team. We heard over the emergency frequencies that the Sheriff just called them for an incident at Duck Lake, so it sounds like your brother and his girlfriend are receiving attention. Our helicopter is ferrying some people down to Lone Pine right now and won't be back until early afternoon. The other big issue is that the winds are strong out of the east here today, and they'll be even worse in the mountains. Even if we can fly there, I don't want to get your hopes up that our pilot will be able to land at Duck Lake, Mr. Ford."

Alpha thought for a moment. The helicopter seemed like his only decent chance to get into and out of Duck Lake before the SAR team. "Are there any other helicopter charters in the vicinity?" he asked.

"Well, there are a few around, some on the west side of the Sierras and then up at Reno and Carson City. But again, the winds are tough today, and I don't think that anyone will want to take the risk, especially if the SAR team is on it."

"That makes sense," said Alpha/Dale. "I'm sitting up by Mammoth Mountain, and the winds are pretty stiff here. I'm just worried about them, my brother and his girlfriend, as you can understand. Could you please call me back when the helicopter returns, and we could check about flying up there? I'm going crazy trying to figure out how to be helpful."

"I understand, Mr. Ford. I have your phone number on my cellphone now, and I'll call you when the chopper returns, and you can talk with our pilot, Eric, and see what's possible. Will that work for you?"

"Oh, yes, yes! Thank you very much! I'm looking forward to his call. Good-bye and thank you very much," said Alpha.

He stored the number of the charter service in his phone to

remember to be in character when they called back. Alpha had some time to kill until he'd hear from the pilot. Off the top of his head, he couldn't come up with any other possibilities for getting Dr. Johnson out from Duck Lake. Every other option required too many people in too short of a time. He could stay here and keep watching cars and trucks, but his mind was racing on how to get to Duck Lake with a team. Rather than sit here and think about it, Alpha decided to head to town, find a quick meal, scout around some more, and consider other possibilities.

After eating a sub sandwich, Alpha checked in with Gamma. "I've been looking at our situation and considering our options. I have one possibility of getting to our friend before everyone else, but it doesn't look good. I'm going to look around for additional opportunities to take control of the situation, presuming that our friend arrives at your location later today. Clear enough?"

"Yep, got it, boss. The other people who are looking for your friend just arrived and should be leaving soon. I'll keep you informed if something changes on my end."

"Gotcha. Thank you."

Alpha had his maps out, trying to piece together the likely routes that the rescue team, and probably an ambulance, would drive to ferry Dr. Johnson from the Duck Pass trailhead to the hospital. There were only two major routes, so his odds were good. The person who had been watching the trailheads at Mono Pass should be getting to town any time now, and the surveillance person from McGee Creek Trailhead had checked in with him over lunch after getting off the exit and heading into town. The last observer on the eastern side of the Sierras watched the Pine Creek Trailhead, and she should be here by mid-afternoon. He figured he'd have enough people available, including Gamma, for any additional interventions.

His next chore was to drive the two major routes from the Duck Pass Trailhead to the hospital. The two obvious choices were Old Mammoth Road and Lake Mary Road. Both routes had open stretches where it would be easy to intercept the expected ambulance. If Gamma followed the ambulance from the trailhead and one or two people waited at the point where Lake Mary Road and Old Mammoth Road diverged, it should be possible to hijack the ambulance and escape, no matter which road the ambulance might take since there were only the two routes. Then they could drive it to a waiting vehicle, transfer Dr. Johnson to the escape van, and head out of Mammoth Lakes. Not a perfect plan, but it's what was available, so he'd have to make it work. He had made more difficult situations work out on other jobs. *Sweet!* Alpha sent a quick message to Omega to give him a status report and let him know that he was planning for several eventualities. One of them should work out in their favor.

Now, Omega was going over the equipment available to him. Everyone on the team had radios and phones, and they all carried sidearms and additional firepower in their vehicles. The most straight-forward approach was not to use weapons but to just be quick and get out of town – that was always his preference. Gunfire just alerted more people that something was going down and brought in even more authorities. The quieter, the better. He also wanted to get to the Duck Pass Trailhead and give Gamma a tracking device so that he could place it onto the ambulance or whatever vehicle used to transport Dr. Johnson away from the trailhead, just in case. No matter where that vehicle went, even if it didn't go to the hospital, it would be easier for him to keep track of it this way. He felt good that he was covering as many possibilities as he could. Something could always go wrong, he knew from experience, but planning and preparing reduced mistakes.

As he considered the next steps, Alpha's cell phone rang; it was the helicopter pilot calling. "Good afternoon, this is Dale Ford."

"Hello, Mr. Ford, this is Eric Kretschman. I'm the helicopter pilot out at the airport. I understand that you want to head up towards Duck Lake, is that right?"

"Yes, sir. My brother and his girlfriend are up there, and he's sent out a distress signal, so I was hoping that we could fly up there and get them out."

"Well, it's not a great day for flying, especially in the mountains. The winds are challenging down here in the valley, and they'll be much worse in the mountains. Also, it's my understanding that the SAR team is out to rescue them, so that's a big relief, I hope."

"Yes, Mr. Kretschman, I know that the SAR team should be on its way, but I'm very concerned, very protective of my brother as well as his girlfriend. What's the likelihood that we could fly up there and pick them up?"

"Well, the chances that we could fly are good, since I just got down. The chances that we could get up to Duck Lake are reasonable, and the chances that we could land there are close to nil. It would be a very rough ride, especially once we get up and over Mammoth Crest. The winds are blowing strong out of the east, and the higher you fly, the stronger the winds blow. On the west side of the crest, the wind likes to roll over on itself, creating a downdraft, sort of like a crashing wave, and the turbulence gets much worse when you fly below the lee side of the crest. That downdraft can push the chopper into the ground if I'm not careful, which is why I'm so leery of flying there."

Alpha took a moment to reply, to act like he was considering his options – he already knew what he wanted. "Well, could we fly up there and have a look at least? You can decide about landing when we get there and feel out the winds."

Eric took a deep breath. "I guess that we could fly there – sure. But no promises about a landing. How quickly can you be here, then? I need to refuel and grab a bite to eat."

"Well, I'm in town, so I should be able to be there in twenty minutes or so. Thank you, sir, I appreciate it!"

"OK, then I'll see you in twenty. Mine is the only chopper out here, so you shouldn't have any problems finding me. It's a small airport. Oh, and you're good with flying in turbulence? I'm not in the mood to clean my bird today."

"Yes, sir, I'm fine with a rough flight. No worries. I'm on my way." Alpha ended the call and quickly called Gamma while he started out of town, letting him know that he was going on a flight and that additional people were either in town or coming soon.

Chapter 36

Alpha quickly found the helicopter on the ramp, near the fueling area at the airport. After parking his SUV, he put a few things into a pack and walked to the aircraft. Eric, he presumed, was tightening the fuel cap and checking the rotors.

"Mr. Kretschman, I'm Dale Ford. I sincerely appreciate you helping us." After shaking hands and a few other pleasantries, they headed to Kretschman's office.

"Mr. Ford, I'll need a credit card to pay for your flight, and you'll need to sign the standard waiver. It's going to be a rough one this afternoon, so I hope that you're prepared and experienced."

"Oh, I should be fine. I served in Afghanistan and had a few chopper flights there that were hairy. At least no one will be shooting at us!" Alpha was trying for some levity and avoiding the truth.

After the formalities, they were ready to go. Alpha/Dale strapped into the passenger seat on the left in the front of the cabin. The put their headsets on, the engine came up to temperature quickly, and they were off several minutes later. Turbulence near the ground decreased as they climbed while the wind pushed them towards town and the mountains. Kretschman wasn't trying to fly fast in these conditions; he was flying safely. After passing the south side of Mammoth Lakes, they banked left and flew up the valley and over Lake Mary. Alpha could make out where he parked and watched yesterday near the trailhead. Duck Pass loomed in front of them.

Over the intercom, Kretschman spoke. "Duck Pass is at about 11,000 feet. I want to clear it by at least a thousand feet to avoid higher velocity winds and turbulence. We're flying southeast, and the winds are strong out of the east. It's going to be rougher until we get back to the east of Mammoth Crest, so hang on tight."

Making altitude in the thinning air and turbulence was difficult for the chopper, and Kretschman circled near the head of the valley to gain more altitude before crossing well over Duck Pass. When the helicopter was high enough to see Duck Lake over the crest, he continued southeastward. Just east of the ridge, the winds gave them an upward bounce that caused Alpha/Dale a bit of discomfort, but not much. On the other side of the pass, Kretschman flew level toward Duck Lake and then beyond, circling back so that he was flying into the rough winds. The pilot kept Duck Lake on his left side so that his client could see it more easily and maybe make out his brother and girlfriend.

Kretschman pointed to something down below them. "That looks like the SAR team, those six or so people, and the horse. They should be down to the lake in ten or fifteen minutes. It looks good for your brother and his girlfriend."

Alpha was calculating in his mind, thinking about whether they could fly in there first. "So, what about landing there and getting them back to safety sooner?"

Kretschman shook his head. "It's not good, not good at all. They're in good hands with the SAR team, so I'm not going to take any risks. I'll try to drop down – slowly – but we'll see."

Alpha/Dale scanned the lake and shore below but couldn't see anyone. He assumed that Dr. Johnson and her savior were sitting under the few trees, avoiding the sun and wind. Alpha pulled a set of binoculars from his pack, but the flying was too rough for him to see any better with them. Alpha wasn't happy that this part of his plan wasn't working out as he wanted, but he wasn't surprised.

As they slowly dropped, the turbulence increased. Kretschman and Alpha were now just below the ridge, and the farther they descended, the rougher the ride became. They were still a good thousand feet above Duck Lake; they could see the wind whipping on the lake surface, pushing the few trees around. "This isn't good," announced Kretschman. "The winds are too squirrelly, and I'm afraid a good gust could push us into the ground. We're heading up and out."

Kretschman tried to climb, but it was difficult, so he turned westward, allowed the wind to push them away from Duck Lake and the rougher air, and he was able to gain altitude as the choppy winds diminished as they flew farther from the ridge. Finally, he climbed and climbed until he was a couple of thousand feet above the crest before heading north and west towards Mammoth Lakes Airport. Once they crossed Mammoth Crest, Kretschman let out a little sigh of relief and relaxed his grip on the controls.

An hour after they started, they were back at the airport. "That was one of the rougher flights in my thousands of hours of flying," said Kretschman. "I'm glad to have that one behind me. I'm sorry that we couldn't do more for your family, but they're in good hands, and we're down safely. Everybody should be safe today. You'll just have to be patient, Mr. Ford."

Alpha/Dale thanked Kretschman and headed back to his SUV. The first thing he did was check in with Gamma and let him know that he was down, the SAR team should be with Dr. Johnson by now, and he hadn't seen anything. Gamma let Alpha know that two of the other team members had arrived and checked in with him, and a third member was nearly in town. "I'm heading up your way," Alpha told Gamma, "so that we can plan this out. I should be there in thirty minutes or so."

Near the Duck Pass trailhead, a small throng of people milled around, watching, and waiting to see what was going on. *Tragedy always draws a crowd*, Alpha thought. He caught Gamma's eye through the group, and Gamma along with two other people walked his way. After greetings and checking in, Alpha spread a map of the Mammoth Lakes area on his vehicle's hood. He explained his thinking to his team, and they considered the possibilities. Without any significant changes, they all agreed to the plan and their roles. They figured they still had a few hours before the SAR team arrived, so Alpha spelled his team so that they could head down to town for something to eat. Before they left, Gamma wandered over by the ambulance and discretely placed a tracking device under the front bumper, out of sight of everyone.

It shouldn't be long now, Alpha thought to himself.

The sat phone in Alpha's backpack buzzed. After he answered, Omega started talking. "Something else has come up. We have a young man on our team who has spent time in the Sierras when he was an exchange student, and he's spent time in Mammoth Lakes backpacking and snowboarding. On a whim, he decided to see if he could hack into any security cameras in the area to see what he might see. He was able to get into a couple of live feeds. What surprised him is that he got into the cameras at a place called Reds Meadow, and he said that he'd been there before. It's a small resort that offers a lot of services for backpackers. On the video from there, he thought that he saw Dr. Johnson.

It wasn't a great or clear picture, but he felt it was her.

"I'm telling you this because his observation makes sense if a backpacker picked her up and someone is trying to throw us off the hunt. I'd suggest that you follow up as best you can and consider alternatives. Make sense?"

"Yes, sir, it does make sense. I'll do what I can to follow up on short notice, and we'll think about contingencies. Thanks for the intel."

After they finished the call, Alpha sat for a moment and tried to figure out the next steps. He had enough people for the moment. Pulling out his map, it didn't look like it was very far to drive from Mammoth to Reds Meadow, and he'd been halfway there a few hours ago.

His next call was to Gamma, who was with the others getting something to eat in town. "Sorry to interrupt your meal. I've just heard that there was a person at a small resort called Reds Meadow who looks like Dr. Johnson. I need one of you three to run up there and check it out."

In the background, Alpha could hear Gamma crushing some papers, likely finishing his meal whether he wanted to or not. "Got it. I'll head up there and send the other two back to you. I can see a map of the area on a sign right in front of me, so it should be easy to get there."

It took Gamma longer than he expected to get to Reds Meadow. Darn those narrow, winding mountain roads! Once there, he parked near the traffic circle and casually walked around, keeping his eyes open. He didn't blend in because he wasn't wearing grubby shorts and a t-shirt, no boots or crocs, no beard or scraggly hair. He looked like a city person and not a mountain man. He sat on a bench, listening for tidbits of conversation, trying to pick up what he could.

He was soon joined on the bench by a couple of backpackers who had just wandered into the resort. They looked beat, he thought. Even though he felt he was sitting upwind, he could detect their distinct aroma. They talked amongst themselves, happy to sit down, take off their packs, and relax, thinking about a hot meal in the café. They loosened their shoes, sat back, and seemed like they were going to nod off.

Before he might lose them to sleep, food, or both, Gamma started to make small talk with them – *How long had they been out? How were the conditions? Where were they headed?* After building some rapport, he got to what he wanted – *Have you heard anything about a lost hiker or backpacker? A young to middle-aged Black woman? I heard some other backpackers talking about her...*

The couple looked at him with befuddled looks on their faces. *Nope, haven't seen or heard anything like that – news to them – and we gotta get some food in us and wash up before we fall asleep*, and they walked off.

After they left, Gamma walked around, listening in on conversations, mostly by the shower and laundry room, sitting by the north end of the general store. He didn't quite stick out like a sore thumb, but it was close. When a fresh-looking, sunburned young man with dripping hair right out of the shower sat by him, drying and dressing, he struck up a conversation, like he'd done a few minutes ago. And the response was the same – quizzical looks and news to me. But, this backpacker had seen a Black woman at the resort earlier in the day who had a backpacking vibe to her, but didn't know where she'd gone. *Maybe I'm getting somewhere,* Gamma thought. He had a photo of Kim on his phone but didn't want to act so obvious by pulling it out. At the same time, he was very curious and knew that the stakes were high, so he risked it. *Yeah, that might be her. I don't know.* Helpful, but not helpful, thought Gamma. He had no idea how tight the backpacking community might be, but he felt that he might be pushing his luck.

After a bit more listening and watching, he wandered back toward his car and pulled out his phone. He spoke with Alpha and told him what he'd heard. Alpha was intrigued but still undecided and told him to stay up there and keep discretely snooping around. Alpha also told him that a couple more helpers had just arrived in town, so he could afford to have him remain at Reds Meadow for the time being.

Well, thought Alpha, *this is a problem. We need to prepare for a couple of possibilities. Either the SAR team is bringing her down or someone's trying to bring her through a back door – assuming that this second possibility even involves Dr. Johnson.* Alpha's mind was in overdrive, trying to figure out what to do, how to handle these possibilities, and manage them all.

Backpackers in the general store were now gossiping about a lost backpacker. Bill overheard them, and asked them for more details, which they didn't really have. His senses tingled much more than yesterday.

Bill stepped out of the general store and stretched. He looked around with intent. It had been a long day, and the guests were just warming up for their wild but short-lived evening. The good news is that backpackers tend to go to bed early, so he could also get some shut-eye. As Bill warily scanned the guests, his gaze stopped on the well-coiffed, clean-looking gentleman who was sitting amongst the backpackers. Most tourists from town look better than the typical bedraggled backpacker and they most likely would have headed back down by now, so this guy stood out. And the town visitors didn't tend to rub elbows with the backpackers.

Playing the game as best he could, Bill moseyed over to the café, checked in on a couple of backpackers who looked like they were hurting some but keeping the object of his attention in his peripheral vision. After these backpackers told them that they'd be fine, he slowly walked past the café, smiled, and waved at some visitors over by the showers, and then made his way to the cabin where he had cloistered his special guests.

After Bill knocked on the door, he saw Beth give him a puzzled look through the window. A moment later, she cracked the door. "Mind if I come in for a minute?" he asked.

Once inside, Bill took off his cowboy hat and gave a respectful smile. "So, I hope that you all are enjoying your stay with us here at Reds Meadow. But that's not the main reason I stopped. There's a fellow at our resort inquiring about a Black woman who might be lost on the trails or something like that. I heard something about that yesterday if I correctly recall, so I found it even more interesting the second time I heard this issue floating around."

Ed sat up on the bed, very alert, as was everyone else. "Can you point this guy out?" Ed asked.

"Yeah, I can. We can't see our inquisitive guest from here, so why don't we walk over towards the other cabins. He sticks out because of his clothing, and you're just as obvious. You almost scream *narc*."

Ed looked down and realized how natty he looked compared to everyone else. "Why don't you take Fred for that walk? He would be much less noticeable than me. And, if this is a real problem – heck, I don't care – then I need to get Kim out of here."

Bill and Fred stepped out of the cabin, ambled about, and whispered. The 'fellow' had moved but was still around the backpackers, and Fred could easily pick him out.

"Any idea who he is?" asked Fred.

"Nope," said Bill. "I saw him earlier, but just assumed that he was a non-backpacking tourist. He's been hanging around for the past hour or so, talking with the backpackers, and hasn't been into the café or store from what I can recall. It's unusual that a tourist doesn't at least stop into the general store, and it's also odd that a tourist spends so much time sitting with the backpackers. The tourists are curious, but not usually as curious as this guy. Now that you've seen him let's head back to the cabin and chat some more."

While they were out, Ed conjured up his next plan. After Bill and Fred returned and Fred concurred that the visitor seemed suspicious, Ed gave his car keys to Beth while Kim and Fred packed their gear. "Bill, could you talk to that gentleman while Kim, Fred, and I head down to the campground? Maybe offer to buy him some dessert or something like that? Beth is going to take my car and meet us down there after she gives us the *all-clear* signal that you're entertaining our new guest some place where he won't see us leave."

Bill gave a polite nod. "Sounds like a plan to me." Turning to Kim, he said, "Good luck, and I'll be watching to see how this all pans out, hopefully for the best!" He gave Kim and Fred warm handshakes and wished them well, and they thanked him profusely, especially Kim. A minute later, Bill strolled across the courtyard, smiling, and talking briefly to guests.

Beth followed him out a moment later and worked her way towards the shower house to watch Bill and where she could be seen by the crew in the cabin. She picked an open spot on the shower house railing from where she had an expansive view of the place.

Bill walked around in a sort of a meet-and-greet fashion, smiling, playing his role well. Beth saw him settle down next to the guy who looked out of place, and he talked with the stranger as pleasantly as anyone else. They both smiled and carried on. Bill soon guided the gentleman to the café like they were a couple of old friends. Leaning on the railing, Beth sat there, head bobbing up and down. A moment later, she saw Fred, Kim, and Ed walk out of the cabin and head north towards the campground. It was her turn to walk to the parking lot and find Ed's car.

Fifteen minutes later and the four of them were driving down to Mammoth. Ed was quiet, brooding, thinking. Finally, he looked at Beth. "For once, I wish that a plan would go as planned. I hate it when someone, something comes along to mess things up. I know that we don't know for certain that guy is looking for Kim, but it's too suspicious and I'm too paranoid. Nobody else has mentioned a lost, Black, female backpacker. I don't know how someone possibly figured out that Kim might be at Reds, or if they just got lucky, but I'm going to assume the worst for the moment. There could be eyes, ears where we don't know, or someone on my team or your department might be selling us out. We don't tell anyone that we think that we've been discovered. I know who to trust with my life on my team, and I hope you have similar feelings for the police department. I'm not changing the plan that we've made – there are too many actors involved at this point, and it's too difficult to make substantial changes. Frankly, I think that they got lucky and decided to look for Kim at Reds; that makes the most sense. We'll make some slight modifications to the plan, though. When we get to town, I'll drop you off at the station, and I'll speak to Chief Madison and let her know what's going on. Does that work for you?"

Beth shook her head, yes. Now it was her turn to speak, but she directed herself to Kim and Fred. She pulled a couple of things from her daypack, turned around so that she could see Kim and Fred in the back seat, and handed them over the seat to the passengers. "So, this being the mountains and all, when things go western, we have some special ways of dealing with problems. Take these and attach the holsters to your wrists. It would be best if you had a long sleeve shirt or jacket to wear, too, to cover them up. You know how to use them, right?" looking directly at Fred.

Fred looked down, then at Kim and then back at Beth. "I've carried many times but never had to pull the trigger."

"Well," Beth said, "let's hope your good luck continues."

Back in Mammoth, the sun sank low over the mountains. They pulled into the police station's back lot. Fred and Kim laid low in the car while Ed went in to speak with the Chief. "Sorry to leave you alone like this, but I figure it's safer for you in the car here than to walk you out in the open for anyone to see. If someone is watching for Kim, this is a likely place for a stakeout."

He was back a few minutes later and passed a sack over the front seat. "I brought some chips and cookies for you from the station – sorry that it's not a better meal, but I hope you understand. I'm not entirely comfortable with how and where to keep you two for now. I don't want you out of the car if someone is watching us here in the police station parking lot. The station is barely covered right now since all the police staff are on alert for this situation, so I don't feel comfortable leaving you in there. I'm not comfortable having you with me, either, but it's my neck if I lose you, so I'm going to keep you close.

"The latest word is that the SAR team is approaching the trailhead on the south side of town. I have a portable radio scanner, and we'll be able to listen to the local frequencies. Chief Madison gave me access to follow the GPS units on Mammoth's emergency vehicles on my computer, so we'll be able to follow them that way, too.

"An ambulance will meet the team at the trailhead and then move injured Kim to the hospital. If all goes well, the ambulance will make it to the hospital just fine. But we think that the routes are exposed and that something could happen along the way, so we'll see. Or they might try to take Kim at the hospital. Once we think that the dust has settled, then we'll get the real Kim out of here. Until then, we'll sit here and listen in. When the ambulance starts moving, maybe we'll head into the main part of town and see what unfolds while we watch and listen."

Chapter 37

The sun had dropped behind Mammoth Crest by the time the SAR team arrived at the trailhead. Riding on the horse was 'Kim' draped in a sleeping bag and wearing booties to protect her damaged feet. Until the paramedics removed the sleeping bag and gently helped her off the horse, it was difficult to tell the gender of the victim or the skin color. A hushed, anxious crowd gathered to watch the commotion, mostly staying out of the way of the rescuers. Watching from the group, Alpha's additional team members – Delta and Iota – figured it was Dr. Johnson. They had a photograph on their phones, but it was difficult to tell for certain that was her because she wore bandages on her head. The distance and poor lighting didn't help, and the rescue team and crowd obstructed their view.

After she slid off the horse, the SAR team and ambulance attendants carefully placed 'Dr. Johnson' on a gurney and checked her vitals and feet better than they had at Duck Lake. The paramedics began an IV to hydrate her.

Gamma was still at Reds Meadow the last Delta and Iota knew and should be coming back to town soon. Alpha was in town awaiting word about the current situation. Since Gamma wasn't available, the plan had changed slightly but should still work fine. Stepping away from the crowd, Delta called Alpha to let him know that Dr. Johnson had arrived and should be transported to the hospital soon.

"We've been following the SAR team's progress on the scanner," Alpha said. "As they load her into the ambulance and before it leaves, move into position at the intersection of Lake Mary Road and Old Mammoth Road so that you can then follow the ambulance and intercept it after it passes."

After stabilizing the patient, rescuers rolled the gurney to the ambulance and loaded it through the back doors. The SAR team gathered and relaxed now that they had completed the problematic rescue, toasting themselves with cans of beer from a cooler in the back of one of their trucks. Delta and Iota were in their car, pulled out with the exiting traffic, and headed to the junction. Shortly, with lights flashing, the ambulance left the trailhead and drove toward town.

Delta and Iota parked on the service road to the Mammoth Lakes water tank. As the ambulance approached, traffic pulled to the side of the road to let it pass. Alert to figure out which way they needed to drive, Delta anxiously watched the ambulance. As he expected, the ambulance continued on Lake Mary Road, and he quickly pulled in behind it. Delta then passed the ambulance, and Iota saw a disgruntled look on the face of the ambulance driver. At the Twin Lakes Vista parking area, Delta pulled in and around the loop and parked on the side of Lake Mary Road, facing the oncoming ambulance. A moment later, Delta and Iota, masks on, dashed out of their car and stood in the middle of the road, handguns prominent, and greeted the slowing ambulance.

Delta and Iota waved their guns, and the ambulance stopped, the driver looking perplexed. Delta approached the driver's door while Iota circled to the rear door. Delta carefully opened the driver's door first, and then Iota did the same with the back door. Inside the cab, the driver fearfully raised his hands, the same as the paramedic in the back.

"*OUT! NOW!*" Delta barked. "Get down on the pavement, behind the ambulance, fingers laced behind your heads."

The ambulance staff dutifully and silently followed directions, got out, and slowly sank to the pavement. Iota quickly frisked the two – no weapons, just radios, shears, and other emergency responder paraphernalia. Iota threw the radios as far away as he could.

Delta and Iota took the seats in the front of the ambulance. As they pulled away, lights flashing and a warbling siren, they were almost gleeful but knew that they still had to get the ambulance to their rendezvous across town without being caught or sidetracked. They drove off at a good clip and hoped to not draw any more attention to themselves than what a passing ambulance might typically attract.

———————

Special Agent Andrews, who had been quietly sitting and relaxing in his car, suddenly sat up. "Well, this is interesting," he said to his passengers while looking at this computer screen. "The ambulance appears to have made an unscheduled, unneeded stop. Now, why do you suppose that it would do something like that?" He grinned and his adrenaline started flowing.

"As Beth said an hour or so ago, it looks like things are going western on us." He started the car but stayed parked, ready to move when needed. "We're going to sit tight and stay out of the way for now and be ready to move at a moment's notice."

Kim and Fred sat up in the car's back seat, peering over the front seat at the computer screen, trying to make sense of the happenings. They weren't feeling nearly as excited as Andrews.

"What do you think they're going to do?" asked Kim, while Fred's eyes widened.

"Well, this being a mountain town, there are few options to get out. They have to head eastward all of the way through town if they're trying to get onto Highway 395, and they have to be careful about getting caught in dead ends or narrow streets. Last night, Chief Madison and I gamed out these kinds of scenarios. We figured that one of their likely moves would be to take the ambulance and then try to either make it to the highway or stop someplace on the eastern side of town and move their hostage into a different vehicle. The ambulance would be obvious, so we're guessing that they're going to try to drive to either a shopping center parking lot or possibly the Mammoth Lakes Welcome Center parking lot. Heading deeper into town, into the shopping areas, makes less sense, but we prepared for several possibilities.

"The ambulance drivers aren't the usual paramedics. They're cops in paramedic uniforms, and we told them to avoid using their radio until after the ambulance drove away, which we hope helps Kim's captors to think that everything is working fine for them."

A moment later, the scanner lit up with radio traffic on the secure channels: *the ambulance had been hijacked and was headed east on Lake Mary Road, lights blazing.* Andrews grinned and shook his head in approval. The plan that he had made with Chief Madison was developing as expected – so far.

"If whoever took the ambulance does as we expect, we have police cars that are going to try to funnel them, herd them towards the visitor center. We don't want this situation to unfold in the center of town. We want to move this party towards a less busy area to avoid innocent bystander involvement. And the hijackers' ruse will also appear more realistic because the visitor center is on the same route as the hospital.

"The hospital is just behind us," he said, pointing through the buildings beyond the back window of his car, south of the Police Station, "and the visitor center is just over there off Main Street." Now, he pointed out the front window of the vehicle and to the right. "One of the reasons that I wanted to just sit here is because I was hoping that the action would come to us. We'll see," he said with a wink.

———————

Just after Delta and Iota hopped into the ambulance and left the driver and attendant lying alongside the road, Iota called Alpha to let him know that they were in control of the ambulance.

"That's good to hear," said Alpha. "Continue to the rendezvous point; we'll see you in a few minutes. Also, do me a quick favor. Can you access the back of the ambulance and take a quick photo of the victim? I want to see her condition so that we know how to care for her."

"Sure, sir. Hang on a moment, and I'll text photos to you. It's a little tight, but I can get back there." Iota wormed his way through the hatch from the cab and into the cabin to snap pictures of their patient. He pulled the blanket back from the unconscious and supine passenger to see her bandaged head better, took a couple of quick photos, and sent them off to Alpha.

On the other end of the text message, Alpha sat in his SUV and looked at the photos. Gamma had just arrived back in Mammoth Lakes and sat in the van next to Alpha. He squinted over Alpha's shoulder. "What do you think?" Alpha asked.

Gamma took the phone, sat there for a moment, and scrolled between the two photos before answering. "I haven't seen her before, but if I were a betting man, I'd say it's not her. There are too many bandages to be certain, maybe she's had some swelling for some reason, but this woman's face looks fuller than Dr. Johnson's, at least from the photos that you shared with us a few days ago."

"That's what I think, too," responded Alpha. "I'm guessing that the police or somebody are setting us up and that Delta and Iota are driving into a trap. We need to be careful so that we don't get sucked into it with them. I'm moving the van across the street so we don't get caught with them if that's the case. I'll sacrifice them before I take a fall for Omega."

———————

Across the city of Mammoth Lakes, as the very last of the day's light glowed over Mammoth Crest, police cruisers and fire engines were on alert and parked on side streets, hidden behind businesses along the main route, engines idling, ready to move. No one knew where the party would be held, but they were expecting a party, and their attendance was mandatory. Everyone followed the progress of the ambulance on their computer screens. As the ambulance passed near some of the vehicles and headed eastward on Lake Mary Road and Main Street, they slowly pulled out and followed from a respectable distance. It was easy to see and follow the ambulance with its lights flashing, and Mammoth's other emergency vehicles ran dark. Traffic flowed back in behind the ambulance after it passed, and the cruisers' and fire engines' headlights blended in. Cars and trucks driving in the opposite direction thought there might be some kind of parade because there were so many emergency vehicles heading east on Main Street.

Andrews, Kim, and Fred sat in their car behind the police station, windows halfway down, and watched the events unfold on their computer screen, the march of ants on the monitor moving towards them. They heard the ambulance siren to the west, and then it went quiet. Andrews sat there, nodding his head, trying to make sense of the ambulance's intentions. He put his car into drive and slowly pulled out of the parking lot, pointing north toward Main Street.

"I'm not certain what they're doing, but I'm guessing that they're quiet now because they're not heading to the hospital, but just trying to make it look like they were. They'll keep driving down Main Street, and, in a moment, I'm guessing that they'll pull into the Visitor Center lot or something like that. My people are getting ready to pounce along with Chief Madison's forces."

Andrews breathed a sigh of relief when the ambulance didn't turn right onto Old Mammoth Road and towards the shopping center a few blocks south. One less risky situation avoided. He could see the ambulance slowing on his computer screen like it was going to turn and head to the hospital. But it didn't. Instead, it turned left at the intersection onto Sawmill Cutoff and then turned left into the secluded Forest Service maintenance lot just off Main Street.

Andrews remarked, "Didn't quite see that coming, but it's pretty similar to what we expected." He waited to pull out of the police station lot and drive towards Main Street. He was in no hurry, wanting the Mammoth Lakes Police to take the lead.

The ambulance turned around in the Forest Service lot so that it could escape or welcome Alpha's and Gamma's arrival. Moments later, several police cruisers pulled into the Forest Service lot, blocking the ambulance from bolting. Spotlights lit up the ambulance and blinded Delta and Iota, hands flying in front of their faces to block the glare.

Across Sawmill Cutoff, Alpha and Gamma watched the ambulance fall into the trap from the campground parking lot. Alpha gave a quick sigh and shook his head. "*FUCK!* Just as I suspected. *Fuck! Fuck! Fuck! Fuck!* Where's Dr. Johnson, then? Now, what are we going to do?" he asked, looking at Gamma while pounding the steering wheel.

More police cars arrived, along with several small fire vehicles. The scene was getting crowded now. Red and blue lights flashed, spotlights brightly lighting the ambulance and Forest Service facility, engines humming. A police cruiser with spotlights burning approached the parking lot from the west, drove through the trees and in behind the ambulance. By this time, Andrews had pulled just onto Sawmill Cutoff, behind several police vehicles and fire department brush trucks. There was no way for traffic to pass on Sawmill Cutoff, and Main Street was blocked to keep gawkers at a distance and an open lane south to the hospital. The party was starting!

After Andrews parked, he stepped out of the car, watching the drama progress in front of them. "You two stay here. I'm going to get closer and try to find Chief Madison. She should be somewhere nearby."

After Andrews left, Kim and Fred sat there for a moment, taking in the action. Overcome with curiosity, they slowly opened their car doors, looked around to see if they were being watched, felt safe in all of the chaos, and then walked around to the front of the car. They leaned against the warm hood, feeling almost hurt that this party was for Kim, but no one had invited them. In a way, though, they were quite content to be observers and not participants. They could see the ambulance through the trees and various vehicles, the two men in the front seat shielding their eyes from the bright lights, pistols in their hands. The ambulance passenger picked up a microphone and spoke through the vehicle's public address system.

"WE HAVE A HOSTAGE IN THE BACK. TURN OFF THE LIGHTS, MOVE AWAY, AND GIVE US PASSAGE OUT OF HERE. IF YOU DON'T, THE HOSTAGE WILL DIE! YOU HAVE SIXTY SECONDS TO TURN OFF THE LIGHTS AND MOVE."

There was no rush of confusion or concern amongst the ranks of the police. They stood there, shielded behind doors and vehicles, comfortable that they were in charge of the state of affairs. They all had received orders to remain calm, that the situation should be in hand, had been told how and why, but to remain vigilant. Sixty seconds passed and the authorities didn't sweat.

"TIME'S UP! WE'LL BE TRUE TO OUR WORD!"

The attendant and driver didn't move, which meant that they weren't quite threatening the hostage, so the police felt no need to intercede – yet. Sharpshooters watched for movement and waited for orders to fire, laser sights dancing on the faces of the two men in the front of the ambulance. Iota held the microphone to his mouth:

"WE WARNED YOU!"

At that moment, a siren chirped from the cruiser behind the ambulance. With the spotlights trained on the ambulance, everyone outside could see the ambulance's cab and that the men were confused. Over the ambulance's speakers came a hissing sound and then *"What the fuck???"* A moment later, the men slumped behind the dashboard and out of view.

Near the front of the phalanx of police vehicles, Kim and Fred could see two officers in tactical gear approach the ambulance, one on each side, sidearms drawn. The officers shined flashlights into the cab, and then one gave a thumbs-up signal. Each officer tried to open the ambulance doors, but the doors were locked. Firefighters hustled to the ambulance and broke out its front side windows while an officer went to the back of the ambulance and opened the cabin doors wide. Paramedics approached the ambulance carrying oxygen bottles and masks. The firefighters released the door locks, opened the ambulance doors and pulled the hijackers out and laid them on the ground. The paramedics were quickly on Delta and Iota, administering oxygen, while police approached and secured them. From the backside of the ambulance, more paramedics pulled the gurney out and gave the victim oxygen while someone unstrapped her. A moment later, she groggily sat up. There were smiles all around!

"What just happened?" Kim asked Fred, a puzzled look on her face. Fred was equally perplexed.

"I'm not certain," he said, "but I'm guessing that they somehow gassed the bad guys, and maybe the agent woman - *Anglin?* - on the stretcher. That's one way to take control of a difficult situation."

Chapter 38

Alpha and Gamma watched everything deteriorate – in their opinion – from the campground parking lot across the street from the Forest Service parking lot light show. They had gotten out of the SUV to see better and stood near Sawmill Cutoff, hidden in the dark under the pine trees. Alpha shook his head, thinking how things had gone from bad to worse. Omega wouldn't be happy with this disaster.

Across the way, they could hear Iota giving his ultimatum to the police, and they could make out the laser lights on their colleagues' heads. *This doesn't look like it will end well*, Alpha thought while he shook his head. He didn't really want to watch the shitshow that unfolded in front of him and turned away, dejected.

His eyes caught on something and a wry smile grew over this face. Alpha nudged Gamma. "Hey, look over there." He was pointing towards Main Street at a car near the back of the assortment of vehicles. "Do you see what I see?"

"What are you talking about? Whaddya see? I'm watching the ambulance." Gamma responded, confusion on his mug. "What do you mean?? I'm not following."

Two people leaned on the front of a car, their faces lit by the glow from the spotlights and red and blue flashes. They were entranced by the show in the parking lot across the street, just as Alpha and Gamma had been a moment before.

Alpha started to grin. "Oh, we may have gotten lucky this time! I think that's Dr. Johnson over there – the woman on the right. Let's go – quietly."

They backed into the shadows and worked their way towards Main Street. The noise and bright lights created an excellent diversion for them. Alpha was almost giddy, going from despair to joy so quickly. *Omega will be happy after all!*

Approaching Andrews' car from the rear, they waited for opportunity to knock, and it did.

"What the fuck???" and people hustled toward the ambulance, all eyes on the drama revealing itself there. Alpha and Gamma took their cue, one slinking up each side of Andrews' car. Shortly, they were beside Kim and Fred with the muzzles of their Glocks in the surprised backpackers' ribs.

With a nudge from the gun's muzzle, Kim sucked in her breath and turned to her right to see what was going on.

"Shit! Alpha, my old nemesis. I was hoping never to see you again. *Shit!"* she muttered and let out a heavy sigh.

On Kim's left, Fred was going through a similar wave of shock and surprise. Gamma was on Fred's left, gun poking him sharply. They all stood there for a moment taking in the growing scene in the Forest Service parking lot. Police and other first responders descended on the ambulance, and the victim - Field Agent Anglin - was slowly up and walking, smiling, happy with her performance.

"We thought that you had escaped, Dr. Johnson. We thought we'd never see you again. I suspected the Feds and police were setting us up but didn't expect you to be so foolish to be here. We'll be on our way now if you two will just follow us."

"Well," Kim replied, "obviously, we didn't know that you knew, although the Feds suspected it. *Shit!"*

Kim looked at Fred and said, "I'm sorry to have gotten in mixed up in all of this. I didn't think that it would come to this. I thought that we were out of the woods, actually and figuratively." Fred looked quite forlorn, muttering *shit* under his breath, not at all pleased with how the events of the last minute had gone.

They were all back in the shadows of the trees now, heading toward the dark campground parking lot and Alpha's SUV, the hostages in front of the captors, walking their walk of shame.

Turning to Fred, Kim said, "By the way, do you remember me telling you about the *bear* that scared Alpha and Beta?"

Fred looked confused for a moment because his mind was elsewhere. "Oh, yeah!" Fred replied and then started chuckling. They stopped walking and turned around to face their captors. Fred then went on, "For future reference guys, here's my suggestion for dealing with problem bears."

Alpha and Gamma were perplexed, standing under the trees, red and blue lights strobing like a disco and silhouetting the kidnappers. They were also annoyed that their hostages weren't moving.

"Let's go!" Gamma barked.

Kim and Fred raised their right arms in unison, pulled triggers, and released an intoxicating cloud of pepper spray. Abruptly, Alpha and Gamma were on their knees, coughing, gagging, doubled over.

Fred stopped spraying; Kim kept going. When her canister was empty, she looked at Fred and shouted, "Gimme your bear spray!"

Fred was baffled by all the chaos and started to hand Kim his pepper spray but pulled back. "Kim, they're down and quite well subdued. There's no need to spray them anymore, and if we need, then we have a bit of spray left." Alpha and Gamma screamed in agony, gagged, and retched, totally overpowered.

As Fred looked over the writhing bodies, he said, "Yeah, Kim, I don't think a second wave is necessary. Do you think that you might have just a teensy, weensy anger management problem?" He was smiling but also gagging a bit himself from the cloud of bear spray.

Kim looked at him, fire in her eyes. "*HELL YEAH!*" she shouted.

Out of the campground shadows, a figure quickly ran toward them, stopped near Alpha and Gamma, and kicked their weapons out of reach. "You two need to be more attentive to loose weapons when you down the bad guys! I tried to get here faster, but when I saw the cloud of bear spray, I decided to keep a safe distance. Aren't you glad I gave you those?"

This sudden interloper caught Fred and Kim off guard but they then smiled and hugged Beth when they figured out who it was. "Sorry, officer, but we haven't been properly trained. We won't let it happen again," was Fred's response. They were all smiling and laughing now, but Beth put some distance between herself and them; the irritant was nearly overwhelming.

As Beth stepped away, she said, "Sorry, you two, but you're making my eyes burn. You're poisonous if you get my drift. And I need to secure these two if they'll just hold still."

Beth looked around and yelled at some firefighters who weren't involved with any other goings-on. "Guys! Bring your truck over here! I need you to wash down my friends – and enemies!"

The firemen were briefly stumped. One walked over to Beth and her little crowd while the other hopped into the brush truck. Beth was cuffing the two victims as best she could while holding her breath. As the first fireman got closer, his nose told him why they needed a shower. When the truck arrived, the firefighters reeled hose out and created a light shower to cleanse the pepper spray away.

Kim and Fred were soaked, happy, elated. Alpha and Gamma were in terrible shape – muddy from being on the wet soil and sick beyond belief. The firefighters did their best to clean the kidnappers' eyes and noses, but it was only a little help. Beth called an ambulance for them. As severely as Kim and Fred had sprayed them, Alpha and Gamma needed serious medical attention and the hospital was just a couple of blocks away.

Beth changed channels, called on her radio and got the attention of Chief Madison. Through the crowd at the Forest Service parking lot, Beth could see Madison look up and around and signaled the Chief to come over their way. Madison got Andrews' attention, and they hustled to the campground parking lot.

"What happened here? Oh shit!" said Andrews when he realized that Kim and Fred were soaking wet and smiling. Beth held two handguns and her own while firefighters attended to the two very sick men rolling in the mud.

"What the hell happened?? I should have left you two locked in the car!"

"Well, yeah, maybe you should have locked us in the car. We also should have been a little smarter and not exposed ourselves – oh well," Kim said. "But it looks like everything turned out fine. This big guy here is one of my kidnappers – Alpha – and I don't know who the other one is."

Andrews was shocked now. "You mean, you two captured them? I don't get it. And why are they such a mess? And..." His voice trailed off. "Ah, I get it now, sort of. I can smell the pepper spray and vomit."

Kim and Fred briefly explained the last few minutes to Madison and Andrews, how they were captured and then sprayed the guys, and how Beth had been watching them the whole time, just in case.

It was Chief Madison's turn to smile now. "Sometimes, my city instincts work pretty well out here in vacationland," she said. "When Officer Collins told me that you two were back in town, I had her keep an eye on you from the police station. When she saw you all leaving, the ambulance approaching and everyone congregating on the Forest Service parking lot, I'm guessing that she watched from the shadows. Am I right, Collins?"

Beth just smiled and nodded her head. Kim and Fred gave her wet hugs and generously thanked her.

Chapter 39

Kim and Fred pulled their backpacks from Special Agent Andrews' car and disappeared into the shadows to change, returned in dry clothes, wet clothes in their hands and backpacks over their shoulders. The scene in the Forest Service lot had dissipated except for the damaged ambulance; a local towing service would be around soon to take it to the city's garage for repair.

Agent Andrews had been on his phone now that Kim and Fred were safe and secure. There were too many people in San Francisco, Washington, and elsewhere interested in this situation's outcome. Chief Madison had to check in with the local media and give them a good story close to the truth but didn't outright name Kim and put Mammoth Lakes in good light and assure the world that tourists were safe and welcome.

Kim used Fred's phone and its last bit of battery to check in with her parents. They were worried since they hadn't heard from her in more than a week, and she hadn't responded to their emails and texts. Kim told them that she had a long story to tell them, but not right now. She was happy and hungry. Kim also checked in with her supervisors to let them in on the good news, but they had already heard through the grapevine that Agent Andrews had initiated. They also granted her a two-week leave to visit her family and start finding a new home, after her debriefing sessions with Andrews.

Fred was pretty much sitting to the side, twiddling his thumbs. Chief Madison told Officer Collins to stay with Kim and Fred and make sure that they got out of town safely – and out of her hair. Fred realized that he was hungry, too, now that the excitement had passed. He seemed to recall having a decent lunch and snacks in the recent past, but it seemed so long ago. Fred still had gorp in his backpack that he could eat while all the excitement played out around him. There also was the issue of getting back on the trail and completing his trip northward. Fred heard a snippet from Andrews that they needed to go to the airport so that he could fly with Kim back to San Francisco tonight, so he figured that he'd need to find a hotel in town. It was too late to head back to Reds Meadow. The weight of the day and all that had occurred dragged Fred down; this was more challenging than a day on the trail.

Kim wandered over to him, handed his phone to him, stood beside him, and then hugged the stuffing out of him. Fred couldn't remember the last time that anyone had hugged him so hard! There were tears in her eyes and his, too. No words passed between them, and yet everything was said in that moment.

Beth watched them, and there were tears in her eyes, too. "Moments like this, winning the day, and watching two grateful people like you are what makes it all worth it." She joined in on the hugs.

Agent Andrews walked over to them, happy to be off the phone. "Hop in the car! We have a plane to catch. I'm guessing that those lights coming over the Sierras are our ride home, Kim." They all looked up and could make out marker beacons and landing lights approaching from the west.

The ride to the airport seemed like it would be quiet because they were all so tired and drained. Their minds were racing despite their fatigue. Finally, Fred broke the silence.

"So, Ed, tell me. What happened in the ambulance there at the end. We were watching, and it seemed like the kidnappers melted or something."

By the light of the dashboard, they could see Andrews smiling. "That was pretty cool, huh?"

"You haven't met her yet, but Agent Anglin looks a lot like Kim. They're not twins, but they look similar enough, especially when you wrap bandages around her head and pull a coat, sleeping bag, or blanket over her. Anyway, last night my team rigged a little surprise in the ambulance. We assumed that these guys would most likely move on the ambulance after it left the Duck Pass Trailhead. There were some other possibilities, but that seemed the most likely. Agent Anglin did an excellent job of playing the role of the dehydrated, injured Kim.

"When the SAR team loaded Anglin loaded onto the gurney, they gave her a remote-control device to hold in her hand and under the blankets. She was immobilized on the gurney like a typical patient but had access to the belts if she needed to escape. It helped to sell her helplessness and be the victim of a backpacking accident to everyone, including the nearby press. The press was one of our biggest concerns because we knew that they'd likely be up close, taking photographs and all. She was fully conscious through everything and just played at being out of it.

"We had a signal set up. As I told you earlier, we figured that there was a possibility that the ambulance would head out of town, but it would be easy to follow. We assumed that Omega's people would stop the ambulance someplace to move Anglin to a different, less conspicuous vehicle, and we thought the most likely place was the tourist information center just down the road. We were a little surprised that they chose the Forest Service lot, but it makes more sense when you think about it.

"Anyway, they pretty much drove into the trap we set. We had several vehicles and lights on their front side and the one cruiser on their backside. They weren't going anywhere, and our biggest concern was that they might try to harm Anglin more quickly than we anticipated. We had the sharpshooters locked on them, just in case, but they didn't make any sudden moves. They were trapped and had no way out, so we hoped that they would just give up. But they didn't. They issued their ultimatums, and we were a little worried that they might harm Agent Anglin.

"If you'll recall, after their last threat, that they were going to harm Anglin, they sat there for a moment, sort of bluffing. One of Chief Madison's people blew a siren squawk on my mark, and that was the signal. When Anglin heard that squawk, she was supposed to push the button on the remote switch we gave her and hold her breath. The remote opened the valves of cylinders under the front seats that contained a fast-acting anesthetic gas that immobilized them and caused them to lose consciousness. It's something that we borrowed from our colleagues in other agencies.

"By the time that they maybe figured out what was going on, it was too late. One good breath of that stuff and they were going to be out. The first couple of officers who approached the ambulance went to make certain that they unconscious and that it was safe. The next people in were a couple of firefighters whose job was to break out the windows so that they didn't overdose on the gas. And we also wanted to get the vehicle aired out and Anglin free so that she wasn't injured. It worked out well, and we're especially proud of Agent Anglin and the risks that she. She'd never been on a horse before today."

A minute later and they were pulling into Mammoth Lakes Airport and headed towards the small terminal. Andrews flashed his headlights, and security allowed him to drive through the gate and onto the ramp. A small jet pulled up to the terminal at the same time as they arrived. "Wonderful!" Andrews said. "Dr. Johnson, our flight is right on time!"

Agent Andrews kept the car near the terminal and parked. The four of them got out; Kim and Andrews reached into the trunk to grab their bags. The jet was shutting down and going through its post-flight checks.

Kim and Fred stood side by side. They looked at each other, weary, happy, emotional, thankful. Fred took Kim into his arms and gave her a big hug and a kiss on the cheek. "Please try to stay out of trouble, OK?" he said.

Kim was slightly tearful. "I want you to know that you've been my knight in stinking armor. You've done so much for me, and I'll never be able to thank you enough. You're a lucky and special man, Timber Wolf." They stepped back from each other and held hands for just that last little bit, proud that they had survived all that they'd been through, proud that they had thrived through it all.

The small jet's door folded out and down, and two people stepped down the stairs, with the first person helping the second just a bit. The airfield was dark; the sun had set long ago. The only real lights came from within the terminal building and from the jet. The two people walked towards Andrews, Kim, Fred, and Beth, backlit by the aircraft's lights. As these two approached, suddenly one figure started running, straight toward Fred. In a moment, he was caught up in a smothering hug and kisses.

"Fred, I'm so happy to see you alive and healthy!" screamed Asta. They hugged and kissed and laughed. After an almost uncomfortable amount of time, Asta let Fred go and stood back, tears in her eyes.

"Honey, I'd like to introduce you to my new friends. This is Agent Andrews and Police Officer Beth Collins. And,…"

Before Fred could formally introduce Kim, Asta gave her as big of a hug as she'd ever received. "If I had talked with them, your family would have told me to give that to you," Asta said. "You'll get many more and then some from them when you see them." Kim laughed and cried, almost uncontrollably, now that the stress was off.

Kim looked at Asta, then Fred, and back at Asta. "So, does this guy torment you and traumatize you when you go backpacking with him?" Kim asked.

Asta grinned but confused. "What do you mean?"

"Like, does he not bring toilet paper into the wilderness when you're out there with him?" Kim prodded.

"Oh dear Kim, I've learned to bring the toilet paper; I don't trust him anymore!"

Everyone was in stitches laughing and enjoying the moment.

"OK, troops, I'd like to get home and sleep in my bed tonight, if only for a couple of hours," announced Andrews, "so if you'll excuse us, we'll be on our way." He picked up his bag and started to slowly make his way to the aircraft, knowing that it was still going to take a couple of minutes.

Kim picked up her knapsack, looked upward, trying to hold back her tears, but it was no use. Fred couldn't hold his tears of joy and thankfulness either. There was time for one last, long hug between them, and then Kim skittered toward the jet. "Good luck, Teddy Bear!" Fred called out.

Andrews got the last word in. "By the way, Fred, Beth made arrangements for you and your wife at a hotel in town for tonight – my treat. I'd appreciate it, too, if you'd get the car back to the rental agency tomorrow. My expense account for these couple of days will be through the roof, and I don't need a stolen car added to it. Besides, if you don't return the car, I'm authorizing Chief Madison to charge you with grand theft. I'll be in touch because there's more that I need from you for debriefing and a long statement from you. Uncle Sam thanks you for your assistance!"

After watching the jet taxi away, Beth, Asta, and Fred got into the car and returned to Mammoth. Beth pulled into a quaint little bed and breakfast and spoke with the proprietor to ensure that everything was in order. Fred looked at Beth and then asked, "Well, how are you getting home? Can I give you a ride?"

"My ride should be here at any moment. A cruiser's going to stop by and take me home. I need a good night's sleep as much as anyone. Everything is taken care of for you two, so relax, shower, and sleep like you haven't slept in days!"

It was now Beth's turn to give Fred a brief hug. "You know, Fred, you were great out there. I've been hiking and backpacking here for years, and you have the story to top all stories. I hope you come back to Mammoth, again and again, but please leave the drama elsewhere." With a parting smile, Beth was out the door.

Fred and Asta stood in front of the B&B for a moment. Fred enjoyed the quiet, the lack of excitement and took a deep, appreciative breath. *What a day*, he thought to himself.

Fred looked at Asta, his shoulders sagging, feeling the weight of the past several days sloughing off him. "You know, honey, I'd like to take and shower and hit the sack. I have too many stories to tell, and I'm too tired to tell them all tonight. I'm just really looking forward to a hot shower, cool sheets, and snuggling with you."

Asta smiled at him, took his arm, and walked inside. "Sounds fine by me, Timber Wolf. You deserve whatever you want tonight, but I was hoping to help you put up your tent pole."

Epilogue

Over the next several weeks, Fred was interviewed by several different agents, each one asking essentially the same questions but in slightly different ways. Fred had been deposed a few times in his life, so running this gauntlet was sort of familiar, and he just went with the flow. Special Agent Andrews spoke with him several times, too. During his last call, Andrews again thanked him for everything that he had done. He also remarked that Kim had been fortunate to have run into him for so many different reasons.

The one person that he didn't hear from was Kim. Fred was irritated a bit, having been with her at such a crucial juncture of her life, and he also knew that she must be going through a hundred times more interviews and other forms of interrogation and debriefings. He thought of her often, as one does after having been through such traumatic times.

About a month after Fred returned home, he remembered that Kim had borrowed his phone to call her parents. Scrolling through his phone, he found a call to a number he didn't know on their last evening together. He pressed on the number, hoping that it was Kim's parents. When a female voice said hello but didn't identify itself, Fred told the distant person who he was and how he knew a woman named Kim.

On the other end of the exchange came a gasp of happiness followed by great gratitude. Fred had reached Kim's mother, and she treated him like an old friend, thanking him lavishly, and asked him to visit or they could visit Fred to express their thankfulness. Fred blushed and said that all he wanted was to talk with Kim and know that she was happy and healthy. Kim's mother told him that she'd get the message to her and then was falling all over herself again, profusely thanking Fred. After he hung up the phone, Fred felt at peace, knowing that Kim was where she needed to be, taking care of herself and healing.

Several days later, Fred's phone rang. He picked it up and looked

– unknown caller. He didn't typically pick up calls like these but decided that he would this time because it just might be Kim.

"Bortz Environmental Consulting, this is Fred Bortz speaking."

For a moment, there was silence. "So, Timber Wolf, if I were you, I'd be watching for a special package to be delivered to my door." The caller hung up. Fred was confused. Smiling, he figured that it was Kim, but had no idea how to call her back.

A moment later, the front doorbell rang; Asta answered the door and was almost shrieking with joy. "Fred, get down here right now!" she yelled.

Fred raced down the stairs from his second-floor office. He found Asta and a very dignified, well-dressed, and beautiful Dr. Kim Johnson at the foot of the stairs. She beamed with joy and gratitude! Fred gave her a long, warm embrace, and it was very mutual.

Kim stepped back from Fred, holding him by the shoulders. "You know," she said, "you look a lot better than the last time I saw you, and you smell a whole lot better, too. You look a lot younger without the gray, scruffy beard." They all laughed so hard!

Asta and Fred invited her in for coffee, lemonade, and biscuits – and margaritas, too! "I'm almost hurt that you're not offering me fresh trout or gorp," Kim said teasingly.

They spent a long time catching up about what had happened over the past several weeks, especially for Kim. As she had said while they were together, she had to sell her house and find a new home. There had been hours and hours of questions, meetings, debriefings, mental exams, counseling, and more. Kim hadn't been allowed access to the programs on which she had been working just before she was kidnapped, but her supervisors assured her that they were working wonderfully well in her absence.

Kim also presented Fred with a very special gift: a brand-new pair of shoes just like the ones he had loaned her! Fred thought that it was a cute and sweet gesture.

Fred said that in his conversations with Special Agent Andrews that they had been able to identify Alpha, Beta, and the others but were unable to tie them back to Omega and his group. Beta's body had been recovered from Duck Creek a couple of days after they left Mammoth Lakes. Andrews' team connected Alpha and Beta to a few past crimes that were also likely affiliated with Omega because of their fingerprints and DNA. Kim was aware of this news.

"OK, enough about me," Kim said. "Did you finish your backpacking trip with less drama?"

"Well, yes and no," started Fred. "Asta and I spent another day in Mammoth, and then she flew home. I took the bus to Reds Meadow and had breakfast with Bill and Missy. They had already heard the stories by that time. I again thanked them for everything that they did for us, and especially for you.

"I started back on the trail again but only made it another few days. The route after Reds Meadow is stunning! By the time I made it to Tuolumne Meadows in Yosemite, I felt that I'd had enough excitement for the summer. It just wasn't the same without you there, Kim! So, I bailed on the last few days of my trip and came on home. Asta and the kids were thrilled that I made that choice."

"Well, I'm sad that you didn't finish your whole route, but I'm happy that you're content with how your journey finished," Kim said.

"Guess what else happened?" Kim asked them. "About a week after the fun in Mammoth, I started to feel sick – fever, diarrhea, not eating much, and lost some weight. I went to see a doctor, and he looked me over, and his staff took some samples. The next day, the clinic asked me to come back. In the exam room, without any prompting, the doctor asked me where I'd been hiking or backpacking. I told him that I'd been out in the Sierras but didn't provide any more details. He just nodded his head and said that's about what he'd expected to hear. Somehow, somewhere I contracted giardiasis."

Fred looked started and sympathetic. "I've never had it myself, but I've heard of a few people who've had it."

"Yeah," Kim replied, "that's what I expected to hear. Let me tell you, it's not fun. I figure that Alpha and Beta were the ones who weren't careful enough with the water we were drinking. That's the bad news. I just finished my antibiotic treatment the other day. The good news is that the doctor is handsome, single, and likes to head outdoors. When I told him a little more about our backpacking trip, he was excited and jealous. We had a hiking date a week later and are going to go out again when I get back." Now, Kim was beaming.

"See! I told you before, that which doesn't kill you makes you stronger! You went through all this difficult stuff, and maybe your life is looking up now. Not that it was so bad before." Fred was proudly smiling. "But I guess that means I'll have to find a different backpacking partner for next summer."

Now Asta gave him a nudge with her elbow. "Thanks a lot, honey."

They talked and reminisced for another hour or so, giving Asta more details that she hadn't been able to drag out of Fred over the preceding weeks.

After a pause, Kim announced that it was time for her to move on, that she had miles to go yet today and tomorrow before getting to Chicago to see her parents. At the front door, there were more hugs and smiles but no tears. Feelings of pride, thankfulness, appreciation, and perseverance. New friends and new adventures.

"The onus is on you to keep in contact, Kim," Fred said. "Your world is too secretive for me, but I'm guessing that you have your ways."

"Hey, I'm not so secretive and hush hush as you think! Let me write down my email address for you before I go."

On a scrap of paper that Asta handed her, Kim wrote out *Sierra_teddy_bear@gmail.com* and handed it to Fred after their last hug, followed by a wink, and she blew him a kiss as she walked down the front steps.

Tim Mulholland is a Midwesterner who enjoys hiking and backpacking. He is an environmental scientist by training, and a landscape photographer who loves to travel with his family. While he has written a great deal in his life, this is his first novel. He loves to backpack in the Sierras, Wind River Range, the Desert Southwest, New Zealand and any place else with his family.

Made in the USA
Las Vegas, NV
26 November 2022

60367902R00201